P9-DEF-875

"You never kissed Cedric
the way you just kissed me."

Her eyes didn't fail him. He could see the truth in them. "No," she said with a little gasp. "No, I mean, I won't discuss it. This can't ever happen again, Your Grace. I'm—"

Trent loved the feeling of Merry's head in his hands. He tipped it backward and took her mouth in a kiss as thirsty and deep as any he'd given in his life.

To this point, first, second, and third kisses had been merely way stations on the road to bed. His mistresses were courtesans, elegant women who chose their own lovers and enjoyed his company as much as he did theirs.

Kissing Merry was no way station. It was like making love. She was kissing him back again, wreathing both arms around his neck.

She was everything he'd ever wanted in a woman, and nothing he'd ever thought to find in a lady.

By Eloisa James

Coming Soon

SEVEN MINUTES IN HEAVEN

ELOISA JAMES

My American DUCHESS

AVONBOOKS

An Imprint of HarperCollinsPublishers

AVON BOOKS
An Imprint of HarperCollins*Publishers*
195 Broadway
New York, New York 10007

Copyright © 2016 by Eloisa James, Inc.
Excerpts from *A Gentleman Never Tells* and *Much Ado About You*
copyright © 2016, 2005 by Eloisa James, Inc.
ISBN 978-0-06-238943-5
www.avonromance.com

First Avon Books mass market printing: February 2016
First Avon Books hardcover printing: January 2016

Avon Trademark Reg. U.S. Pat. Off. and in Other Countries, Marca Registrada, Hecho en U.S.A.
Avon, Avon Books, and the Avon logo are trademarks of Harper-Collins Publishers.
HarperCollins® is a registered trademark of HarperCollins Publishers.

Printed in the U.S.A.

10 9 8 7 6 5 4 3 2 1

This book is dedicated to two young
English people, Joe and Leanne, who came from
York, England, to our apartment in New York for a visit.
Joe carried a diamond ring hidden in his pocket
for four days before he found
the perfect spot in Central Park.
May your lives together be as romantic as this
novel—and as Joe's proposal, which, frankly,
was a romance novelist's dream.

Acknowledgments

My books are like small children; they take a whole village to get them to a literate state. I want to offer my deep gratitude to my village: my editor, Carrie Feron; my agent, Kim Witherspoon; my partner-in-crime, Linda Francis Lee; my website designers, Wax Creative; and my personal team: Kim Castillo, Anne Connell, Franzeca Drouin, and Sharlene Martin Moore. In addition, people in many departments of HarperCollins, from Art to Marketing to PR, have done a wonderful job of getting this book into readers' hands: my heartfelt thanks goes to each of you.

Chapter One

April 6, 1803
Lady Portmeadow's ball in honor of
   the East End Charity Hospital
15 Golden Square

At 9 pm sharp, Lord Cedric Allardyce gracefully fell to his knees, signaling his intent to request Miss Merry Pelford's hand in marriage.

Merry stared down at his buttery curls, scarcely believing this was actually happening to *her*. She had to force back a nervous giggle when Cedric complimented her finger for its slenderness before slipping on a diamond ring.

It felt as if she were on a stage, playing a role meant for a delicate, feminine Englishwoman. That actress hadn't shown up, and storklike Merry Pelford had taken her place.

But at 9:02, after Cedric's lyrical proposal drew to a close, she forced back a nervous qualm and agreed to become his bride.

Back in the ballroom, Merry's guardian, her aunt Bess, didn't seem to realize that Cedric and Merry were mismatched. "The two of you are exquisitely suited, like night and day," she said, eyeing Cedric's yellow hair. "No, midnight and the dawn. That's not bad; I'll have to write it down."

"My aunt is a poet," Merry told Cedric.

Before Bess could prove her credentials by tossing out a line or two, her uncle Thaddeus—who was bluntly unsympathetic to rhymes of any kind—dragged Cedric off to the card room. Merry instantly pulled off her glove and revealed her diamond ring.

"Cedric is friends with the Prince of Wales," she whispered.

Bess raised an eyebrow. "It's always helpful to be acquainted with those in power, though I can't say I view the man as a desirable acquaintance on his own merits."

Merry's aunt had grown up in that cradle of American high society known as Beacon Hill; her father was a Cabot and her mother a Saltonstall. Her staunch belief that she represented the pinnacle of society had remained unshaken in the presence of the most haughty noblemen.

"Cedric believes that His Highness has been portrayed unfairly," Merry said stoutly. She was marrying an Englishman, and that meant she had to adopt English ideas.

"The only prince I've met to this date is that Russian who courted your cousin Kate," Bess said. "There's nothing worse than a man who bows too much. He popped up and down like a jack-in-the-box; it gave me a headache just to look at him."

"Prince Evgeny," Merry said, nodding. "He was always wearing white gloves."

"White gloves on a man have their time and place. But what with the gloves and the bowing, he was like a rabbit, one of those that flashes its tail before it runs off."

Aunt Bess certainly had a lively gift for metaphor.

"What a lovely evening," she continued. "The only thing better would be if your father was with us, but I'm certain that he and your sainted mother are watching over you. Likely he was the one who put the idea for this visit to England in my mind!"

Merry nodded, though she was less certain about her father's approval. Mr. Pelford had been a patriot to his core, and had been elected to represent Massachusetts in the Constitutional Congress, after all.

He had made his own way in the world, taking the profits from a successful patent for a weaving machine and speculating in real estate, then standing for the House of Representatives. In fact, if he hadn't succumbed to a heart ailment, Merry thought her father could have ended up President of the United States.

Her aunt's thoughts must have followed hers, because she added, "Though now I think on it, your father might have disliked the idea. More likely, 'twas your mother. I know she loved the land of her birth."

Merry brushed a kiss on her aunt's rosy cheek. "My father wouldn't have a single complaint. You and Uncle Thaddeus have been the best possible guardians."

"Such a sweet child you were, from the very day you came to us," Bess said, her eyes turning misty. "You make up for the lack of my own children tenfold. I can scarcely believe that my niece will be an English lady."

Merry couldn't quite imagine it herself.

"Lord Almighty, this room is overheated!" Her aunt started fanning herself so energetically that the feathers on her headdress billowed like a ship's sails. "I feel as hot as a black pudding."

"Why don't we go onto the balcony?" Merry suggested. Its doors stood open in a fruitless attempt to cool the room.

"If it's stopped raining," Bess said dubiously. Once in the cool night air, she quickly recovered. "Your Cedric is dazzling," she exclaimed, snapping her fan shut. "A title is all very well, my dear, but I think it's better to judge a husband on his own merits—on the plain naked man, if you take my meaning."

"Aunt Bess!" Merry tugged her from the open doorway. "You must watch what you say. English gentlewomen aspire to modesty."

It hardly need be said that Bess didn't share their aspirations. "That ballroom is full of women pretending never to have gawked at a man's wishbone," she pointed out, "whereas in reality they walk around the room like butchers' wives at a fish market."

"Englishwomen have very refined manners," Merry objected.

"So they'd like to think. The proof of the pudding is in the eating, m'dear. Look at the fashions here. I appreciate those silk pantaloons as much as the next woman."

Merry rolled her eyes. "Aunt Bess!"

"You're betrothed again, so I can speak my mind," Bess replied, unperturbed. "Mind you, speaking of pantaloons, your Cedric is certainly a well-timbered fellow." She gave a throaty chuckle. "That reminds me—I promised to dance this quadrille with your uncle. He's as clumsy as a June bug, but he does enjoy a nice gallop around the room. Come along, dear."

"If you don't mind, Aunt, I'd rather stay here for a few minutes."

Her aunt gave her a squeeze. "How I love that smile of yours! Your Cedric is a perfect lady's playfellow. Come your wedding night, the two of you will be as merry as crickets in a fireplace."

With that, her aunt reentered the ballroom, feathers and fan flapping.

Merry wrapped her shawl around herself to ward off the April air and tipped back her head to look at the sky.

She kept forgetting that no stars shone above London, rain or no. Fog and smoke turned the streets dark by four in the afternoon.

But Cedric loved the city, so they would live here. There was no point in longing for starlight. Or gardens, for that matter.

Merry had a passion for gardens that went beyond her school friends' delight in arranging bouquets. She liked to "muck about in the dirt," as her uncle called it, rooting up plants and rearranging them until she had laid out the perfect garden.

Just then a man shot across to the balustrade and muttered a string of oaths that no young lady was meant to overhear.

She drifted a step closer, pleased at the opportunity to augment her vocabulary of forbidden phrases. Alas, the only word she caught was "bollocks," and she already knew that one. As she watched, his fingers curled around the rail in a controlled but furious gesture.

Most likely, someone had snubbed him, and he'd come out here to regain his composure. English aristocrats, as she'd discovered since her arrival in London, had a penchant and a talent for delivering withering remarks. She'd seen her own darling Cedric issue several snubs himself, though only when mightily provoked.

Why, if she were the type to take offense, she'd be cross at half the guests here tonight, given the way they mocked her Boston accent.

The man glowering down at an innocent whitethorn hedge was probably from one of the lower rungs of the social ladder, someone whom most people in that ballroom would look right through.

In America, he would be free to make his own way, judged on his merits, not his birth. But here? One was born into a social class, and in that class one remained until death.

The man certainly wasn't wealthy. Cedric's attire glittered with gold thread and gilt buttons, but this fellow's coat was as plain and black as a Quaker's.

Even from where she stood, she could tell that his cravat had no more than a touch of starch and was tied in a simple knot. In fact, he might be without the services of a valet, as his hair was cut short and wasn't in the least modish.

Perhaps he *was* American. It would explain his unfashionable hair and coat. With a surge of patriotic fellow-feeling, she moved over to him and lightly touched his sleeve.

When he turned to face her, she knew instantly that she'd been wrong not only about his nationality, but about his rank. The hard line of his jaw and the arrogance of his manner marked him, without question, as a member of the British peerage. Even his hair, the color of tarnished guineas, looked aristocratic.

"I beg your pardon?" His voice was deep—and she thought she heard disdain. He glanced down at her hand, still resting on his sleeve, and she snatched it away.

Oh dear.

English ladies never spoke to strangers, so he probably expected her to cower like a chambermaid. In that case, she would disappoint him. No American flinched before an Englishman, noble or otherwise.

Head high, she met his eyes straight on, and sure enough, a distinct flash of surprise crossed his face. "Please forgive me for disturbing you, sir," she said, curtsying. "I mistook you for one of my countrymen."

She could scarcely believe she'd felt pity for the man, because now she had the impression that she was sharing a small space with a large predator. She fell back a step with the aim of returning to the ballroom, but he moved forward and blocked her flight.

"There are a great many Americans in London this season, are there not?" he asked.

Goodness' sake, the man was ferocious-looking. It was difficult to imagine who would have had the nerve to affront him; in comparison, her combative former fiancé Bertie Pike was as placid as a cow.

He had made her so rattled that she spoke before she thought. "According to the *Times*, there are at least three times as many Americans in London as there were a decade ago."

Her former governess, Miss Fairfax, had always said that no man wished to be thought ignorant, but Merry was certain that this man wouldn't give a damn—because he was absolutely confident about what he did know.

Sure enough, he merely cocked an eyebrow and asked, "Did the *Times* offer an explanation for the swell in your numbers?"

"It did not. But did you know that Americans often study in your Inns of Court? Five men who signed our Declaration of Independence were educated at the Middle Temple."

She nearly clapped a hand over her mouth. She had gone from inappropriate to objectionable; American independence was hardly a subject about which English aristocrats were enthusiastic.

She dropped a hasty curtsy. "If you'll excuse me, sir, I shall go fetch my next dance partner."

Laughter gleamed in his dark eyes. "If I might offer you some advice, no English gentleman wishes to be 'fetched.'"

His evident amusement eased her nervousness. "My experience of London is not great, yet I have already discovered that there are any number of English gentlemen eager to be 'fetched,'" she said, giving him a wide smile before she remembered that young ladies weren't supposed to do more than demurely curl their lips.

"I surmise that you are referring to gentlemen who seek to enrich themselves by marrying a woman in possession of a fortune. Are there no adventurers of that kind in America?"

His tone made it clear that he was not a fortune-hunter. Merry had grown tired of gentlemen subtly informing her that her fortune trumped her "unfortunate" nationality.

"Of course," she said. "But at home they aren't so condescending. Here they act as if they're doing one a favor, whereas to my mind the truth is quite the reverse."

"You make a good point," he conceded.

"Though I'm not being entirely fair. English gentlemen have titles for sale, and even my cousins—who are Cabots and quite powerful in their own right—don't have anything attached to their name that directs people to bow and scrape before them."

"I gather you are not inclined to bow and scrape before a titled gentleman?"

He didn't seem in the least critical, which was a relief. "I am not. I prefer to judge a man on his accomplishments and character. If you have a title yourself, sir, I apologize for being so direct."

He smiled, which she took to mean that he was untitled. "Have you met many peers . . . any dukes, for example?"

"I have met the Duke of Villiers, and just last evening, the Prince of Wales." Merry lowered her voice to a whisper. "To be frank, each seemed to feel that his titles made him as special as a five-legged calf. Though, to be fair, the duke might expect reverence on the basis of his coat alone."

His bark of laughter appeared to surprise him as much as it did her.

"Now if you will excuse me, sir, I must return to the ballroom." Merry was fairly certain that Cedric had no concerns about her faithfulness, but there was no reason to cause a scandal by being caught in a tête-à-tête.

He didn't move. "Tell me, do you consider yourself representative of American ladies?"

"In some respects," she said, hesitating.

His smile deepened. "How do American ladies compare to their English counterparts?"

"Well, American ladies prefer to speak rather than warble," Merry said, with a mischievous grin. "We never faint, and our constitutions are far hardier than those of delicate English gentlewomen. Oh, and we add tea to our milk, rather than the other way around."

"You are of the impression that 'delicate' characterizes the fair sex as represented tonight in Lady Portmeadow's ballroom?"

Merry pursed her lips, thinking of the hawk-eyed ladies who ruled over London society. "Perhaps it would be more accurate to say that Englishwomen *aspire* to delicacy, and American women do not. For my part, I believe that a woman's temperament is something she ought to be able to decide for herself. I have no plan to have an attack of the vapors now, nor shall I in the future."

"I've heard about these 'vapors,' but I have yet to see a woman faint," he said, folding his arms over his chest.

He had a nice chest. Her eyes drifted all the way down to his powerful thighs, before she recovered herself and snapped her gaze back to his face. His expression was unchanged, so hopefully he hadn't noticed her impropriety.

Still, in the back of her mind, she decided that Aunt Bess was right: on the right man, snug silk pantaloons were an undeniably appealing fashion.

He was patiently waiting for her to respond. He had a kind of power about him that had nothing to do with fashion. Now she thought of it, she had seen that kind of self-possession before: in a Mohawk warrior she'd once met as a girl.

She shook her head, pushing the thought away. "Not even once? In that case, you're either lucky or remarkably unobservant. Didn't you notice the fuss earlier this evening when Miss Cernay collapsed?"

"I arrived only a quarter of an hour ago. Why did Miss Cernay faint?"

"She claimed a mouse ran up her leg."

"That is highly improbable," he remarked, a sardonic light in his eyes. "Lady Portmeadow is notorious for her frugality, and not even mice care to starve."

"Miss Cernay's claim is not the point," Merry explained. "She was likely groped by Lord Ma— by *someone*, and fainted from pure shock. Or perhaps she feigned a swoon to avoid further indignities. Either way, I promise you that an American lady would have taken direct action."

He unfolded his arms and his eyes narrowed. "Am I to infer that you know who this blackguard was because he groped you as well?"

" 'Grope' is perhaps too strong," Merry said, noticing the air of menace that suddenly hung about those large shoulders. " 'Fondle' would be more accurate."

Her clarification didn't improve matters. "Who was it?" he demanded. His brows were a dark line.

She certainly didn't want to be responsible for an unpleasant confrontation. "I haven't any idea," she said, fibbing madly.

"I collect that *you* did not faint."

"Certainly not. I defended myself."

"I see," he said, looking interested. "How did you do that, exactly?"

"I stuck him with my hat pin," Merry explained.

"Your hat pin?"

She nodded, and showed him one of the two diamond hat pins adorning the tops of her gloves. "In America, we pleat silk gloves at the top and thread a hat pin through. They hold up your gloves, but they can also be used to ward off wandering hands."

"Very resourceful," he said with a nod.

"Yes, well, the lord in question *might* have squealed loudly," she told him impishly. "Everyone *might* have turned around to look. And I *might* have patted his arm and said that I knew that boils could be very troublesome. Did you know, by the way, that a treatment of yarrow is used for boils, but it will also stop a man's hair from falling out?"

She could feel herself turning pink. He had no need of that remedy. Although cropped short, his hair was quite thick, as best she could see on the shadowy balcony.

But he gave a deep chuckle, and Merry relaxed, realizing that it was the first time all week—perhaps even all month—she felt free to be herself. This man actually seemed to like it when a bit of information escaped from her mouth.

"Happily, I am ignorant about boils," he said. "Are American ladies typically knowledgeable about such matters?"

"I can't help recalling facts," she confessed. "It's a sad trial to me because it's hard to remember in time that they ought not to be shared."

"Why not?"

The corners of the man's stern mouth had tipped upward in a most beguiling fashion. In fact, she found herself starting to lean toward him before she caught herself.

"There are few acceptable topics of conversation in London. It is quite wearying to try to remember what one is allowed to discuss," she said with some feeling.

"Bonnets, but not boils?"

He must be something of a rake, Merry decided. The way his eyes laughed was very alluring.

"Exactly," she said, nodding. "British ladies are discriminating conversationalists."

"Don't tell me you have ambitions to master the art of saying nothing."

Merry laughed. "I fear I shall never become an expert at fashionable bibble-babble. What I truly dislike," she said, finding herself confiding in him for no reason other than the fact that he seemed genuinely interested, "is that—"

She stopped, realizing that the subject was leading her to insult his countrymen. She was still a guest in this country, at least until she married Cedric; she should keep unfavorable opinions to herself.

The expression in his eyes was intoxicating, if only because no one else she'd met was interested in the impressions that an American had of their country. She loved London, if only for its marvelous public gardens, but there were aspects of polite society that she found tiresome.

"It's the way people speak to each other," she explained,

choosing her words carefully. "They are clever, but their cleverness so frequently seems to take the form of an insult."

Merry felt her cheeks growing warm. He must think her a complete simpleton. "It's not that I don't appreciate a witticism. But so very many remarks come at someone's expense."

He frowned at that. "Such people talk nothing but nonsense, and you should ignore them," he ordered.

"I can't, but I am learning to control my temper."

"I believe I'd like to see you in a passion."

"You may mock me if you like, sir, but I can tell you that it is perishingly difficult for an American to transform herself into the perfect English lady! You should try it."

He had a very appealing dent in his cheek when he smiled. "I'm quite sure I would fail. For one thing, I wouldn't look anywhere near as appealing in a gown as you do."

He was right about that. He was uncommonly large. Of course, so was she: much taller than any lady had a right to be, as Miss Fairfax had remarked any number of times.

"Do you, in fact, know why Americans add tea to their milk rather than the other way around?" he asked, returning to her earlier claim.

"Because it is the *correct* way to do it, of course," she said, twinkling at him.

He shook his head. "Here's a fact for you. Your countrymen add boiling tea to their milk in order to scald it, in case its quality is not all one would wish."

"Oh for goodness' sake," she cried. "Don't tell me you're as ignorant of Americans as everyone else at this ball! My aunt's housekeeper would die of humiliation before she would serve milk that wasn't absolutely fresh."

"Then why do Americans put milk in their cup first?"

"It tastes better. The only reason English people do the reverse is to demonstrate that their china is of the very best quality and won't break. Inferior china cracks immediately if you pour in scalding water without first cooling it with milk. And before you ask, we Bostonians drink from the very best Chinese porcelain."

Rats. She'd been waving her hands about, which was one of the habits she was determined to curb. Cedric had mentioned once that ladies should not resemble Italian opera singers.

The way this gentleman could smile with only his eyes was quite . . .

She really should return to the ballroom before she did something foolish. "If you will excuse me, sir, I must allow my dance partner to find me." She gave him a smile. "Or rather, *fetch* me. I'll bid you good night."

When he still didn't move, she began to edge around him.

"Do satisfy my curiosity," he said softly. "Why on earth did American gentlemen leave you free to voyage to England and enjoy our season?"

He had no business looking at a betrothed woman with that gleam in his eye, though of course he was unaware she was engaged, since her diamond was concealed by her glove. He took a step toward her, close enough that she could feel the heat of his body.

And then his eyes moved to her mouth, for all the world as if he were as consumed by desire as Bertie used to be.

That was a nonsensical comparison, because he was an English gentleman and even a fool could tell that this man had complete control over himself and his emotions.

His eyes moved lower still, to her gloved hands. He frowned. "Are you married?"

"No!" she said hurriedly. "The truth is . . . The truth—"

She should tell him that she had become betrothed to Cedric that very evening. But for some reason she blurted out a different truth.

"I earned myself a reputation."

He stared at her for a second. "You surprise me."

"Not *that* sort of reputation! It's just that I—well—to be honest, I have fallen in love more than once. But I wasn't truly in love, because each time I came to see that it had been a terrible mistake. I had to break off two betrothals."

He shrugged. "You've learned a valuable lesson about that overrated emotion, love. Why should that earn you a reputation?"

"I'm appallingly inconsistent," she explained. "I truly am. I made a particularly regrettable choice with my second fiancé, who was far more interested in my fortune than my person. He sued me for breach of promise, and everyone learned of it."

"Surely that speaks ill of him, not you," he said, clearly amused.

"There was nothing funny about it," she said tartly. "Dermot had borrowed on his expectations. That is, the expectation that he would marry me."

"Did the suit go to trial? I can't imagine that a jury would award damages to such a b—" He stopped. "Such a blackguard."

"Oh, it didn't go that far. My uncle settled the case. But I'm afraid that the news spread, and because I'd broken off my previous betrothal, there are those who said that I am . . ."

"Chronically faithless?"

And, at her nod, "What happened to your first fiancé?"

"Bertie had a lovely nose, but he was terribly bellicose," she confessed.

"I have never thought much about noses," the gentleman observed. He bent slightly to look at her nose, almost touching her.

Merry's mouth went dry. He smelled wonderful, like starched linen and wintergreen soap. She licked her bottom lip, and for a second his eyes caught there before he rocked upright. He looked completely unmoved, whereas Merry's heart had started pounding in her chest.

"Your nose is quite lovely," he said.

"As is yours," she blurted out. It was. Merry was something of a connoisseur, and his nose wasn't too sharp or too narrow or too wide. It was just right.

"Still, I could be bellicose," he suggested.

Merry felt a sense of breathless pleasure that almost made her giggle. "Have you engaged in any duels?" she asked, putting on a severe expression.

"Not one."

"Bertie had two."

"That seems—"

"During the first month we were betrothed," she clarified.

"Perhaps he was provoked?" There was something thrilling in his eyes. "I can imagine that a man betrothed to you would not take kindly to other gentlemen's attentions." His eyes stayed, quite properly, on her face, and yet her entire body prickled with heat. "I expect you garner quite a lot of attention," he said softly. "I wouldn't blame Bertie for wanting to keep you all for himself."

Merry's pulse was beating so quickly that she could hear it in her ears, like a river rushing downhill. "Both opponents had accidentally jostled him in the street," she managed. "The duels had nothing to do with me."

"Bellicose, indeed," he murmured.

His voice enveloped her like a warm cloak, and Merry

had the sudden dizzying idea that the balcony had broken away from the rest of the house, leaving the two of them stranded on a dark, warm sea.

"When I returned his posy ring, I thought I might be challenged," she said, trying to lighten the atmosphere.

"He gave you a posy ring? In England those are exchanged between young girls. An apprentice might give one to his sweetheart."

"It was quite pretty," she said, defending Bertie. "The flowers spelled out my name."

"Really," he drawled. Somehow, she didn't know quite how, he had eased even closer to her. She could feel his warm breath on her cheek. "How in the hell does a posy spell anyone's name?"

"With the language of flowers," she said, starting to babble. "Each flower means something, so you communicate as if you were speaking French." Her voice faltered because his dark eyes were so intent. "Or something," she whispered, her voice just a thread.

A sudden burst of music sounded from the ballroom and Merry jumped. "I should—"

"But first you must tell me the rest of the story."

Something about his voice commanded obedience, and even though Merry never allowed herself to be ordered about, she found herself answering. "It's not merely a *story*," she said, giving him a little frown. "I was heartbroken to return Bertie's ring. And Dermot's as well."

"So you returned Dermot's posy as well."

"He didn't give me a posy," Merry said, biting back a smile. "He was very proud of his golden hair, and so he had a ring made from it."

A moment of dead silence followed, and then the gentleman threw back his head and roared with laughter.

Dermot's lawsuit had been so unpleasant that Merry tried never to think of their betrothal, but laughter made the pinch of humiliation easier to take.

"So you came to London as a result," he said, finally.

"My aunt feared that no one would wish to marry me." She shouldn't be on a balcony, in the dark, talking to a man like this. She should tell him that a gentleman had, indeed, asked for her hand and she had accepted.

"Your aunt undervalues your charms. I am certain that most men in America would simply assume that you had yet to meet the right man. And that when you did, you would settle as happily as a bird in its nest."

His eyes were on her unfashionably full lips, and then they drifted down to her equally unfashionable bosom, covered by little more than a few twists of rosy silk.

She took a deep breath, which didn't help things because she caught a whiff of starched linen again and, beneath that, something more elusive, more compelling. Male. Color was rising in her cheeks, so she fixed her eyes on his jaw.

"In my opinion, it wouldn't matter if you had discarded three or thirty fiancés," he stated.

When she ventured to glance back at his eyes, she saw that he was addressing her forehead in a most proper fashion. All the same, the roughness in his voice sent a wanton thrill down Merry's legs. She suddenly imagined him rumpled and sweaty, his chest heaving.

Her own foolishness was like a shower of cold water. What on earth was she doing? "Thank you," she said, nodding madly. "That is kind of you, and it has been a pleasure to converse." Without further ado, she stepped around him and turned toward the ballroom.

A large hand curled around her waist, neatly spinning her about and bringing her up against him.

Sensations skittered through her at the press of a hard male chest against hers. Miss Fairfax would have been appalled. Yet rather than pull away, Merry froze, looking up at him with her heart pounding in her ears.

"Who groped you?" he demanded.

"Who had made you so angry before you came onto the balcony?" she countered. What—or who—on earth would enrage a man like this?

"My fool of a brother. And now I'd like you to answer my question."

She had already forgotten what he had asked. His gaze was so intense that she felt confused and flushed. She would never allow a man—a complete stranger—to kiss her, if that's what he was contemplating.

"What was your question?" she asked, wincing inwardly when her voice came out as breathless as a siren's.

"Who groped you?" he repeated.

He had that warrior look in his eyes that Merry found absurdly compelling. She came out with the truth before she could think better of it. "Lord Malmsbury . . . Lord Malmsbury lets his hands stray where they shouldn't."

"Stay away from him," he said, scowling.

"I appreciate your concern," Merry said with dignity as she pulled free and stepped back, "but there's no call to order me about. I have already decided to avoid his lordship—not that he has shown the slightest inclination to deepen our acquaintance, thanks to my hat pin."

"Between your weapon and his boils, I doubt he will risk further encounters." His smile reappeared. "I trust that after we are formally introduced, I may request a dance, if I promise not to grope you."

It occurred to Merry that she would rather like to be groped by this man. It was an appalling realization. She was *betrothed*.

He executed a perfect bow.

She dropped a curtsy, and this time did Miss Fairfax's instruction proud, nearly grazing the ground with her knee.

Merry walked back into the ballroom without looking back; no matter what her governess thought, she possessed self-control. Plenty of it.

She had almost reached the other side of the room before she turned her head and looked back.

He was nowhere in sight.

She took a seat along the wall and gave herself a good talking-to. What on earth was she thinking? Was she truly as fickle as the gossips back home believed? She might have made mistakes choosing her first two fiancés, but she had never been truly capricious.

She had truly believed that she was in love with both Bertie and Dermot. She had never flirted with a man while betrothed to another.

Not that she had precisely *flirted* with this man.

All right, she had flirted.

Merry groaned silently. Why hadn't she slapped him when he caught her around her waist, or at the least announced her status as a soon-to-be married woman? Instead, she had just looked up at him like a silly widgeon waiting to be kissed.

No wonder he'd been so amused. He likely thought her the veriest green girl, knocked head over heels by the magnificence of his black-clad presence.

It was all so embarrassing.

The next time she encountered him, she would have to emphasize that she was in love, and had scarcely given their conversation a second thought. Perhaps she would say something like, *Oh, we've met, have we not? I declare, I forgot all about it!*

"There you are, m'dear," her aunt said, appearing before

her. "Cedric came by with a glass of wine for you." Bess thrust a brimming glass into Merry's hand. "The boy is endlessly considerate, I must say."

"Thank you," Merry said.

"He returned to the card room with your uncle," Bess said. "You'll see him later; we'll be taking your beau home in our carriage, because his vehicle threw an axle or something of that sort. You should have seen how graciously he accepted your uncle's offer. His manners are just miraculous! Why, he's as polished as wax."

"'As polished as wax,'" Merry repeated, pulling herself back together. That conversation on the balcony meant nothing. She'd probably never meet the man again. "Aunt Bess, that doesn't make any sense. You use wax to polish things."

"You know what I mean," Bess said, unperturbed. "The boy shines like brass."

Merry frowned.

"Oh, tut!" her aunt said. "You're lucky to have him, my dear, and that's all I'll say about it."

As Merry began to explain (not for the first time) the concept of mixed metaphors, one of her suitors, a Mr. Kestril, approached, and after greeting them both, said, "Miss Pelford, I believe you granted me your next dance."

"Certainly," Merry said, smiling at him. Cedric had suggested that Merry keep Mr. Kestril at a distance because he wasn't "good ton," whatever that meant.

But Merry liked him; Mr. Kestril was not only taller than she, but he knew a lot about gardening.

"As shiny as an ingot from a fairy hill," her aunt said abruptly.

Mr. Kestril's forehead creased. "I beg your pardon?"

"I had described Merry's fiancé, Lord Cedric, as being as shiny as brass, but I'm trying to come up with something better," Bess explained, neatly dropping the fact Merry was now betrothed into the conversation. "My Muse just suggested a comparison to a fairy ingot."

"My aunt is a poet," Merry told Mr. Kestril, whose mouth had pulled tight at Bess's news.

"Nothing so grand," Bess said, fanning herself. "A *poet* implies subtlety and genius. I merely dally with words."

"There's a touch of genius in your comparison of a fairy ingot to Lord Cedric," Mr. Kestril said dryly.

Merry frowned. "Why so? A fairy ingot is gold, isn't it?"

"And Lord Cedric's hair is golden-colored," Bess explained.

The strains of a country dance started up. "Miss Pelford," Mr. Kestril said, bowing deeply and extending his hand. "If I may?"

She put her hand in his. And with that, they were away, capering down the room, and smiling every time they met and parted, and met and parted again.

Merry kept her eyes on her partner's face and glanced neither right nor left. Not that there was anyone she'd want to see in the ballroom.

Other than her fiancé, of course.

Chapter Two

Octavius Mortimer John Allardyce, the sixth Duke of Trent, returned to the ballroom feeling as if he'd taken a sharp blow to the gut.

Earlier that evening, Trent had no sooner presented himself at Lady Portmeadow's ball, kissed his hostess's hand, and entered the ballroom than his twin brother, Cedric, had appeared and announced, loud enough so that anyone within a stone's throw could hear, that he was now betrothed to marry.

Although Trent's first impulse had been to give a howl of joy, he had pushed it down and instead offered his brother a congratulatory nod.

He had been just about to request to meet his future sister-in-law when Cedric had added—as casually as if he were discussing the weather—that he had given his betrothed a diamond ring.

Their mother's, to be precise. The ring was worth more than any other piece of jewelry in the family estate, but its value was symbolic as well as financial: it had been worn not only by their mother, but by their father's mother before her.

In other words, his brother had given away the ring that was traditionally worn by the Duchess of Trent, the ring that family lore dictated should grace the finger of his own bride. Perhaps Trent should have locked it away, but it had never occurred to him that Cedric would take it.

In another man, theft of a diamond ring might reflect avarice. That wasn't the case with Cedric; he was jealous of Trent's title, but he wasn't greedy. Cedric's eyes had been bright with glee. He intended, very deliberately and simply, to provoke.

Equally clearly, Cedric had made his announcement at a ball in the hopes that Trent would lose his temper before an audience that included most of fashionable London. The scandal resulting from a lady's betrothal ring being wrenched off her finger would be discussed for years.

Trent would be damned before he gave his brother the satisfaction of a public dispute, even though the ring belonged to *his* descendants, not to Cedric's. The very idea of reclaiming the diamond from his future sister-in-law, who was the innocent in this whole business, was extremely distasteful.

Without a word, he had turned on his heel and taken himself out onto the balcony. He had been staring into the dark garden when he had felt a touch on his arm, turned—and met her.

Now, back in the ballroom, he stood at the edge of the whirl of music and color and thought about what had just happened.

He didn't even like Americans.

They were overly bold, in his experience—and she was no different. She had looked him in the eye as if she were a member of the royal family: direct and unwavering, without a hint of respect for his title.

Yet she was the prettiest thing he'd ever seen, with riotous curls the precise color and sheen of a ripe chestnut, and a mouth like a lush rose, without the aid of sticky paints. Her figure was luxurious and trim at the same time, and she was tall enough that he could kiss her without getting a painful crick in his neck.

But what had made him lose his equilibrium were her eyes. He was pretty certain they were misty gray, but it had been hard to tell on the shadowy balcony. What he did know was that they sparkled with laughter and intelligence. And they changed with her every emotion, her every thought clear.

Her openness was a welcome change from his family's furtiveness. His father, like any man who drinks to excess, had harbored secrets on secrets. What his mother had thought of that, no one knew. Trent had no memory of her expressing any opinion or emotion other than a generalized, withering discontent.

Everything the American thought and felt, by contrast, was written in her eyes and—as far as he could tell—fell straight from her lips. She would never be guarded with her thoughts: more likely, whomever she married would spend a good deal of time laughing as she informed him, all too bluntly, exactly what she thought.

Trent had never contemplated laughing with a wife. To the extent that he'd thought about his duchess, he'd imagined a reserved woman, who would make no scenes of any kind. She wouldn't cling to him, create fusses, or make incessant demands, particularly of the emotional sort.

But he was used to making rapid decisions when presented with new evidence.

He would marry this lady because he liked everything about her, from her husky giggle to those facts she loved so much.

She wouldn't be a properly respectful wife, or even be an obedient one. But she would never be sly, either. She would be a very different duchess than his mother had been—which would be all to the good.

He had had no idea that he'd been waiting for a particular woman, but it turned out he had been waiting for an American with glossy curls who would look him straight in the eye and not give a damn that he was a duke.

Cedric's bride could keep the diamond ring. Trent would buy his American a new ring. She was from a new country, after all.

He would buy her a ring worth twice the purloined diamond. They would start a new tradition, and *his* ring would grace the hands of future Duchesses of Trent.

Now he merely had to discover her name, arrange a proper introduction, and inform her chaperone that he intended to pay her a morning call. The request would speak for itself: anyone who overheard it would suspect that she was to be the next duchess. The gossip would be all over London by morning.

Trent only discovered he was smiling when he met the puzzled eyes of a man he'd been to school with.

"Excellent champagne, isn't it?" Lord Royston said, raising his glass.

"Yes."

"You haven't any."

"I will," Trent said. "If you'll excuse me, Royston, I must find our hostess."

"You should get some champagne before it runs out. Last I saw, Lady Portmeadow was lurking near the refreshments table, no doubt to ensure that no one takes too much."

"Right. Well—"

"Shameful, the way she laid out a plate or two of cucumber sandwiches and tried to pretend it was a spread," Royston continued, staring so hard that his eyes bugged out a little.

Had he really become so grim that acquaintances found a smile shocking? The man was looking at him as if he were a five-legged calf, as the American had described. The memory made him smile again.

His lordship blinked uncertainly. "Heard your brother has found a wife."

"We both have," Trent stated.

"Have you indeed! Who is your duchess-to-be?"

"I have yet to ask her, so I'd best keep it to myself."

Wry humor crossed Royston's eyes. "Of all the men in London, you needn't worry about a refusal, Duke." He raised his glass. "I'll drink to the prospect of matrimony, since it's making you so cheerful. Don't think I've seen you smile in years."

Trent bowed and made his way toward the refreshments table, in an anteroom off the entrance hall. He probably hadn't smiled often, not when every minute of his day was consumed by saving the estate his father had almost bankrupted.

But that would change after he married an American who had promised never to swoon, but who had looked slightly dazed after examining him from head to foot.

Especially after perusal of his midsection.

His body had responded to her gaze with a surge of raw lust. If they hadn't been so close to the ballroom, he would have kissed her. Hell, he would have snatched her up and ravished her . . . after obtaining her permission, naturally. The thought sent another wave of heat through his loins.

More than once during their conversation he'd had to fight an impulse to claim her lips. Claim all of her, in truth. Push her up against the balustrade and kiss her until those intelligent eyes were blurred with desire, and her clever brain forgot every fact it had ever contained.

Sure enough, as Royston had predicted, Lady Portmeadow was hovering beside the refreshments table, watching cucumber sandwiches disappear down her guests' gullets.

He helped himself to a sandwich, just for the fun of it, and ate it as her ladyship rounded the table to him. Then he took another and ate that, too.

"I am so honored that you were able to join us tonight," Lady Portmeadow said with a pinched smile. "It's at times like these that I miss your dear mother."

Trent had no idea what she was talking about. He took another sandwich. They were small, but surprisingly good.

"How have you been, Lady Portmeadow?" he asked.

"The same, the same. My daughter Edwina is . . . oh, you likely know that. After all, you've come to her coming-out ball."

Trent frowned, confused. Wasn't this ball in honor of the new hospital that his brother had championed?

"I saw no reason to go to the expense of two balls," Lady Portmeadow explained. "Edwina is making her debut this evening, which is fitting, as your mother was her god-mother."

Trent bowed slightly.

"I shall take you to Edwina," Lady Portmeadow said,

taking his arm and drawing him back to the ballroom. And away from the sandwiches, Trent couldn't help noticing. "She has changed a great deal since you knew her as a child. I am happy to report that those unfortunate freckles have disappeared."

"I am certain she is most lovely," Trent murmured. He remembered Edwina without enthusiasm. She had been about as interesting as a bread pudding.

In fairness, she had been only ten years old at the time.

"Your brother told me that you have been very busy with the House of Lords since the season began," Lady Portmeadow said, as they crossed the entry, heading toward the ballroom. "Have you seen Lord Cedric tonight? He must have told you his happy news."

"He has." Trent nodded to an acquaintance.

Lady Portmeadow lowered her voice. "I am so *pleased* for him. You must know, of course, how much your mother worried. I've thought of her a hundred times in the last few years, watching the two of you grow to be men. Younger sons frequently pose problems. It's such a burden for a man to grow up without an inheritance."

Trent kept his mouth shut. The fact Cedric had gambled away an estate was thankfully not common knowledge.

"There are some unfortunate aspects to his proposed marriage," Lady Portmeadow whispered. "Prudence dictated that your brother chose from a limited selection."

Hell. Cedric must have found an heiress with buck teeth or a squint.

Trent tried to feel sorry for him, but he couldn't keep his mind on it.

He kept thinking about his American. Not a few English maidens would consider themselves compromised merely for having conducted a long conversation with a man on a shadowy balcony. But his American had no interest in the sophisticated games that members of English society amused themselves with.

She had walked straight up to him and touched his arm—but not because he was a duke. She hadn't the faintest idea who he was. In fact, he had the distinct impression that if she had known he was titled, she would have marched off in the opposite direction.

Trent grinned to himself, looking forward to the moment when he was introduced, title and all.

"Now where could my daughter be?" Lady Portmeadow asked, pausing at the entrance to the ballroom and holding on to Trent's arm with a grip that suggested she thought Edwina would make a fine duchess. "Ah, there she is, dancing with Viscount Bern."

Trent seized his moment. "I shall be delighted to dance with Miss Portmeadow later this evening. But meanwhile, I wonder if I might request a favor?"

"Certainly, Your Grace."

"I would be most happy to be introduced to a young lady whom I glimpsed in the ballroom."

"Certainly," her ladyship repeated less readily, reluctance warring with curiosity.

Trent guessed that motherly instinct told her to secure a duke as her son-in-law, but that she would love to be the hostess who had introduced one of the most eligible, yet elusive bachelors on the market to his future duchess. Just imagine the story she could weave about the moment they met.

He gave a mental shrug and looked around the crowded room for his American. He found her within seconds, happy to learn that she was just as delectable in the light of the chandeliers as she had been on the balcony.

She stood only a few yards away, a glass of lemonade in her hand, next to a scrawny yellow-haired girl with a petulant mouth. The yellow-haired girl was nodding at something Nigel Hampster was telling them.

"Delectable" wasn't quite the right word. The American had a heart-shaped face and a turned-up nose. Turned up in the right way: adorably. She would probably reject that characterization, but it struck him as correct. She was adorable.

Except that word wasn't right, either, because he could see her curves more clearly now that she stood directly under a chandelier. She wasn't wearing white, like most of young ladies around her; her rose-colored gown hadn't even a hint of virginal chastity about it.

Instead, it was caught up under her plump breasts and clung to her body as if she had dampened her petticoats. The bodice was cut low, at the very edge of propriety.

She looked expensive. Sensual. Complicated.

Innocent.

And adorable—all at once.

Hampster was telling jokes to the yellow-haired girl, even though any fool could tell that he was really performing for the girl who stood to the side. She was looking straight through him, a fixed smile on her lips.

Trent found he was grinning again. She would be a magnificent duchess.

"Whom would you like to meet, Your Grace?" Lady Portmeadow prompted, following his gaze. "Oh, I see—Lady Caroline! She does have lovely hair, and she's considered a diamond of the first water. She's Wooton's daughter, though rumor has it that her dowry is not commensurate with her status."

Her ladyship swept on without waiting for confirmation, lowering her voice a trifle so that only the ten closest people could hear.

"I am also told that she doesn't even speak French. In

fact, unkind people have jested about whether she speaks *English*. It need hardly be said that a man of your stature must find a lady who has a command of languages, perhaps three or four."

Edwina must be able to speak in tongues, considering the force with which her mother was advocating the duchess-as-linguist idea.

"In fact, I was speaking not of Lady Caroline, but of the young lady next to her," Trent said.

Lady Portmeadow squinted. "Oh, of course, you were," she said, to Trent's surprise. "Now, where can your brother be?"

"I beg your pardon?"

"Where did I last see Lord Cedric?" She rose on her toes and peered over the heads of the crowd.

"My brother is undoubtedly in the card room," Trent said. He had a sudden unwelcome thought.

"Quite likely," Lady Portmeadow said. "I'll be happy to introduce you to Miss Pelford, and then I'll take you to meet Edwina. Did I tell you that she began learning German last year, purely for the joy of speaking the language? Not that I mean to imply that she's a bluestocking . . ."

Trent had stopped listening.

Pelford. He had heard that name before.

From his brother.

He wasn't a man who swore, silently or otherwise. He considered vulgarities a sign of lost control.

Fuck.

Chapter Three

Earlier that evening . . .

Her heart bounding, Merry gazed down at Lord Cedric Allardyce's curls as he knelt before her, his proposal of marriage being offered with exquisite eloquence. Outside Lord Portmeadow's library, a rainy April held London tight in its dark, wet grip—but Merry was oblivious to it, for Cedric had just compared her to "a summer's day."

Merry had not given up hope that men existed who were as kind as they were handsome, but she had given up hope of finding one. She had finally vowed to herself that even if she couldn't find a perfect man, her third engagement ring would be her last.

But now she understood that the old saying had come true: the third time really *was* the charm.

She couldn't imagine changing her mind about Cedric. He was as handsome as her second fiancé, Dermot Popplewell, but he was a good man, which was far more important than a pleasing profile. Directly after meeting him last month, she had learned that Cedric was instrumental in raising funds for a charity hospital being built in Spitalfields, in East London.

What's more, he was unfailingly gracious. He noted her Americanisms but never scolded her for them. Every word he uttered was eloquent. By contrast, after her first fiancé, Bertie, proposed, he'd told her that she was "as pretty as a red wagon."

A red wagon! She should have known from that very moment he was unsuitable, but she'd been infatuated.

Cedric, however, had just compared her to a "darling bud of May." Would *Bertie* have sworn that he loved her to distraction?

Inconceivable. The only thing that distracted Bertie was a new rapier in a shop window.

Cedric didn't give a flip about her money, either. He was a duke's son, for goodness' sake. Her uncle Thaddeus had told her that very afternoon—while noting that Lord Cedric had his permission to propose—that his lordship had no need of her fortune.

Honestly, Cedric was almost too good to be true. She felt a twinge of worry, but she pushed it aside.

He was perfect for her.

As she watched, rapt, he caught up her left hand, delicately removed her glove, and slid a diamond ring onto her finger. Emotion was pressing so hard on the back of Merry's throat that she hadn't even croaked "yes" before he touched his lips to her fingers, and rose as gracefully as he had knelt.

Cedric smiled at her and ran a finger down her cheek.

With a thrill, Merry realized that he was about to kiss her for the first time. He leaned forward, and a shiver ran through her.

"I'm morally opposed to kissing young ladies to whom I am not affianced, Merry. Will you say yes?"

He was so ethical, so unlike the lecherous boys she had known back home. "Yes," she breathed. He bent toward her again and Merry's eyes drifted closed. His lips brushed hers, once, then again.

She swayed toward him, tilting her head to receive another kiss, a real kiss this time, one where he would draw her into his strong arms and kiss her as if he was scarcely able to contain himself.

No kiss came.

She opened her eyes. Her fiancé had turned toward the library table, and was picking up the glass he had carried with him from the ballroom.

With a start, Merry remembered her governess's instruction. An English lord would never be as indecorous as Bertie, who stole kisses every chance he got. Even worse, if Bertie managed to catch her alone, he would caress her in most inappropriate ways.

She wouldn't like Cedric to behave in such an unseemly fashion. Well, perhaps she *would* like it, but it would never happen because Cedric was a true gentleman, as principled as he was handsome.

"I don't suppose you ever imagined as a little girl that you would marry into the English peerage," Cedric said.

"No, I hadn't," Merry admitted. After a brief encounter with a Mohawk warrior at age eleven, she'd always imagined herself as the adored bride of a man with high cheekbones and the touch of wilderness in his eyes—most assuredly *not* an English peer.

That girlish foolishness had led directly to her accep-

tance of Bertie's proposal. Obviously, Cedric was as unlike
Bertie as a swan to a potato.

Lord Cedric epitomized British aristocracy. If she was a
summer's day, he was the glitter of sun on snow.

As dazzling as the ring he had slipped onto her finger.
"Did you know that the first diamond ring in honor of
a betrothal was given by the Archduke Maximilian of
Austria to Mary of Burgundy?" Cedric asked, nodding
at her hand. "I chose this ring because you are as lovely
as that lady."

"I'm honored," Merry breathed. As much as she had
loved Dermot's hair, his woven-hair ring was revolting
when compared to this. "It is exquisite. I love rose-cut diamonds."

"Your ring finger is as perfect as the rest of you." He
smiled down at her. "Just imagine what your friends will
think when they learn of Lady Cedric Allardyce. Surely
to be a lady is the dearest wish of every schoolgirl in
America."

Merry bit her lip. She was certain he didn't mean to con-
descend. But before she could offer her opinion about the
ambitions of an entire nation of schoolgirls, Cedric added,
"I say, have I put my foot in it? Did you have a governess
rather than go to school? I have no idea whether there are
governesses in the United States, what with the wilderness
aspect and all. I do apologize."

His worry about insulting her was typical of Cedric's
sweetness. His knowledge of New England was very limited, but that was true of everyone she'd met in London.

Earlier that evening, for example, Lady Prunella Smith-
ers had been astounded to learn that Bostonians drank tea.
"For some reason, I thought you threw it all in the harbor,"
she had said, puzzled. "I distinctly remember my governess telling me that Americans abhor tea."

"Boston is quite civilized," Merry informed Cedric. "Though as it happens, I had an English governess."

"Indeed? Ah, that explains your charming manners. She must be very proud of her charge," Cedric said, returning her glove.

In fact, Miss Fairfax would likely faint from shock when she heard the news.

Back in the summer, her governess had vehemently protested Aunt Bess's decision to take Merry to London for the season, arguing that no English gentleman would want to marry her charge, whom she deemed entirely deficient in ladylike graces.

"Let me be the first to admit that I have failed, after a lifetime of instructing the very finest young ladies," she told them shrilly. "I have failed!"

"Merry's reputation has suffered from two broken engagements," Aunt Bess had pointed out. "Mr. Pelford and I both believe that it would be advisable to go farther afield."

It wasn't as if Merry had left Bertie and Dermot at the altar. She'd ended things as soon as she'd recognized her mistakes, although regrettably she hadn't been certain about Bertie until the day before she was due to marry him.

Gossips back home were calling her "Mary, Mary, Quite Contrary" behind her back. What sensible man would trust her to keep her promise?

"Well, this is a thirsty business, proposing," Cedric said, as Merry carefully drew the glove over her newly bejeweled hand. "Why don't we find you some lemonade?"

Merry had discovered earlier that evening that the lemonade on offer looked like piddle and tasted like water. Not that she had voiced this observation, because—*thank you, Miss Fairfax!*—she was perfectly capable of tact.

The lemonade served at balls in London never tasted like much, which suggested it was a taste peculiar to the

English, or at least to the refined segment of London society in which she found herself.

Cedric was likely drinking something other than lemonade; gentlemen usually had different, and presumably better, drinks than did the ladies.

"May I try yours instead?" she asked, reaching toward the glass he held.

Cedric fell back a step. "Snatching a drink from a man's hand is simply not done, darling. But don't fret; I shall guide you through the thickets of English decorum, pointing out your little faux pas before anyone else notices them."

Merry felt her cheeks warm with embarrassment. "I'm sorry. I shall be very grateful for your advice."

"British ladies do not imbibe brandy, but that doesn't mean I'm not sympathetic. I'm sure I can find you something better than lemonade."

He turned and headed for an array of decanters that stood on the sideboard. "I can't imagine why people believe that the lemon is an adequate substitute for the grape." Just as if he were a son of the house, he started pulling the stoppers from the decanters and sniffing them.

"I believe you'll enjoy this," Cedric said, handing her yet another pale yellow drink.

She thanked him and took a tentative sip. It was like wine, but sharper and more flowery. "This is lovely," she said, beaming at him.

"Canary wine looks just like lemonade, so no one will know," he said conspiratorially, clicking his glass against hers. "Here's to your health!"

He refilled his glass and then ushered her to the sofa, respectfully seating himself at the opposite end. Merry could hardly believe that this was actually happening to *her*.

She was betrothed to an English lord, who was telling her in his delicious accent where they would live once they were married. Naturally, he owned a house in one of the city's most genteel areas. Too dazzled—and frankly, too ignorant of London geography—to contribute to the conversation, she finished her wine in silence.

Cedric bounded up and refilled it for her. He settled himself back into his end of the sofa and began telling her about the previous day, when he had wagered against the Prince of Wales at cards, and won.

"I informed the prince that I was thinking of marrying a granddaughter of Lord Merrick," he said. "I told my brother the same, last evening."

"I have yet to meet your brother," Merry said, seizing an opportunity to change the subject. "I always wished I had had a twin sister."

"Later, I shall introduce you. His Grace is rarely seen in a ballroom," Cedric said, sighing. "The duke isn't at home in refined surroundings. He wasn't lucky enough to inherit . . . shall we say, my *aplomb*? I've already told you how resentful he's always been of me. The fact I have won the hand of such a beautiful woman will make him more petulant than usual."

A beautiful woman! Merry generally thought of herself as pretty, but never beautiful. "Beautiful" was a word reserved for women with yellow locks and emerald eyes.

Merry's hair was thick, unfashionably dark, and curled too much to grow past her shoulders. Her eyes weren't starlike, her lips weren't rubies, and her height meant she often looked straight into a man's eyes—so being told she was beautiful made her feel a pulse of pleasure that went right to her toes.

Bertie's red-wagon remark had dealt a blow to her self-esteem. But Cedric's compliments were in an entirely different realm—gracefully delivered, with such deep sincerity. She couldn't stop smiling.

"I feel I must warn you: you mustn't expect His Grace to greet you with open arms," Cedric was saying. "My brother dislikes both America and Americans, I'm afraid. He always votes against you in Lords."

Oh dear. Well, it was better to be forewarned. Merry made up her mind on the spot to avoid the duke whenever possible. The last thing she wanted was to cause Cedric any strife owing to her nationality.

"His opinion is unimportant," Cedric said, sliding closer, a debonair, rakish look lighting his eyes.

Merry's heart instantly beat faster. He was going to kiss her—really kiss her. Pull her into his arms and . . .

He pressed a kiss on her lips.

"You look quite flushed," Cedric said, pulling back. "Perhaps the wine is a bit strong for you?"

"Oh no," Merry cried. "I love it. I love canary wine!" She hastily drained her glass, set it down, and snatched up her fan. He probably thought she was a country bumpkin. "Did you know that laudanum is sometimes made with a base of canary wine?"

Too late, she remembered that her governess had deplored Merry's tendency to rattle off facts when she was embarrassed.

"If a gentleman doesn't know something," Miss Fairfax had said over and over, "it is not for one such as you to mend his ignorance. Besides, facts are boring."

Cedric raised an eyebrow, but tactfully ignored her inept question. "Permit me to refill your glass," he said, and stood.

"I shouldn't drink any more wine," Merry said, not wanting to admit that her head was spinning. But, well, it *was*. Spinning, that is.

She felt distinctly tipsy.

"But we must share a private toast to our betrothal,"

Cedric said, turning around with a decanter in his hand. With his wavy locks falling over his eyes, he was heart-stoppingly handsome.

She nodded, wondering if she ought to simply confess how gauche she felt. They were going to be married, and he would be her most cherished friend in the world. And he was so sweet that he would instantly understand. She opened her mouth—

Cedric said, "You must be feeling terribly out of place."

He *knew*.

He understood her!

"Americans often feel out of place when they first come here to London," he continued, seating himself again.

Merry frowned. She didn't think it was a question of nationality.

"The prince said it best," Cedric went on thoughtfully. "Prinny noted just the other day that the spirit of English-men is entirely different from that of Americans. You can perhaps see it most readily in the servant class; ours are not only more obliging and industrious, but better pleased and happier."

"Well," Merry began, hardly knowing where to start.

"*You* are a natural inhabitant of my country," Cedric said. "Prinny was most reassuring about that. You may be American now, but in short order, your mother's blood will prevail, and you will find yourself refined by the very air of England."

Merry felt as if she'd lost track of the conversation some-time ago. "By the air?" she echoed.

"You will quickly learn all the little things that charac-terize an English gentlewoman. The habits of mind that bespeak gentility without words. For example, I have heard that in America, a man might eschew tongs entirely and pick up a lump of sugar with his fingers."

"A pair of tongs is certainly more proper," Merry ventured, beginning to wonder how much she should defend her countrymen.

"Yet Americans are innocent of a charge of nastiness," Cedric said earnestly. "Where there are no rules, one cannot be wrathful about such an abomination, but in England, things are quite, quite different."

Merry knew very well—because Miss Fairfax had informed her again and again—that she didn't possess a proper delicacy of mind. Obviously, this was a sign of it, because she often snatched up a lump of sugar and dropped it into her tea without a second thought. In fact, she had occasionally done the same when serving her uncle.

Panic fluttered in her stomach. Hopefully, the air of England would start working on her before Cedric realized what she was truly like. What if London's civilizing effect didn't work its magic?

She couldn't—she simply could *not*—break off another engagement.

"Merely by living in this great city, a person acquires elegance of manners," Cedric concluded, setting his empty glass to the side. "Shall we return and announce the happy news that you have accepted my proposal?"

As they reentered the ballroom, Merry saw at once that there was no need to make a formal announcement of their betrothal; twenty or more heads swiveled expectantly in their direction. She glanced up to find her fiancé smiling tenderly at her, for all the world as if she were Juliet and he her Romeo.

Her heart thumped again.

The third time truly *was* the charm. Cedric was ideal.

All she had to do was make herself as perfect as he was.

Chapter Four

Returning to the present . . .

Nigel Hampster, Merry decided, bore a tragic resemblance to his furry little namesake. His nose twitched when he was excited, and since Lady Caroline was encouraging his dull stories by giggling, he was practically wiggling with excitement.

She kept trying to listen and then finding herself succumbing to yet another wave of anxiety about her forthcoming marriage.

Her doubts surely stemmed from the fact that Cedric had proposed and then abandoned her for the card room. It had nothing whatsoever to do with the pleasure she'd felt after coaxing a stranger on the balcony to laughter.

That was foolishness, a symptom of the fickle nature she

had developed in the last few years. What sort of woman had she become? One who could never keep a vow? A capricious flibbertigibbet?

Her father would be so ashamed.

She was ashamed.

After she'd returned Bertie's ring, eight months had passed before she'd met Dermot; then another thirteen between her disengagement from Dermot and meeting Cedric. This time, she was scarcely betrothed to one man before thinking about another. She shuddered, thinking of her own inconstancy.

A momentary foolishness on a balcony was forgivable. But she refused to be a flighty, vacillating little fool who would consider ending things with Cedric for such a stupid reason.

With that thought, she made up her mind to find her fiancé in the card room or wherever he was and demonstrate how much she cared for him.

No, adored him. How much she *adored* him.

A lady wasn't supposed to express affection in public, but he would simply have to endure it. She glanced at Lady Caroline and Mr. Hampster, but they were paying no attention to her. She walked a step or two away so that she could set her wineglass down on a small table. Then she tugged off her left glove, followed by her betrothal ring, and replaced them, this time with the diamond ring outside the glove.

She didn't care for the look, but there were women who did. Some had four or five rings crammed over their gloves.

Her ring sparkled in the light thrown by the chandeliers. It really was beautiful. A woman who wore a diamond engagement ring, she reminded herself, did not throw over the fiancé who had presented her with that ring.

"Miss Pelford."

Merry picked up her drink and turned to greet her hostess with a sigh of relief. Itemizing the defects in her character was making her head ache.

"Miss Pelford," Lady Portmeadow said, "I am honored to introduce you to the Duke of Trent, who expressed a wish to meet his future sister-in-law. Your Grace, this is Miss Pelford, who hails from Boston, originally. In America, you understand."

Merry looked up. And froze.

She should be curtsying. She should be saying something—anything! Instead, she stared silently and then, as if she were assembling a puzzle, his face began to look familiar.

Before her stood the austerely dressed man from the balcony. Or, as he had been introduced, the Duke of Trent.

Cedric's twin brother.

His hair was dark and gold, the color of winter wheat, whereas her future husband's hair was lighter, like chaff in the sunlight. She hadn't see his eyes clearly in the dusky light outdoors, but now she discovered they were blue—not Cedric's lazy, sweet blue, but a dark, demanding hue.

He was more muscled than Cedric—she disliked exceptionally muscled men, she reminded herself—but she would guess that he was the same height, to the half inch.

She should curtsy.

"Oh, for heaven's sake," she exclaimed without thinking. "Did you know who I was?"

"You've met," Lady Portmeadow cried, her head swiveling between them. "Your Grace, why did you—"

"We had not been formally introduced," the duke bit out. "And no, Miss Pelford, I had no idea who you were."

He appeared unamused. Merry's heart sank to the

bottom of her slippers. Likely he thought that Cedric should have introduced the two of them. Merry had to admit that she agreed.

But he bowed, so Merry responded with a hasty curtsy. As she straightened, she glanced around, hoping to see Cedric. Her mind was reeling with the fact that she had unwittingly engaged in a tête-à-tête with her fiancé's brother.

It was unthinkable. How could the laughing stranger on the balcony, the man who made her feel witty and desirable, be the brother whom Cedric had described with such disdain?

There was something very unsettling about having had a flirtatious conversation with one's brother-in-law.

Almost brother-in-law.

"I look forward to dancing with your daughter later this evening, Lady Portmeadow," the duke said, his tone strongly suggesting that their hostess withdraw. The lady's eyes were eagerly darting between the two of them as if she were taking notes for the twopenny press.

There was no need to be impolite to their hostess merely because she was a bit nosy, so Merry gave the duke a look that said as much. "I expect you'll wish to ask Miss Portmeadow for a minuet, Your Grace. She is one of the most accomplished young ladies of my acquaintance, and she dances beautifully."

"Spoken like the sister you shall soon be!" Lady Portmeadow exclaimed. "Now that your brother has found a wife, Your Grace, you must look for a duchess. Why, we scarcely see you in society!"

"I do not enjoy dancing," the duke stated.

"Ah, but Miss Portmeadow is divinely graceful," Merry insisted. If there was one thing she was certain of, it was that she didn't want the duke to think that *she* had any interest in dancing with him.

"Miss Pelford, when will you marry Lord Cedric?" Lady Portmeadow asked brightly.

Merry winced inwardly. Taking a deep breath, she reminded herself that her third engagement would be her last.

"We have yet to make plans." She forced her mouth into a smile.

The duke's expression darkened as if he might explode. Apparently, he disapproved.

Cedric had described his brother as dictatorial, not to mention ill-disposed toward Americans. As head of the family, he might believe that he had power over his brother's decisions.

If that was the case, His Grace would have to learn differently. American women did not allow themselves to be pushed about by a man simply because he was titled.

Merry straightened her shoulders and turned to their hostess. "You must put the duke down for Miss Portmeadow's supper dance," she said sweetly. "As part of the family, I shall make it one of my first tasks to see that His Grace finds a wife."

Lady Portmeadow seemed surprised by the suggestion, but as Merry surmised, she was not one to look a gift horse in the mouth. If the Duke of Trent took Miss Portmeadow in to supper, eligible gentlemen would take notice. She smiled, waggled her fingers, and slipped away before His Grace could say yea or nay.

They stood looking at one another silently. The duke had a cross look on his face. Even so, he was wickedly handsome—as handsome as Cedric.

In that instant she realized exactly why he didn't care for the idea that Cedric was marrying her. It had nothing to do with her nationality or his right to approve of his brother's spouse.

It was their conversation on the balcony. The duke thought she was a trollop, a woman who accosted utter strangers and flirted with them in the near dark.

It was unfortunate—indeed, it was humiliating—that they had met under such improper circumstances. But it had happened and there was no wishing it away. They had to acknowledge it and move on.

With that in mind, she pushed her untouched glass of wine into his hand. He took it, looking faintly surprised.

Then she put her hands on her hips, just as Aunt Bess always did when she was vexed. "Why on earth are you dressed so plainly? You don't look like a duke."

"How would you possibly know, Miss Pelford? I can assure you, if you didn't grasp it yourself, that the Duke of Villiers's sartorial foibles are not representative of those of his rank."

"I cannot be the first person who has misconstrued your rank. You look like a Quaker—certainly not ducal."

"I needn't dress to advertise," he said dryly. "People give me the same admiration as a five-legged calf without prompting."

Well, spit. He was a living example of why people bowed and scraped in front of dukes. There was something so powerful and just plain imposing about him that even she had the impulse to try to assuage his temper.

She took her hands off her hips, because the posture wasn't natural for her.

"May I return your lemonade now?" he asked, a sardonic look in his eyes.

The last thing she wanted was for him to think she was as impressed as everyone else. As a member of the peerage, His Grace was used to being fawned over. He would need some time to grow accustomed to a sister-in-law who treated him as though he walked on the ground with the rest of humanity.

Merry put her hands back on her hips, the better to show off her indifference to his title. "You don't appear to be happy that I'm joining your family," she observed.

"I am not."

His voice was a growl.

If Merry's voice were capable of that register, she would have growled right back. He was making her a little nervous, so her breath felt tight in her chest and her voice was a near whisper. "You don't feel your brother has made a suitable choice?"

His eyes narrowed, but he didn't reply.

It had to be said. "I much enjoyed our earlier conversation, Your Grace. I should be sorry if you feel I am an inappropriate spouse for Lord Cedric in light of it. Let me assure you that I do not make a habit of conversing with strangers."

"You misunderstand me." Something almost violent, a kind of controlled fury, colored his words and ran over Merry's skin like the touch of his finger.

"I am aware that you and your brother are not on good terms," she observed, taking the bull by the horns.

The duke was again silent.

"I expect you underestimate him," Merry suggested. "He does the same of you."

His jaw tightened. Perhaps the duke didn't know that Cedric's characterizations were so harsh. "I've noticed that siblings are often blind to each other's best qualities," she added hastily. "But surely you are aware that your brother is a very kind and thoughtful person."

The duke just stared at the floor for a long moment. Cedric was right; bitter jealousy had divided them. What a shame. A drop of confusion slid down her back like icy water. The duke was so very different from Cedric's description of him.

But it was true that they were opposites. If Cedric dazzled, his brother was dark, and possibly dangerous.

Well, that was overstating it.

"I suppose that is possible," the duke said finally, lifting his eyes to hers.

"I was an only child, but I gather it is quite common. In time, you will come to recognize each other's good qualities," she said encouragingly. "Why, I expect you have no idea that Lord Cedric is deeply romantic."

A moment of silence followed. "You are right about my ignorance of that trait," His Grace said.

What did it say about her own character that she could scarcely recall why she had agreed to marry Cedric? At this very moment she was having trouble remembering to breathe properly; she found the duke's glower absurdly thrilling.

She wanted to make him laugh again. She wanted to lean forward and tempt him into looking at her breasts.

She wanted . . .

"I think I fell in love with him when he compared me to a summer's day," she cried, rushing into speech. "A summer's day," she repeated firmly. For some reason, it didn't sound quite as romantic as it had when Cedric, kneeling at her feet, had first murmured it.

Another silence. Then: "I certainly didn't know my brother was capable of quoting Shakespeare," His Grace drawled.

Of course, Cedric had been quoting poetry. How stupid of her not to have recognized it. The English were forever trotting out a line or two of the Bard and then waiting for her to applaud. She was getting sick of the man's name.

" 'Shall I compare thee to a summer's day?' " the duke recited in a flat monotone. " 'Thou art more lovely and more temperate.' "

His intonation made it clear that he found her neither lovely nor temperate, whatever that meant.

"Cedric's poetic nature makes it easy to understand why I fell in love with him so quickly!" The sentence came out in a chirping voice that didn't sound in the least believable.

" 'Cedric'?" His Grace repeated.

"We are not so ceremonious in America," she said, defending her informality. "Indeed, as we will soon be family, you may address me as Merry, if you wish. Not Mary, as in Mary, Queen of Scots," she added, "but Merry, as in Merry Christmas. My mother was a rebel."

He gave her a questioning look.

"She was English, and Christmas was not well regarded in Boston when she first arrived," Merry explained. "Observing an English holiday was considered rather inflammatory at that time. I never knew my mother, but my father told me that she wanted me to have a name that reminded her of home."

"I gather she would have approved of you marrying an Englishman."

Merry nodded. "I think so. It was one of the reasons that I—that I came here. Besides the reason I told you about, I mean."

The duke had forgotten that the glass he held was actually hers, because before she could warn him, he took a swallow, then sputtered. "Bloody hell, what is this?"

"Canary wine," Merry said hastily. "But I hadn't yet tasted it, Your Grace. You may drink the rest."

He put the glass down on the table. "You were telling me that you fell in love with my brother after he quoted some lines from Shakespeare."

"I must confess that I didn't recognize the quotation. I

could never bring myself to read poetry, let alone memorize it."

"Shakespeare wrote that poem for a young man," His Grace observed.

Merry wasn't sure what to make of that. "My governess despaired of me," she said, trying to lighten the atmosphere. "I can't make poetry stick in my head. I managed to memorize only a line or two, and those badly."

"You, who have all those facts at your command, can't remember more than two lines of poetry?"

"Not even that. 'Ye little birds that sit and sing amidst the shady valleys . . .' something, something . . . 'Go pretty birds about her bower, sing pretty birds, she may not . . .' something . . . followed by a lot of warbling." She wrinkled her nose.

For a second, she saw a gleam of laughter in his eyes, but then it disappeared. "Yet Cedric's use of poetry was persuasive. Were your other fiancés similarly literary?"

Merry was wrestling with herself, because it seemed that, contrary to her previous conviction, she did like muscular men, at least the one standing before her. The mere sight of the strong column of his throat as he drank had sent a shiver straight through her. She'd never felt *that* before—not with Bertie, nor Dermot, nor Cedric. She tried to banish the thought the moment it surfaced, but panic spread through her like black oil across a puddle.

What's more, the duke was close enough that she could smell wintergreen soap again, and it was intoxicating.

Far more than Cedric's musky cologne.

The evidence was inescapable. She truly was an awful person, fickle in every way. She was attracted to her fiancé's brother, which probably broke some sort of ecclesiastical law.

She could control these disgusting urges. It was simply a

matter of taking her marriage vows. After she and Cedric were wed, it would all be different.

Avoiding the question of literature—Bertie's "red wagon" spoke for itself—she answered his real question. "As I mentioned on the balcony, I believed myself to be in love before, but it feels very, very different this time."

He didn't look convinced.

"Do look at my betrothal ring," she chirped, lifting her hand so that the diamonds caught fire from the chandelier. "Cedric—*darling* Cedric," she amended, "chose it for me because he said I remind him of—well, of some duchess who was given a diamond ring by an archduke."

The duke's large hand lifted her small one toward the candlelight. For a moment they both stared at the sparkling cluster of diamonds she wore. "It was the Archduke Maximilian of Austria."

"You know the story?" She was surprised. Cedric was interested in objets d'art, jewelry, and fashion, but His Grace didn't seem to be that sort of man. She'd assume him to be an expert about horses, politics, science . . . things of that nature.

"Our father gave a diamond ring to our mother, and so he liked to tell the story of the first such token."

Merry felt her lips curl into a genuine smile. "You see how romantic Cedric is? He must have bought me this ring because your father did the same for your mother. My mother died when I was born, but . . ." She trailed off.

"But?" The duke shot her a look.

"My father buried my mother with her wedding ring. He told me that she was so happy on their wedding day that he knew she would haunt him if he took it away from her, even to give it to me."

His Grace said nothing, so Merry gave him a crooked grin. "Theirs was a love match, you see. A mésalliance."

"How so?"

"Oh, my mother was from a respectable English family, visiting her cousins in Boston when she met my father. His ambitions were not small, but he wasn't wealthy when they wed."

The duke's eyes were intent on her face, making her heart skip a beat.

"I would guess that your father became highly successful," he observed.

"He was a member of our Constitutional Congress." Merry raised her chin, as proud of her father as she was of her country's fledgling republic, where there was no House of Lords, and no one was born into power.

"If he was anything like you, I suspect he would have become president."

Something about the duke was turning her into a woman she wouldn't recognize. A dishonorable woman, who thought it would be a good idea to smile at her own fiancé's brother.

Not just smile, but *smile*.

"I like to think so," she said briskly. "Your Grace, it is nearly time for your dance with Miss Portmeadow. I haven't seen your brother in some time, so I must find him."

She tried to infuse her voice with adoration for Cedric but ended up sounding like a bleating goat.

The duke's mouth tightened, then he said, "Of course. It is hard for lovers to be apart for long."

There was definitely a rough edge to him. It was as if that Mohawk warrior had put on a coat and strode into a London ballroom. He didn't belong amid all these polished gentlemen. Cedric was right about that, at least.

"Do you know," the duke said conversationally, "that no one except yourself has gone head to head with me in years?"

She couldn't stop herself from smiling at him. "That

is all too apparent, Your Grace. Clearly, you have been shamefully cosseted. Your mother is likely to blame."

His mother must have adored having little twin boys. Merry could just imagine what they had been like, with hair like shiny golden coins, blue, blue eyes, and sweet smiles.

To her surprise, the duke's expression turned bleak. A footman came past, offering a tray with glasses of lemonade. Merry shook her head.

"You don't care for lemonade?"

"No, thank you," she said cautiously. Something had changed in the very air. His Grace looked as if he'd come to a conclusion—one that didn't please him, but one to which he was grimly resigned.

"Your choice of beverage, canary wine, is not customary for English ladies, as I suspect you are aware."

He was cooler, distant. She hadn't realized his eyes were warm until they were . . . not.

"I find lemonade unsophisticated," Merry said, managing a careless smile. "I prefer something stronger."

"I wasn't aware that Lady Portmeadow offered a choice."

"She doesn't. But Cedric brought me a special drink. He is most thoughtful."

"'A special drink,'" the duke echoed, his voice neutral.

She was starting to feel nettled. "Do Englishwomen restrict themselves to lemonade? Because my English governess unaccountably neglected to teach me that rule."

"Am I to take it that American ladies drink fortified wine on each and every occasion?"

"What if we do?" Merry retorted, raising her chin. "What possible reason could you have to condemn or approve the practice?"

His eyes drifted over her, and not in an agreeable way, not in the appreciative manner that he'd looked at her before. Something was different about him now. He looked every inch the aristocrat.

"As you mentioned earlier, Miss Pelford, you are clearly in need of instruction about how to comport yourself in English society. Permit me to note a rule that your governess overlooked: young ladies do not drink spirits. You will have to take care not to display inebriation."

"I have never been inebriated," she said hotly.

"I am relieved to hear it. I have one more point to make, and then I'll escort you to my brother."

Merry ground her teeth. "Please do," she managed.

"My brother is overly fond of brandy."

For a moment Merry couldn't imagine whom he referred to. Was there another Allardyce brother, one whom Cedric had neglected to mention? No, of course not. The duke meant Cedric. It was slanderous, and proved that this estrangement was far worse than she'd believed.

She had to defend her betrothed. "You are mistaken," she said, letting her voice have a distinct edge. "I have never even seen Cedric tipsy."

His gaze was rock-steady. "You will."

To her dismay, Merry realized that the duke's stubborn insistence meant that one of her fiancé's claims about his brother was indeed true. Cedric had once told her that the duke spread lies about him throughout London, including a fantastic tale about how Cedric had once almost shot a bishop.

And now His Grace was telling her that his brother—her fiancé—was an inebriate. She made a silent apology to Cedric, resolving to say as much when she saw him next. She was ashamed that she hadn't entirely believed him.

"His claims are absurd," Cedric had told her, "but you know how it is. Some people will believe anything."

She couldn't abide underhanded men, not after Dermot

had sneakily borrowed against his expectation of marrying her.

She let some of her disdain creep into her eyes. His Grace shouldn't be allowed to think that everyone would believe the lies he told about his own brother. She, if no one else, would always take Cedric's side.

"I gather you do not believe me," he said.

Merry didn't know how to answer. She could hardly inform the duke that Cedric had warned her that his brother would try to ruin his reputation.

The duke's eyes rested on hers for a moment and then he looked past her at the crowded ballroom. It was remarkable that no one had interrupted them, but the ball seemed to be swirling on, taking no account of the two of them. Of course, everyone knew they would soon be family members, and there was nothing very interesting in the chatter of a brother- and sister-in-law.

"Has he told you how our parents died?" he asked, with an abrupt change of subject.

"He has not."

"Then I shall tell you. Seven years ago, on a fine spring evening, my father took my mother out for an airing in a light phaeton."

Merry felt a trickle of dread.

"Phaetons require deft handling and can be dangerous even in the best of circumstances." His voice was even, but something flickered in his eyes that could only be pain. "And easily fatal, if the driver has consumed the better part of a bottle of brandy before taking up the reins."

The implication was plain. "Tell me your mother didn't die in that carriage accident," she whispered.

"They both did."

Her stomach clenched. "No," she breathed. "I'm so sorry."

"Sadly, my father often drank to excess, and Cedric

takes after him in that respect." His voice didn't invite pity; without question, he would damn the pretensions of anyone who offered sympathy.

Her fingers twitched with a ferocious wish to put her hand on his cheek and soothe the pain that he felt. No wonder His Grace was so worried about Cedric's drinking. The family had experienced a terrible tragedy, all of it springing from one evening of Bacchanalian excess.

But it wasn't her place to offer the duke consolation. All she could do was try to mend the breach.

"You are mistaken about Cedric," Merry said, gentling her voice. "I assure you that he will not cause an accident like your father's, because he does not overindulge. He has been courting me for well over a month, and I've never seen a sign of dissipation."

He had been looking at the floor, but now his eyes cut to her. "I must ask you to not drink even canary wine around my brother. Your future husband needs his wife to help curb his worst habits rather than join in them."

Before she could respond, she heard Cedric's welcome voice coming from behind her. Merry whirled in relief. Even though they were surrounded by people, somehow this conversation had become more improper, more intimate, than the one she and the duke had had on the balcony.

"Lord Cedric," she said brightly, "your brother and I have been acquainting ourselves."

"I'm sure that has been a charming experience," he said.

"It has been most interesting," His Grace said blandly. "You have made an excellent choice. The future Lady Cedric will make us all proud."

"I can't tell you how happy it makes me to have your approval," Cedric replied.

"There was no question of my refusal," the duke said. "I know you are eager to set up your own household."

Merry felt as if small knives were flying around her head, slicing through the air so quickly that she couldn't see them.

"Miss Pelford showed me her ring," His Grace continued. "A diamond cluster for a diamond of the first water."

Cedric's lips widened. No one could call his expression a smile, though there was something satisfied about it. "I gather you applaud the wisdom of my decision?"

Merry frowned. Another, silent, exchange was taking place, which she couldn't begin to interpret.

"As pertains the ring," the duke said. "Certainly." He shrugged.

"What on earth are the two of you talking about?" Merry asked.

"Your ring," Cedric said. "You are wearing a ring that belonged to our mother, the late Duchess of Trent. But as the duke well knows, she would want my wife to have it, not his."

Merry looked at the duke, whose face was utterly expressionless. "*What?*" she cried. She turned to Cedric. "But—but you said—"

"I said I chose it for you," he said silkily, "and I did."

"I assumed you bought it for me." She caught herself. She didn't want to sound like a disappointed child. With a swift tug, she removed the ring. "This ring is meant not for me, Your Grace, but for your bride. You must keep it for her."

"My brother is rich enough to buy his wife any number of rings."

Merry dimly registered that she did not like Cedric's tone. He sounded vaguely spiteful, which she didn't like in women, and even less in men.

That wasn't important at the moment.

The duke had shifted position. He was leaning against

the wall and staring down, as if there was something fascinating about the floorboards at his feet. "I believe my mother would be quite happy to see her ring on the hand of the future Lady Cedric," he agreed.

Well, spit. There was something she didn't understand here, something about the duke and his mother.

His Grace looked as calm as a fishpond, but she saw through him. There was a secret attached to the duchess's ring.

"You two may dislike each other," she said, giving first one, then the other, a pointed frown. "But I would be grateful if you could stop this childish game of insulting each other in my presence. I feel as if I'm breaking out in hives."

"Hives?" Cedric repeated with palpable distaste.

"Hives, or boils?" the duke murmured, sounding amused.

Merry revised the image of their mother smiling lovingly at her sweet little boys. The poor duchess had likely found herself in the midst of a pitched battle from the moment they spoke their first words.

The problem was that they were both stubborn, willful, and English. There was something to being English, she was discovering, just as there was something to being American.

She understood the inherent character traits of Americans: they were open-minded, ambitious, independent, and brave—sometimes to the point of foolhardiness.

The British, however? Perhaps it was a hallmark of their nationality that these two men were so stubborn that they could choke on it.

Feeling a wave of exhaustion, she tucked her hand into the crook of Cedric's arm. "I'd like to go home, please. Aunt Bess mentioned that you would accompany us, because the axle on your carriage is broken, isn't that it?"

If she hadn't been looking straight at Cedric, she wouldn't have seen his eyes fly to his brother's and then look down. "Something like that," he murmured.

"Miss Pelford," His Grace said, and swept her a magnificent bow.

"Your ring," Merry said, and held it out to him.

"Oh for God's sake, just keep it," her fiancé said sharply.

"This is the future duchess's ring," Merry stated. "While I appreciate the sentiment with which you chose it for me, Lord Cedric, I cannot wear a ring that will, by rights, belong to my sister-in-law."

"I am giving it to you, Miss Pelford," the duke said. "You are in love with my brother. It will serve as my wedding present."

"No, thank you," she said. Proving that an American could be as stubborn as any Englishman, she held out the ring once again.

"We could sell it," Cedric put in—most unhelpfully, she thought.

The duke muttered something under his breath and accepted it back.

Merry just wanted to go home. A part of her wanted to go all the way home to Boston, where brothers didn't growl at each other like bears sharing a too-small cave.

Lady Portmeadow appeared. "My butler will be calling the supper dance in a few minutes!" she said brightly. "May I say that it has been such a pleasure to see the three of you chatting so cheerfully? I know that my dear friend the late duchess would have been very happy." She beamed at Merry. "Our sex serves as nature's peacemakers, don't you agree?"

Her ladyship hauled the duke away before His Grace could express his opinion about Merry's peacemaking abilities, though not before he threw her a glance that reminded her it had not been his choice to sup with Miss Portmeadow.

"We need a drink," Cedric said, breaking the silence. "I always need a drink after spending more than five minutes with my brother. Though I must say, you did quite well with him. I thought I'd find the two of you at each other's throats."

"Why?" she asked, startled. "Surely you don't believe me capable of such incivility."

"The duke despises Americans. Told you that before. Oddly enough, I got the impression he actually likes you. I'll fetch you a glass of wine from the library."

"I'd rather go home." She'd had enough of the ball, the betrothal, and all these exhaustingly fraught exchanges.

"One more drink," Cedric insisted, taking her by the wrist and drawing her toward the door. "I couldn't possibly face the ride to Portman Square in a closed carriage with your aunt without first cushioning the blow."

Merry had felt worry before; when, for example, she'd come to see that life with Bertie would mean watching her husband hack his way through forty or fifty duels, if he even survived to his third decade. Later, she'd fretted over the depth of Dermot's attachment to money—and the depth of his enthusiasm for spending hers.

But it was not until this moment, hearing her fiancé refer scornfully to the person she loved most in the world—the person who had raised her, and had sacrificed so much to ensure her well-being—that she experienced true panic.

She started to say something—*You don't really mean that!*—but stopped herself. He *did* mean it. He'd met Bess only a handful of times, but he'd clearly made up his mind.

"My aunt is very dear to me," she said forcefully.

Her tone of voice obviously sank in.

"She's very colorful," Cedric offered. "It's just that colorful can be so exhausting in large doses. All that poetic fervor . . . not very good ton."

"My aunt *is* the very best 'ton,' " she said, rattling the word off as if she hadn't had to ask their butler what it meant. "Her decency and kindness are infinitely more meaningful than any pedigree."

"I do realize that your aunt is representative of the best people to be found in America," Cedric said hastily.

Her fiancé could be a real dunderhead sometimes, Merry thought. But wasn't every man like that on occasion?

She was glumly certain that she knew the answer to that. Her uncle Thaddeus had an alarming propensity toward belligerence for the sake of it; he and Bertie had been hens of the same color. Indeed, either of them would have challenged any man who labeled him a hen.

Her aunt was always pulling Uncle Thaddeus away just before he could throw down the gauntlet. It was part of marriage, putting up with men and soothing over their foolish quarrels.

Merry saw the duke again about an hour later in the foyer, after she had finally persuaded Cedric to leave. His Grace bowed so stiffly that her aunt bridled visibly, and announced in the carriage that Merry's future brother-in-law didn't appear to be a nice man.

"I apologize for being overly forthright about a family member," Bess told Cedric, "but there's no reason for His Grace to be ill-mannered. I cannot like it. Is he always like that?"

Cedric was lying back in the corner of the carriage, his legs stretched out between them. "Have you heard of Jaquet-Droz's automaton?" he inquired, by way of response.

Merry's uncle had been drowsing in his corner, but

he opened his eyes at this. Like her father, Thaddeus was an inventor, and there was no well-known machine that he hadn't investigated. "Made entirely of bits of wire and the like, and yet it can write with ink and a quill pen."

"My brother's just like that," Cedric said. "A man of wire and brass. Except I think I'd compare him to John Dee's wooden beetle. The beetle could actually fly, you know." He chuckled to himself.

If Merry hadn't already realized it, she'd know it now. Cedric liked his brother about as much as the devil likes holy water: to wit, not at all.

"I don't know about auto-men," Bess said, "but the duke was not very nice, considering that he was meeting his future relatives."

Merry bit back an instinct to defend His Grace. The duke wasn't mechanical or unfeeling, as Cedric had implied. Indeed, Merry had the idea that he was all raw flame underneath his chilly exterior.

What would have happened to her if there had been such a breach in the family that her uncle and aunt had refused to open their home to an orphan after her father died? The tension between Cedric and his brother was unacceptable, if only for the sake of the children she hoped to have.

"You won't see much of him," Cedric reassured her aunt. "He departs tomorrow—apparently he's planning to spend upwards of three weeks mucking about in a slate mine he's bought in Wales."

That was just as well. Out on the balcony, she had responded to the duke in an entirely inappropriate way, and it was even worse when they talked of his parents' death. This was the best of all solutions.

In the next three weeks, she would grow closer and fall

more in love with her fiancé. By the time the duke reappeared in London, she would be able to greet him without a trace of self-consciousness.

That balcony foolishness would be forgotten, and they could forge a relationship as brother and sister, just as they ought.

Chapter Five

*T*rent walked up the stairs to his bedchamber in the hours just before dawn, weary to his bones. He'd stayed out half the night the better to avoid his brother, which was a damned foolish reason.

Over the years, he'd grown used to the peculiarities of being a twin. He and Cedric were as dissimilar as two people could be—and yet they often hit milestones at very nearly the same moment. They'd taken their first steps together; spoken their first words to each other; lost their virginity on the same day, albeit in different counties.

But nothing like this had ever happened before.

It had to be some odd alignment of the planets. Or perhaps it was because the Allardyce brothers were particularly suited to American women. Aye, that was likely the answer.

He merely had to find another American, one who hadn't already accepted a ring from Cedric.

If only a man could go to a horse fair and pick out a wife. Then it occurred to Trent's exhausted brain that, in fact, Almack's was the human equivalent of that horse fair. Unfortunately, he detested the bloody place.

He entered his bedchamber and came to a halt. Cedric was lying in wait for him. Literally.

His brother was asleep in an armchair next to the fireplace, a boozy mess. His mouth hung open and he was listing to the side like a fir tree heavy with snow. His cravat was crumpled and his yellow curls were closer to a tangle than an elegant tumble.

"Cedric," Trent said wearily. "Wake up."

He dropped his coat on a chair and wrenched off his neck cloth. In telling contrast to his twin's fawn pantaloons and rose-colored coat, his coat was black, his pantaloons plain, and his boots hadn't a single tassel.

He had to repeat himself a few times, and had stripped to the waist and was washing at the basin before his brother finally stirred.

"Oh, for God's sake," Cedric drawled behind his back, "don't tell me you're still washing behind your ears every night, like a good little boy."

Trent straightened and turned as he toweled off his shoulders. "What are you doing in my chamber?"

"It pains me to say it, but you are verging on burly," Cedric said, his eyes resting on Trent's chest with distaste. "You would present a far more fashionable silhouette if you took a carriage around London like every other peer. Clearly, you are exerting yourself too much."

Cedric affected a shudder that set Trent's teeth on edge. His brother had never been like this when they were boys. These days it was as if he concocted new mannerisms every day just to irritate.

"I have no interest in debating the merits of a slender physique," he replied, "especially after spending the entire bloody afternoon listening to arguments about the failure of the Peace of Amiens, followed by that charming incident at the ball. What the hell was that about? You had to steal Mother's ring behind my back?"

"A nobleman ought to at least make an effort," Cedric said, entirely ignoring his question. "You represent the family, *Duke*—though God knows, you don't bother to play the part, or even look it."

Trent always used to be Jack to his twin, if to no one else—until their father died. Since he'd inherited the title, Cedric had addressed him only as Duke, the term uttered with obvious distaste.

Cedric scowled when he didn't respond. "Forget the diamond. I had to catch you before you left for Wales. Lady Portmeadow has sent you no fewer than five missives regarding the East End Charity Hospital, and you haven't paid her the courtesy of a response."

"What does she want?" Trent bent over to pull off a boot. The letters must be in the stack that his secretary deemed personal—which he never bothered to open. Years ago, he and his twin had neatly divided the responsibilities of an English lord, and Cedric had appropriated all those involving social events—particularly those at which strong drink flowed like water.

"You never looked at them, did you?" Cedric asked with a sniff. "Did you even realize that you hosted tonight's ball in honor of the hospital with her ladyship?"

Trent straightened, boot in hand. "What?"

"You know, two hosts, one party. She's as stingy as they come, so she leapt at the idea. You paid for the champagne."

"How did that come about, given that I know nothing of it?"

"I'm certain I told you weeks ago. Or perhaps I forgot. It was one of my more brilliant ideas, that you and Lady Portmeadow should share the expenses, if not the duties."

Cedric pushed himself out of the chair and walked unsteadily to Trent's dressing table, where he propped himself on one hand and leaned close to the mirror. "Now the ball is over, Lady Portmeadow would like you to release funds for the wing of the hospital. They're going to break ground next week."

Trent dropped the boot with the thump. "I'm building a hospital wing?"

"I've put a year into ensuring that hospital breaks ground. You didn't really think that our family wouldn't contribute, did you?" Cedric turned, a sardonic twist on his lips. "The Duke of Trent is building a wing on the hospital in memory of his oh-so-beloved parents. It's only a few thousand pounds."

"You have no right to promise thousands of pounds to anyone," Trent stated.

"Lord Portmeadow," his brother drawled, "is the head of that precious Committee on Standing Orders that you are always complaining about."

An all-too-familiar frustration rose in Trent's throat. After inheriting the dukedom seven years before, he'd succeeded in turning his impoverished ancestral estate into a flourishing concern that employed hundreds, but the one person he had been unable to master was his twin.

"You should be glad that your hoard is going to good use," Cedric said, with a squinty-eyed smile. He was happiest when he managed to provoke Trent—and he knew exactly how to do it. He apparently devoted his sober hours to dreaming up new ways to force Trent to fall in with one of his schemes.

Trent picked up the dropped boot and tossed it in the general direction of the wall. Cedric was right: it was too late to withdraw his sponsorship without offending the lady and her husband, who was one of the most powerful men in the House of Lords.

More importantly, he had always meant to support the hospital, though he would have preferred to be consulted about his donation. That charity was the only thing Cedric had done in the last year other than order new coats and drink himself into a stupor.

God knew why his brother had taken on the task, but he had talked an impressive number of people into supporting the project.

"The wing is in memory of our parents?" Trent asked.

"Yes," Cedric said, his voice taking on a false sweetness that Trent loathed. "I thought of specifying Mother, but I had the idea you might object."

Trent didn't answer. The late duchess had never pretended not to favor her younger son. And to despise her elder.

"The wing will be devoted to the care of impoverished orphans," Cedric continued. "We *are* orphans, after all."

"I scarcely think that we qualify as orphans, in that we were twenty when the duke and duchess died," Trent said, tugging off his second boot.

"*I* for one am practically impoverished," Cedric said.

"You have a tidy income, and the house in Berkeley Square," Trent said, adding, "not to mention the fact that you are affianced to an heiress." It was ridiculous to feel a twinge at the memory of Merry Pelford laughing about English fortune-hunters.

Trent should be happy about his twin's betrothal; it

meant Cedric would finally establish his own household. A few years ago, Trent had deeded him a townhouse that had belonged to an aunt, but Cedric had declined to leave Cavendish Square. He liked playing the duke too much.

For example, he had taken the ducal town coach to Lady Portmeadow's ball, leaving Trent to make his way in a curricle. But Cedric would have to buy his own carriage now. Hell, he would have to buy his own engagement ring; the ducal diamond felt as if it were burning a hole in Trent's pocket.

"You never said what you think of my fiancée," Cedric said. "I know she's American, but Merry's mother was one of Lord Merrick's daughters."

"Merrick?"

"A Hertfordshire baron who fled to Boston after winning a duel in which he killed his opponent. Not the most desirable connection, but she's apparently as rich as Croesus, so who cares? I've put our solicitor on to an assessment of the money. I'll be damned if I marry a pig in the poke. I want every penny documented before I see her in church."

"Why the solicitor?" Trent asked. "Didn't Miss Pelford's father provide you the details when he gave permission?"

"Gave permission? As if an American would quibble with his daughter marrying a lord? The man's dead, in any case, and an uncle is managing her supposed fortune."

Cedric dropped back into the armchair. "I'm just not convinced she's good enough to become my wife. What does she contribute besides filthy lucre? She's a Yankee, and no one would describe her as a diamond of the first water. She's a long Meg, for one thing. Feel as if I'm dancing with a man."

Trent had a sudden vision of Merry's luscious figure, and his fist curled instinctively. It wasn't his business.

"I'm the son of a duke. She's from one of best families over there, but is that really such a distinction?" Cedric's mouth twisted. "I heard a rumor that her uncle made a fortune inventing some sort of barnyard geegaw. If that's the case, I'm definitely selling myself short."

Their mother had always reasoned that since the entire estate would one day be Trent's, he must learn to be generous to his brother. No matter what Cedric had wanted, he had got: on one notable birthday, even the tin soldiers that had been meant for Trent.

As a consequence, Cedric had grown up viewing life as a competition in which he, owner of the lesser title, was always deserving of more.

"You know best," Trent said.

"Now I think about it, I'm too young to marry," his brother said moodily, pulling a flask from inside his coat and taking a swallow. "Perhaps when we're thirty. You haven't even considered the question of an heir, have you? You wouldn't be the first to have a cod instead of a cock."

Bloody hell. Cedric must have already drunk a bottle of brandy. He was deemed throughout polite society to have exquisite manners, but when he was drunk, his conversation veered between crass and vicious.

One would suppose Trent could have helped his brother stop drinking, but no. He had emptied the wine cellars that had been started by the first duke. He had stopped drinking himself. He had cut off Cedric's allowance. He had reasoned with him, and wrestled with him, and given him ultimatums.

Nothing had made the slightest difference.

"Maybe if I wait, I can find a grocer's daughter," Cedric said now, with a bark of laughter that had nothing to do with humor. "Don't you love that idea? A grocer's daughter becoming a lady."

"In fact, I had the same thought you did," Trent said. "I, too, intend to marry by the end of the season."

"Just how are you planning to meet the lady?" Cedric inquired. "Are eligible misses to be found in the slate mines these days?"

"It's only April," Trent said, shrugging. "There's time after I return from Wales."

"It'll be easy enough, since you don't need a dowry. It's only poor bastards like myself who have to sell our bodies and our titles to the highest bidder in order to keep bread on the table. I suppose I might as well stick with the heiress I've got."

Trent pulled his shirt on again. In this mood, Cedric could blather on for hours, remaining on the knife edge of inebriation before passing out. "I'm going to find something to eat," Trent said, heading toward the door. "Would you like to join me?"

"For God's sake," his brother said with disgust, "would you just ring the bloody bell the way every other man of our station does? The servants have nothing to do until you ask them to put together a plate of food."

The knife boy slept in the kitchen. If the bell rang, the boy would awake the butler, who would dress hastily and rouse the cook, Mrs. Button, who would rouse the housekeeper, in order to get the keys to the pantry. A kitchen maid would get out of bed to get the banked fire back up—and two hours later, a splendid supper would appear on a tray, brought by a footman who was half awake, but dressed in livery.

"I only want bread and cheese," Trent stated. "I'll walk you to your room."

"As if I needed a bloody escort," his brother said, lurching to his feet. "I can find my own bloody chamber."

They walked down the corridor while Cedric muttered

about bread and cheese, which—according to him—no one above the rank of a tapster would eat unless stranded in a snowstorm. "And perhaps not even then. A refined palate needs to be coddled. Assaulting it with bitter flavors and coarse grains will leave it unsuited to appreciate delicate flavors."

He sounded so earnest that Trent grunted some sort of response.

"It's the difference between sipping wine from crystal and throwing back beer from a redware mug in the pub."

Trent had no idea what redware was. But a pub? He loved a dark pub and a hearty ale. Which just went to show that somehow he and his brother had got mixed up in the womb: he had the title but plebeian tastes, whereas Cedric had all the polish and gentility that signaled the bluest of aristocratic blood.

Once his brother wandered into his chamber, Trent headed down the backstairs to the kitchens.

Mrs. Button, bless her heart, knew what he liked, and had left out a loaf of crusty bread, a slab of sharp cheddar, and a jar of her best tomato pickle.

He sat at the kitchen table and ate, listening to the even breathing of the knife boy curled in the corner of the warm room.

In the last few years, Cedric had lost a respectable fortune playing vingt-et-un, and been expelled from divinity school after he'd shot off the Bishop of Winchester's miter at fifty paces. He was an excellent marksman and hadn't harmed the bishop, but that didn't excuse the escapade; he might have taken the man's head off.

On the basis of that skill, Trent had purchased a commission for him in the Queen's Regiment of Light Dragoons—a

waste of money, for within the year Cedric was unceremoni-
ously discharged for drunkenness and sent home.

That led Trent to thinking about what it would be like
once Cedric married and moved to another house.

He reckoned it would be heaven.

Pure heaven.

But . . . not if Cedric's wife was Miss Merry Pelford,
American from Boston.

Chapter Six

Trent woke the next morning with a devil of a headache and an even worse temper. Merry Pelford was in love with his brother.

The end.

Full stop.

It was just as well he was going to Wales. For one thing, he shouldn't think of her as "Merry," although she had given her permission. She belonged to his brother, and he had to stop thinking of her altogether.

"The traveling coach has been made ready, Your Grace," his valet informed him, as Trent was toweling himself off after bathing.

He nodded. "Tell Woods I've one errand in London first, and I'll go from there to the Holyhead Road. No need to tire the horses with London streets; I'll take a hackney." He'd like to be off for Llanberis immediately, but there was one pressing item that he had to see to on his way out of the city.

Lord Malmsbury had a freehold apartment in the Albany, which Trent knew about because he'd tried in vain to interest his brother into moving into one of the sumptuous gentlemen's apartments.

Trent had a vague idea that Malmsbury was in demand as a single gentleman. He was a doughy fellow who was all smiles, flattery, and pale eyes, just the sort whom Trent had no time for, the kind who made up the numbers at a dinner party and could be counted on to dance with one's wallflower second cousin.

And who took a fondle of the girl's rump as payment, apparently.

It wasn't long before the hackney drew up in front of the Albany. He told the driver to keep the horses standing, as he wouldn't be more than ten minutes, if that.

Cedric always complained that Trent had no manners, but Trent reckoned he had just enough. Since he *was* polite, he waited until Lord Malmsbury's man left the room before he pulled off his coat.

"Your Grace?" Malmsbury stuttered, as Trent tossed the coat onto a chair.

Trent strode forward, caught the rogue by his neck cloth, and slammed him against the wall. "I gather that you amuse yourself by touching young ladies in ways unbecoming to a gentleman."

"Never!" Malmsbury gasped.

"You never groped a woman, let's say, at Lady Portmeadow's ball last night?"

The man's eyes shifted; Merry was right about him. Trent slammed him against the wall once more.

Malmsbury said something unintelligible, but then, it's hard to make yourself clear when your air is cut off.

"You're developing quite a reputation for pinching young women, you disgusting bucket of lard," Trent stated. He let Malmsbury drop to the ground.

Things got no better once the man found his voice; he started spluttering something about how Elisabeth Debbledon was no better than she should be. Debbledon? Trent knew of his advances upon Merry and the swooning Miss Cernay. Miss Debbledon made it three ladies in one night . . . at least.

Trent's fist smashed into Malmsbury's jaw, spinning the man about and sending him into the wall with a thud. Trent leaned in. "If you ever again touch any lady—no, any woman—who isn't your wife, you may expect another visit from me."

"I don't have a wife!" Malmsbury squealed, clutching his jaw, where a red patch signaled a bruise to come.

"Then you have no one to grope, have you?"

Somewhere in the back of his mind, Trent was surprised by the way he was responding to the idea that this scoundrel had touched Merry.

But mostly he was enjoying himself.

"If I even see you within ten yards of Miss Pelford, I'll find you and I'll touch *you*, Malmsbury. After which, you'll be singing soprano, if you understand me. Men never touch ladies without permission." He bared his teeth like a feral dog. "I shouldn't have to teach you that lesson."

"I won't touch her," Malmsbury blubbered. "I won't touch her. I never touched her."

"Good," Trent stated, pulling down the cuffs of his linen shirt. He retrieved his coat and shrugged it back on. If he adhered to Cedric's ideas of fashion, he would never have been able to land a punch like that, because his coat would have been too tight to remove without a valet's help.

Malmsbury had his hand cupped over his jaw and was

taking in sobbing gasps. A young maid entered with a tray holding glasses and a decanter and stopped, mouth hanging open.

"I don't have time for a drink," Trent said as he passed her. "But thank you nonetheless."

He paused at the door, and looked back at Malmsbury. "If I ever hear that a woman has been pinched on the ballroom floor or anywhere else, I shall know whom to look for."

"I haven't." His voice came out in a ragged whine. "Damme, you've broken my jaw!"

The maidservant didn't say a word, but the satisfaction on her face was unmistakable.

Trent couldn't think of any real reason to tell Merry about what had just happened, but he found himself directing the hackney to the Pelford residence in Portman Square anyway.

He had the idea that Mrs. Pelford had been affronted by his manner the night before. The sight of Merry on his brother's arm had been a blow; he'd barely stopped himself from ripping her away. But he refused to play out some childish competition with his brother.

He would stop by the Pelfords and clarify to everyone concerned that he was very happy that Cedric had found such a lovely woman to marry. He might as well inform his future sister-in-law that Malmsbury would never again offer her the smallest affront.

What's more, he had made up his mind that Merry must take back the ring. For one thing, the estate was thriving and he could easily afford to buy his future wife a brand-new ring.

And for another, Cedric was indisputably right. The late duchess had adored her younger son, and she would have been happy to see her ring on Cedric's wife's finger.

His mother's blatant partiality had caused him some

pain during his childhood, but from this distance, he had decided that her favoritism had been a positive thing. It taught him early not to be dependent on a woman.

That lesson would enable him to use rational criteria to choose a wife. Obviously, he had responded so strongly to Merry because it was time to marry; he and Cedric were once again in tandem.

He could find a lady of her temperament. Besides, she might be overly emotional for his tastes. His last mistress, Elsa, had been entirely pleasant during the liaison's earliest months, but after a time she'd become maudlin and tearful, and began hinting about wedding rings.

When he had declined, Elsa had wept bitterly, although the terms of their agreement had been established at the outset. He gave her a ruby as a farewell gift, but the memory still pricked at him, as if he'd betrayed her somehow.

He didn't want another mistress; ergo, he had to find a wife. A wife who wouldn't throw that sort of scene. Merry said that London was thronged with Americans, so it shouldn't be hard to find another woman who was independent, opinionated, and straightforward. And beautiful, of course.

Trent strode up to the Pelford townhouse, resolved to get this over quickly and be back on the road.

The sight of Merry jolted his body with the searing power of a lightning bolt.

She was seated beside her aunt, wearing a gown that was more demure than that she wore the previous night. It was pale pink, nothing special, but even so, her breasts almost spilled over the bodice, as luminous and white as the best sugar.

Sweet, like sugar. He'd like to—

He must be losing his mind. He should probably take

a mistress as soon as he returned to London, just until he found the right lady to marry.

"Mrs. Pelford," Trent said, bowing. "Miss Pelford. I hope you will forgive me for coming upon you unannounced. I am on the verge of leaving for a trip to Wales, but I wanted to pay respects to my future sister-in-law somewhere other than in a crowded ballroom."

"Your Grace," Merry said, with a lovely smile. "What a pleasure. Please do join us."

He hadn't realized how plump her lower lip was. He needed an American with lips like that. And breasts.

Nothing else would do.

Trent lowered himself into a chair, keeping rigid control over his expression to ensure that he had an affable and pleasant air. Sure enough, Mrs. Pelford was regarding him cautiously, as if she found herself entertaining a crocodile.

"A happy surprise," she said, not entirely convincingly. "May I offer you some tea, Your Grace?"

Trent never took tea. Daylight hours were short, and at this very moment he should be well on his way to Wales. But he found himself accepting a cup as well as a crumpet, though he wasn't hungry.

"We have been talking of our gardens in Massachusetts," Mrs. Pelford told him. "My niece has designed all nature of charming aspects on the estate."

"Are the gardens very large?" Trent asked, wondering what she would consider an estate. The gardens at his country seat, Hawksmede, covered nineteen acres.

"Oh yes," Mrs. Pelford said. "Quite large."

She did not seem inclined to specify, so Trent turned to Merry. "May I know something of your designs?"

"Last summer, I made two little terraces at the end of the great walk, raised twelve steps each," Merry said. She started waving her hands and talking about climbing roses and trellises and a gazebo with Ionic columns.

"My husband was not happy with that gazebo," Mrs. Pelford put in. "Two hundred dollars for a structure that won't even keep out the rain!"

"If the gazebo had walls, they would obstruct the prospect," her niece replied, clearly not for the first time. She turned back to Trent. "You can't imagine how splendid the view is. It overlooks the orchard, and beyond that, the forest and the river. There is no other spot on the estate so well situated to an open structure."

Trent was getting the idea that the Pelford estate might well rival his own. He tried to think if there were any "prospects" in his gardens, but nothing came to mind.

One thing he did know was that the townhouse he had deeded to Cedric had no more than a forlorn patch of ground in the rear. Perhaps they would buy a house in the country.

"You'll have to forgive me my chatter," Merry said sheepishly, handing him a plate with a thick piece of gingerbread. "It's springtime, and so of course I find myself thinking of the gardens. I have an apricot tree that has never bloomed; I had hopes for it this spring, since I had a wall built to shelter it."

" '*Come then and see this lovely Seat,*' " Mrs. Pelford recited out of the blue. " '*So healthful, happy, and complete!*' "

"My aunt is a poet," Merry said, with a practiced air. "Her specialty is commemoration."

"A lovely couplet," Trent said. "I should be happy to hear the rest." He had eaten the crumpet without noticing, so he started on the gingerbread.

"In that case, do have another cup of tea, while I fetch

the entire poem," Mrs. Pelford said, jumping up and beaming at him. "I shall return directly."

Of course, Merry and Trent rose as well. The moment her aunt left the room, Merry turned to him with an adorable wrinkle of her nose. "You must change your mind directly and leave," she whispered. "My aunt's poetry is not for everyone."

"I can spare a few minutes," he said, thinking that he should not. At this point, it would be well past dark before he reached the inn where he planned to spend the night.

"Her poem addressing my gazebo is more than seven hundred lines long! Don't worry, I can make your excuses."

"I paid a visit to Lord Malmsbury this morning," Trent said. Even as he spoke, he remembered that ladies didn't appreciate talk of fisticuffs. His mother had paled at the mere suggestion that he and Cedric had fought, although there were years when they pummeled each other daily.

Her eyes widened. "Is he a friend of yours?"

Trent tried to think how to phrase his account delicately. "Lord Malmsbury is merely an acquaintance. After our exchange this morning, he won't be eager to deepen the association."

Merry gave him a delighted grin. "Please tell me that you punched him?" At his nod, she clapped her hands. "Bravo! He's such a little weasel. I thought later that I should have poked him harder with my hat pin. I should have drawn blood."

American ladies, it seemed, had no qualms about fisticuffs.

"He will never touch you again," Trent vowed, and a bit of the steely anger he felt at the thought leaked into his voice.

"I daresay, not after being drubbed by a duke."

"An elegant turn of phrase," Trent said, feeling that unfamiliar smile on his lips again. "Do you rival your aunt in poetic prowess?"

"I have no such aspirations." She took his arm and began to draw him toward the door. "You truly ought to leave, Your Grace, before my aunt returns. She will be so happy to have an audience that you may well be unable to stir for an hour. And Lord help you if she decides you would also appreciate her poem describing the entire park."

"Very long?" Trent inquired.

"Over one thousand lines."

He was unable to suppress a groan.

"In couplets!"

"As it happens, I am leaving for Wales on matter of urgency," he said.

Her smile sparkled. That was a silly way of putting it, but it was true.

"I think your brother said you own a mine there?"

"Yes, I own a slate mine near Blaenau Ffestiniog."

Merry repeated the name, her soft voice mangling the Welsh characters. "Welsh is such an interesting language. What will you do there?"

"I'm not satisfied with the safety conditions," Trent said, wondering why he was coming out with details that no lady—

"Of course, there was that terrible accident in Yorkshire a few months ago," she said, nodding.

"In Barmby Furscoe," he confirmed. "Some reports put the deaths at thirty pitmen."

"What causes an explosion like that?"

Her eyes were bright and interested. If Trent had mentioned the disaster to Cedric, he would have received a blank stare. "That colliery was sunk by the Low Moor

Company," he explained. "From what I've heard, they didn't set proper rules, and someone brought an unprotected flame below."

"So you're going to establish regulations about the kind of lamps allowed below ground?"

"And make certain that the tunnels are adequately ventilated and supported. But before I depart, I wished to return your ring." Trent pulled the diamond from his pocket.

Merry's brows drew together. "Absolutely not."

"I was wrong to accept it from you last night."

"Someday you will give this ring to the woman who will be your wife. Imagine what she would think upon learning that the ring that had belonged to her predecessors had been given away."

Sunlight was pouring through a window, revealing Merry's skin to be precisely the color of ivory, save for the smallest spray of freckles across her nose. He couldn't help grinning at her. "Being such an avid gardener, I am surprised that you don't have more freckles."

"Thanks to bonnets," Merry said, with loathing. "I have any number that fit around my face like a horse's blinkers. My aunt has always been fearful that my freckles would multiply and I would never make an appropriate match."

"I like them," Trent said.

She stood before him, glowing like the most delectable apricot that ever grew on an American branch—or an English one, for that matter—and her aunt had worried about her attractiveness? No matter where she went, men would fall at her feet.

He picked up her hand and pressed the ring into her palm.

She shook her head. "Your Grace, I must insist that you take the ring."

Before she could stop him, he slid the ring onto her finger.

"I want you to have it," he stated, curling her fingers closed and wrapping his own around them. "My *mother* would want you to wear it."

She didn't attempt to break free, just looked at him with a puzzled frown. "Didn't you say that this ring is always worn by the duchess?"

"My mother had a decided preference for Cedric," Trent said lightly. "I assure you that the estate can more than bear the charge of another such ring for my wife."

Merry stiffened. "Your mother had a *favorite* child?"

"Cedric was the sort of child whom a lady enjoys," Trent explained. "Summoned to her boudoir, I was guaranteed to break something, whereas Cedric could be counted on to take an interest in her coiffure or her attire. Or both."

Her hand felt small in his, as if he'd trapped a bird.

"Her Grace was wrong to act in such a manner," Merry said bluntly. "A mother ought to love all her children equally."

Trent shrugged. "It didn't hurt me." In reality, he thought Cedric had had the worse end of the bargain, because their mother's constant fretting over his status as a second son ensured he never forgot it.

Merry apparently didn't agree. She started embroidering on the theme of mothers, but Trent wasn't listening. She had the ripest pair of lips he'd ever seen.

He'd like to kiss her until they looked bee-stung, the lips of a woman who had been bedded hard and furiously, who had—

Bloody hell. He had to take hold of himself.

"Your Grace?" the lips asked.

"I beg your pardon, Miss Pelford. I lost track of the conversation."

A look of distinct sympathy came into Merry's eyes. "I'm so sorry! Of course, your mother must pose a difficult subject for conversation. I should have been more sensitive."

He could have explained that he didn't give a damn about his mother and hadn't since the tender age of eight, which was when he fully understood his place in the hierarchy of her affections.

But there was no real point. "Yes, well, you can see why I've decided that I'd prefer my wife to wear a different ring," he said briskly, releasing her hand.

Just as they had the night before, they gazed down at the diamonds gracing her slender finger.

"I don't know," Merry said hesitantly.

He couldn't stop himself; he ran his fingers lightly down the back of her hand until they reached the ring. "It belongs to you. It fits perfectly." He felt the rightness of it deep in his gut.

Their eyes met, and he noticed with a pulse of surprise that hers were gray, but with a circle of violet at the very edge. He'd never seen eyes like that.

She licked her bottom lip and Trent froze. He couldn't kiss her. Just because he was standing so close that he could smell her skin, and she had his ring on her finger, and she was looking at him with confusion but not denial . . .

Shit.

He had almost kissed his brother's fiancée. Again.

"Right," he said, taking a step back. "That's settled, then. You are once again in possession of the ring."

Merry turned her head away quickly but he saw a rosy flush in her cheeks.

No. He was mistaken.

She loved Cedric. She'd told him so several times the night before, and Merry was not a liar.

Trent cleared his throat. "I must be off. But—" The words stuck in his throat, but he forced them out. "I just wish you to know that I'm very glad that you will be my sister-in-law. I believe you will make a splendid wife for my brother."

"Thank you," Merry said slowly.

"I'm sure that Cedric will curtail his drinking once you are married. My comments last night were inappropriate, and I apologize."

"Your Grace, I'd like you to consider that your worry is unwarranted. Lord Cedric mentioned at some point that you dislike both wine and spirits, and I am sure that you are very prudent in your behavior."

"Not always," Trent said wryly, thinking that he was a fool to have visited her.

"Most young men are not abstemious, but that does not mean they drink to excess."

"I am aware of that," Trent said. He didn't know what else to say. She'd have to see it herself.

"Cedric, for example, is a consummate gentleman." A trace of defiance edged her voice. "As I told you, I've never seen him even the least tipsy."

No one had ever come to Trent's defense the way Merry was coming to Cedric's. Not that Trent had the faintest need for protection.

But Merry belonged to his brother, and she would make certain that Cedric didn't harm himself while in his cups. Trent had known her less than a day, and he could say that with absolute certainty.

She was the best possible wife for his brother.

He forced himself to smile and bowed again. "I am leaving London for some weeks, Miss Pelford, but I shall look forward to seeing you and your family again upon my return."

Just then, Mrs. Pelford trotted back into the room. It seemed the poetess could not find her seven-hundred-line poem in honor of the gazebo, but while searching her study she had fished up a sonnet sequence describing a three-sided Chinese house.

"I regret to say that I must postpone the pleasure," Trent said, bowing over the lady's ink-stained fingers. "I am leaving for Wales, and should have left London some hours ago."

"You are leaving the city?" Mrs. Pelford's face fell. "But you will return shortly, will you not?"

"In a few weeks."

"I imagine Lord Cedric has mentioned this, Your Grace, but my husband and I are eager to return home to Boston. We have asked that the betrothal be a matter of a few months."

That made him feel slightly cracked but Trent pushed the thought away. He wanted Merry, more than any woman he'd ever seen, but she would be the salvation of his twin. That was far more important than his response to her.

"I am happy to hear it," he said, more firmly than he might have. The sooner Merry married Cedric, the sooner she would begin to solve his brother's problems.

Mrs. Pelford patted his arm. "You shall come to tea again as soon as you come back, Your Grace, and I will read you the entire sonnet sequence."

"It will be a pleasure," he murmured, and made his escape.

It would be Cedric, and not himself, who would be obliged to endure nine hundred lines, or even more, commemorating the wedding. He had the distinct impression that Mrs. Pelford would write such a poem in a matter of a week, perhaps on the ship back to Boston.

He also had the awful feeling that he himself would have listened to all nine hundred lines, if it would make Merry happy.

Hell, he would listen to ten thousand lines, if he could sit next to her and entwine her fingers in his. And think about just what he was going to do to her in their bedchamber after the poetry reading was over.

Trent flung himself into the carriage with relief.

A slate mine could be dangerous.

But just at this moment it seemed far less dangerous than the brightly lit drawing room he had just left.

Chapter Seven

In the days that followed, the spark of anxiety Merry had felt about her cultivation of mind—or lack thereof—grew larger and larger. Every time she turned around, someone was gazing at her in horror.

She laughed too loudly. She slouched in her chair. She yawned when she was bored. Call her a rebel, but seven courses at one meal was insufferable, especially when one was only permitted to speak to the persons on one's left and right but never, ever to the fascinating person across the table.

She seemed incapable of making any self-improvements whatsoever. It was enough to make her think that her governess had been right. She could still hear Miss Fairfax lamenting, "Merry has none of the discretion, modesty, or reserve required of those who marry into polite society."

Aunt Bess had only laughed and said that when it came to marriage, a fortune trumped discretion.

"*That* is an American belief," Miss Fairfax had retorted. "Ladylike accomplishments are more important than worldly goods, and your niece has none."

"Well, spit," Merry had protested. "You've taught me how to embroider *and* how to make wax flowers."

Miss Fairfax's yelp of anguish had probably been heard in London itself. "No lady would allow such a vulgarity as 'spit' to pass her lips!"

Her governess's criticisms had usually bounced off Merry like rain from a tin roof. But that one had stuck, and night after night she lay awake, wondering if she and Cedric could be happy together. Clearly, he expected his wife to excel at something more refined than molding wax flowers.

Absurdly, sometimes she found herself wondering what it would be like to be a duchess. The very idea was ridiculous: a duke might flirt on a balcony, but he wouldn't consider actually marrying a woman like her. He would marry someone like Lady Caroline, a noblewoman who knew the ins and outs of society.

Not that she would ever want a position like that anyway. All eyes followed a duchess. She could scarcely imagine the storm of gossip that would result if a duchess made a faux pas, the kind she made every day.

But then the duke hadn't seemed to be as concerned about etiquette as Cedric was. She even thought he might join a conversation across the table, though that was probably wishful thinking on her part.

And irrelevant, of course.

In desperation, she began to compile a list of etiquette rules that included the correct use of sugar tongs, as well as a reminder to never say "spit." A young lady at a musicale had practically swooned when Merry growled it after tearing her hem.

Two weeks into her betrothal, the list had grown to four pages. When she had questions—Why *are* morning calls often conducted in the afternoon?—Cedric was happy to elucidate.

"No one is awake in the morning," he explained. "Except servants, of course, which reminds me that you mustn't greet your butler with such familiarity. I realize that you value Jenkins. But we show our respect by keeping a certain distance."

Even an hour with her fiancé was liable to result in one or two new rules.

Not that she saw Cedric very often. If she'd had her way, she would have liked to spend part of every day with him. To her dismay, Cedric was rarely free, and when he was, he often seemed to be late for an important appointment.

Still, he always put his name down for two dances at every ball. He never failed to bring her a glass of canary wine, a gleam of conspiratorial mischief in his eyes. He seemed amused by the idea that his fiancée was too sophisticated for lemonade. Cedric had a marvelously world-weary, sardonic manner that Merry was trying, albeit with little success, to imitate.

She watched her fiancé for signs of inebriation, but never saw any. Which meant that she spent more time thinking about when the duke would return from Wales than she ought, but only because she looked forward to setting him straight about his brother.

And it was only out of dutiful family feeling for her future brother-in-law that she daily scoured her uncle's newspapers, to reassure herself that there had been no mining accidents in Wales.

After an uneasy fortnight, she had to admit that the

twinges of doubt she felt could no longer honestly be called "twinges." She was at a crossroads. She could become a selfish, vacillating woman, who fell in and out of love as casually as she changed her gloves, casting men to the side as she might a boring novel.

Or she could become a true wife to Cedric, loving and loyal in the way that Aunt Bess was to Uncle Thaddeus.

Merry's challenge was not to mimic an English lady. No: she had to become a better person. The duke would return any day—not that his return was relevant—and sometime after that, she and Cedric would marry.

Sometime? There was a precise date set now, in June. It was easy to forget, because Bess had hired a secretary to manage all the details. Still, Merry was due for a second fitting of her wedding dress, an idea that made her feel a little faint.

In the end, she wrote a strongly worded note to Cedric, asking him to join her for a morning ride in Hyde Park. They *had* to spend more time together before they vowed to love each other to the end of their days.

Besides, it would give her a chance to practice being a better person.

The next morning Cedric appeared at the prescribed time in an extremely elegant riding coat, and they set out for Rotten Row in Hyde Park. He wasn't precisely cheerful—Cedric was clearly not a morning person—but she appreciated the fact that he made the effort.

Overnight rain had scrubbed the coal smoke from the sky, and for once London smelled fresh and clean. The sky had the color and shimmer of mother-of-pearl, as if the very air was made of water.

The only sound was that of hooves squelching in the puddles that dotted the paths, and occasional plops as drops found their way from leaves above to the ground.

Merry couldn't stop smiling, even though Cedric was grumbling because her "summons," as he put it, had rousted him from bed. No one of note could be seen on the Row this early, and indeed, they passed only a couple of grooms exercising horses.

Most unhappily for Cedric, a small gust blew just as they rode under a particularly low-hanging branch, sending rainwater cascading onto his hat and splashing in all directions, making it look as if his head were a tiny fountain. Merry laughed, but stopped immediately, because naturally Cedric's headache was worsened by this indignity.

"Perhaps we could gallop for a few minutes," she suggested. "We haven't seen a soul other than those grooms, so no one would be affronted to see me riding above a trot."

"That is because no one of countenance is out of bed. If you think that I will ever ride with you again at this hour, you are mistaken. I am mortified to discover that I am in the company of servants."

Well, spit. He really was annoyed.

"Shall we try a gallop, Cedric?" Merry asked again.

"What you don't seem to understand, *Miss Pelford*," Cedric said with dreadful emphasis, "is that a lady is a lady all the time, not merely when she is within view of polite society. Gentility must needs be internal. Even though we find ourselves in a throng of servants, it behooves us to behave with utmost circumspection."

They were hardly in a "throng"; in fact, the grooms had apparently taken themselves back to the mews, and there wasn't a soul to be seen in the park.

Cedric warmed up to his topic while Merry reminded herself that his irritability was entirely understandable. He had asked her repeatedly to address him by his title in public and she kept forgetting.

She nodded, and nodded again. And when she frowned,

it was merely because she heard something other than Cedric's nettled—if well-bred—tones. She pulled up her mare, Dessie, and strained to listen.

Cedric didn't notice, riding on with one gloved hand waving in the air as he emphasized his point about the delicacy of the British temperament.

There it was again—a whimpering sound, like an animal in distress.

"Why have you stopped?" Cedric said, turning about. "Oh bother, this damp has entirely wilted my neck cloth! I shall look no better than a milkman."

Merry slid off her mare and draped the reins over the pommel. Dessie shook her head and stamped her hoof a few times, but stayed put, so Merry headed toward the hedgerow lining the south side of the Row.

"What on earth are you doing? Don't touch those branches; you'll become wet."

"I think I heard something," Merry explained, pulling a branch aside. Rainwater bounced off the leaves and splashed over her.

"What did I tell you?" Cedric demanded. "I suppose we'll have to return home so that you can change."

Before she could answer, she heard another scrabbling noise, and a plaintive whine that sounded like pain. She ignored Cedric, bent down, and pulled another branch aside.

Through the foliage she could see a small space within the hedge, and within it, a black-and-brown puppy, about the size of a loaf of bread. It must be trapped by its collar, because its round rump was wiggling in the air as it tried to free itself.

Cautiously, she reached through the dense branches until she touched wet fur. Rolls of loose skin moved under her fingers. The puppy whined again and twisted around to lick Merry's wrist.

"Hello, little one," she crooned. "You mustn't worry. We'll have you out of this hedge in a trice."

She managed to get a firm grip around his middle, and gave a tug. This made him squeal with pain, so she stopped and gave him a pat. Her shoulder jogged the branches above her, sending rainwater onto her bonnet, which lost its shape and molded itself unpleasantly to her neck.

"Cedric," she called. "I need help. There's a puppy!"

She couldn't turn her head far, because her arm was inside the hedge, but after a moment Cedric appeared in her line of sight. He had dismounted and was tying his reins to an overhanging bough. "A puppy," he said with disgust. "You sound like a schoolgirl."

The little dog had begun snuffling her hand, and a floppy ear, as soft as cashmere, fell on Merry's wrist. "We're going to rescue you," she promised, stroking the mounds of soft fur covering his middle. "How long have you been stuck here, poor baby?"

"How is he trapped?" Cedric asked, making no attempt to help.

She inched her hand forward until it reached a piece of cord tied around the puppy's neck, caught so tightly that she couldn't get even a single finger under it. It must be cutting viciously into his skin.

"There's a cord around his neck," she said, giving the puppy another pat before removing her arm from the bush. "Can you try to break it, Cedric? I'm not strong enough."

Her drenched bonnet was funneling rainwater down her back and soaking her to the skin. Though her fingers were cold, she managed to undo its strings and toss it on top of the hedge. Its fashionable ruffled brim was ruined, and it looked like nothing so much as an old tea cloth.

Cedric peered through the branches. The puppy had begun whimpering again.

"Don't worry, darling," Merry said. "I won't leave you. We are going to save you." She could see one trustful brown eye looking up at her. It was rather bulging, but in an adorable way.

"He must have run under the hedge to get out of the rain," she said, turning to Cedric. "And now he's caught fast. Can you break him free?"

"Not if there's a cord around his neck," Cedric said. "I'd probably strangle him. We shall inform the parish constable and he will send someone with a knife. Come along. I'll pay the man to make sure he finds a home for the animal afterward."

"Oh, Cedric, we can't leave him!" Merry cried.

Her fiancé's mouth tightened and she remembered—again—that she was to address him as Lord Cedric out of doors. "Of course we can," he said, straightening. "It's about to start raining again, and there's nothing we can do for the animal." Another whimper came from inside the hedge. "We are merely prolonging his agony."

"I'll stay, and you go," Merry said, turning her head as a horse came into sight, galloping toward them. "Or perhaps we can send whoever this is to get help. It's probably another groom exercising a horse."

Lord knew, no one other than a groom would dare to take his horse above a trot, what with all those rules that Cedric had laid out for her about not galloping in Hyde Park and never, ever putting a horse on a lead line.

She said none of this aloud, though, because she was practicing prudence and restraint.

"If you insist, we will instruct the groom to remain with the animal until the constable arrives."

"No, I will stay here until he's free." She reached into the hedge again and caught up one of the puppy's ears.

"I must ask you not to squat on the common roadside,"

Cedric said stiffly. "I could not leave you here unprotected."

"Don't be absurd!" Merry cried, exasperated. "What harm could possibly come to me in broad daylight?" A warm tongue licked her hand again. "Oh, you are a sweetheart, aren't you?" she breathed. "You'll be out of there in no time and I'll ask Cook to give you some scraps of beef. You would like that, wouldn't you?"

The horse and rider were still pounding down the path toward them. Merry tried again to get a finger under the cord, but it must have hurt as the puppy uttered a little yip.

"Lord Cedric!" she called, "Do you see anything sharp we could cut the cord with? Perhaps a rock?"

"A *rock*?" her fiancé answered, managing to sound bored and irate at the same time—quite a feat, though his accent was a great help. Merry had observed that an aristocratic accent lent itself to expressions of irritability.

"Thrashing about in the sand is ruining your skirts," Cedric added. "Get up."

"If I let go, he'll begin crying again," Merry replied, her voice becoming a bit sharp despite herself.

Cedric looked over her head. "Well, well, what a surprise. It seems it wasn't a groom riding in such a reckless fashion."

She heard the thud of boots hitting the sandy path as the rider dismounted, though she couldn't turn her head far enough to see him and still keep her hand on the puppy. "Could whoever just arrived *please* fetch a constable so we can cut this poor animal free?" she called.

"It's the duke," her fiancé said acidly. "Did I neglect to mention that His Grace is once again honoring London with his presence? Who else would be galloping such an ungodly large horse?"

Merry twisted about and looked up.

The Duke of Trent was walking toward her, tall and imposing, his inky blue eyes on her face. In that instant, her stomach tightened and her heart thudded . . . and then she remembered.

Brother-in-law.

Brother-in-law.

Chapter Eight

*T*rent was getting some exercise after a brutal week on the road from Wales, when he spied the unmistakable figure of his brother in the middle distance.

That was surprising, considering that Cedric had been drunk as a wheelbarrow when he arrived home the night before. Even more surprising, Cedric was leaning against his horse, looking down at a woman who was crumpled on the ground next to him.

He pulled up, dismounted, and approached the pair, his gut tightening as he recognized that the woman on the ground was Merry. She was not crumpled after all, but kneeling with her back to him, with one arm thrust into the hedgerow.

As he approached, she made no move to stand, or even withdraw her arm from the hedge but she twisted around and looked up. "Good morning, Your Grace."

He was mesmerized by the sight. Merry's hair was curling in the damp as if it had a life of its own, springing free from whatever pins she had put in it that morning. She wore a tight—and wet—riding habit, with buttons that ran down the front in a way that emphasized her magnificent chest.

Her face, like her coat, was streaked with rain and her lips were wet. He was struck by a violent urge to bend over and pick her up. He would bury his hands in that glossy hair and kiss her senseless. Kiss her until her cheeks were pink and her lips were warm.

Lust rolled over him like fog coming in from the ocean.

He swallowed a curse and flexed his hands. These bouts of lust were remarkably inconvenient.

Belatedly, Cedric's voice penetrated the fog of desire. "You're kneeling in the dirt like a chambermaid lighting a fire. Get up!"

Without thinking, Trent snarled, "Do not speak to her in that manner."

Cedric's eyes narrowed. "*You* are giving *me* lessons in comportment?"

"Gentlemen!" Merry called. "I'd be grateful if you could save your bickering for later."

Trent dropped into a crouch beside her. "What is inside that hedge, Miss Pelford?"

She withdrew her arm and held the brushes back so he could peer inside. "A puppy with a cord around his neck. Whenever I stop petting him, he pulls and I'm afraid that he's going to strangle himself."

Trent reached into the tangle of bushes and after some maneuvering, managed to find the puppy's neck. "Bulldog, I would say." And then, a heartfelt "Damn, that's wet," as the hedge dropped a load of cold water over him.

"I suggest we leave," Cedric said in a clipped tone, "and send a constable who will cut the animal from his bonds. He could have been freed by now," he said to Merry.

The household servants quavered with fear in the face of Cedric's reprimands, but Merry seemed unmoved by his displeasure.

"Please, could one of you fetch some help? I shall remain here." She added the last firmly, without the slightest contrition in her voice.

"I can't wrench the cord free without injuring him," Trent said, straightening. "But I've got a knife." He went to his horse. Like any man who spent most of his time in the country, he kept a knife sheath mounted on his saddle. He undid the flap and pulled out his blade, listening to Cedric and Merry squabble over what to do with the dog.

Leaving them to it, he crouched down again and began to work on cutting the cord where it was caught in the bramble.

Cedric and Merry's exchange was building into a proper row. He could have told her that it wasn't worth the energy; his twin had the endurance of Hercules when it came to arguments. At the moment, Cedric was characterizing Merry as "an uncaring foe to all animals," because she had refused to leave the dog.

The cord gave way at last, and Trent got a good grip on the wriggling puppy and hauled him, wet but otherwise unharmed, out of his leafy prison.

Merry uttered an enchanting squeak of delight.

"You did it!" She reached out and took the puppy, bringing his face up to hers. "He's the most darling dog I've ever seen!"

The pup resembled a bulldog, given his snub nose and loose, rumpled skin. But there might be a few other breeds mixed in as well. His coat was longer and wirier than a bulldog's; perhaps he had some terrier in his family tree.

"Look at that tail," Cedric said with disgust. "It's curled like a piglet's."

"Just look at his face!" Merry cried. "Half of it is white and the other brown. Well, brown-black. And he has a patch over one eye! Isn't he adorable?"

In the Portmeadow ballroom, on the night they'd met, he had found Merry beautiful. But seeing her now, her hair falling to her shoulders, her riding habit plastered to her breasts . . .

She made Trent feel a little insane.

"I think I'll call him George. Doesn't he look like a George?"

"He looks like a street mongrel," Cedric stated. "I trust you are not thinking of keeping it," he added, displaying a positive genius for saying the wrong thing at just the wrong moment.

Merry pushed a mass of shiny ringlets behind her ear. "Of course I'm keeping him. You don't think that I would abandon him, now he's been freed? Your Grace, do you suppose that you could remove the cord from around his neck?"

She parted the folds of skin bunched around the puppy's neck, exposing the much-too-tight cord.

"Keep him still," Trent said.

Merry nodded and held the dog close against her.

Trent carefully inserted the tip of his knife under the cord and began to saw as gently as he could.

"Poor baby," Merry told the puppy, who was crying as his hind legs scrabbled against her chest. "It'll be over in a moment."

"If that coat wasn't already ruined, it is now," Cedric said. "For God's sake, Miss Pelford, put the animal down and let my brother take care of it. The duke prides himself on his barnyard skills; he's always out and about birthing a sheep or building a privy just for the fun of it."

At that moment Trent's blade broke through and the cord fell away.

"Oh, thank you!" Merry cried, giving Trent a huge smile. She cradled the dog belly up, and bent to kiss his nose. "That feels better, doesn't it?"

"The animal is not an infant," Cedric pointed out unnecessarily. "I would strongly suggest you put the mongrel down. I can smell him from here, and you may well catch fleas."

Merry gave her fiancé a cool stare. "George is unbathed through no fault of his own."

Trent looked at his brother with some interest. It was obvious that nothing short of an act of God would separate Merry from that puppy. Cedric should simply reconcile himself to a dog in the marital bed.

The thought of that bed chilled him more than the rainwater had. He should just get back on that horse and head off to his country estate.

Now.

Before Merry smiled at him one more time.

Or before his eyes drifted to her bosom again because damn it, that riding coat had been made by some devil who wanted men to crumple to their knees.

He'd be happy to fall to his knees. He would take the wet hem of her skirts and draw them slowly up. He would have to warm her legs with kisses, of course. She must be chilled through.

Pallid where she ought to be pink.

"That is *not* a lady's dog," Cedric declared. "You are holding a bulldog. It will grow into a monstrosity."

His brother was making one mistake after another.

Eyes flashing, Merry drew herself upright like an enraged statue of Juno.

If he were betrothed to Merry, he would beg her to wear that riding habit every time it rained. Toss that. He wouldn't take her out in the rain. He'd just take her into the bath—

Bloody hell. Trent wrenched his mind out of the gutter once again.

"I have always wanted a dog like George," Merry announced.

"You didn't even know what a bulldog looks like," Cedric retorted.

"It's possible we don't have the breed in the United States," Merry admitted. "Is his skin supposed to be so loose or is he very hungry? Just look at his darling expression. He's so sad." She dropped another kiss on the puppy's round head. "There's no need to be sad, George. I'll take care of you. I'm going to feed you until you don't have any wrinkles left."

"You cannot possibly keep that dog," Cedric said, true alarm leaking into his voice.

Not being stupid, the puppy twisted around so he could lick Merry's chin.

"Not only will he grow to be large, but he will snuffle and drool. A bulldog is *not* a lady's dog; they were bred for bullbaiting."

Merry was tickling the animal, blind to his ridiculous pug nose, or the grime that had turned its white parts dingy. "You like being called George, don't you?" she whispered. "Yes, you do. Hello, George."

"Why George?" Trent asked. It was the name of the sovereign, and one of his school friends, and the local bishop . . . it didn't jump out to him as a name for a fat puppy.

She gave him a mischievous grin. "George, for George Washington."

"You're naming the dog after your first president?"

She nodded. "We Americans love General Washington." She bent over and kissed George. "And I love you," she told him.

The little dog seemed to have a sweet temperament, since his only response to the indignity of being held like an infant was to lick Merry's hand every time he had a chance.

"I think there are many who would find it an insult to the founder of your country," Cedric pointed out, "though it is no concern of mine, I suppose."

"I suppose not," Trent murmured.

"If you insist, we will give him to my groom," Cedric announced. "That way you could visit the dog in the mews."

Trent sighed inwardly. His brother had a lot to learn about women. Even he—who had always avoided complicated relationships with women—knew that Cedric was about to go down fighting.

"You don't mean that," Merry stated.

"I do mean that. Now we must return to your house before anyone catches sight of you. Your appearance is unacceptable."

Merry had been kissing the puppy's snub nose, but she slowly raised her head.

Trent braced himself. He scarcely knew his future sister-in-law, but he judged that she was as strong-willed a woman as he'd ever met, and not someone to take an insult without a rejoinder.

But she surprised him. She did not lose her temper.

Instead, he watched with some fascination as the rage melted from her face. "In that case, I suspect that you won't wish to hold George while I mount Dessie." There was even a faint thread of amusement in her voice.

He'd forgotten that she was in love with Cedric. Love could blind someone to a person's worst traits—one of the many reasons he considered himself fortunate to have avoided the emotion altogether.

"Absolutely not," Cedric replied.

Trent reached out and plucked the puppy from her arms. George began enthusiastically licking his hand. "He's a charmer. I like the dark circles around his eyes. Very fetching."

"Like a streetwalker in Whitechapel," Cedric put in.

Merry was looking up at her mare. Even though she was on the tall side for a woman, she undoubtedly used a mounting block.

Trent glanced at his brother, but Cedric had taken out a handkerchief and was using it to wipe rainwater from the glossy surface of his tasseled boots. Trent could have put George down, but he didn't want to have to chase him down the path.

So he draped the puppy over his shoulder, put his hands on Merry's waist, and hoisted her onto her mount.

She smelled of perfumed soap and wet woman, a combination so potent that it almost knocked him down. She fit his hands as if she'd been made for them.

This was ridiculous. One look, one touch, and he felt starkly possessive.

It wasn't merely that she belonged to his brother, which she did. Nor that if anyone could pull Cedric out of a cloud of brandy fumes, it was Merry.

Most importantly, Trent didn't want to feel emotion like this toward the woman he married. He wouldn't countenance an unfaithful spouse, but he also had no intention of running around London like a jealous fool, warning people away from his flirtatious wife.

George liked being on Trent's shoulder. He scrabbled around, caught Trent's neck cloth with his teeth, and shook it with a little growl.

"No," Trent stated, his voice an adult version of that growl.

The puppy froze. As he pulled him off his shoulder, George hung his head, looking like nothing so much as a kitten being hoisted in the air by its mother.

"What the hell," Trent exclaimed, feeling something warm running down his back.

Cedric gave a bark of laughter.

"I'm so sorry!" Merry cried, reaching out her hands. "George is sorry, too. He's just a baby."

Trent handed the dog over. He thought of using his handkerchief to blot the urine, but what would be the point? His black coat disguised the stain, but he smelled like a pisspot.

He untied his horse and leapt into the saddle. "I shall escort you back, since I'd better change my coat before my first appointment."

"Surely that little episode settles it," Cedric said, as they turned the horses back toward Portman Square. "The dog is fit for the stables, if that."

Merry had settled the puppy in the crook of her arm again. She smiled at Cedric without a trace of irritation in her face. "His name is George."

Trent was impressed by her self-control. She didn't appear ruffled by Cedric's colossal rudeness. In fact, he had the feeling that his brother had finally met someone who was as stubborn as he was.

His hands tightened on the reins and he was aware that his heart had started thudding against his ribs in an uncivilized manner. He scarcely knew Merry Pelford, so why did he feel this wave of possessiveness? Desire felt inked on his skin, as if it were visible to everyone.

He glanced over to see Merry's slender arm cradling the dog, and felt another stroke of jealousy.

Envious of a damned dog. That was a first.

He had a sudden chilling awareness: he was losing his mind, probably from some sort of twisted fraternal jealousy. That he'd met Merry without knowing she was Cedric's fiancée—and within minutes had decided to marry her—just made it more twisted. Those stories people told about twins were coming true.

Except they weren't.

Because he'd be *damned* if he felt anything for a woman whom his brother had selected to wed. That was perverse.

Merry spent the ride home talking in a low voice to George, while Cedric amused himself by disparaging a musicale they had both apparently attended the night before, from the hostess's refreshments to her guests.

As they neared Pelfords' house, Cedric made one last attempt to separate Merry and George. "If you want a dog," he announced in a generous tone, "I shall buy a suitable one for you. Some ladies do have dogs, after all."

He sounded as if he were trying to convince himself, Trent thought cynically. "The Princess von Aschenberg has a dog," he heard himself saying.

Cedric frowned.

"It has a decided resemblance to a hairy rat," Trent clarified.

"Of course!" Cedric turned to Merry. "The princess's Maltese can be a guide. You should think of a dog as part of your attire, like a bonnet or reticule."

A flare of wicked amusement led Trent to chime in. "I believe the princess changes the ribbon on her dog's topknot to match her costumes."

"Like a maypole?" Merry sounded dubious.

Trent dismounted to say good-bye, as did Cedric.

A footman ran over and stood at Merry's horse's head. Waiting for a groom to bring over a mounting block, she tickled her puppy under the chin. "George would look very well with a ribbon."

"Where, on his tail?" Cedric scoffed.

Trent held back a grin. George's tail was not one of his best features.

His breath caught at the generous curve of Merry's smiling lips. If she had been his fiancée and she smiled at him in that reckless way, as if what he'd said was foolish but she forgave him for it, he would have kissed her until they were both senseless.

He watched her lean forward so that the groom could help her dismount. Her riding coat was still damp and clinging to lush breasts.

He would have pulled her off the saddle and carried her inside where no one could see them. Then he would have torn open her coat, cupped her breasts in his hands, and licked every drop of rainwater from her skin.

"I'll pay you a call tomorrow," Cedric was telling Merry. "I'll bring a dog for you, a more appropriate dog."

Merry frowned. "I have a dog."

"Now that I know you want a pet," Cedric observed, about an hour too late, "I shall find you an animal that will enhance your countenance rather than diminish it, as this cur will necessarily do."

"George—" she began.

"That dog will urinate on you if given the chance. Moreover, you are holding the animal in a manner that could be deemed offensive, considering that his undercarriage is entirely visible."

Merry bit her lip. The sight sent a bolt of lust down Trent's thighs. He had to get out of here.

"I will bid you both good day," Trent said. He bowed to Merry. "Miss Pelford, it has been a pleasure. Cedric . . . George."

Merry made a perfunctory curtsy and disappeared with her puppy into the house.

Cedric turned his scowl to Trent. "Even *you* must understand that a lady of breeding cannot bring that mongrel into polite society."

Trent shrugged. "Why not make fashion rather than follow it?"

"Miss Pelford is not yet in a position to make fashion," Cedric said.

"That seems a harsh appraisal," Trent observed.

"It's drudgery, training an American to be a proper lady. I wish I'd never taken it on."

"Surely you don't mean it."

Cedric ran a hand through his hair. "You needn't start worrying about whether you'll have to share your ha'pennies with me again. I've committed to marrying her. It's just that her instincts are invariably incorrect," he went on, as they both mounted.

"How so?"

"One could almost say that she is instinctually immodest. Hell, she's like you in that. I suppose *you* would think that it's perfectly fine that she cart around a mongrel with his clothes peg waving in the air. An indiscriminate pisser, moreover."

"The puppy had been frightened, cold, and no doubt hungry for God knows how long," Trent pointed out. "He only piddled because I startled him. And who gives a damn how she carries the animal?"

Cedric shrugged. "The dog is merely a symptom of the whole. Merry Pelford has no ladylike instincts." To Trent's surprise, his brother looked genuinely stricken.

"I'm sure that you can steer Miss Pelford in the right direction."

"It's so much work. Who would have thought? She had an English governess, after all."

Trent had no answer, so they headed toward Cavendish Square. That exchange cleared his mind. He refused to be the bastard who stole his brother's fiancée away. In fact, as a family member, he should try to help calm the waters.

When they were back home and grooms rushed out to take the horses, he said, "I don't think Miss Pelford will relinquish George, even if you do find another dog for her."

For all his fussiness, Cedric was an excellent horseman. He turned from instructing a groom to make both horses a hot mash.

"Nonsense. I know where to find the right sort of dog, a white Maltese. I'll buy one that will not urinate in the house, let alone on Merry herself."

"It won't work."

"You scarcely know the woman, I might point out."

"I had a lengthy conversation with her at the Portmeadow ball, before I realized she was your fiancée," Trent said.

"Indeed?" Cedric said sharply. "And where was that?"

"On the balcony. Neither of us had any idea that we would soon become family." Trent nodded to the groom who was taking his mount, but he could feel his brother's eyes on his back.

"I'll bring along the new dog tomorrow and make a trade," Cedric said, after they left the stables. "You don't understand: women are flighty, not to say fickle. Surely you heard the gossip about my fiancée?" he asked, striding ahead in order to climb the front steps before Trent.

The orders of precedence decreed that Trent go first, but Cedric never allowed Trent to precede him. Trent didn't give a damn about whether a duke should pass through a doorway before a lord, so they never quarreled over it.

"I have heard nothing about Miss Pelford, but she herself told me of two broken engagements in her past."

Cedric had drawn out the flask he always kept in his coat, but it proved empty. "I think it's more accurate to say that she has *had* two men in her past."

The door swung open but Trent jerked his head at the butler, sending him scurrying back into the house and out of earshot. He joined Cedric on the top step and growled a question. "Are you implying that Merry—Miss Pelford—has been less than chaste with her previous beaux?"

"You really know nothing of women, do you?"

Trent was starting to think that he knew a damned sight more than his brother. Merry was a virgin; he'd bet his life on it.

"Without question, she made sport between the sheets. But I'm smarter than the two fools who came before me. I haven't even given her a proper kiss—just busses on the lips—and believe me, she's as hot-blooded as any wench you might meet in Covent Garden."

Trent fought back an impulse to tear his brother limb from limb. "You are wrong," he said, finally, voice clipped but under control. "Your fiancée is chaste."

Cedric threw him a condescending glance. "You mustn't rely on appearances, Duke. She clearly tired of the others when they didn't satisfy her."

"You are wrong."

Cedric walked across the threshold, remarking over his shoulder, "I've kept her wanting, and she's in the palm of my hand."

Trent had cultivated an iron control since the time he was eight years old, and that control kept him in good stead now. He would gain nothing—*Merry* would gain nothing—if he knocked out his brother.

Even so, he strode forward and caught Cedric's arm. "Do not *ever* speak about your wife-to-be in that manner again," he said through clenched teeth.

Cedric gave a startled cough.

"Merry Pelford is in love with you. She deserves your every respect, in public and in private. She would never engage in intimacies outside of marriage, and if you can't see her bone-deep virtue, then you don't know her at all."

Cedric began to struggle.

"She's an innocent and you'll need to keep that in mind on your wedding night. Do you understand me?" Trent hardly recognized his own voice, it was so deeply and viscerally enraged.

"You're nothing but an animal," Cedric said, his mouth contorting into a petulant sneer. "One would think that brothers—*twins*—could be honest with each other, but that's not the case with us, is it? Here you are, instructing me to lie to you, not to mention the whole world."

"There's no lie involved, simply a modicum of respect for the woman who will bear your children." Trent dropped his hand.

"I need a drink," Cedric said, brushing off his sleeve. "What with my fiancée demanding my presence at the break of dawn, and you displaying all this newfound love of etiquette, I have the head of a Drury Lane doxy after a hard night."

It couldn't be much past ten in the morning. Cedric gave Trent a mocking smirk. "I don't suppose you'd like to join me in a constitutional, Duke? No? I do wonder what you get out of denying yourself pleasure."

"Don't be an ass," Trent said flatly. It was horrifying to realize just how relieved he felt to learn that Cedric had not yet kissed Merry.

Another sign that he'd lost his mind.

He should avoid Merry until after the wedding. Until she had become Cedric's, in the most basic and primitive of ways.

That would change everything. He would stop feeling this ungodly compulsion that was urging him to get back on his horse and return to Portman Square.

Ask to see her. Ask to see George. Use the puppy as an excuse to flirt with his future sister-in-law.

Trent gritted his teeth and tore off his urine-stained coat, making up his mind not to think about Merry.

He succeeded—until much later that night. Asleep, he rolled over in his bed and discovered Merry lying beside him in a tangle of glossy curls.

His blood thrumming with deep joy, he raised himself above her on his hands and knees, lavishing kisses on her.

He was running a hand down her sleek side, about to round the curve of a generous breast, when she murmured something.

Trent froze.

Her eyes opened, beautiful . . . tearful?

"Merry?" he whispered. "What is it?"

"Cedric?" she asked, her voice trembling.

The name ripped through Trent's dream like a gunshot. He awoke, gasping, fists clenched, sweating.

There was nothing he hated more than losing control.

She belonged to Cedric, damn it. He'd go to hell before he became the person who stole her from his brother. It struck him that perhaps lusting after one's sister-in-law *was* hell, but he shoved the thought away.

Yes, it was inconvenient that he felt such a raw passion for Merry. But all that meant, really, was that it was time he found a wife.

It was probably the same for wild beasts. The time had

come, and being twins, he and Cedric had responded to it at precisely the same moment and to precisely the same woman.

He stared into the darkness, trying to convince himself that being a twin meant accepting oddities.

It didn't work.

Chapter Nine

Like any self-respecting dog, George clearly felt that the bath and flea treatment were unnecessary, but he didn't hold a grudge.

"Just look how *good* he is," Merry told her aunt. They were supervising as a groom scrubbed George down. "He's not even complaining, though you can tell by his eyes that he is dreadfully offended."

Once clean and sweet-smelling, George was even more adorable than before. Buying items that every presidential dog needs—a china bowl, a blanket, a collar made of Spanish leather—took the better part of the afternoon, after which the family spent the evening trying to teach George to sit on command. He didn't seem to be able to sit, and toppled over if they pushed his little bottom to the ground.

After he had fallen over twenty times, he began toppling every time they said, "Sit." Another ten times, and he began rolling over if one of them caught his eye.

"He must think we're deranged," Bess pointed out. "Why would we want him to roll over so many times?"

Merry scooped up her puppy and gave him more kisses. "He has such a sweet nature that he'll roll all day just to please us."

"He'd do anything to get more of those meat scraps," Thaddeus said crustily. Alas, George had discovered that Thaddeus's boots were helpful for teething, and Thaddeus hadn't taken it well.

The boots were not George's sole transgression; he'd also had an accident in the dining room. After that, the knife boy was enlisted to escort him to the back garden once an hour.

The following morning the secretary whom Bess had lured away from a countess arrived to detail the wedding preparation. Merry had been enthusiastic in planning her first nuptial ceremony, matter-of-fact about the second, and could only be called tepid when it came to the third, so Bess sent her off to teach George to walk on a leash.

"It was a complete and utter failure," she told her aunt at teatime.

"He'll learn," Bess said, leaning down to greet George, who was so happy to see her that his tail wagged his entire body. "I cannot imagine why we never had a dog before."

"I can point to one reason: those boots took me three months to break in," Thaddeus said. "I don't have time for tea because I'm meeting a man who swears he's got a remarkable improvement on the water closet. Something to do with a self-filling cistern, whatever that is. I've no doubt but that it's all nonsense, but I might as well take a look."

Merry's uncle had made his first fortune by inventing a mechanical poultry feeder, and his second and third by investing in the inventions of others. He'd yet to find a workable apparatus in London, but he was endlessly curious, and counted a day lost in which he didn't inspect some new device or other.

"How was the mechanical hairbrush yesterday?" Merry asked.

"The Portable Rotary Hair Brushing Machine? Foolishness, my dear, pure foolishness. No lady would want it spinning around her head, and gentlemen don't brush for more than a few seconds. I suggested that it might have purpose as a clothing brush in a coal mine or such."

"Perhaps as a dog brush?" Merry suggested.

"Dogs would take fright at the mechanism's grinding noise." And with that, Thaddeus clapped on his hat and escaped out the front door.

Bess handed Merry a teacup. "My dear, have you noticed that we haven't had a single caller this week?"

She had noticed. But what was the point in fretting about her lack of social success? "Invitations arrive for every event that matters. Perhaps people aren't venturing out in the rain."

"No one is talking of anything but the charity hospital," Bess said, "which speaks highly of your Cedric, I must say. However, I was less pleased to learn from Mrs. Plessel about a supper party in honor of the hospital, to which we are not invited."

"Who is giving the party?"

"Mrs. Bennett."

"I suppose that may be a snub," Merry said. She couldn't bring herself to care very much. George was lying politely at her feet, but the look in his eyes made it clear that he would like to eat a buttered crumpet.

"It is a definite snub. I dislike that woman, and I gather the feeling is mutual."

Merry tried to remember what Mrs. Bennett looked like. "Is she the lady who wears sables even when the sun is shining?"

"No, you're thinking of Mrs. Raddlesby. Mrs. Bennett always wears pearls and manages to make the choice look virtuous." Bess snorted. She was of the opinion that pearls were aging, but that diamonds took ten years off a woman's face.

"I can't seem to place her," Merry said, racking her memory. London was full of ladies with pious expressions and pearls.

"She's one of those women who lives in a hive with other women buzzing around her, and they aren't buzzing compliments, either. She looks at me as if I were the gardener's wife. No: the *under*-gardener's wife."

"Oh, I know who she is! Mrs. Bennett is the daughter of a viscount," Merry explained. As part of her preparation for life with Cedric, Merry was trying to memorize *Debrett's Peerage of England, Scotland, and Ireland*. It was slow going, but she had made it past the nobleman whose daughter had married a common Mr. Bennett.

"I don't care if she's the daughter of the sultan himself," Bess retorted. "I am almost certain that her pearls are paste, and yet she and her friends smirked at my emeralds as if I'd chosen to wear a necklace of embalmed ants."

"'Embalmed ants'?" Merry repeated. "Ants aren't even green, Aunt Bess." George had rolled over and was begging, but she shook her head. "No crumpet for you, Master George! You don't need to grow any plumper."

"She thinks I wear bottle glass around my neck. As if you weren't truly an heiress, but some sort of conniver, wearing paste jewels in order to catch a titled man."

"That's absurd."

"I'll tell you what's absurd," her aunt said moodily. "It's

the way all these English girls wrap themselves up like little snowflakes and drift around the edges of the room."

Merry grinned at her. "In that analogy, Lady Caroline would be a blizzard. She has vowed to wear only white until she marries."

"There's another one I can't bring myself to like. She told me that Americans were ungrateful, unreasonable, and unjust, and when I gave her a look, she said it was only her opinion, and meant as a helpful observation."

"I'm sure she thinks it's unjust of me to have visited London and snatched Cedric from the market. I believe she would like him for herself." Merry reached for another crumpet. Being snubbed made her irritable, and that wasn't good for her soul.

"She can't afford him," her aunt said flatly.

"What?" Merry fumbled her crumpet and it dropped onto the tray.

"Your fiancé is a second son," Bess said. "Surely you are aware that Cedric must marry an heiress?"

"He's not Dermot. He's the son of a duke!"

"Here in England, the eldest son inherits the estate." She patted Merry's arm. "That doesn't mean Cedric won't make an excellent husband."

"I didn't know," Merry said, shaken. How could it be that Cedric needed to marry an heiress? He dressed . . . well, he dressed far better than did his own brother, the duke.

Back home in Boston, the Pelfords lived in a mansion, surrounded by the houses of relatives and friends. The Cabots were the Cabots, and they were friends with the Peabodys, and that was about all there was to it.

In London, on the other hand, all sorts of people pretended to be richer or higher-born than they were. Or even lower-born, as the duke had in his plain black coat.

That just led to Merry telling herself—for the hundredth time—that she had no business thinking about the duke. She should think about her fiancé, her handsome, generous fiancé.

Cedric, the man of her heart.

She had just reached for the dropped crumpet when the door opened and Jenkins announced, "The Duke of Trent. Lord Cedric Allardyce."

"Oh, hello!" Merry cried, leaping up and coming around her chair. The duke halted and bowed first in the general direction of her aunt, who remained seated, and then to Merry.

Cedric fell back a step, and swept into an elegant gesture. Since he couldn't see her in the depths of his bow, Merry gave her buttery fingers a quick lick before picking up her skirts and dropping a curtsy.

The duke saw her do it. There was a peculiar expression in his eyes, but it definitely wasn't censure.

When everyone was once more upright, Merry said, "How lovely to see you both again." If she sounded a bit dizzy, it was only because the look in the duke's eyes had unnerved her.

George was racing around and between their legs, so excited that he didn't even yap.

"As regards that dog," Cedric began, "I have brought a gift for you."

"How thoughtful," Merry exclaimed.

When she had first met the duke, she'd found his eyes rather cool, even hard; now she wondered how she ever thought that. He was obviously on the verge of laughing aloud.

Cedric headed back toward the entry, and Merry turned to the duke. "Your Grace!" she said with mock severity. "What is that naughty expression you are wearing?"

"'Naughty'?" he echoed. "Do you know that no one has accused me of that in years?"

"Very naughty," she said firmly. "Clearly, you know someth . . ."

Her voice trailed off because Cedric had reappeared, carrying a dog.

Or perhaps one should say half a dog, or a third of a dog. Poised on his arm, looking rather like an outsized parrot, was a tiny white dog with beady black eyes. The long hair on its head had been pulled into a topknot and tied with a ribbon.

"No!" Merry said, looking instinctively at the duke. "That is not what I think it is."

"This is Snowdrop," Cedric said. "She will help bring you into fashion. I have been assured that she never forgets herself."

"Snowdrop?" Aunt Bess put in, finally coming to her feet and joining them. "Who gave her that absurd name?"

"I did," Cedric said, chill shading his voice. He turned to Merry. "Perhaps you didn't think that I would follow through on my promise? I promised you the perfect accoutrement for a lady."

Merry looked from Cedric to the dog and back to the duke. Then she looked down at George, who was running circles in a frenzy of excitement.

"I warned my brother that his chance of separating you from the puppy was close to nil," the duke said. The glint in his eye showed that he was enjoying this, even if she wasn't.

She did not care for the fact that her fiancé had ignored her express wishes, but she was not going to air that opinion in front of the duke. "I suppose that Snowdrop can keep George from feeling lonely when we are out of the house."

"George will be happier in the stables," Cedric said. "Not only is Snowdrop a better breed, but her grandmother belonged to Queen Charlotte."

The duke snorted. "George may grow to be a capital ratter; this one has nothing but a pedigree to recommend her."

Bess shook her head at the duke. "We have no need of a ratter in this house, Your Grace."

"There is no room for a *ratter* in any lady's household," Cedric put in. "That proves my point precisely." He deposited Snowdrop on the floor. "One need only regard the two animals in proximity to determine which is the finer animal."

George instantly scooted over with his usual look of jolly expectation, sliding the last few inches on his too-large paws. Snowdrop flattened her ears and tucked her tail firmly between her legs. She allowed herself to be thoroughly sniffed, albeit with the air of a queen suffering a necessary but objectionable visit from a physician.

"Dogs have no delicacy of mind," Bess commented. "I should greatly dislike it if people took to sniffing each other as a form of greeting."

Merry was used to her aunt's ruminations on life and didn't turn a hair, but Cedric's mouth tightened.

Just then Snowdrop let out a surprisingly loud bark, and George instantly backed away and sat down.

"Look at that!" Merry cried. "He *can* sit!"

"Every dog can sit," the duke stated.

"We thought perhaps his back legs were too short to sit. Or his bottom was too plump. He usually falls over."

George did not topple, although he leaned back and away from Snowdrop, who pranced up to him and emitted a low growl.

This intimidated George so much that his plump little

body trembled all over. Merry bent down and snatched him up into her arms. "I'm afraid that they will never be friends."

"Snowdrop is an Amazon, despite her size," the duke said appreciatively.

"They need not be *friends*, as George will be living in the stable," Cedric put in.

Merry shook her head at him.

"The rugs in my house in Berkeley Square have not been subjected to urine," he said, adding acidly, "I prefer to keep it that way."

Merry forced herself to remain silent. He didn't mean it. In time Cedric would realize how dear George was.

Snowdrop, meanwhile, had started prancing around the duke's feet with a coquettish waggle. When he ignored her, she sat back, lifted her button nose into the air, and yapped.

"I believe that was a command," Merry observed.

"Miss Pelford, I beseech you to put that animal down and pick up Snowdrop, or she will become confused about her owner," Cedric said.

Snowdrop put a paw on His Grace's boots and whined.

"She is not confused," Merry pointed out, nestling George even closer. "She's in love. With the duke."

"She is destined to have a broken heart," His Grace said, paying her no attention.

"She and George would not be happy in the same house," Merry said, "but you could take Snowdrop, and they could visit each other occasionally."

"She would not be happy with me, either," the duke stated.

"Snowdrop would do so much for your countenance," she said mischievously, letting her eyes drift from his black coat to his plain black boots. "I think we would all agree that a touch of fashion could do wonders."

Cedric's face had grown even more chilly during this exchange; he turned somewhat abruptly and walked over to join Bess, who had returned to the tea tray. His rigid shoulders conveyed his offended sensibilities.

"Did you really think that dimple of yours could persuade me to adopt a dog, which is not only *not* a ratter, but which from a distance might be confused for rat?" the duke asked quietly.

Merry bit her lip to stop herself from laughing. "She could ride on the seat next to you. Think of the two of you, bowling around Hyde Park in the spring, Snowdrop adorned with a new ribbon . . . lavender, perhaps?"

Snowdrop was now positioned squarely in front of the duke, dotingly gazing up at him.

"There is no space in my vehicle for an animal," the duke stated.

Under Bess's supervision, Jenkins had replaced the teapot with a fresh one and supplemented the crumpets with several kinds of cake.

"Your Grace, Merry," Bess called, "I think that is more than enough conversation about dogs. Please, do join us for a cup of tea."

Merry nodded, and looked to the duke. "A cat may look at a king, or so they say."

"They can say whatever they like."

"It would make your brother very cross if you took her . . ."

He gave her that crooked smile, the one with more than a drop of sardonic amusement about it. "I see that you are acquainting yourself with our family politics, Miss Pelford. However, I am not so easily baited."

He walked over to Bess without another glance at poor Snowdrop.

Merry knelt and put George on the floor again. There

was no help for it; she was going to be the owner of two dogs. "Snowdrop, I want you to be a good girl, because George is only a baby."

Snowdrop snarled, tiny upper lip curling ferociously.

George trembled—and piddled. On the Aubusson rug and, distressingly, on the hem of Merry's gown as well.

In the ensuing furor, Snowdrop paraded around in triumph while Jenkins exhibited the first signs of a nervous collapse. Bess was sympathetic. Cedric was decidedly *not* sympathetic.

"That dog is not fit to live indoors," he thundered. "You are being cruel by acquainting him with the comforts of this house because he will have to live in the stables."

"He will never live in the stables," Merry cried, snatching up George again.

There was a significant silence.

Merry looked to the duke for help, but he had strolled over to the fireplace and was gazing down at the burning logs as if reading ancient runes in the flames.

"I will not share my house with an incontinent animal," Cedric announced.

"George is almost trained," Merry said. The puppy looked thoroughly ashamed.

Snowdrop, meanwhile, was amusing herself by circling Merry's feet, head cocked, beady eyes fixed on George.

"I *promise* that there will be no further accidents," Merry added.

Cedric looked at Bess. "Mrs. Pelford, I regret to say that my interest in a piece of cake is quite overset by this incident."

"I completely understand," Aunt Bess said. "I—"

"You will have to choose between us," Cedric said, cutting off Bess as he turned back to Merry. "Lady Cedric

Allardyce must be a woman of fashion, and a woman trailing an incontinent bulldog does not meet that standard."

His bow was perfunctory, with no added flourish at all. He swept through the door with all the outrage of an affronted emperor exiting the stage.

The duke crossed the room and tapped Merry's chin. Despite herself, tears were welling in her eyes.

"Ah, damn," he said softly. "You really do want him, don't you?"

Merry swallowed a sob. "I do."

"You shall have him." It was a promise. And anyone could tell the duke always kept his vows.

It wasn't until later, after he had taken his leave, that it struck Merry that His Grace might not have been referring to George, as she had assumed.

He might have been asking if she really wanted Cedric.

Chapter Ten

There was only one way to make certain that Cedric went through with the marriage, and Trent grimly decided to do it.

"I'll take the dog," he said abruptly to his brother, much later that evening. They were at the table, having just finished a mostly silent late supper—during which, Trent reckoned, Cedric had drunk far more than he had eaten.

"What?"

"I'll take George and the white dog, too, when you marry."

"Why would you do that?" Cedric tried to narrow his eyes but failed, and closed one of them instead.

Trent shrugged, rounding the table. "If you don't want her, I'll take Merry as well." The words escaped his lips as if they had shaped themselves.

"She's mine," Cedric said flatly.

That was exactly the response that Trent was pushing him to say. Of course it was. He hoisted his brother upright and deftly wedged his shoulder under Cedric's arm; he was well practiced at this ritual. "Time for bed."

"You know," Cedric said, when they were halfway across the dining room. "My earliest memory of this room is seeing Father collapse and fall to the floor. He nearly hit his head on that andiron over there."

Trent grunted. His brother was remarkably heavy for such a slender man.

"Drunk as a beggar," Cedric muttered.

The words started a horrible train of thought in Trent's mind. Merry might die the way their mother had, thrown from an overturned phaeton. His father had never realized what he'd done; he'd sustained a grave injury to his brain and succumbed after two days without regaining consciousness.

Cedric had once told Trent, in a late-night drunken fit that neither of them ever mentioned again, that he begged his mother not to get in the phaeton that evening. "Told her if she loved me, she wouldn't go," Cedric had said, slurring voice growing darker. "She said that I was becoming stuffy. Tapped me on the cheek as if I were five years old."

The thrill of terror that had shot through Trent's veins calmed. Cedric had not driven a carriage of any kind, let alone a phaeton, since their parents' accident. He always took a coachman.

Merry would be safe.

His brother didn't reappear until luncheon the following day, when he joined Trent at the table looking half dead and exuding a sickly sweet smell of liquor despite the fact his hair was wet from a bath.

"I'm going back to bed," Cedric said a while later, breaking the silence.

"Right."

"I don't remember much of last night." No shame was evident in his tone; he was matter-of-fact, as if he were remarking that he had misplaced a pair of gloves.

Trent saw no reason to reply.

"But I do remember that you promised to take both dogs upon my marriage," Cedric went on.

"Yes." Trent helped himself to another slice of roast beef.

"Do you suppose she'll agree to that?"

Trent had been certain that Merry would never relinquish George. But considering how she had reacted to the possibility of losing Cedric, it was possible that she would reconcile herself to the dog being in a good home.

She could always visit George, after all. His mind conjured up an image of his sister-in-law traipsing in his front door with those shining eyes and that hair and bosom and . . .

No, she could not visit the dog.

"I'll send both animals to Hawksmede," he said.

Cedric's lip curled. "We'd have to have all the carpets taken up, in that case. It will reek when summer comes."

"They can live in the gatehouse with Mrs. Plunket and her husband."

"That's not a bad idea," Cedric allowed. He pushed back from the table unsteadily. "Damme, but I was really soaked last night."

Trent couldn't think of an appropriate response.

A flush rose in his brother's cheeks. "You're such a sanctimonious prig."

Trent chewed his beef without answering.

"I shall take Merry for a walk in Hyde Park this afternoon," Cedric said, after a moment. "I shall explain to her that she has a clear choice. She can either keep the dogs, or she can give them to you and marry me."

"She loves you," Trent said, raising his eyes from his plate.

"She does, doesn't she?" Cedric mused. "I suppose you think that's a terrible mistake on her part."

"Not if you were to stop drinking," Trent said.

"Perhaps I will after I'm married," Cedric said, to Trent's surprise. "I have a devil of a head. It's not worth it."

Perhaps Cedric's marriage would be his salvation. "In that case, why not allow Miss Pelford to keep her dog?" he suggested. "George is just a puppy, and they grow up quickly. Don't you remember Blossom?"

As boys, they had shared a dog, a bloodhound with a heart as big as the whole county. For a few particularly miserable years, Blossom was the only thing that made Trent's life worth living.

A muscle worked in Cedric's jaw. Then he said, "I suppose you're right. I'll tell Merry she can keep the dog but only if she's not seen with him outside the house."

Trent had serious doubts about the way his brother seemed to think his fiancée would follow his bidding, but it was not his business. "George can stay in the buttery when you entertain people."

Cedric rubbed his face wearily. "I'm not even married yet, and I can already feel the bloody ball and chain dragging at my ankle."

With that charming remark, he made his way from the room and, presumably, up to his bed.

Chapter Eleven

Merry entrusted George to the knife boy when Cedric arrived to take her for a stroll in Hyde Park.

"That dog will have to be locked away when we have guests," Cedric announced as they set off down the path. "I also request that he not be allowed in the drawing room until he can be trusted."

"Certainly," Merry exclaimed, wondering what on earth had caused Cedric's change of heart. Presumably the duke had intervened. "George is learning to wait for the garden, unless he is startled."

With the question of George resolved, they walked along in silence, Merry racking her brains for an acceptable topic of conversation.

"I look forward to seeing your hospital when the building is completed," she finally said. "It's truly a magnificent thing you've done."

"Regrettably, you won't be able to visit the building, as it is in a part of London that respectable ladies do not frequent. I shall commission drawings so that you can obtain some sense of the edifice, at least."

"Surely I could pay a short visit," Merry said, startled by the unconditional sound of Cedric's decree.

"Not only is the area dangerous, but the patients, too, will be of a rougher sort. Though come to think of it, you Americans are so brash and straightforward; it's not as if you are as delicate as an English lady. I suspect that you could fight off an Indian attack all on your own."

He laughed, so Merry joined him, her laughter a little hollow. "I doubt that one of my hat pins would fend off a tomahawk."

"A toma-what?"

"Tomahawk. It's the weapon used by Indian tribes that's very similar to a hatchet. In any case, Spitalfields is no more dangerous than any large city," Merry asserted. "I read in the *Times* that the most vicious criminals live in an area called the Devil's Acre, near Westminster Abbey, and I've been to the Abbey many times."

"It's out of the question," Cedric stated. "There's another thing I've been meaning to suggest. I think we should consider engaging a tutor who specializes in elocution."

Refining her accent would not address the larger problem: the actual words Merry spoke. According to Miss Fairfax, English ladies were like deep, still pools. "Opinions are accursed," her governess had repeated over and over. "Gentlemen treasure a quiet nature."

Merry was many things—and she truly could fashion a wax flower if required—but she wasn't a deep, still pool. For example, she had a very negative opinion of Cedric's declaration that whole swaths of London were off limits.

"Oh, I meant to tell you that I accepted an invitation to

Mrs. Bennett's for dinner on your behalf," Cedric said. "As well as your aunt and uncle, of course."

"At such late notice?" Merry asked, rather startled. "My aunt was under the impression that we were not invited."

"The dinner will honor those who contributed to the hospital fund," Cedric said. "Mrs. Bennett was happy to add yourself and Mr. and Mrs. Pelford after I pointed out her oversight. Even my brother has engaged to attend, since he funded the Allardyce Wing."

The duke would be there.

The duke *might* be there.

Not that it mattered to her. He was nothing more than her future brother-in-law.

"Shall we retrace our steps? The mist is frizzling your hair, and it is beginning to resemble moss." Cedric chuckled at his own joke.

Merry touched her fringe as they turned. The curling irons her maid, Lucy, used every morning to shape fashionable corkscrew curls were the culprit. This morning she had put on a straw bonnet adorned with small plumes, but she probably should have worn a cottage hat with a wide brim.

The truth was that she was beginning to feel certain that she could not achieve the level of refinement required of Lady Cedric Allardyce. Elocution lessons wouldn't help. She felt stubbornly more American every day, not less.

Cedric patted her hand as they climbed the marble steps to Uncle Thaddeus's townhouse. "You mustn't take it to heart."

Merry turned to him, grateful that he understood the distress she was feeling. "Oh, Cedric—I mean, Lord Cedric—I do feel wretched."

"Everything can be mended," he said, in a consoling voice.

"Do you think so?"

"We will have to dismiss your maid and hire someone French."

"But—"

Cedric smiled. "Shakespeare praised his beloved for the 'black wires' on her head."

"Really?" If Merry heard about that playwright's stupid opinions one more time, she really *was* going to spit.

"Regrettably, in this civilized age, we require a great deal more from the gentle sex's toilette."

Had Cedric just said her hair was two centuries out of date?

If Merry hadn't sworn—no, *vowed*—that she would never again jilt a man, she would have parted ways with Cedric then and there.

But she couldn't. She had given her word.

She said good-bye to Cedric and went to find her aunt, all the while trying to ignore the persistent voice in the back of her head that said an elocution tutor and a French maid wouldn't do it. Nothing would make her an acceptable English lady.

Bess turned out to be in the small sitting room with the dogs.

Snowdrop had appropriated George's new velvet pillow, leaving the puppy to a spot on the floor. He got up so quickly when Merry entered that he tripped over his paws before bounding up again and coming to greet her.

"Good afternoon," Merry called, crouching down to scratch George's ears.

"Good afternoon, dear." Bess narrowed her eyes. "Upon reflection, I do not care for that bonnet. The feathers are going every which way, like a hen in a fit."

Merry straightened, and gave her pelisse and the offensive bonnet to Jenkins, who retreated into the hall.

Then she scooped up George and carried him over to the sofa.

"I shall ring for more crumpets," Bess said, doing so. "I seem to have eaten them all."

Merry was desperately trying to decide whether to confess her worries about the upcoming marriage. "Aunt Bess," she finally said, "I have a problem that I wish to discuss with you."

"Your problem is what we should do about your hair," Bess said, eyeing her. "That coiffure is not pleasing to the eye. I think we'll have to send Lucy back to Boston and hire someone from Paris."

Jenkins reappeared, so Merry ground her teeth while she waited for Bess to detail precisely how many crumpets she would like.

"My hair is frizzled because you insist that Lucy shape it into ringlets," she said, when they were again alone.

"Fashion is a harsh mistress," Bess said airily. "Lucy should apply a remedy. The *Lady's Magazine* suggested applying a tincture of sesqui-something to the hair."

"Sesqui-something? What on earth is that?"

"Something like iron. Obviously, I am misremembering the name." She frowned. "Perhaps the effect as well. It might have been to color one's hair."

"My hair will have to remain this color, Aunt Bess, because Cedric just informed me that he prevailed upon Mrs. Bennett to include us in her dinner party tomorrow evening."

"So I gather," her aunt said, gesturing toward a card on the table beside her. "An invitation arrived an hour ago."

"He believes that our lack of invitations was an oversight."

"Most unlikely," Bess said cheerfully.

Merry leaned forward, pinched a lump of sugar with the

tongs, and dropped it neatly into her cup. *This*, at least, was a nicety of etiquette that she had mastered. "I'm sure that Mrs. Bennett was quite disgruntled when Cedric pointed out her omission."

"There is no question but that we must attend," Bess said with a sigh. "She writes that Lady Caroline will be in attendance. I think that young lady can't afford Cedric, but she doesn't seem to agree; she would love to steal your fiancé. You mustn't allow that to happen, Merry."

"Well, but—"

Her aunt held up her hand, giving her a commanding look that suggested she had guessed Merry's doubts and did not approve. "Thank goodness, you caught Cedric's attention before your hair reached this state," she added. "A third broken engagement would be disastrous, my dear, as we agreed before reaching these shores."

Sometime later, Merry retreated upstairs, thinking about the morrow. If she were inclined toward dramatic turns of phrase, she would say that the dinner was shaping into a gladiatorial contest between herself and Lady Caroline.

The perfect English lady against the flawed American.

She only wished that she cared more. It was hard to put a finger on what had gone wrong with her engagement. It wasn't just her awkward manners. Cedric had never looked at her with the glint that had shone in Bertie's eyes—and yes, in Dermot's as well.

She ruthlessly pushed away memories of the way the duke looked at her. Whatever emotion was in *his* eyes was monstrously improper. It made her feel warm to the tips of her toes to even think of it, which was monstrously improper as well.

At length, Merry decided that she owed it to Cedric— and indeed to herself—to try to improve herself one more time. She devoted most of the next day to preparing for Mrs. Bennett's dinner, sitting on a low stool and reading a book about table manners while Lucy tamed her frizzled tresses.

Clear consommé was drunk from the bowl; other soups were not. One should delicately lift the finger bowl from the plate and place it to the left. And so on.

She could do this. American women regularly forged paths through the wilderness. A London dining room was hardly the wilderness, even though her uncle Thaddeus had come to the conclusion that Englishmen in groups resembled a pack of jackals. "Red in tooth and claw," he kept repeating darkly, refusing to accompany them to Mrs. Bennett's.

Would it be possible to fend off a jackal with a hat pin? Merry shook herself and dove into a chapter entitled "On the Peculiarities of Dress, with Reference to the Station of the Wearer."

A few minutes later she dropped the book to the floor.

She and Bess had spent three months in Paris before traveling to London. While in France, they had spent many pleasurable hours poring over French fashion plates, Dutch lace, and Italian linens—and that time and attention were reflected in the wardrobe Merry had brought across the Channel.

The watered silk she intended to wear in the evening was trimmed in pearls and silver lace. It cost the earth but was worth every penny.

It was better than a hat pin.

It was like a suit of armor.

Chapter Twelve

Mrs. Bennett's dinner party

Merry and Bess walked into Mrs. Bennett's drawing room that evening to find it already populated with philanthropic gentlemen and ladies. Footmen moved among the guests, offering drinks on silver trays.

Lady Caroline was posing in the center of the room, though no one stood near her. She had the air of a Greek goddess who finds herself unexpectedly without acolytes.

"Look at that," Bess muttered. "Englishmen are not as foolish as one might take them to be. They'd rather talk to each other than suffer that woman's lisp."

"She is quite attractive," Merry replied, keeping in mind her vow to be a better person.

"What does she attract? Pond life? There's your Cedric."

Aunt Bess nodded toward a man at the far end of the room with his back to them.

"No, that's the duke," Merry replied, without hesitation. His Grace was notably sturdier than his twin; the duke's shoulders had to be a third again as broad as Cedric's. In fact, he was bigger from head to toe.

"I do love pantaloons," Aunt Bess murmured, as the Duke of Trent turned around, revealing gray silk stretched over powerful thighs.

Other male guests wore embroidered coats in a dizzying array of colors, but the duke's black coat wasn't even fashionably tight. It looked as if he could shrug into it without help from a valet.

Merry bit back a smile thinking of the battles Cedric must wage with his brother over sartorial matters. Her fiancé took the art of dressing very seriously.

The duke, on the other hand, couldn't have done more to make it clear that he was uninterested in the whole business. These days, most younger men didn't powder their hair, but they used pomade to coax it into waves approximating a wig's curls. Not His Grace, whose tousled hair showed no signs of a valet's hand.

Catching her glance, he raised an eyebrow by way of greeting.

Raised a dark, sardonic eyebrow, and then turned back to his conversation.

"Not polite," Bess said with a sniff. "He can be charming if he wishes, but he doesn't act like a duke, for all Mrs. Bennett looked as happy as a boa eating a goat."

Their hostess had not endeared herself to Bess when she greeted them with the whispered information that they would find a duke *and* a duke's daughter in her drawing room. "Very shabby genteel to boast about one's guests," Bess added.

"Hush," Merry said, declining a glass of lemonade. She was determined to be fashionable in every respect.

Her aunt ignored that. "All this fawning has led to His Grace thinking he's the cock of the walk."

"Please don't use that word in public, Aunt," Merry said, through gritted teeth.

"You're turning into a regular Puritan," her aunt retorted, taking a sip from her glass. "For goodness' sake, Mrs. Bennett's cook must have used one lemon for the entire punchbowl. As watery as Communion wine. Oh, there's Mrs. Avedon. I must compliment her on her elegy to a dead rabbit."

"A dead rabbit?"

"Quite heartbreaking and difficult: a hundred lines, all in rhymed couplets. What rhymes with 'rabbit,' after all?"

Merry sighed and went over to greet Lady Caroline. "I hope you are quite well?" she asked, dropping a deep curtsy that acknowledged the lady's lineage. She positioned herself with her back to the duke, facing the door leading to the entrance hall. Surely Cedric would appear any moment.

Lady Caroline greeted her with a smirk and a bob of her knees. "I cannot complain." Her accent, in combination with a slight lisp, made her sound like a parrot that'd been trained to talk. "Cannot" turned to a high-pitched "cawnawt."

"Your gown is lovely," Merry observed, unable to think of anything else to say. "I am partial to whitework embroidery."

"I wear only white," Lady Caroline remarked. She lowered her voice and added, "In England, it is seen as a mark of one's station; in fact, my mother turned away her maid for wearing a white gown."

"That seems unfair, considering that gentlemen are free to dress like peacocks," Merry said.

"A lady must be particularly careful to avoid vulgar display."

Her pointed glance suggested that wearing pearls on one's sleeves constituted just such a vulgar display.

"I am glad that we Bostonians do not adhere to the same precepts," Merry said with a smile. "White is so difficult to wear, as it makes my skin look sallow. Though not yours, of course."

The footman came around again. "Juice is ruinous for the waistline," Lady Caroline declared. "I shall take a glass but I won't allow even a drop to touch my lips."

Merry promptly changed her mind and accepted a lemonade. At least drinking it would give her something to do.

"You do see that your future brother-in-law is in attendance, don't you?" Lady Caroline whispered. "Such a shame that the duke didn't deign to greet you, but, well, one cawn't blame him, cawn one?"

"One cawn," Merry said, unable to stop herself.

Lady Caroline didn't notice. "His Grace rarely attends society events, but my father has long intended to promote a match between our houses. Imagine, Miss Pelford, that would make us sisters."

She didn't summon up a smile at that thought, and neither did Merry.

"A consummation devoutly to be wished." The deep voice came from behind Merry.

Really?

Did everyone in London deem it necessary to fling around big words?

Lady Caroline smiled lavishly. "Your Grace!"

Merry turned. The duke was bowing, so she curtsied in reply, taking care not to spill her lemonade.

"That wasn't very graceful," Lady Caroline said with a giggle. "You look like a chambermaid caught in the hallway with a pile of sheets. Not that I mean to imply the least similarity."

"Of course you didn't," Merry agreed. "Your Grace, might I ask you to translate your greeting for me? What is a 'consummation'?"

His eyebrows rose again, and Merry felt her cheeks turning hot as she suddenly remembered that consummations were the natural consequence of weddings.

Lady Caroline tittered and flipped open her fan. "Really, Miss Pelford! Your plain-speaking American ways are disquieting to those of us accustomed to a more circumspect manner of speech."

"It was not I who raised the subject," Merry said, giving the duke a hard look.

"I was quoting *Hamlet*," he said apologetically.

Was it a requirement of British subjects that they commit to memory the entirety of the Bard's work? Lady Caroline launched into a speech about how she so, so loved Shakespeare's plays while Merry puzzled over the duke's quotation.

Could he really have meant that it would be a good thing if she and Lady Caroline became sisters-in-law? That implied he intended to marry the lady. Her heart sank. When she and Cedric married, Lady Caroline would presumably become part of her circle of acquaintances, but it would be awful if she became part of the family.

Lady Caroline had started twittering on about how the weather cawn't have been better at some house party she'd been to—which allowed her to emphasize the circles to which Merry had no entrée.

"You really should have gone, Your Grace!" she cried. "I cawn't tell you how lovely it was, so, so comfortable because it was all people like ourselves, if you take my meaning."

A grin tugged at the corner of the duke's lips, which was a very good look for him. He did not appear to be regarding Lady Caroline with anything resembling romantic fervor. But if Merry was interpreting his Shakespeare quote correctly, he had to be considering marriage to her.

Unless he had rattled off the line without thinking about it.

"'Devoutly to be wished'?" she mouthed, nodding toward Caroline. "*Sisters?*"

Merry watched as that sank in. His jaw tightened. Apparently, he hadn't considered that she and Caroline could only become as close as sisters through a marriage that involved himself.

She grinned. "'A consummation devoutly to be wished,'" she mused, taking advantage of a momentary pause in Lady Caroline's monologue. "You *do* grasp the import of His Grace's quotation, don't you, Lady Caroline?"

"I certainly do." The lady sniffed. "Shakespeare's immortal words run through the veins of every English subject. Even more so in my case, since those plays were written by one of my distant relatives. Everyone knows that the Earl of Essex was the real author of the plays."

The duke was glowering at Merry, likely because he was afraid she would explain the whole "consummation" business—which Lady Caroline would instantly translate into a proposal.

If the duke were wearing a ring, she'd probably rip it right off his finger and put it on her own.

"Shakespeare was *not* the Earl of Essex," the duke stated.

Oh dear me. His Grace was feeling a little irritable.

Merry beamed, letting her eyes reveal how much she enjoyed having him in her power. "We Americans are woefully ignorant. All I remember is that my governess said Shakespeare was a glover's son. And wasn't there something about how his father was fined for having a dunghill outside his house?"

She and Miss Fairfax had toiled through *Romeo and*

Juliet, after which Merry had relegated drama to the same category as wax flowers; to wit, best avoided.

Lady Caroline sighed gustily. "Really, Miss Pelford, I must ask you to refrain from talk of dunghills. I gather that all sorts of vulgarity are acceptable in the Colonies, but not here."

The Colonies? The war had ended twenty years ago, for goodness' sake.

"During his lifetime, everyone in London knew Shakespeare," the duke said. "They saw him writing in pubs, and they talked about him."

Lady Caroline was clearly torn between offending an eligible duke and burnishing her claim to Bardian blood. Nature prevailed over policy. "No man of low blood could have written such immortal lines," she pronounced. "Why, you might as well say that he was—" She stopped.

"That he was American?" Merry suggested. She tapped her chin with her finger. "Why didn't I think of that? Perhaps I, too, am descended from the Bard!"

She took a sip of her lemonade, which might as well have been plain water, just as Bess had said.

"Is that canary wine?" the duke asked, rather grimly.

"Canary wine?" Lady Caroline repeated, mystified.

Merry gave the duke a wry grin. "Do you think me Cherry Merry, Your Grace?"

"Cherry Merry?" Lady Caroline echoed, sounding more like a parrot every moment.

"Drunk," Merry explained. "When I was little, people would tease me if I stumbled, calling me Cherry Merry."

Lady Caroline sniffed and turned up her nose. "I am happy to say that no one has *ever* entertained the idea that I might be fuddled by alcohol."

Chapter Thirteen

It wasn't Trent's business if Merry Pelford was as drunk as a lord, which she clearly was not. But then she gave him that smile again, the one that sent lust roaring down his legs—and there *was* something a bit inebriated about it. Damn it.

He snatched the glass from her hand and took a swig, not because he truly believed his future sister-in-law was addicted to the grape, but because—well, because he wanted to see her mouth open with surprise and her eyes widen.

He was as capable of a spontaneous gesture as the next man.

"I had no idea you were so thirsty," Lady Caroline cried. "You must have my glass as well, Your Grace. I assure you that my lips have not touched the rim."

That was when he realized that his real motive was that Merry's lips *had* touched the rim.

Just now she pursed her lips to blow a stray ringlet out of her eyes, and he had to choke back a growl because of what happened to his body at the vision.

"I'll take my empty glass back so that you can drink more of this refreshing beverage," Merry said cheerfully.

She was being purely devilish, because the lemonade tasted like dishwater, but there was no help for it. He took Lady Caroline's glass and drained that as well.

"Your Grace?" Lady Caroline began.

She had an odd lisp. Trent arranged his face into an approximation of a smile. "Yes?"

"You must be so, so thrilled that Miss Pelford has consented to marry your brother."

"I am, I am," Trent agreed.

He was interested to see Merry's smile vanish.

"Generally speaking, those of our rank don't see many love matches," Lady Caroline went on. "But it has been so, so romantic to watch Lord Cedric win Miss Pelford's heart and hand."

"Indeed," Trent responded.

"The third time is the charm!" Lady Caroline said brightly, managing to insinuate all sorts of things with one short sentence.

Merry's eyes rested thoughtfully on the lady for a moment, and then she said, "In truth, I erred in my first two choices. I find that men are like walnuts: you never know if there's anything rotten inside until they're cracked."

God, she was magnificent.

"Whereas I think that marriage is like religion or medicine," Trent countered, handing Lady Caroline's empty glass to a footman, then taking Merry's and giving that over as well. "All three have to be taken on blind faith."

Lady Caroline's head swiveled between them. She must have been taught that charm meant perpetual smiling.

"You have been neither married nor betrothed, am I right, Your Grace?" Merry asked, as her eyes met his over the fan she had just unfurled.

"That is correct," he allowed. That errant ringlet had fallen over her forehead again. She had so much hair that a man instinctively pictured it spread across a pillow.

No.

What was he thinking? Sister-in-law.

Sister-in-law.

It was time to change the subject. "Why on earth hasn't my brother arrived yet?"

Lady Caroline looked around with an unmistakably eager flutter of her lashes. It could be that Cedric had indeed undersold himself. Perhaps he could have married a duke's daughter.

"His carriage may be snarled in a crowded street," Merry said, fiddling with a circlet of pearls and diamonds at her wrist.

For God's sake, how rich was the woman? Not that he cared, except as regarded her ability to support Cedric. If he were marrying her, he'd make her put her money in a trust for their children.

He would support his own wife.

He shouldn't be thinking along those lines.

Nor should he be looking at the contours of Merry's body. She would tempt an archbishop, though. She couldn't be wearing stays; her gown was designed so that the slightest touch would have pushed her bodice below her breasts.

It was clear to everyone that her breasts were round and high, as if they naturally presented themselves for kisses. For adoration.

"If marriage is indeed like religion, I think it will be a paradise," Lady Caroline chirped.

Trent and Merry turned to her at the same moment.

"How very quixotic of you," Merry said.

"In fact, I believe that romance is possible in daily life," Lady Caroline breathed, her eyes roaming over Trent's face and straying down his neck and arms.

Perhaps Cedric did not have a chance.

"For those of our station, marriage is, of course, a matter of bloodlines and family connections," the lady continued. "Yet love is certainly possible within the bounds of that agreement. In fact, I think that marriages amongst ourselves are far more likely to flourish than amongst servants, whose pairings are the result of animal instincts."

Merry seemed to be grinding her teeth. Interesting.

"Don't you agree with my broader point about marriage, Your Grace?" Lady Caroline asked.

"To some extent," he said, thinking of the romantic streak that Merry thought she saw in Cedric. "I believe that a man and woman are far more likely to live in harmony if emotion plays no role in the choice of spouse. On either side."

He glanced down to find that Lady Caroline had laid her hand on his sleeve.

"It is such a pleasure to realize how much we are in agreement, Your Grace. You are so wise in comparison to us two foolish women."

Merry's jaw tightened again.

"Oh, I wouldn't say that you are foolish, precisely," Trent said, baiting the tiger.

"How kind of you," Merry said. "I imagine we only seem so in contrast to your wisdom."

Lady Caroline's lashes fluttered some more. She took her hand from his sleeve about a second before he was going to shake himself free.

"Does love have no place, then, in those marriages you deem successful?" Merry inquired.

A little stir reached them from the other end of the room, and Trent knew without turning to look that his brother had finally arrived. Cedric never slipped into a room. He issued salutations and compliments the way a priest doles out Communion wafers. Everyone lined up, and everyone was blessed.

Interestingly enough, Merry's eyes didn't shift from Trent's face, though Lady Caroline was leaning sideways to see around Trent's shoulder.

"I am firmly of the opinion that it does not. I haven't experienced the emotion and I shouldn't care to."

"One needn't have love for a marriage to be successful," Lady Caroline agreed, smiling at him so lavishly that he could see her upper gums. She had been listening, then, even if she had been gawking at Cedric.

"What do *you* think of love and marriage, Miss Pelford?" Trent asked, in the brief interlude before Cedric, who was making his way down the room, came within earshot.

"How can you ask me that when I am betrothed to your brother?" she asked. Her words may have been playful, but her eyes were not.

"I am inquiring in the abstract," he said, "with no reference to the particulars. I am aware that yours is a love match."

"In the abstract, then," she replied, "I would worry that a marriage arranged purely on the grounds of suitable lineages and property contracts would be like the circus: very gay and shiny on the outside."

"And on the inside?"

"Prosaic at the best, and torture at worst. At least, from the point of view of the animals forced to dance for their dinner."

Cedric had reached them and was bowing so deeply that

his chin nearly touched his knee. Trent found himself staring blankly at his brother's hand tracing flourishes as he bowed.

Miss Merry Pelford had a steel backbone. She would survive marriage with his brother, for all of Cedric's flaws. If anyone could save Cedric, it would be Merry.

But, for the first time, he thought about what that marriage would be like for her.

What kind of marriage would it be? Once a bear is trained to dance for his dinner, what does he think of his trainer?

That might have been the question in her eyes, but perhaps it was only wishful thinking on his part.

"Your Grace," Lady Caroline said, her hand on his sleeve again. "Mrs. Bennett has signaled that we should remove to the dining room."

Sure enough, their hostess was trilling something about how formal processions by rank were fusty and old-fashioned, and they should all proceed at their leisure.

"Yes, of course," Trent said. Mrs. Bennett had claimed Cedric; they were walking from the room together, his head close to hers.

Lady Caroline's hand tightened on his arm. "I am sure neither of us considers such rules passé."

Trent didn't give a damn who reached the dining room first. He didn't respond, just began towing her to the door.

"I trust that you are not worried that your brother will be left at the altar, Your Grace," the lady said, changing the subject. For whatever reason, she had decided to mount a campaign against Merry.

"That is for Cedric to worry about, not me," Trent pointed out.

"But, Your Grace, you do realize that Miss Pelford is betrothed for the *third* time?"

Trent shrugged.

Merry had taken Kestril's arm. He was a decent fellow, though young and—now Trent thought of it—fairly dim. His lands ran along the western border of Trent's country seat, and they'd always maintained an amicable relationship.

Even so, the way Kestril was looking at Merry made Trent's eyes narrow.

If she were his fiancée, he would never allow her to sit at a different part of the table. Hell, he wouldn't like it if she smiled at another man the way she was smiling at Kestril.

He might become shameless, holding her hand in public. Kissing her in public. Worse, even.

In carriages.

Trent suited his stride to Lady Caroline's mincing steps while he deliberately allowed the devil to tempt him. Between a gap in the couples ahead of them he could just see Merry's back.

Back?

Who cared about backs?

He did. It turned out that he cared about necks as well, because her hair was swept up and then fastened to the side in ringlets that bared her neck. It was a delectable neck. A kissable neck.

Below that was a sweep of creamy back, and then below that, a rump as rounded and perfect as he'd ever seen.

"Do you agree, Your Grace?" Lady Caroline asked.

He had no idea what she had asked him. Glancing down at her, he saw her eyes were eager. He hedged. "I expect so."

"Your brother is so, so beneficent and altruistic."

He murmured something.

"You can even see it in his choice of bride," she said, with a touch of malice.

Trent looked up just in time to see Merry smiling at

Kestril and then slipping away down the hallway, likely heading toward the ladies' retiring room. Sure enough, as they reached the door to the dining room, he caught sight of her gown's floating hem disappearing up the stairs.

He drew Lady Caroline into the room, started automatically for the head of the table, and paused. As the highest-ranking gentleman and the highest-ranking lady, the two of them would ordinarily be seated close to their hostess.

As with most time-honored conventions, there was rhyme and reason behind the rule of precedence regarding entry to the dining room: to wit, it dictated the order of seating down the table.

Mrs. Bennett's dismissal of the usual order of things had resulted in guests' seating themselves hirdy-girdy. Cedric had seated himself in the place that, strictly speaking, should have been occupied by the highest-ranking gentleman in the room: himself. The empty seat next to Cedric would do for Lady Caroline.

The only other unclaimed seats were toward the opposite end of the table—beneath the salt, as the old saying went. For a second he entertained the idea of escorting Lady Caroline to one of them, just to see her outraged expression.

Mrs. Bennett hopped to her feet. "Oh no," she cried, recognizing the problem too late.

"That's quite all right," Trent said cheerfully, depositing Lady Caroline next to Cedric with no further ado. "Precedence is out of mode, as you say, and I'm happy to sit wherever there's a free place. If you'll excuse me for a moment, I shall return directly."

He tried not to exhibit undue haste as he made his way from the room. The butler started toward him, but Trent waved him aside.

What the hell was he doing?

He climbed the stairs, cursing himself. He was following Merry Pelford like a damned lapdog.

As he reached the top he had a moment of clarity. He was following her because, of everyone in London, Merry met his eyes squarely and didn't look away. She didn't cringe or fawn.

In fact, she was downright disrespectful. She lived in a universe where men were not adulated simply owing to an accident of birth.

No one he'd ever met had looked at him and seen anything other than his duchy, like a medal on a heavy gold chain, determining his every interaction. Even Cedric saw only the title that had been snatched from him by an accident of birth, not the twin brother who stood before him.

He turned the corner at the top of the stairs and there she was, just closing a door behind her. She had rubbed a dark rose color on her lips.

She didn't need it. On the other hand, it made her look naughty . . . and absurdly enticing.

"Your Grace," she said, her voice clear as a bell in comparison to Lady Caroline's. Merry's thick black lashes framed eyes that seemed as changeable as the weather. You could see emotions going straight through them. Right now, she was surprised.

He'd be damned if she was in love with his brother, as she claimed to be.

"I wanted to thank you privately for not informing Lady Caroline about the consummation that I certainly do not wish for," he said, walking toward her. "I spoke carelessly."

"Trying to be witty by spouting quotations," she said, grinning at him. "Tut, tut, Duke. Your pretension could have had grave consequences."

"More than grave," he said truthfully. "Lethal."

Her eyes crinkled. Since when did crinkling eyes send a bolt of desire through a man's body?

"I am so sick of Shakespeare," she confided. "To be honest, I wish the man had never written a line. I'm starting to hate him."

"There's many a schoolboy who agrees," Trent said, abandoning caution and taking another step toward her. "Hereafter, I shall curb my cleverness."

"There's a sacrifice that will change the world," she said, laughter running through her voice. It was heady stuff, that laughter.

Something must have showed on his face because she went still.

"It's remarkably easy to make an idiot of oneself trying to show off for a lady," he admitted, the huskiness in his own voice surprising him. "You'd think I would have learned that lesson in my salad days."

He was staring at her the way a lad gapes at a buxom barmaid, not the way a gentleman—a *duke*—eyes a lady. But he couldn't seem to turn away. Merry Pelford's clear eyes smashed through all his defenses.

She finally broke their gaze by looking at the floor, color flooding into her cheeks. It wasn't merely on his side, then. She felt it.

"If you'll excuse me, Your Grace, I must return to the dining room."

"As must I." He offered his elbow and enjoyed it far too much when she slipped her hand through.

A large, overly ornate mirror hung facing the bottom of the stairs, presumably positioned so that the lady of the house could glance at herself one last time before leaving. It was impossible to avoid one's reflection.

He never spent time gazing at his own face, but if he happened to catch sight of himself in a glass, he was accustomed to seeing an indifferent, sardonic aspect on the face looking back at him.

That expression was nowhere to be seen.

In fact, if he were given to poetic fancy—which he was not—he might have described his expression as smoldering. It gave him a queer sense of vertigo.

As they entered the dining room together, he had the uneasy feeling that the face in the mirror reflected things he'd rather not think about.

Emotions.

The idea was so perturbing that he allowed a footman to pull out Merry's chair while he seated himself beside her.

"Your Grace," said a feminine voice on his left. Please, let it not be a marriageable young woman.

Benjamin Trewell, a decent fellow he'd known since university, nodded to him from across the table. "My wife."

Trent smiled at her. "Mrs. Trewell, it's a pleasure."

They chatted for a moment, but a footman intervened, pouring wine. Trent turned to Merry, and groaned inwardly. He could see directly down her bodice. Belying his earlier impression, she *was* wearing stays; he could see them as well. They pressed against her breasts, making them even plumper and higher than they would be naturally.

He shifted in his seat, cursing his damned silk pantaloons.

The gentlewoman beside him was talking on and on about a dog she was training. Or perhaps it was a child; he had missed a crucial detail.

Disgust curdled in his gut. What in the living hell was he doing at this dinner party? If he was honest with himself, he'd only come in order to see Merry Pelford.

That would be: to see his future sister-in-law.

Right.

Well, he'd seen her.

And lusted after her.

She was delicious. His cock was threatening to burst out of his pantaloons. If he wasn't careful, he might finally see a lady faint—after glancing at his lap.

The hell with it. With an abrupt gesture he reached forward and flicked his wineglass so that it tipped over, sending a wave of claret across the tablecloth and into his lap.

Mrs. Trewell gave a little scream; Merry said nothing, but drew away slightly. He was sufficiently overheated that the cool liquid was a relief. And brought him under control.

"I must apologize," he said, rising from his seat and handing his sodden napkin to the footman who had rushed forward to assist. The entire table stared at him, every conversation cut short. "I shall have to return home and change my clothing. I have no other choice."

At the other end of the table, his hostess had leapt up with a look of horror; too late, Trent realized that she—and everyone else—would assume that he was leaving the party because he was insulted at being seated among less honored guests.

"I would prefer to stay," he said, bowing to his hostess. His lie would have no effect; he could see people whispering to each other, and Mrs. Bennett looked stricken.

He gave a mental shrug and then a general bow to the table.

Chapter Fourteen

Merry watched in astonishment as the duke stalked from Mrs. Bennett's dining room.

"Apparently, His Grace didn't care to be seated with mere mortals," Mr. Kestril remarked.

Had the duke overturned that wineglass on purpose? Could he truly have been so irritated at not having been granted the precedence he considered his rightful due that he'd left a dinner party before it even started?

She wrinkled her nose in disappointment. He hadn't seemed like that sort of person, but he was a duke, after all.

"I am rather surprised," Mr. Kestril said, echoing her thoughts. "My lands run beside his, and he's never put on airs. But I gather he's courting Lady Caroline, and perhaps he felt the meal was beneath his notice when he was not seated beside her."

With the duke's abrupt departure, the party felt flat and

tiresome. Cedric was seated far above her at the table. Lady Caroline was flirting with him with an ostentatious intensity that should have made Merry jealous. It didn't.

Fortunately, Kestril was happy to talk. It turned out that he was a bird enthusiast who could list which birds she might glimpse in Hyde Park but would never see at home in Boston.

Seven courses later, Merry had become an expert on London's winged residents, and the dessert course, an array of confections and sweetmeats, was finally being served. She sampled each of them, as etiquette demanded, but in truth the only thing she wanted was a piece of the pineapple in the center of the table. She had been craving a taste since she'd entered the room and seen it crowning an elaborate tower of more prosaic fruits, as unexpected and exotic a sight in damp, sooty London as a Mohawk brave in full regalia.

She had tasted her first pineapple the day after she'd arrived to live with her uncle and aunt. She had been a young girl, grief-stricken, tired, and lonely. Bess had told her that pineapples arrived on ships that sailed to Boston from islands where the sun always shone, and people wore folds of cloth around their middles and danced from morning to night.

For the first time since her father died, the heavy, gray cloud that had clung to Merry like a second skin lifted. To this day, she could remember her first bite, how it tasted like honey and happiness, an emotion she'd forgotten in her grief.

The tower of fruit was being dismantled, and a footman made his way around the table to inquire about preferences. When it was her turn, she asked for a slice of the pineapple.

As the footman retired to slice the fruit, she heard a very

old man across from her say distinctly, "She's asked for the pineapple!"

If Merry's etiquette books hadn't been so emphatic on the incivility of speaking across the table, she would have asked him why he was surprised. Instead she watched silently as he summoned back the footman and requested a slice himself as, indeed, did everyone else at her end of the table.

"They are devilishly difficult to grow in our northern climate," Mr. Kestril informed her. "As you may know, they originate in the tropics, where the days are long."

"I am surprised that they can be cultivated in England," Merry said, taking a bite of the presumably English pine-apple.

"They have to be grown in a hothouse with a pineapple stove. Chelsea Physic Garden has a number of thriving plants, I believe."

"A pineapple stove?" Merry echoed, just as their hostess signaled that the ladies would now retire to the drawing room.

"If you are interested, I could arrange a visit to the garden," Mr. Kestril said, as they all rose.

"That would be lovely," Merry said, beaming at him. "I am interested in plants of all kinds, and I would dearly like to see that stove."

Cedric appeared. "Kestril," he said, bending his shoulders slightly, rather than bowing at the waist.

"Allardyce," her dinner companion replied, bowing, though his countenance was cool.

"Mr. Kestril has kindly offered to arrange an outing to the Chelsea Physic Garden," Merry told Cedric.

"Perhaps you will have time after we return from our wedding trip," Cedric said languidly.

This was the first Merry had heard of a wedding trip, but she knew better than to question him in public. Besides, Aunt Bess arrived, slipping her arm through Merry's to lead her away; the butler was waiting to escort the ladies to the drawing room.

Immediately upon entering the room, Aunt Bess was waylaid by a poetry enthusiast and drawn into a discussion of sonnet form, which left Merry to sit between Lady Caroline and Mrs. Bennett. How wonderful.

She had scarcely seated herself when Lady Caroline glanced at Merry's midsection and said, "I do hope that pineapple was your own, Mrs. Bennett, since Miss Pelford was so hungry."

Lady Caroline's peculiar elocution turned simple vowel sounds nearly unrecognizable—but even after Merry untangled the "paheenawpple," she had no idea what the lady was talking about.

"I would never *buy* a pineapple," Mrs. Bennett replied airily. "Their appearance pleases me, hence I rent one to create my table's centerpiece, but most people I know can't abide the flavor."

At that, the ladies all fell over themselves to assure her that they, too, loathed pineapple and had only accepted a slice from politeness.

Rent?

The pineapple had been *rented*?

Who rented food?

"What next?" Lady Caroline said, laughing. "Will guests begin to swill the violets in the finger bowls?"

Who would have dreamed that a hostess could rent a pineapple for a dinner party? Yet Londoners did, apparently, and it had been profoundly gauche of Merry to request a slice.

Embarrassment flooded through her, spreading right to the very tips of her fingers. "I was not aware the pineapple was merely a decoration," she said apologetically. "We do eat them back home. In fact, Mr. Kestril told me that King Charles the Second enjoyed the first pineapple grown in England back in 1675."

The silence that followed was familiar; no one ever seemed interested in the sort of information that stuck in Merry's memory.

"I am truly sorry for eating your centerpiece," she added quickly.

Lady Caroline leaned toward her and patted her hand. "No one can blame you for your ignorance of polite society."

Merry told herself that Lady Caroline was likely so poisonous because she was hungry. Starvation did that; it turned otherwise decent people into cannibals.

"If you don't mind the hint, Miss Pelford, I would suggest that you stay away from sweet fruit. I'm sure you are hoping to look your best on your wedding day, and staying slender requires willpower." Lady Caroline glanced down at her rake-thin body with satisfaction.

Maybe the lady *was* starving. Did it really give her the right to be so perishingly obnoxious?

Bess came to the rescue before Merry could say something she might regret. "Mrs. Bennett," she said, smiling at their hostess, "I must reiterate my niece's apology. I assure you that I will have a replacement pineapple delivered to your door tomorrow morning."

Mrs. Bennett's eyes narrowed, and Merry's heart sank. Her aunt meant well, but the implicit reminder that Bess's emeralds were not green glass was not well received.

"I have a wonderful idea," Bess continued, widening her smile to include the whole circle. "We shall serve pineapple at my niece's wedding breakfast. I am certain that tasting the fruit will change your minds. It is remarkably beneficial for the skin."

Oh no.

Lady Caroline bridled, and the red patches around her jaw deepened in color. "Really, Mrs. Pelford," she said shrilly. "One would almost think that you imagine a few pineapples could serve as an entrée to polite society."

Her aunt had raised Merry to turn the other cheek, and never lower herself to respond to a snub. But now Merry felt a slow boil rising to the surface on her aunt's behalf. It was one thing for Lady Caroline to be rude about America—but now she'd been hateful to the person Merry loved best in the world.

"I did not have that in mind," Bess said calmly, picking up her teacup. "It would be a fine thing to be a part of the British nobility, of course, but not everyone has ambitions to that elevated station. As I'm sure you know, in America we favor democracy rather than a constitutional monarchy."

As the person of highest birth in the room, Lady Caroline clearly took Bess's indifference to the nobility as a personal insult. She tossed her head, like a horse about to rear on its hind legs. "You will forgive me if I point out that the smell of the shop lingering around your niece's betrothal suggests that *she* has precisely that ambition. As I understand it, Lord Cedric's tailor is already celebrating, though the wedding has not yet taken place."

This audacious statement was followed by a long moment of dead silence—a moment in which Merry discovered that the civilizing effect of London air had its limitations. Resentment that she had repeatedly pushed to the back of her mind turned to a rage that swept her like a fever.

"As *I* understand it, Lord Cedric had a wide choice of

heiresses," she said, keeping her tone sweet. "I know we are all sympathetic, Lady Caroline, regarding any disappointment you might be feeling."

"Mrs. Bennett," Bess said in a slightly raised voice, "This tea is truly marvelous. Will you tell me where your housekeeper finds the blend?"

Brick color had flooded Lady Caroline's cheeks. "At least I will not have to bribe people to attend my wedding breakfast with the promise of pineapples!"

"Well, spit," Merry retorted, "I can't say that it had occurred to me that a pineapple or two gave one entrée to the haut ton. Imagine what one could do with a crate of oranges."

All the ladies turned their heads expectantly toward Lady Caroline—except Aunt Bess, who gave Merry a look that sent a shock of shame through her.

"I beg your pardon," Merry exclaimed, at the very same moment that Lady Caroline turned her shoulder and whispered loudly to their hostess, "One cannot expect persons from the Colonies to understand civilized behavior."

"I declare that I would be *terrified* to travel into the wilderness, where no rules of polite society pertain," Mrs. Bennett agreed. "Why, I wouldn't be surprised to find a naked savage serving the table instead of a footman in livery! I shouldn't have the faintest idea how to conduct myself as, indeed, is clearly the case for some who travel to our shores."

With this, Aunt Bess rose, gathering her shawl and reticule. "I have most unfortunately developed a headache, and I'm afraid that I must take my leave."

All thought of further apology had flown from Merry's head. She leaned forward and smiled at their hostess. "I do assure you, Mrs. Bennett, that were you to visit my country, you would find our customs easy to negotiate. For example, in America, you won't find even a single stalk of asparagus on the table unless your hostess wishes you to eat it. And unless your hostess owns the vegetable in question."

"*Niece*," Bess said, with dreadful emphasis.

Merry felt a bit dizzy—though whether with triumph or shame, she wasn't certain. She jumped to her feet as her aunt gave Mrs. Bennett a polite thank-you that avoided any mention of ornamental produce.

Their departure had the effect of spurring the other guests; by the time they made their way out the door, ladies were milling about and donning their pelisses; husbands had been summoned from cheroots and port.

"You were strongly provoked," her aunt said the moment their carriage door closed and they were alone. "Nevertheless, I am sorely disappointed in you, Merry. I hope I have taught you that kindness is always the better alternative."

"I do know that," Merry said. Her anger was seeping away, and she began to feel acutely ashamed. Had she really taunted Lady Caroline because Cedric hadn't chosen her as his bride?

"Mind you, Lady Caroline's remarks were remarkably ill-bred," Bess allowed.

"She implied I was fat, and she was unforgivably rude to you."

"She wanted to provoke you, and you allowed it."

"I know it doesn't excuse what I said. I'm tired of remaining silent while people say ignorant things about America."

"England is your mother's country," Bess pointed out. "What's more, you have made a solemn promise to an Englishman to wed him and live here for the rest of your life. Your children will be English, Merry. For your own peace of mind, you must stop taking offense at such silliness.

Mrs. Bennett's remark said more about her character than about our country."

Merry nodded.

"Unfortunately, I'm fairly sure the pineapple was rented in order to provide the illusion that Mrs. Bennett could afford to offer her guests exotic fruit."

"Wasn't it part of the decoration? She said that I had eaten the centerpiece."

"I had the impression that Mrs. Bennett was disguising a harsher reality, and your misstep may inadvertently have caused the lady a financial hardship. I took a closer look and her pearls are definitely made of paste."

The carriage turned a sharp corner and Bess lost her balance, pulling herself upright again with a muttered exclamation. "I shall never get used to these London streets! At any rate, I will send over a replacement pineapple tomorrow. They are dear in Boston, but they must be an extravagance here."

"I shall write Mrs. Bennett an apology," Merry said unenthusiastically.

Bess nodded her approval.

"I suppose I can apologize to Lady Caroline in person." That was not a conversation Merry was looking forward to.

"There is always a silver lining, my dear," Bess said, more cheerfully. "We shall not receive any more invitations from Mrs. Bennett."

They sat in silence while Merry thought over the conversation. "I do have one question," she said at length. "Lady Caroline's remark about my betrothal seemed very pointed."

"Marriage *is* a commercial transaction for those in our station," Aunt Bess replied. "You are an heiress, Merry, and it does no good to pretend that men don't take it into account. Though as you know, your uncle structured your settlement so that your fiancé has no claim on your money until the marriage actually occurs."

"But Lady Caroline made it sound as if Cedric had received money in return for his proposal," Merry said. "She was only referring to the dowry, then?"

To her alarm, Bess hesitated.

"No," Merry breathed.

"It isn't the way it sounds," her aunt said hastily. "Not a penny of your fortune has gone to your fiancé, and none shall until you're fast married."

"Then?"

"Your uncle did pay some of Lord Cedric's bills."

"Bills? What bills?"

"Oh, merely some accounts at the tailor's and so on." Bess waved her hand dismissively. "So that the two of you can begin married life with a clean slate."

"How much money did Cedric owe?"

"As to that, I really couldn't say. If your uncle wishes to make you a wedding present, he is well within his rights to do so."

"The debts must have been quite substantial if everyone knows that they have been paid." Merry straightened, and asked fiercely, "When exactly did Uncle Thaddeus pay those bills? Was it a condition of my betrothal?"

"Oh, goodness, no!" her aunt cried. "Never think that, my dear. Your uncle found out a week or so ago that Lord Cedric had a couple of annoyingly persistent creditors. He paid the debts and gave his lordship some sound advice about not going into arrears."

That sounded like her uncle: generous to a fault, though prone to giving advice where it might not be welcomed.

In Boston, one did not order French gowns unless the

money was readily available to pay the dressmaker. Cedric, it seemed, took a more cavalier attitude toward balancing his accounts.

"I'm certain it was a trifling amount," her aunt concluded.

"You don't think that I've once again betrothed myself to a man with no money?" Merry asked. She had a sinking feeling.

Bess shook her head firmly. "Your uncle made certain of that. Lord Cedric is not penniless. Though he does not currently live there, he owns a house in Berkeley Square, which is an excellent address. He has an income inherited from his mother. Your uncle wished to make the gesture of settling some minor debts, and I approve of it."

The gentlemen had only just left their port when she and her aunt made their farewells, so Merry had done no more than nod and smile at Cedric. By now he would have learned about the pineapple fiasco, in fact, probably the moment the front door closed behind them.

Lady Caroline, if no one else, would detail every faux pas Merry made that evening, undoubtedly while announcing that the finger bowls were at risk.

Never mind what her aunt thought; her third betrothal was clearly in its death throes.

Their carriage became caught behind some farm wagons, and after a while Bess slumped into the corner and went to sleep.

Merry remained bolt upright, thinking about Cedric.

The problem was that her mind kept snapping back to the way the duke had looked at her when they encountered each other upstairs.

He had almost kissed her. But that didn't mean she had the option of marrying him.

No man would ever marry a woman who was once betrothed to his brother. And no duke would marry someone like her. Not only was she American, but her reputation was already damaged; imagine what would happen if she discarded yet another fiancé.

She had only two choices.

She could marry Cedric, or she could jilt him and return to Boston.

Chapter Fifteen

That night Merry dreamed that the pineapple turned into a golden egg sitting on the table of an ogress who shouted "Fe, Fi, Fo, and Fum!" and threatened to grind her bones into a loaf of bread unless she turned the egg into an omelet. She woke up with an echo of that furious ogress in her ears.

George had hopped off the bed and was dancing around the feet of her maid, wagging his tail.

Lucy was at the window. "You must rise, miss," she said, struggling to pull back the heavy velvet drapes. "Your aunt is making such a fuss as you wouldn't believe. She sent a footman out for a peenacle and when he came back without one, she was not happy. Luckily, he finally managed to find two."

"Not 'peenacle,' *pineapple*," Merry said, swinging her legs over the side of the bed.

"That's right, pineapple. You'd think they was made out of gold. They're that dear."

"So I understand," Merry said with a sigh. George danced back over to her and rolled onto his back.

"The boy's waiting out in the hallway for the puppy."

"Where's Snowdrop?"

"Mr. Pelford took her for a drive. That dog is a terrible flirt. She's even trying to make up to Mr. Jenkins!"

Lucy liked Snowdrop, but she had not succumbed to George's charm, probably because Jenkins was always on the alert for an impending accident. The household always took its tone from the butler.

Merry pulled on her wrapper, opened the door, and handed over the wriggling puppy.

"Your uncle is less than pleased that both pineapples were delivered to someone's house, given how much they cost, but the missus said they were by way of apology." Lucy's eyes were gleaming with curiosity.

There was no need to keep it a secret; Merry supposed that the better part of fashionable London was aware of her faux pas by now. "Last night, at Mrs. Bennett's house, I asked a footman for a slice of pineapple."

Her maid's eyes widened. "Are they poisonous?"

"Not at all; they're delicious. The problem was that Mrs. Bennett had rented the pineapple. It was temporarily decorating the table on its way to another dinner party."

Merry wasn't the only one who hadn't heard of rented food. Lucy just kept repeating, "Why, I never."

As she waited for her bath to be filled, Merry added "Avoid Lady Caroline" to her etiquette list, and underlined it for emphasis. Just below it, she wrote, "Avoid pineapples."

She kept thinking about those new rules while she soaked in the tub. They weren't precisely matters of etiquette. They could be termed guidelines for survival.

All the same, she was losing faith in her list. She was exhausted by the pursuit of perfection. Miss Fairfax had probably been right: she wasn't capable of cultivation of mind.

The truth was that Cedric didn't want someone like her for a wife. If they married, she would be chipped into little pieces by his disapproval before their first anniversary.

She had to return the ring Cedric didn't buy her. Her heart skipped a beat at the thought—but it didn't crack. If anything, she felt relieved.

Recognition of her own fickle nature caused the most painful wrench in her heart. Twice before, she'd concluded that she could not bring herself to marry a man after solemnly promising to do so.

And now she had reached that conclusion a *third* time?

Maybe she was heartless and unable to truly love.

Or perhaps she was incapable of loving one man for her entire life. She had truly believed that she was in love with Bertie. She had loved his enthusiasm, and the way he called her his "best girl." And then she'd swooned over Dermot's golden hair, the same as all the girls had. And then Cedric . . .

Yet in every case, she had discovered later that she didn't really like, let alone love, her future spouse.

Not for the first time, she felt an aching wish for the mother she'd never known. Bess and Thaddeus were very dear, but they weren't the same as parents.

Maybe that was the problem. She had a coldness in her heart from being orphaned. But it sounded like an excuse, the kind of thing a fickle woman would tell herself in order to soothe her guilty conscience.

She couldn't stay in the bath forever, and in any case, the water had grown cold. It was time to get dressed and face the day.

She wouldn't be surprised if she were about to get those callers her aunt had missed—though now they would come for the wrong reasons.

Just in case, she dressed for a jury of her peers, putting on a blush-colored morning gown copied from a Parisian fashion plate. After the debacle of her first broken engagement, she had discovered that French fashion was a great help in assuaging anguish.

The gown was styled for morning wear, but it was silk rather than the usual muslin, and it fell gracefully from its high waist and swirled a little at her ankles. But the *coup d'éclat* were the matching shoes. They were made of pink kid, slashed to reveal stripes of the same glossy silk as her gown.

Not only were they exquisite, but they had heels. She fancied that her bosom looked a bit more in proportion when she wore them.

Merry stared at the glass and felt more like herself than she had in a month. Last night she'd lost her temper, but all the same, she had drawn a line in the sand.

In Boston and New York, people *liked* her. They considered her reasonably witty and kind, and not unattractive.

But in London . . .

English polite society determined one's worth by criteria at which Merry would never excel. Her awkward manners and frizzled hair all seemed of a piece, somehow. Right then and there, she made up her mind that there would be no more curling irons. Her natural curls would have to do.

Once downstairs, it appeared at first that her pink shoes had been donned in vain. Uncle Thaddeus informed her that they would accept no callers because the excitement of the morning—the initial inability to find a pineapple followed by the footman's successful acquisition of two—had sent Bess back to her bed with a sick headache.

After her uncle left for his club, Merry informed Jenkins that she was "at home" for Lord Cedric Allardyce.

Uncle Thaddeus would not approve of Merry's entertaining her fiancé without a chaperone. But unlike Bertie, who would have toppled her onto a sofa in five minutes, Cedric would never take advantage of the opportunity. And it was essential that they talk.

She felt much better after playing with George in the back garden. Cedric might not think she was perfect, but George made it clear that *he* thought she was absolutely splendid.

When they returned to the drawing room, she sat down at the escritoire and George slumped onto his stomach, put his head on her shoes, and fell asleep.

For a while, Merry just stared through the window at Portman Square. Cedric would presumably pay her a call soon. If he didn't, she'd have to summon him. Her throat felt as if it would close, thinking of the conversation that lay ahead of her.

She just kept telling herself that Cedric didn't want her. It wouldn't be like Bertie, whose eyes had filled with tears. Or Dermot, who had spat out his intent to sue her, and had done just that. Cedric would be happy to see the back of her.

Finally, she forced herself to take out the design for a new garden at her uncle's summer house that she had put to the side with the excitement of coming to London. She wanted blossoms to cascade down the hill in front of the gazebo constructed the summer before.

That was one happy aspect of breaking her third betrothal: she could create the new garden. She could watch her apricot tree mature. Maybe she'd even acquire one of those pineapple stoves, whatever they were, and bring it back with her.

At precisely eleven o'clock, carriages began to roll up in front of the house. Grooms rushed from carriage after carriage, calling cards in hand; the front door opened and shut repeatedly as Jenkins politely turned them all away.

When Merry finally heard the noise of Jenkins actually ushering someone into the house, she sprang from her desk. She was shaking, but desperate to get it over with.

Her fingers curled around the back of a chair as she told herself that she could work on her uncle's gardens for the rest of her life. She had no need of a husband. Her hand closed so tightly that her knuckles turned white.

She was almost certain that she would have no need to say a word. Cedric was surely devastated by her last, largest gaffe. As a gentleman, he could not call off the engagement, but they could dissolve the betrothal with only a few words.

As Cedric walked through the door, she swallowed hard. Should she open the subject? Would he say something?

No sooner had Jenkins tucked George under his arm and left, than Cedric stopped, flung out an arm, and demanded, "Am I a connoisseur of the best the civilized world has to offer, or am I not?"

Merry's heart skipped. "I beg your pardon?"

He strode toward her, fell back a step, and swept her a magnificent bow. " 'Oh nymph, in thy orisons be all my sins remembered!' "

"*What?*" Merry cried.

He straightened and said with a shrug, "The analogy doesn't quite work, but that's no matter."

"What is an 'orison'?"

"An eye. No, no, what am I saying? A *prayer*." He reached for her hand and brought it to his lips, his eyes holding hers captive. "You have the power to forgive my sins."

"I have what?"

"Merry, you are not simply in fashion," Cedric cried. "At the moment you *are* the fashion!"

She felt as if the world was reeling around her. "Why? Surely not because I ate Mrs. Bennett's pineapple?"

"Precisely!" His smile was toothy . . . triumphant. "I will not pretend that I haven't had moments in which I doubted my judgment, fearful that you would not join me at the pinnacle of society. Moments when I wondered whether the role of Lady Cedric Allardyce might prove overtaxing for an American."

Merry sank into the chair she'd been clinging to.

He took the chair next to hers, and angled it so that their knees brushed. "You have pointed up the empty pretentiousness of households such as Mrs. Bennett's. I am shocked to think that I accepted her invitation."

Cedric didn't seem to notice that Merry had been struck dumb. "Last night you conducted yourself as befits the wife of a duke's son. *Everyone* is talking about it. Prinny himself—the Prince of Wales—congratulated me on finding a wife with such a clear sense of propriety, not to mention the ability to give a withering set-down that rivals Brummell's. He particularly enjoyed your comment about a 'pilfered pineapple.'"

"What? I said nothing of the sort!" Merry cried, finding her voice.

"Unimportant," Cedric declared, waving his hand in the air. "Everyone is saying you did. The story of your victory is circulating all over town."

"I thought you would be angry with me."

"One mustn't always rigidly adhere to rules," Cedric announced. "We leave that to the lower classes."

That was not what he, or anyone else, had intimated to

Merry before today. Her heart was beating so fast that she felt ill.

"With one small gesture, asking for a slice of pineapple—the *rented* pineapple—you revealed the true colors of Mrs. Bennett's shabby gentility." Cedric sprang from the chair and crossed the room in order to straighten his neck cloth in the Venetian mirror. "The woman pushed her way into the highest circles by means of that hospital committee, but believe me, no one will fall for her pretenses again."

"Is everyone speaking of Mrs. Bennett in such terms?" Merry's stomach clenched.

Cedric turned back to her. "I shall be most interested to see her reception at the Vereker ball tonight. *If* she dares to attend. In the future, I intend to demand a slice of pineapple whenever I see the fruit on a dining table. Those airing an empty pretentiousness that merely gestures at our ranks must be put in their places."

"Oh no," Merry cried. "I would never want Mrs. Bennett's reputation to suffer through my ignorance."

"She brought it on herself." Cedric paused. "The five pineapples delivered to her house this morning might have been a touch heavy-handed. One must avoid vulgar display even in service of a well-deserved snub."

"My aunt didn't mean it as a snub," Merry gasped. "She sent the pineapples to Mrs. Bennett with her most sincere apologies, and there were only two."

Cedric laughed. "Brilliant! From the mouths of babes, et cetera." He waved his hand again. "On that same subject, I must say that I was pleasantly surprised when my brother actually behaved like a man of his rank and left Mrs. Bennett's table after being roundly insulted by his hostess. I would have expected him to lounge at the bottom of the room and demand a mug of ale."

Merry came to her feet. "I cannot allow Mrs. Bennett to suffer from my foolish error!"

"It was *her* foolish error. She placed a duke below the salt, and she boasted of pineapples that weren't hers. Now she's a pineapple pariah." He laughed. " 'Pineapple pariah.' I amuse myself."

"But Cedric—"

"Admitting no callers this morning was also a brilliant stratagem. All of London will be desperately attempting to befriend you at the ball tonight." He pursed his lips thoughtfully. "You must utter another such riposte. Perhaps I shall steer Algernon Webbling in your direction. He has that hilarious stammer. Alas, I regret I must be off, but I am certain that some clever bon mot will come to you. You might plan it this afternoon."

"No, don't go," Merry cried, catching his sleeve, though she dropped it instantly when Cedric glanced at her hand. "We must talk."

"I am due at my tailor's thirty minutes hence," he said. "I ordered a new coat for the ball."

Merry couldn't think straight. She had to figure out a way to make amends for her insult to Mrs. Bennett. And there was the matter of their betrothal to discuss. "Could you possibly delay the trip to your tailor?"

"Alas, no," Cedric said firmly. "My coat was ready yesterday, but brass buttons have become entirely too common. As you might have noticed, even Kestril was wearing them last night, and he is no more than a country bumpkin. I told my tailor that he had to swap the buttons or I wouldn't pay a ha'penny for the coat."

"Buttons," Merry repeated.

"Buttons should come as a surprise," Cedric informed her. "The new ones are ebony with inlaid brass flowers. My tailor swore on his mother's grave that they are the only such buttons to be found in all England."

Likely her uncle had paid for those buttons—or, even more likely, the new coat was bought on credit and waiting for their marriage before the bill was settled.

"Cedric, we *must* talk," Merry insisted.

But her fiancé just pushed open the door to the hallway, where Jenkins was waiting.

"I am very proud to be marrying a woman whom all of London admires," Cedric said, bowing.

"I didn't mean to ruin Mrs. Bennett's reputation!"

"Style, not sincerity, is all that matters." And with that he brushed a kiss on her cheek, not seeming to notice when Merry recoiled.

Jenkins helped Cedric shrug on his close-fitting overcoat. With a flourish and another bow, her fiancé clapped on his hat and left.

Over the course of the morning, so many cards had arrived that the silver tray in the entry overflowed with them. Merry slipped back into the drawing room just as the door knocker sounded again.

It was quite ironic that Cedric had finally looked at her with the admiration she had hoped for . . . but for all the wrong reasons. Now, too late, he was apparently hers, for better, for worse—at least until she managed to break it off in person, or send him a letter to that effect.

Merry shook her head. Jilting Cedric was not a problem; God knows, she had experience in that.

The real problem was Mrs. Bennett. Merry sank into a chair, feeling truly ill. The thoughtfulness that is never mentioned in books of etiquette seemed to be as rare in London as pineapples—but that didn't mean that she should have lowered herself to be as spiteful as Lady Caroline.

What must poor Mrs. Bennett be thinking? A wave of nausea came over Merry and she fought back tears.

Her father would be ashamed of her for more than one reason. But that didn't mean she couldn't fix the situation.

She had to make amends to Mrs. Bennett. Casting off Cedric could wait, but atoning for her rudeness could not.

Just paying a visit to the lady would do nothing. She had to make a public announcement of some sort, tonight, at the Vereker ball.

After which she would break her third engagement.

Chapter Sixteen

Lady Vereker's ball

Trent made up his mind to attend the Vereker ball for one reason, and one reason only: to find his own American to marry. His fascination with his brother's fiancée was entirely inappropriate and must cease.

Naturally, the first person he saw upon his arrival was Cedric, holding court amid a cluster of gentlemen and ladies with sharp faces and predatory eyes, vultures who dressed impeccably and always seemed to be murmuring something at once clever and unpleasant.

In short, Cedric was in his element.

Trent headed in the opposite direction. It was slow going because ladies with eligible daughters in tow stopped him every few feet. Every one of those girls was dressed in white; they looked like a crowd of vestal virgins who'd left their lamps at home. Their bodies blurred together, making their heads stand out.

Miss Chasticle with the red hair—God, no. Miss Petunia with the squint—unlikely. Lady Sissy Royal, with the snub nose—not even if hell froze over.

It had just occurred to him that he hadn't met a single woman who was worthy of serious consideration—where were the American ladies this evening?—when Lady Caroline emerged from the pack with all the demureness of a hungry jackal.

Perhaps that pinched aspect of her face had nothing to do with him, and she was simply hungry. Her white gown had a low neck, which had the unfortunate effect of giving her collarbones a marked similarity to the ridges on the backs of sea monsters depicted on medieval maps.

Here be dragons, he thought unenthusiastically.

"Duke!" Lady Caroline cried, with an archness that was acceptable, and a familiarity that was not. "It's such a pleasure to see you a second night in a row. Dare we hope that you plan to assume your rightful place in society?"

Just in time, Trent bit back the *God, no* he was thinking. Rather than answer, he bowed and kissed the lady's proffered hand, wondering what she would think if he told the truth: he'd come to the ball to find an American wife.

But even as he formulated the thought, he knew he was lying to himself.

He'd come to the ball to find one particular American, and no other woman of any nationality or attributes—no matter how pleasing—would do.

Hell and damnation.

Cedric already thought Trent had stolen the title that was rightfully his, and now he was going to steal his fiancée.

"I was so, so horrified at the affront you received last

night," Lady Caroline said, lowering her voice and drawing closer. Her hair brushed against his cheek, each strand rigidly set in place, as if her curls had been starched. "Although I have been friendly with Mrs. Bennett in the past, naturally I revised my feelings the moment I saw how *you* were treated."

"I have no idea what you're talking about."

"Such an extraordinary insult, to seat a duke at the bottom of the table! Thank goodness, you did not tolerate her disrespect. I recounted the event to my father upon returning home, and he agreed that we members of the peerage must insist on the rights and privileges to which we are entitled. I assure you that I have heard nothing but the most supportive remarks from all quarters."

"I left only because I spilled wine on my garments," Trent stated.

Lady Caroline twinkled at him. "Of course, Your Grace. You are the soul of discretion. But a disregard for precedence was not the only blunder at last night's dinner. I suppose you have heard about the pineapple incident?"

Trent glanced over her head at the room. Not that he was searching for Merry. Oh hell, he was searching for Merry.

"I have not," he said. "If you'll excuse me, Lady Caroline—"

She put a hand on his sleeve and drew close to him again. Trent felt a prickling in his shoulders that suggested a sizable portion of the ballroom was watching them closely. Tonight White's betting book would include wagers in favor of Lady Caroline's chances of becoming a duchess.

"Your future sister-in-law created quite a bother last night," the lady whispered.

Trent froze. "Miss Pelford?"

"I would not have believed her to possess such refinement, but that just goes to show that one cannot judge on appearances, as my sainted grandmother often reminded me before her death."

Trent waited while Lady Caroline related some fool thing about a rented pineapple.

"Now everyone is gushing about Miss Pelford, repeating her clever remarks." Her expression curdled a little. "For my part, I don't think it appropriate for those of our station to makes jests about those who are lower in status."

That didn't sound like Merry.

"Miss Pelford apparently labeled Mrs. Bennett a 'pineapple pariah.' It is not precisely *kind*, you know, but there are those who seem to find the term amusing, and everyone is talking of it." Lady Caroline hunched one thin shoulder with an expression of disdain.

"Have you seen Miss Pelford this evening?" he inquired. "I ought to greet her."

"I last saw her around the lemon grove at the end of the ballroom," the lady said with a sniff. "I am aware of the mania for hothouse plants, but Lady Vereker erred by bringing so many trees into the room. The ballroom's size is insufficient."

To Trent's relief, a gentleman appeared at her side and bowed. "Lady Caroline, I believe this dance is mine."

Trent disengaged himself from the hand clutching his arm, but before he could make an escape, she leaned in again and murmured something about the supper dance. Then she gave her dance partner a condescending smile and left before Trent could answer.

The forest of plumes waving above ladies' heads prevented Trent from seeing whether Merry was still somewhere near the "lemon grove." Worse, a stout lady immediately slipped into the space left by Lady Caroline and thrust her daughter forward as if the girl were a posy of white carnations peddled outside a music hall.

Trent managed to bow, even in the cramped space. In the back of his mind, he was evaluating Lady Caroline's story.

Unless he was sorely mistaken about her character, Merry had no hidden capacity for viciousness. Even had she lost her temper, he'd wager that she wouldn't stoop to insulting people. She'd probably fish up a fact or six to demonstrate why she was right.

The thought brought a wry grin to his lips and too late, he realized that the young Miss Randall-Barclay, to whom he had just been introduced, had taken the smile as encouragement. She started flapping her lashes as if she'd been caught in a high wind.

"Forgive me," he said, "I'm afraid I didn't catch your remark."

"I asked if you were enjoying the season?" she breathed. "It's my first."

It couldn't be easy having your mother parade you in front of prospective husbands, and he liked the optimistic bravery in her smile.

"I haven't any sisters," he said, "but I understand that a lady's first season is a taxing adventure."

Her smile broadened. "I assure you that if you had been trapped in a schoolroom for fourteen years, you would have no complaints about going to balls, and eating ices."

She would make a lovely wife for someone, just not for him. He was too . . . too ferocious. Strains of music sounded, and a flash of hope crossed her eyes.

"May I have the honor of this dance?" he asked.

Miss Randall-Barclay beamed and curtsied, and then he placed her among a long line of women standing opposite their dance partners, freeing him to go back to thinking about his American.

Merry would never come up with a spiteful term like "pineapple pariah." If she were insulted, she would get excited, and wave her hands about, and turn pink. She might utter a snappy retort. He'd bet she could be kissed out of a bad humor.

He was finally thinking clearly. Yes, there had been a chance that Merry would coax his brother into sobriety if she loved him. He'd bet his right arm that Merry did not love Cedric.

She might have thought she loved him, but she didn't.

As the music drew to a close, he was reunited with Miss Randall-Barclay. Her yellow curls were bouncing on her shoulders and she was glowing with happiness.

She was pretty.

Merry wasn't.

Merry was too intelligent, and too voluptuous, and too funny to be merely pretty.

Hell, he kept coming around to the same realization he'd first had on the balcony at Lady Portmeadow's ball.

He didn't want another woman to look at him the way Lady Caroline had. Or touch his arm.

He wanted Merry on his arm.

He wanted Merry in his bed.

Mrs. Randall-Barclay accepted her daughter back with the controlled triumph of a woman certain that her daughter would have a brilliant season, if only because the most elusive bachelor in London had shown every sign of interest.

Trent kissed both ladies' hands and, determined not to be waylaid again, went in search of Merry. He made it to the bottom of the ballroom just in time to find the main actors in the previous night's melodrama, Mrs. Bennett and Merry, coming face-to-face.

Last evening, Mrs. Bennett had had the self-confident attitude of a woman enjoying a social triumph. Tonight, she looked like a mouse who had been befriended by a playful cat.

Obviously, she was well aware of her new status as a pariah.

For her part, Merry cast him a harried look and sank into a curtsy in front of Mrs. Bennett before he could greet her.

"Mrs. Bennett," she said, as she straightened, "Please allow me to apologize again for my gauche behavior in eating your centerpiece."

"I don't regard it," Mrs. Bennett squeaked.

Trent groaned inwardly. The lady should either make a joke of the whole affair or defend herself; if she didn't show spirit, she would indeed become an outcast.

"I promise you that you need not fear that I'll consume your table decoration, if you are gracious enough to invite me to your house," Merry said, trying again.

Mrs. Bennett murmured something without looking up. If she didn't show some backbone, her invitations would dry up like a puddle in August.

"I imagine Lady Vereker is worried that I shall abscond with a lemon from these lovely trees," Merry insisted, sticking it out, although her eyes had a desperate look. "She informed me that they were *rented* from the Chelsea Physic Garden."

Mrs. Bennett's mouth wavered into a smile, but at that moment Cedric stepped forward, brushing invisible lint from his brilliantly embroidered cuff.

Trent's jaw clenched when he saw that his brother's eyes were glassy. Cedric was drunk. Not entirely soused, but well on the way.

"Are we to begin renting apparel now?" Cedric drawled. "Perhaps there are those in this very room whose attire comes from another's dressing room."

Merry narrowed her eyes at her fiancé. "Your lordship, that is not an appropriate subject of conversation."

"We already have a pineapple pariah." Cedric paused just long enough to allow an appreciative titter of laughter to subside. "And now I, for one, begin to suspect that we may well discover there is a similarly invidious practice of leasing evening gowns. Bogus ball gowns, in short."

"Lord Cedric!" Merry cried, as high color suffused Mrs. Bennett's cheeks.

Cedric pulled out his quizzing glass and directed a hideously enlarged eye at the costumes around them, pausing for a moment on Mrs. Bennett's ruffled hem.

To Trent's mind, Merry looked like Venus in a rage. Her head was high, her eyes stormy, and every magnificent inch of her quivered with rage.

"Lord Cedric!" she snapped again.

No, shouted was more accurate.

Every head in the vicinity, including Trent's, turned to see how Cedric would respond.

"Miss Pelford," he acknowledged with a world-weary sigh, allowing his quizzing glass to fall. He looked for all the world as if he were a bishop whose homily she had interrupted.

"Wouldn't you agree that it is more invidious to depend upon a woman to *pay* for your clothing than it would be to rent it?" she demanded.

The awful silence that followed was like the pause that follows a crack of thunder.

"After all, if you had rented that magnificent coat you are wearing, at least you would have paid some of your own money for it, rather than having to rely on my uncle to ensure your tailor was compensated."

Dents appeared beside Cedric's mouth.

"As a newcomer to London society," Merry went on, seemingly without pausing for breath, "I did not understand that an unpaid-for pineapple could decorate a table. But I also had no idea that an entire wardrobe of unpaid-for clothing might be worn without disgrace. We do not have a high opinion of that sort of behavior in Boston, though I suppose it seemed good to you at the time."

Cedric's eyes shone with an arctic light but his mouth remained tightly closed. He gave Merry a furious, high-nosed stare, turned on his heel without a word, and left.

Trent glanced back at Merry to find a bleak look in her eyes. She had either just recognized that she was in need of a husband, or she had realized that her spirited exchange with Cedric would do nothing to resurrect Mrs. Bennett's reputation.

He had every intention of solving her first problem and he could take a stab at the second. He stepped forward and bowed. "My dear Mrs. Bennett, good evening." He consciously embellished his words with the rich, plummy tone of a duke of the realm.

"Your Grace," Mrs. Bennett whispered.

"I must apologize again for leaving your dinner so abruptly." He hesitated, as if wondering whether to speak intimately, then lowered his voice just enough so that everyone in the vicinity could hear him. "A rather extraordinary realization drove me from your table."

Merry nodded madly. "Oh, do tell us, Your Grace," she trilled. "What was it?"

"I made up my mind to ask a lady for her hand in marriage," Trent announced.

"Oh!" Mrs. Bennett yelped. "You did? That is, you are? A lady at my table?"

"When I realized the depth of my passion," Trent said, "I could not remain at the dining table. I had to . . . to *muse* about my passion."

A chorus of gasps was heard. Trent glanced at Merry, whose face had gone utterly blank. Surely she realized he was fabricating all this for her sake.

"I am honored!" Mrs. Bennett exclaimed.

"Please do tell us more about your musings, Your Grace!" a woman standing beside her asked.

"I cannot share my thoughts, as I have not been able to make my address," Trent said gravely. "To this moment, I have no idea whether the lady in question will agree to become my duchess or no. But it was at your dinner, Mrs. Bennett, that I became conscious of the truth of my heart."

More twittering.

A glance at Merry showed that she was now struggling to hold back a giggle. At least one person realized he wasn't the sort to muse about passion.

"I feel certain that you will be able to persuade the lady," Mrs. Bennett said eagerly. "Perhaps I—"

He interrupted her. "Had I remained at your table, my dear Mrs. Bennett, I trust that I could have steered your guests away from devouring the centerpiece. I know that *my* housekeeper would be quite dismayed, Miss Pelford, if you grazed on her elaborate displays."

"Graze?" Merry repeated, picking up his cue like an experienced actress. "I beg your pardon, Your Grace! Cows *graze*; ladies such as myself do not."

"I hope the bovine association did not insult you."

"I am not cross," she said piously. "Only hurt." She heaved a dramatic sigh.

"My butler has rented many a pineapple," Trent said, untruthfully. "I shall warn him about your penchant for the fruit before you dine in Cavendish Square."

His butler would sink with mortification at the suggestion that the ducal household had ever rented an item of food—or anything else—but, alas, the household reputation had to be sacrificed at the altar of Mrs. Bennett's redemption.

"I know you Americans think that lemonade is an insipid beverage," Trent concluded. "Yet I must entreat you not to strip our hostess's trees. The Chelsea Physic Garden will surely wish them returned with their fruit intact."

He cleared his throat and glanced about. "It must be time for the supper dance." The crowd watching them obligingly melted away.

Two ladies pounced on Mrs. Bennett and drew her away, chatting animatedly. He assumed they would spend the rest of the night going over the marriageable damsels on her invitation list. In his estimation, the lady's reputation would not die, but blossom.

He turned to Merry.

Chapter Seventeen

The duke had saved her—or rather, he had saved Mrs. Bennett.

For a moment Merry felt nothing but happy relief. But a second later, her spirits crashed as she remembered Cedric's petty, cruel behavior. She would never have believed him capable of such abhorrent conduct.

Mrs. Bennett had done no more than put on a dinner party in Cedric's own honor, and he had mocked her. How could she possibly have misjudged yet another man so badly? She was an idiot, a perfect idiot.

Language that no lady should even know, much less utter, ran through her head.

"The performance is over," said a deep voice at her side.

She looked up at the duke. Her head felt hot and sick, as if a fever was coming on. "I should apologize for being so rude to your brother, but I will not," she said fiercely. "I know my reputation is ruined, and I've effectively broken off a third engagement, but I don't care."

"I don't believe your reputation is entirely ruined," he replied, looking unconcerned. "But another public scene might prove the coup de grâce." He took her arm and guided her through the lemon grove to a secluded bit of space between the trees and the wall. On the other side, the ball carried on without them.

"It's not as if I have to give him his ring," Merry burst out. "I can just give it to you, since it is yours!" She began to tug off her long glove, but the duke put his hand on hers.

"Tomorrow."

"I must find my aunt," Merry said, giving up the battle of the ring. "Maybe I can persuade her to arrange passage for us on a ship leaving immediately."

"No, you won't," the duke replied.

Merry scarcely heard him. "I shall never come back. The way everyone laughed at poor Mrs. Bennett was despicable."

Although they were isolated from the ballroom by a screen of trees, she imagined the dancers colliding as they tried to get a look at the two of them, when they should have been minding their steps.

She had no illusions about her status as a spectacle; Miss Merry Pelford and her American ways would be the subject of conversation for years. She'd let down herself *and* her nation.

"I must go," Merry said. She was shattered. "My aunt will hear the gossip in a moment, if she hasn't already."

"My brother was drunk," the duke said.

Merry turned to face him. His Grace was leaning against the wall next to her, with that careless look he had sometimes, as if he were indifferent to how those around him felt. And yet he had been the only person other than herself to come to Mrs. Bennett's defense.

"Drunk?" she repeated, frowning at him.

"Three sheets to the wind. Possibly four sheets. Typically, Cedric waits until he arrives home before he permits himself to become quite so inebriated."

"If you are making an excuse for him, it won't wash," Merry said bluntly.

The duke shrugged. "All I am saying, Miss Pelford, is that when my brother is that deep in drink, he'll say anything for a laugh."

"I noticed no signs of intoxication." Weren't drunken men supposed to stagger and slur their words? All the same, the certainty she'd felt about Cedric's temperance was no longer unshakable.

"Did he bring you canary wine tonight? I assure you that Cedric was not holding a glass of lemonade."

"You're saying that he drinks to excess, even here, but displays no obvious sign of it?"

"I tried to warn you."

That was true, and she'd dismissed his attempt as the lies of a jealous brother. Lady Portmeadow's ball might as well have been a century ago, so much had happened since.

Merry stared at the glossy leaves of the lemon tree in front of her, trying to think it through. There had been an odd agitation about Cedric, a raw eagerness that she hadn't liked.

"But we danced, and he didn't stagger," she said, offering the one indication of drunkenness that she knew of.

"Cedric staggers only when he's into a second bottle of brandy."

"Second bottle," she said faintly. "You didn't say—I didn't understand."

"Few people do."

His expression was so dispassionate that he could have been discussing the weather. Merry scowled at him. "Why haven't you done something? You're his brother. He was *cruel* to Mrs. Bennett."

"You raise an interesting question. What can I do for my brother? Hide the brandy? I've done that already. Cedric shows no desire to limit his drinking, and believe me, he is well aware of my feelings on the subject."

She lapsed into silence again. He was right. Cedric was an adult. "Does this occur with regularity?"

"Cedric began drinking more and more after our parents died," the duke said, as casually as if they were talking about a penchant for something as innocuous as collecting rare books. "After a few embarrassing episodes, he more or less learned how to control his conduct in public—although he didn't succeed tonight."

"I have appalling taste in men," Merry said under her breath.

"It does seem that way," the duke agreed. He was a deeply annoying man, because one moment his blue eyes were chilly, and the next they were so warm that a person—even one like herself, in the depths of despair—wanted to smile.

"I shall leave this ball in even more disgrace than I left Mrs. Bennett's house last night," Merry said gloomily. "I might as well get it over with."

They emerged from the partial seclusion of the trees and started walking the length of the ballroom.

In the back of her mind, she was thinking about the fact that the duke had apparently decided on a bride—or had he? She was desperate to ask whether he had invented his revelation merely to provoke the crowd's curiosity . . . but she couldn't think how to phrase such a question.

Surely he wasn't speaking of Lady Caroline.

Merry couldn't delude herself about the streak of pure,

blind jealousy she felt in response to that idea. She was the biggest fool in the world. Who goes straight from being besotted by one man to being infatuated by his brother?

The duke may have been Cedric's twin, but everything about him was darker. They talked differently; they moved differently. Cedric was supple and graceful, his steps in the quadrille a thing of beauty. He twirled and whirled, and other dancers stepped aside to watch him.

She'd never seen the duke waltz, but she would guess that he would hold a lady at arm's length and lead her around the floor briskly, as if he couldn't wait for the music to end. She couldn't imagine him giving a final flourish as he bowed, or spinning his partner one last time as the music faded.

They reached the great doors leading from the ballroom without encountering her aunt or uncle. If she had had any doubts about how fast gossip could spread, the fact that every person in the ballroom turned to watch the two of them walk the length of the room would have dispelled that.

"I have to leave," she hissed. "I can't walk through the reception rooms looking for my aunt. This is intolerable."

The duke nodded, drawing her down the corridor until he opened a door and whisked her through it, closing it behind them.

The chamber they found themselves in was quite dark, save for what little light was emitted by a fire burning low in the hearth; Lady Vereker had no doubt left the lamps unlit in an effort to discourage her more adventuresome guests from straying into the private chambers.

Once her eyes adjusted to the dimness, Merry was able to make out book-lined walls, a large table in the center, and a great many comfortably padded armchairs arranged in clusters.

The duke glanced down at her. "I'll leave you here, and look for your aunt and uncle myself, Merry."

"I can't believe that I've done it again," Merry whispered, her voice catching. "There's my third betrothal gone. I'm such a fool."

The duke sat down on a large leather chair and then, before she could react, pulled her into his lap.

"Your Grace!"

"Hush," he replied, and eased her against his chest. It was very large and comforting chest. She laid her cheek against his shoulder, even though it was monstrously improper.

"Do you think something is wrong with me?" she asked. "Never mind, that was an absurd question."

"You would have been the salvation of Cedric," His Grace said, running his hand comfortingly down her back.

"I very much doubt that," Merry said. "He made it quite clear that he had no respect for me." She tugged off a glove and used it to wipe away a tear. The duke's hand paused for a moment and then resumed a slow caress.

"I have effectively purchased proposals from two fiancés," Merry said, wiping another tear. "It's so *humiliating*."

More tears pressed on the back of her throat so she removed her other glove, concentrating on the task so that she'd stop crying.

"I know he didn't show to his best advantage tonight," the duke said, "but my brother is capable of great generosity. He did spur the building of the charity hospital."

"Don't even dream of trying to persuade me to take him back!" Merry cried. "I shall return to Boston, and I shall never marry, because I have no aptitude for choosing a husband."

"You shall marry," the duke said with calm certainty. He pressed a large linen handkerchief into her hand.

"You are that sort of man," she said damply.

"A marrying man?"

"The sort who always has a handkerchief when one is needed," she explained, pressing it against her eyes. "My first fiancé, Bertie, was the same."

"Oh God," the duke groaned.

"What?"

"You're not one of those women who always harp on about their previous husbands, are you?"

"I haven't had any husbands!" Merry objected.

"You know what I mean." Then, putting on a Cockney accent, "Mr. Watson, he were my first, he were such a good man to me, he were, always took me to the panto at Christmas. Terrible short-tempered, though."

Merry gave a little hiccup of laughter. Who would have guessed that the Duke of Trent had it in him to sound like a flower seller from the East End?

The duke settled her more securely against his shoulder. She ought to find her aunt. She didn't move; instead, she just lay against him, thinking about starched linen and wintergreen soap.

"Then there was my second, that would be Mr. Tucker," the duke said, in a cheery falsetto. "He was all very well in his way, but short with money. Poor as a church mouse, really."

"I have George," Merry said, running her finger around one of the duke's buttons. It wasn't brass, or inlaid. It was just plain black. "In time I will forget all of my fiancés."

"The first three, anyway."

Merry managed a weak smile. "If you would be so kind, I think it'd be best if you found my aunt now."

Trent knew very well that he should be feeling sympathy, and not lust.

But lust it was.

He had Merry on his lap, and she was a lapful of soft curves. She felt wonderful, and she smelled wonderful, and what's more, she was no longer betrothed, and thus was free to be kissed.

Naturally, she felt wounded and distraught; she would need time to recover. He could wait. If she hadn't just gone through a despicable scene with his twin, he would have kissed her so ferociously that she'd have no uncertainty as regards her future.

"You will marry," he assured her again, giving in to impulse and pulling her so close that his chin rested on a cloud of fragrant hair. "I'm glad you haven't stuck a bunch of plumes on top of your head. I couldn't hold you."

"You shouldn't be holding me like this." But she didn't pull away. "I shall not marry, because I fall in and out of love at the drop of a hat. The truth is that I have a shallow soul."

"I don't think you're shallow." He could just hear the faint hum of well-bred voices coming from beyond the library's thick door.

"I am wildly in love at the start. And then the truth grows on me that it's not love at all, and in fact, I don't even *like* my fiancés very much. If I am completely honest, I've known how I felt about Cedric for some time."

"You're proving the point I made at the dinner party," Trent said with satisfaction. "Marriage should never be arranged on the basis of emotion. It's a highly unreliable gauge of a potential spouse's worthiness."

"Do you agree with Lady Caroline, then, that marriages should be a matter of bloodlines, as if one were breeding rabbits?"

"Where do rabbits come into it?" Trent inquired.

"One of my cousins, the summer when we were both nine, decided to breed a brown rabbit."

"Why on earth? Brownish rabbits are exceedingly common."

"He wanted to make his own, using a white rabbit and a black rabbit. He got the idea because his father breeds racehorses."

"Did it work?"

"Not exactly, but after a few generations if you stood a fair distance away and squinted, the babies almost looked brown."

Trent decided that he *would* kiss Merry, and be damned to the whole idea of giving her time to recover. He could be respectful. Gentle.

"Why are we discussing brown rabbits?" he asked.

"Lady Caroline thinks of marriage as if it were as logical as pairing rabbits by the color of their fur."

"In that case, she's attracted to my fur. She informed me earlier that she was giving me the supper dance and I had the distinct impression that she would announce our betrothal if I were fool enough to show up for that dance."

"You might want to avoid being as kind to her as you are being to me," Merry said, nodding. "She told me that the two of you were ideally suited."

"No one will ever trap me into marriage," he replied calmly. "That's one good thing about being a duke. I don't give a damn what anyone says; I'll not marry a woman merely to satisfy society's dictates, any more than I would marry for love, if I were to feel that emotion."

Merry twisted to look up at him. "We should not be even in private together. Your future bride would not be pleased. But just so you know, Your Grace, I would never make any assumptions on the basis of your kindness." She lapsed back against him and resumed tracing circles with her finger.

His future wife was terribly obtuse if she thought he often—or ever—took young women into his arms in order to comfort them.

"You are a good friend," she said.

Trent managed not to snort.

"I've never had a male friend before." The surge of desire that went down Trent's body when their eyes met had nothing to do with friendship. But Merry looked at him earnestly and said, "I'm so grateful to you for rescuing Mrs. Bennett in the ballroom, Duke. I wish there was something I could do for you. Before I depart for America, I mean."

"Don't you think that, as near family, we might do away with my title?"

"As I understand it, addressing a duke by his title *is* informal address for use only between family and close friends. I am counting myself among your friends, even though I am no longer betrothed to your brother."

"You will always be in my family," Trent said.

"I can be a distant cousin. Someday you will bring your son—the one who will inherit your title—to Boston, and I'll teach him to be an American."

"Will that make him a better duke?"

"Oh, absolutely."

Finally sounding less dejected, Merry proceeded to regale him with an assortment of facts about American men. Could it be that she really assumed they would be merely friends in the future? The idea was so unpleasant that Trent succumbed to impulse and interrupted her monologue with a kiss.

He had promised himself he would be gentle when he kissed her. He was wrong.

It was a greedy kiss. He had never realized that a lady's lips could be as voluptuous as a courtesan's—but that the addition of surprise and innocence would make it a far headier experience than he had ever experienced.

To this point, Trent hadn't particularly enjoyed kissing. It was too intimate. He'd never been selfish about giving pleasure, as he enjoyed bodily intimacy. All the same, he didn't care for kissing.

Not until now.

When Merry started kissing him back, the shock of it sent a hum down his limbs that brought with it a strange feeling, as if the world were shaking around them.

One of her hands came around his neck and buried itself in his hair. Her mouth had been sweet, but now it was silk and fire. Her innocence was still there, but alongside it, a searing urgency.

Trent lost himself. Their tongues danced together and he felt a shudder go through Merry's body. She made a whimpering sound in the back of her throat, and desire exploded down his spine.

It wasn't until he became aware that one of his hands had settled on her thigh, and that certain parts of his body had taken on an ungentlemanly life of their own, that he regained a measure of sanity.

He drew his mouth away from hers, just far enough that he could still feel the erotic heat of her breath. He watched her face, his heart pounding unsteadily, as she opened her eyes.

A man could get lost in those eyes. Desire shimmered between them like a haze on a hot day in August.

Would she be outraged? Surprised?

She was dismayed.

"I *loathe* myself," she mumbled, closing her eyes in anguish.

"It wasn't a bad kiss." Trent's voice had a rasp that he'd never heard in it before.

Her eyes opened again. "You have the oddest sense of humor," she said, frowning.

"Did you enjoy the kiss?"

"It was a very nice kiss. In fact—"

She caught back whatever she was about to say.

"I am a despicable person," she said, her voice ragged.

He suppressed a smile. "I strongly disagree."

Descriptions and details began tumbling out of her—about Bertie, who used to kiss her on a sofa (if Trent ever met him, he'd have to kill him for that), about Dermot, about Cedric . . . In short, the whole sorry saga of Merry's romantic life thus far.

Trent didn't want to discuss the three men she'd fancied herself in love with. He didn't want to imagine that they had touched her. Or kissed her.

As Merry recounted her supposed sins, Trent cupped her face in his hands and lowered his lips to hers, so close that their noses brushed. She went silent. "You never kissed Cedric the way you just kissed me," he stated.

Her eyes didn't fail him. He could see the truth in them. "No," she said with a little gasp. "No—that is to say, I won't discuss it. This mustn't ever happen again, Your Grace. I'm—"

He took her mouth in a thirsty, deep kiss.

Before now, first, second, and third kisses had been merely signposts on the road to bed. His mistresses had all been courtesans, refined women who chose their lovers and enjoyed his company as much as he did theirs.

Kissing Merry was no signpost. It was like making love, something he could do all night. She was everything he'd ever wanted in a woman, and nothing he'd ever thought to find in a lady.

Their kiss grew ravenous and wild, her tongue sliding against his with a passion that couldn't be shammed, especially when a quiet moan floated into the dark room and was answered by his growl. This was a kiss from which he might never recover.

Finally he pulled back, because it was that or ravish his future bride in the middle of a ball, which he refused to do. Merry's lips were cherry red and swollen, and her eyes heavy-lidded. He desperately wanted what he could not have . . . yet.

"I will find your aunt and uncle," he said, his voice rasping as he stood, drawing her to her feet. "I'll tell them where you are. I think it's best that I don't escort you home myself."

He wouldn't be at all surprised if every single person in the ballroom knew that the two of them had retreated to this room together.

The glow of pleasure drained from her face instantly. "You don't think anyone knows we're here? That would be terrible."

Almost . . . he could almost sympathize with her horri-fied expression.

"I certainly don't want you to feel trapped into marrying me, Your Grace."

He stopped feeling sympathetic. Merry needn't be quite so vehement about insisting she wasn't compromised. To his mind, the only thing that could have compromised her more was if he had given in to impulse and drawn up her skirts.

"No one could possibly trap me into marrying, if I didn't want to," he told her. "As I have already stated."

Relief spread across her face. In fact, another man might find it discouraging, how relieved she appeared.

But he had just kissed her. She had quivered under his touch, and moaned aloud. She wanted him.

Trent bowed, but then paused in the doorway. "I shall

pay you a call tomorrow morning," he said. She murmured something, and looked down so that a thick fall of curls hid her eyes and the lovely line of her jaw.

Merry was his, and that was all there was to it.

She would have to get used to it.

Trent left the premises without a lady at his side, and without a glass slipper in his pocket. But just like the prince in the fairy tale, when morning came, he was determined to find his princess.

Chapter Eighteen

Merry's mind reeled as she sank back into the chair, watching the door close behind the Duke of Trent. One minute she had been talking to him about her forsaken betrothals, and then she had found herself being kissed more passionately than ever before in her life.

She put her hand to her mouth, as if his lips had left an imprint there. At first, he had been comforting. But there had been nothing soothing about his kisses.

They were untamed, ferocious, demanding.

Even thinking about them made her pulse pound in her ears. As soon as his mouth touched hers, she had felt as if she were melting inside. As if she might open her mouth and embarrass herself.

No.

They were only kisses. He was a duke, a man who would never marry someone like her. They were intended to make her feel better after the unpleasantness with Cedric.

Just as she tried to decide whether men actually kissed in an effort to comfort—she had the strong feeling that Miss Fairfax would not agree—a noise startled her.

She looked in the direction of the sound, the part of the room farthest from the door, and she was stupefied to see Cedric emerge from behind an armchair.

Her hand fell from her face. Her mouth opened in astonishment, but she was incapable of speech. Cedric ambled over and seated himself opposite her, making certain that his pantaloons were perfectly smooth before he crossed his legs.

"That is an extremely unattractive expression," he observed. "You should close your mouth."

With this insult, she found her voice. "What are you doing here?" she squeaked. It was the least of her questions, but the first to come to mind. He'd heard everything. He must have heard everything. Oh God, he must have heard her kissing Trent.

"I retreated to think over your charming remarks in the ballroom. When you and my brother entered, I could hardly leave. One hesitates to interrupt people who are so passionately engaged in the fine art of betrayal."

Yes, he heard her kissing Trent.

"Betrayal!" Merry cried, though she could scarcely deny it. She *had* betrayed him. Still, she had to try to defend herself. "That would imply that our betrothal was still intact, which any person in the ballroom could tell you was not the case."

It wasn't very convincing, even to her own ears. It was despicable to kiss another man five minutes after breaking an engagement.

Cedric rose, drew a cheroot from his inside pocket, and lit it with a rush he took from the fireplace.

"I didn't know you smoke!"

"Apparently, there are many things that neither of us knew of the other." He turned back from the fire. "For example, I knew you were a lusty wench, but I was still surprised to see you so enthusiastically returning my brother's, shall we say, addresses? Though perhaps advances is a more accurate word."

"He was merely trying to reassure me," Merry said, knowing her excuse sounded feeble.

"No, he wasn't," Cedric stated, sitting back down. "I informed my brother a few days ago that I had never kissed you properly, and he snatched the opportunity to score a point against me."

Merry must not have heard correctly. "You discussed kissing me? With your brother?"

He shrugged. "Likely you don't understand sibling behavior. By kissing you, the duke just won that round. He'll gloat later because he stole a march on me."

Merry gasped. "That is revolting."

"We're twins." Smoke wreathed Cedric's head. Together with the glow of the fire behind him, he resembled an elegant Beelzebub. "There's nothing closer than blood, for all we snarl at each other. I told Trent that I had no plans to take you to bed until our wedding night. I didn't want you to tire of me, as you had of the others."

The humiliations Merry had felt after she ended her engagements to Bertie and Dermot were nothing compared to this. For a moment, she couldn't breathe. A ghastly memory of the times she had swayed toward Cedric, her eyes closed, expectant, flashed through her mind.

"To be blunt," he said impatiently, "it was obvious that once you sampled the wares, you quickly came to the conclusion that you'd had enough and need not marry the poor fools. I kept my hands off you in order to hold your interest. I think we can both agree that my brother enjoyed usurping my place."

"If I understand you correctly," Merry said, the words strangled by disbelief, "I have never consented to—to sampling any man's wares!"

"That's what Trent said." Cedric tipped his head back and blew a perfect ring of smoke. "He as much as dared me to try it on, but I thought I'd better heed my instincts and stay out of your bed."

They—did they laugh over the way she—

"The duke advised you to stay out of my bed?" The question was dust in Merry's mouth. She wouldn't have believed humiliation could be this vivid, as if someone had stripped her of clothing and dragged her in front of a crowd.

"No, no," Cedric said genially. "The opposite. I'd worked *that* out myself."

Something about this story was wrong. The duke was steadfast. Honorable. She was certain of it.

"I don't believe you," she said, each word dropping into the silence like a wooden block. "I don't believe that your brother would discuss intimacies. Not with you or anyone else. His Grace is neither vulgar nor dishonorable."

Cedric snorted. "You understand so little about men, my dear. Though anyone could deduce that from your romantic history, could they not?"

"Ignorance alone cannot explain my rotten choices," she said, rather sharply.

"Trent and I discussed that very thing—intimacies with you—later in the day on which you found that dreadful dog in Hyde Park," Cedric said. "We had returned to Cavendish Square and were on the threshold, just about to enter the house. If it makes you feel any better, Trent sent the butler back into the house when the conversation began."

There was something so bluntly factual about his report that a lump of ice began to form in Merry's chest.

"You talked about me on the front steps?" Against her better judgment, she almost believed him. Almost.

"I told him that I didn't plan to tup you until marriage, and that I hadn't kissed you because I felt you were the sort to lose interest. How right I was. I must say that you take faithlessness to an extreme," he added, drawing on his cheroot so sharply that it made a hissing sound.

Merry had the irrational sense that he was crushing her heart, physically compressing her chest. She wanted to tell him to stop, but instead she just sat rigidly in place.

"You must understand, we are exceedingly competitive," Cedric continued. "Our mother used to egg us on, which didn't help. Trent even tried to turn my betrothal to you into a contest, but I needed your dowry and of course, as duke, he could never marry someone of your nationality and stature. Though he did have one go at you before I stopped him."

Merry felt as if she'd descended into some sort of nightmare in which no one was who she'd thought he was. "You mean . . . on the balcony?"

"You didn't really believe that he had no idea who you were when you first met, did you? I had told the duke that I was planning to propose to Miss Pelford the night before the ball where you met him."

"Oh."

"I warned him off," he said, pity leaking into his voice. "I told my brother that you were so in love with me that he had no chance. But as you see, he waited until there was a breach between us and leapt on you like a fox snapping up a chicken."

In that moment, Merry understood that her heart *was*

breaking—though the heartbreak had nothing to do with the end of her engagement.

Cedric caught her expression and misunderstood it. "The duke wouldn't have ruined you or, God forbid, compromised you. He's not that wicked, and besides, he wouldn't risk being forced to marry you. He understands that his spouse will need to come from the peerage. He just wanted to score points against me."

Did Cedric think that she would applaud a cruelty that went only so far? Nothing between the duke and her was real, not the way he smiled at her, talked to her, or teased her. And yet their friendship had felt more real and more true than any relationship she'd ever had with a man.

Cedric shrugged, and blew another ring of smoke. "He won that round. The sport of betrayal, as played out between brothers."

He gave her a look that was oddly sympathetic. "If it helps any, it has nothing to do with you. We came out of the womb fighting for the same toys. The estate has never been enough for him. He wants everything that's mine: he even told me that he wanted the dogs. He offered to adopt both of them."

Merry tried to think of something cutting to say, but even when she was furious, she'd never been any good at coming up with insults.

She did the only thing she could think of: she began to tug off the diamond ring. "I'll return this to you."

"No need."

"There's every need," she said, trying to stop herself from crying. "I don't want your ring. I mean, of course, I won't keep your family ring."

"I do not accept your breaking of our engagement," Cedric said casually.

"What?" Merry's head jerked up. "What did you just say?"

Cedric flicked the ash from his cheroot. It landed on the carpet to the side of his chair. "We will marry just as planned. It was extremely gauche of you to air our private business in the ballroom earlier, but we'll put it about that it was a lovers' quarrel."

"We are not marrying!" Merry glared at him. "You must be very drunk. Either that, or you're cracked."

"As a matter of fact, I'm neither," Cedric replied, sounding a little surprised. "I was trapped in that chair with no more than a sip of brandy for what felt like hours while you and the duke pawed each other."

Merry's thoughts were so jumbled that she couldn't form coherent speech. She should get up and find her aunt, and never mind the fact that everyone would gape at her. Surely they all knew, even if she hadn't, that she had been no more than a pawn between rival brothers.

No, it was worse than that. She was seen as a lascivious American heiress who sampled and discarded men the way other women did hats. No wonder Bess had been so worried about the damage to her reputation if a third fiancé was jilted. Merry's naïveté had protected her from understanding the ugly conclusions people were drawing.

Merry felt a stab of longing for her father so acute it almost took her breath away. Her father would never have let her betroth herself to three despicable men in a row. Well, two despicable men; Bertie was only hot-tempered.

Her father would have put his arms around Merry and made everything all right, the way he had when she was a little girl with a scraped knee.

Cedric flicked another ash, indifferent to where it landed. "Actually, I've come to a decision about our marriage. I know we're supposed to marry in June, but I think we'll marry two days hence instead."

"No!"

"I don't trust you to stand by your word as time passes. This must feel tiresomely familiar, but if you refuse to marry me, I can and will sue for breach of promise."

"You should be ashamed of yourself!" Merry whispered. But she straightened her spine and met his eyes. "You are immoral to do this to me. You and your brother, both of you."

"It is not *I* who nearly did the blanket hornpipe with a man to whom you are *not* engaged, in the Verekers' library—where anyone might have entered." Cedric pointed at her with his cheroot. This time, the ash dropped onto the chair and he flicked it away.

"In fact, there's enough shame to go around. You will marry me, Merry Pelford, because the moment you accepted my proposal, you promised me that money. Moreover, when you told all and sundry about the unpleasant state of affairs regarding my debts, you made me look like an ass. You damaged my chance of making a satisfactory marriage in the future."

The feeling of being caught in some sort of odd, distorted nightmare was only growing stronger. Merry tightened her lips before she said something irrevocably unladylike. Perhaps that etiquette list had been good for something.

"So you must marry me or I'll sue you *and* your uncle," the fiendish man opposite her said. "I'll give him some credit: as soon as Pelford realized I was having second thoughts, he popped out with that offer to pay off my debts. Here's my thinking: You may be something of a sow's ear, but you can be shaped into a purse full of guineas. Or however that goes."

"You are a contemptible person," Merry said stonily. "I am not a sow's ear. And only a boor and a parasite would allow another man to pay his debts."

"I don't think we should exchange insults just yet, do you? It seems so connubial, and we aren't there yet."

"Why must you make yourself seem clever by using big words?" Merry cried.

He raised an eyebrow. "Your paltry vocabulary is hardly justification for such hostility. I would venture to call it— forgive me—a trifle ill-bred."

"If I were to enter the church with you," Merry stated, "I would never say yes. Unless in answer to the bishop's question whether anyone had just cause to stop the wedding."

A faint smile curled Cedric's lips. "I have every faith that you will respond appropriately—in other words, with a yes."

"I've been sued by one avaricious man," she pointed out. "I have an attorney already."

How could she have ever thought that Cedric had warm eyes? They were cold as ice. "In fact, you will marry me."

Merry jumped to her feet. "You've lost your senses, perhaps owing to an overindulgence in spirits. I shall return to Boston as soon as I can arrange passage."

If she thought about the fact that the duke and his brother had discussed her; about the fact that the duke had kissed her merely to score points against his brother; about the fact that she was nothing but a shuttlecock batted between insolent, titled Englishmen, she would cry.

No, she would sob.

She pushed the thought away and started for the door. She'd been deceived before. She would survive this.

Just as she reached for the latch, Cedric caught up with her, and spun her around. He leaned in close and Merry recoiled, her head jolting against the door.

"You will marry me," he stated, eyes holding hers. "My suit against you will not only refer to a broken wedding contract. After your not-so-delightful display this evening, I will also sue for slander."

Merry could not believe her ears. "No one will credit that foolishness!"

"Oh, but they will." He smiled. "I have a roomful of witnesses to the fact you besmirched my character. You broke off two previous engagements; obviously you are not to be trusted. Everyone knows that you paid off one of the men. Likewise, everyone now thinks that you paid for me. You are American. People will believe anything of you."

Despite herself, a tear rolled down Merry's cheek. "You are nothing but a liar and a cheat," she managed.

Cedric raised a hand to her chin and forced it up. "Darling, do you really think that I give a damn about insults from a fiancée whom I caught groping my own brother?"

"Then sue me. Ruin me!" Merry cried, choking back a sob and getting control of herself again. "I would rather be utterly ruined than marry you."

"What of your uncle?" Cedric asked softly. "Your hotheaded, good-hearted uncle. Not even Mr. Pelford has bottomless pockets."

Merry stared at him. Her uncle stood to lose his fortune because of her inability to keep her promises. Because she was a vacillating fool.

Her heart thumped. Thaddeus would be outraged.

He would challenge Cedric.

"I might add that I am a crack shot, and quite good with a sword," Cedric said casually.

"Why would you do such a monstrous thing? Who *are* you?"

"There's no need to be histrionic. I don't want to sue you; I want to marry you. You owe me money, and you've damaged my reputation. The only way to gloss over that vulgar public performance tonight is for you to walk down the aisle of St. Paul's looking as if I fulfilled your heart's every desire."

Merry pressed her lips together tightly. The nightmare she'd found herself in was growing worse by the moment.

"It's not as if you have a chance in hell of becoming a duchess. I thought my brother could have been a wee bit more polite when he announced that he would never marry you," Cedric said. "Don't you agree? After all, he had just kissed you, for all the world as if he were genuinely interested. Maybe he was; his mistresses are generally fleshy in the bosom."

Merry might be a plaything between warring brothers but they seemed to have their own queer code of honor. The duke had punctiliously informed her—twice—that he would never be coerced into marriage. He had never allowed her to delude herself into thinking his kisses meant anything.

"You don't want to marry me," she said desperately.

"That is true. What you said in the ballroom was so vulgar that I don't even like you very much at the moment. However, needs must. A lawsuit might get me money, but I'll end up without a bride, and my reputation in tatters. I won't be able to find a suitable wife of my own rank. Therefore, we shall marry."

"I'll give you ten thousand pounds," Merry offered. "It cost me five thousand dollars to get rid of Dermot; that's more than double."

"I'm worth at least that. I have a title, and I am not graced with the laughable name of Dermot Popplewell. Really, how could you? Merry Popplewell. It sounds like a nursemaid. A governess at best."

"I'll give you fifteen thousand pounds," Merry said desperately. "In a year or two, no one will care whether I paid your tailor's bill."

Cedric raked his fingers through his hair. She watched with loathing as a lock fell into precisely the right place over his forehead. "Merry, Merry, Merry. You still don't understand, do you?"

"Apparently not."

"My brother *wants* you. He wants you merely because I found you first, but that's irrelevant."

Merry felt sick. She edged sideways. "Let me go."

"As long as you understand that we shall leave this room arm-in-arm, and you will smile with girlish pleasure as you inform everyone that you hadn't understood the nature of your Uncle Thaddeus's gift, and that we are quite reconciled. I shall announce that I've decided to purchase a special license tomorrow, and we'll marry the following morning."

"No," Merry gasped.

"Oh yes," he said calmly. "The wedding will be a spectacle to remember; I'm quite certain that most of London will contrive to appear, even with this brief notice. But I do have one request. You've had your last kiss from my brother, if you please. I think we'd better say no family dinners for a good period, don't you think?"

Her heart was broken, but that didn't matter. She had to protect her uncle. Thaddeus couldn't lose his fortune, and possibly his life, owing to her mistakes, to a feud between heartless aristocrats.

"Very well," she said dully. Voices were coming down the corridor. Cedric caught her wrist and pulled her away from the door.

"One complaint to your uncle and aunt, or to my brother,

and I'll throw down a gauntlet that will end in a duel," he threatened. "You may take me at my word, Merry." Anyone meeting his icy gaze would have no doubt he meant it.

The door opened and Aunt Bess walked into the room. To Merry's horror, Lady Vereker crowded through after her. "My goodness!" the lady cried. "I thought His Grace was with you, Miss Pelford."

"Good evening, ladies," Cedric said, bowing. "My brother has been and gone. He played the peacemaker, escorting Miss Pelford to me after my fiancée and I had a most foolish squabble." He slipped an arm around Merry and gazed down at her lovingly.

"It appears to have worked," Aunt Bess observed, her tone approving. "I'm happy to see it. Unfortunately, gossip is flowing through that ballroom like water. I cannot understand why people are so convinced that the duke would try to steal his own brother's fiancée. The very idea!"

"The chatter stems from the fact that we've seen these two young men grow up, you understand," Lady Vereker said. "And they've always been . . ." She paused delicately.

"Antagonistic," Merry put in dully.

"I was about to say competitive," the lady clarified.

"Only over trifling things," Cedric said. "Never over something as momentous as marriage, Lady Vereker."

"Of course not," Aunt Bess said. "In the end, family are all you can count on."

"Lady Vereker," Cedric said, "could we count on you to sort out any little confusion that might pertain in the ballroom as to my brother's intentions? I certainly don't want his future bride to have a mistaken impression. As you may know, he has chosen a duchess."

"Lord Cedric, have you any idea about the identity of the lucky bride?" Lady Vereker asked eagerly.

"It wouldn't be my place to confirm anything. But I can

say that I have noticed he seems quite taken with Lady Caroline," Cedric told the lady.

In years after, Merry never could remember how they managed to leave the Vereker townhouse.

She only remembered the moment in which Cedric jerked her to a halt before their host and hostess, and said ruefully, "My fiancée and I owe you our humblest apologies for causing such a contretemps during your ball. What fools we made of ourselves! A lovers' quarrel. One has to think of Shakespeare's immortal words: 'Lord, what fools these mortals be!'"

He threw her a melting glance. "My darling misunderstood the import of a gift from her uncle. Happily for me, I was able to enlighten her."

Merry smiled.

Weakly, but she smiled.

Chapter Nineteen

Dear Lord Cedric,

I was unable to sleep all last night. I understand that I am nothing more than a tennis ball batted between you and your brother, but please do not make this worse by insisting on proceeding with a ceremony that is surely repugnant in the eyes of God and man.

Believe me, yours respectfully,
Miss Merry Pelford

Dear Merry,

Why, there is no end to the novelties left in store for us. I had no idea that you placed so much faith in the wisdom of the Almighty. Or was it merely that you believe I shall end up in a dark and thorny place? No, really, my dear, I must insist upon marriage.

Yours ever,
Lord Cedric Allardyce

Dear Lord Cedric,

I will give you £20,000. It is the whole of my fortune, but I am prepared to surrender it in order to extricate myself from this situation. Please.

With sincerity and respect,
Merry

Dear Merry,

Money is but one of the reasons I am marrying you, and by far the least important, if you will have the truth of it. Imagine: the duke has been rather apologetic about the whole affair. He seems sincerely regretful to have conducted himself so inappropriately with my fiancée.

I am hopeful that this marriage will begin a new era for myself and my brother. I believe it might be the mending of the family.

Yours ever,
Lord Cedric Allardyce

Dear Cedric,

I beg you to release me from my promise. I would embark for America tomorrow morning, if it were possible. You need not worry about the competition with your brother; I would not have anything to do with him if someone were to pay me £20,000. As such, there is no need to go to these extremes.

Yours most sincerely,
Merry

Dear Merry,

I am happy to inform you that I have procured a special license from Doctors' Commons. Furthermore, I have confirmed with the registrar at St. Paul's that we shall be able to marry at ten of the clock tomorrow morning. Although we are marrying with what some might term undue haste, I dislike the idea of marrying you in a manner beneath our dignity, and I was happy to confirm that the Bishop of London will wed us. Footmen are busily running about London spreading the joyous news.

Ever yours,
Lord Cedric Allardyce

Dear Cedric,

You cannot want a wife who would rather find herself at the bottom of the sea than joined to you in holy matrimony.

Merry

Dear Merry,

The revelations go on and on. Who would have imagined that the stubborn young American lady had such a poetic soul?

On a less poetic note, as I am sure you are aware, your uncle and I have brought our final contractual negotiations to a satisfactory conclusion. I am not sure whether your uncle has informed you, but my brother has involved himself in the business. He has been insistent that your settlements are most generous— not that I would not have been, but I admit to feeling a touch of pique as regards your behavior with him.

He and I have talked extensively today, and he is right: pique has no place in marriage. I am writing to tell you, Merry, that I forgive you. You can trust me never to mention again the kisses you shared with the duke.

It is in the past; we begin with a clean slate.

Ever yours,
Cedric

Merry stared at Cedric's final sentence for some time. She had spent most of the night sleepless and crying uncontrollably, and the whole of the day composing letters that she hoped would persuade Cedric to relent. But now it was ten in the evening, and they were set to marry in twelve hours' time.

He wasn't going to relent.

The duke . . . the *duke* had insisted that her settlements be generous. She understood the impulse behind that: he was ashamed of having kissed her—not the kiss itself, but his motive for it. As well he should be.

Bess and Thaddeus seemed positively ecstatic that their niece would at last make it all the way to the altar. Bess hadn't even asked whether Merry truly wanted to go through with the marriage. Merry quickly scolded herself for that self-pitying thought. She had to stiffen her spine and get through this.

She went to bed feeling like a prisoner facing the gallows, exhausted and terrified. No matter how fiercely she willed herself to stay asleep, it was impossible. She kept jerking awake, mind whirling.

She had a feeling many women neither liked nor respected their husbands. But was there any woman who had felt such a deep yearning for her brother-in-law that as soon as her eyes closed, she dreamed of kissing him? Especially a brother-in-law who had behaved so despicably?

How would she ever look at the duke without remembering his kiss?

Better question: How would she ever look at her husband without loathing him?

By the time dawn arrived, she had, thankfully, cried herself into a state of numbness. It felt as if she were enveloped in a cloud that moved with her wherever she went. It muffled the world, and made her aunt's chatter fade away.

She floated through Aunt Bess's brief but informative discussion of the wedding night, registering just enough information to conclude that she would have to join Cedric in swilling brandy in order to survive that.

During her wretched night, she had somehow arrived at several important decisions.

The first was that, for once in her life, she would keep her promise. She would be honorable, if nothing else. She understood English society well enough to know that if she jilted Cedric and absconded back to America, he would be ruined.

Who would marry him? She suspected that fathers of eligible English lasses already viewed him as a drunk and a fortune hunter.

When would the next American heiress come along, ready to be dazzled by borrowed poetry and ignorant of the fact that a man can be befuddled by brandy and still dance a quadrille?

Never.

No, she had made a final, fatal choice when she had accepted Cedric's proposal, and she must carry it through.

Second, she would allow a year or two to pass before she encouraged reconciliation between her husband and his twin. She would spare herself the company of the man who had kissed her for such a terrible reason, whether His Grace was repentant or not.

And finally, but certainly not least, Cedric would have to give up brandy. In fact, she would insist he give up wine and spirits altogether. She refused to accept a drunkard for a husband, even if she had to take him to an island off the coast of Wales and keep him there until he forgot what brandy smelled like.

Her life would be good. Even her married life would be good, because she would make it good. She would have children, and she would love her children, and spend time in the garden.

Her plans churned through her mind even as their carriage rolled up Ludgate and into St. Paul's churchyard, which swarmed with all manner of carriages. Cedric was right: even with such short notice, most of fashionable London had managed to gather.

A few minutes later, standing with her uncle in the great doorway at the western end of the aisle, her daze finally evaporated and panic took its place. She had gone to bed feeling like a condemned prisoner; at the opposite end of the aisle was her gallows.

Before she stopped herself, an image of the duke laughing at her analogy popped into her head. He would think she was absurd. But *he* wasn't marrying a drunken, unpleasant lout.

Ice trickled down her spine and her extremities tingled. Her feet wanted to run, just as fast as they could.

Out of St. Paul's for a start, followed by out of England.

How could she have ended up in this situation? The last two days had passed in a frenzy, each hour propelling her closer and closer to this moment. Yet some small part of her mind had been certain that it wouldn't actually happen.

Was it too late to change her mind? Merry clutched her uncle's elbow and peered through her veil up the aisle. The veil was Belgian lace, bought optimistically during their Paris sojourn, and so difficult to see through that it might as well have been fashioned as a tablecloth.

"Uncle Thaddeus," she whispered.

Of course it was too late. Her uncle couldn't even hear her over the chatter of the hundreds of people who had congregated to see the wedding.

Were the English always so boisterous? In Boston, guests waited in dignified silence for the bride to arrive, with merely rustling or a hastily suppressed whisper here or there.

"Uncle!" Merry tightened her fingers around his elbow.

She glimpsed through the veil that he had turned his head to look at her. He may have smiled, but the lace blotted so much of her view that it might as well have been a blindfold. She felt as if she were standing in a very small and very hot white cave.

Thaddeus leaned close, bringing with him a reassuring whiff of the best tobacco and strong coffee. "There's nothing to worry about," he rumbled in her ear.

Merry swallowed hard. "I just—"

The organ swelled, downing out her voice with its jubilant announcement of the bride's appearance. Thaddeus began to guide her slowly forward, as she trembled from head to foot within the grotto of her veil.

There is no going back. The words beat relentlessly in her head, keeping time with her uncle's slow pace.

The nave seemed endless. Her veil moved a little with every step, but not so much that she could see anything other than the black-and-white checkers beneath her slippers. The pews and their occupants were nothing but a haze. She couldn't even distinguish the faces closest to the aisle.

It made her feel like a pawn, advancing up an endless checkerboard. Her uncle played her piece, not she—but again she had to tell herself not to be sorry for herself. *She* made the choice to marry Cedric, and this sorry situation was no one's fault but her own.

The checkerboard abruptly changed pattern, giving way to radiating circles of checkers. She was fairly certain that meant they'd entered the transept. Not far now. With every step, her heart beat faster, and her hands trembled.

A swell of noise filled the cathedral and she detected

movement at the edge of her vision; it seemed Cedric was walking forward to meet her.

Her uncle brought them to a halt and for a moment all she heard was an excited murmur echoing throughout the vast space.

"Uncle?" she asked, turning her head.

He brought her forward two more steps. "Merry," Thaddeus said, lowering his voice. "You must trust me, my dear. You will be happy."

He was wrong, so wrong. Her heart was shattering. Still, there had been brides like her throughout history. They had survived. She would survive.

Merry turned her head toward her groom, but her cursed veil prevented any but a general sense of his person. Wordlessly, he took her arm from her uncle and moved to stand beside her, facing the bishop.

At least Cedric didn't reek of cologne this morning. He seemed to own more vials of scent than she did, but this morning he smelled quite nice, with merely a touch of wintergreen soap about his person.

"Dearly beloved," the bishop intoned, and Merry's heart gave a painful thump. This was unbearable.

"We are gathered together here in the sight of God, and in the face of this congregation, to join together this man and this woman in holy matrimony."

She heard Cedric take a deep breath next to her. Panic flared again. The bishop rattled on with the rite but she couldn't concentrate.

She should have stayed with Bertie. True, he had compared her to a red wagon, but he had adored her. Truly adored her.

With a start, she realized that the bishop was addressing Cedric. "Wilt thou have this woman to thy wedded wife, to live together after God's ordinance in the holy estate of matrimony? Wilt thou love her, comfort her, honor, and keep her . . ."

Honor?

She neither liked nor respected Cedric; how could she be expected to honor him? Or, for that matter, *obey* him? Her heart pounded so that she did not hear Cedric's response over the rushing in her ears.

He must have said, "I will," because moments later she found herself vowing to honor and to obey, in addition to keeping herself only unto him and all the rest of it.

The bishop turned to Cedric again and rattled on about how he should love and cherish her.

A choked scream pressed on the back of Merry's throat. But rather than scream, when a hand encircled hers, she obediently parroted everything the bishop told her to say, the words emerging from her mouth like smoke, as if they meant nothing.

Do vows that a woman doesn't hear matter?

The bishop said something else. A different voice interrupted her hysteria. "With this ring I thee wed," her groom stated. "With my body I thee worship, and with all my worldly goods I thee endow: In the name of the Father, and of the Son, and of the Holy Ghost."

What a liar he was.

What a liar *she* was.

A ring slid over her finger. "Oh no," she whispered under her breath. "No, no."

But that plea went unaddressed, because hands gently turned her, and then gathered and lifted her veil.

Light struck her face but Merry was looking at the marble floor, at the toes of her elegant slippers.

Slowly, she raised her head, steeling herself.

And met her husband's eyes.

Chapter Twenty

Trent was prepared, if necessary, to catch his swooning wife when she discovered whom she had married. When he entered the cathedral, he had not expected Merry's veil to be so thick that he couldn't even make out her features—which made him doubt that she had seen his face.

In short, she might think she had married Cedric. He had a shrewd idea that her aunt had depended on just that.

He lifted her veil and met Merry's eyes. Sure enough, they widened in shock. She opened her mouth, perhaps to scream.

Instinctively, Trent took a step forward and covered her mouth with his own.

He meant to merely brush her lips but he deepened the kiss instead, willing her not to protest. Sensation shot all the way down his body.

Merry was his wife now. He hadn't stolen her; he had

only taken what his brother had tossed aside. His hands circled her waist and he bent his head, memorizing the shape of her lips, and when she gasped, her taste.

No matter how it had come about, she was his now.

Merry's veil had disappeared, and instead of Cedric . . .

The duke.

Her husband?

Impossible. *Impossible.*

Yet the duke was kissing her, and Cedric was nowhere to be seen. His Grace's kiss felt unhurried, as if there was nothing else that either of them should be doing. There was no self-consciousness about it, either, even though a church full of onlookers sat before them and a bishop stood behind them.

He didn't pull her improperly close, but she could feel the strength in his hands through her gown.

Merry felt her eyes closing. The duke made no sound but his approval shimmered through her. For one second, their kiss became something completely different: sensual, daring, scandalous.

The congregation! The bishop!

Her eyes popped open and she pulled away.

The man she had unwittingly married was looking down at her, his eyes unreadable. "My brother relinquished his claim to your hand," he said, in a voice only she could hear. Her hands came up without her volition, grasping his forearms.

"He did what?"

"We shall give it out that I fell madly in love with you, and my brother gave you up from the goodness of his heart. People expect that sort of thing from twins."

"He gave me up," Merry repeated.

Well, obviously he had, because Cedric was not standing in front of her. The relief that abruptly flooded her body was so acute that her knees trembled.

Alarm crossed the duke's face. "You've done so well. Please don't be the first woman to faint in my presence."

"I shall not," Merry said, willing her knees not to buckle.

"I forgot that Americans never swoon," he murmured, and she saw a flash of amusement in his eyes.

Somehow, her prayer had been answered. She had not opened her eyes to discover that she had become Lady Cedric Allardyce.

"Where is he?" she whispered.

Her husband turned them to face the assembly—which caused a commotion that would have counted as a roar in a Roman amphitheater—and leaned over to speak in her ear.

"He embarked for the Bahamas on last night's tide."

Merry could scarcely hear him through the tumult. She curled her fingers around his elbow. Her breath was coming quickly . . . From the shock? From the kiss?

She told herself to smile, and began the return journey down the aisle. Their marriage must be legal. The scandal would be far too great otherwise.

Beside her, His Grace was nodding to people as he walked. Just as if there was nothing out of the ordinary in marrying his brother's intended.

Merry had the queer feeling that she had toppled straight into a novel, one of those that appeared in three volumes with special bindings. Miss Fairfax had always pointed out sourly that life wasn't like a novel.

Miss Fairfax, it seemed, was wrong.

In more than one way.

The girl who was too tall, who had no manners, whom no Englishman would want to marry . . . that American girl was now a duchess.

Chapter Twenty-one

Thaddeus Pelford met Trent's eyes with a knife-edged nod that said as clearly as a cocked pistol that Trent had better make his niece happy.

He would.

He hoped.

He glanced down at Merry. Yards of billowing lace set her off like a jewel, emphasizing her silky hair, wide eyes, rosy mouth. Her train was long enough to sweep the widest path in Hyde Park. Like a peacock dragging its tail on the ground, she looked magnificent, if slightly ludicrous.

They emerged from the great doors into May sunshine to be met by a shout of excitement from the crowd gathered outside. A cluster of journalists from the gossip rags sprang forward screaming questions. Clearly, news of the bridegroom swap had spread.

Footmen clothed in the ducal livery stood shoulder to

shoulder in two rows, creating an aisle to the carriage door. The crowd stretched as far as Warwick Lane, jostling shoulders and craning necks to see the beautiful heiress from America whom a duke had stolen from his own brother.

Merry made a little sound, and her hand tightened on his arm. But then she smiled and raised her right hand in a wave.

A romantic gesture was clearly called for, so Trent scooped her up. The curves of Merry's body fit his arms as if she'd been designed for them. In the sunlight, the violet in her eyes was the color of forget-me-nots.

The crowd roared with approval.

He nodded at a footman, who sprang forward and gathered up the yards of lace spilling on the ground behind them. At the carriage door, Trent leaned in and placed his bride on a seat, then climbed in after her, and sat down opposite.

Any man would be moved by Merry's curves. Any man would feel a possessive thrill. It was probably a requisite part of the wedding ceremony, invoked by the vows that had bound her to him.

The footman pushed an armful of lace through the door and closed it. The coachman instantly loosed his reins, and the throng parted as the carriage started slowly forward.

As if they'd been alone together a hundred times, Merry reached up and began pulling out her hairpins, creating a little pile on a seat until she was able to pull her veil free.

Trent watched silently, feeling a throb in his groin. He wanted to pull her onto his lap, take out every single pin, and watch her ink-dark hair fall around her shoulders. Hell, he'd like to start unbuttoning that gown, baring creamy flesh that no man other than himself would ever see.

She seemed to be in lace from head to foot. Could she

be wearing only lace under her gown? He'd never seen a lace chemise, but he could imagine it playing hide and seek with rosy nipples.

He'd like—

"Duke," she said.

Their eyes met.

"Should I say, husband?"

"Is that a genuine question?"

"Was that ceremony a farce? How can it possibly have been a lawful wedding?"

"It was a legitimate ceremony. You are now the Duchess of Trent by special license." He hesitated. "I realize that your veil obscured your vision, but the bishop did say Octavius Mortimer John Allardyce, rather than Cedric Mortimer Allardyce."

She raised an eyebrow. "Your names are quite similar."

"Every male in my family is named after Mortimer, the first duke."

"I had no idea that you were standing in for your brother," she said, confirming his impression. "Does this mean you have won the competition, or has Cedric won, and I'm the consolation prize?"

Competition?

"There was no competition," Trent said, adding honestly, "but I will admit that by marrying you I consider myself a victor."

A moment of silence followed, in which Merry bundled her veil into a reasonably neat pile on the seat. "Cedric told me all about the conversation you had with him on the steps of your house," she said finally.

Trent frowned.

"In which you discussed the fact that Cedric had not bedded me," she clarified. "I believe that is the term he used. I might add that I find it reprehensible that the two of you would talk about me, or any other woman, in such a manner."

He must have a streak of perversion, because the fact that his new duchess was scowling at him just made Trent desire her even more. "I entirely agree with you."

"I suppose Cedric brought it up," she said, jumping to the right conclusion when he didn't say anything else.

"Did he tell you that we were competing for your hand?" Trent asked, wondering exactly what his brother—who had a positive genius for delivering half truths—had told her. "As I recollect, Cedric announced that he had refrained from kissing you in order to keep your interest."

She flinched, and looked down at her lap. "I can't believe I thought I was in love with a man who is so coarse and cold-blooded. I am such a fool."

Trent didn't like the humiliated ache in Merry's voice; his words came out more fiercely than they might have. "It was the opposite of a competition. I was trying to convince myself that I had no right to woo my brother's fiancée."

Her head swung up.

"It wasn't working," he said, watching her closely. "The only thing I remember of the conversation was gratitude that he hadn't touched you."

"Cedric told me that you only kissed me at the ball in order to score a point against him."

He felt a prickle of irritation. "Do you really think that I give a damn about *scoring points*? I have never kissed a woman for any reason other than the obvious." He gave her a hard stare that had so much lust in it that his American, innocent as she was, had to know exactly what he felt.

Sure enough, her cheeks turned a little pink. But her expression didn't soften. "I would have thought that you would never discuss bedding a lady. But I was wrong."

Trent's jaw tightened. He felt as if he'd spent his life wading through muck that his brother had spread at their feet.

"So yes," Merry said fiercely, "I found it *entirely* possible that you and your brother would engage in a form of sibling rivalry involving a scoring system of one type or another."

"You are incorrect." Despite himself, his voice turned a bit chilly. Merry had come to a fair assumption, given that she didn't know him well. But it rankled. "Cedric was deliberately untruthful. An honorable man considers his brother's intended out of reach, and that's not taking into account the fact that you told me you were in love."

"You wanted—you thought about wooing me?"

He nodded.

"Why?" she asked, her American bluntness coming into play. "You have no need for my inheritance. Cedric thought that my nationality and lack of gentility would tarnish his title; just imagine what it will do to yours. Or did your brother force you to the altar?"

Damn it, most young ladies would love to marry him. Apparently he'd ended up with the one woman who would prefer disgrace to being a duchess.

"If the wedding had been called off, especially after Cedric's behavior at the Vereker ball, the natural assumption would be that you had jilted him, just as you did Bertie. Your reputation would never recover."

"So you sacrificed yourself for my good?" In a heartbeat, she'd gone from angry to utterly furious. She pulled off the wedding ring he had slid over her gloved finger in the cathedral. "Hold this a moment, please." She dropped the ring into his hand and began removing her gloves— with the help of her teeth.

"What?" she said, catching his eyes. "Have you any idea how much lace gloves itch?"

"I've never seen lace gloves before."

"You'll never see me wearing them again." She tossed the gloves on the seat beside her veil. She had every right to be so angry. Hell, if someone lured him to the altar under false pretenses, he'd be livid.

"In the midst of your concern for my reputation, why didn't you just tell me?" she demanded. "Forgive me, but what sort of man thinks it's acceptable to marry a woman without asking her beforehand?"

He'd known this moment would come. He just hadn't pictured the pain in her eyes. Damn it, he should have followed his instincts, not listened to her aunt.

"I asked to speak to you yesterday. But Mrs. Pelford felt—"

"Aunt Bess knew all this?" Her voice rose. "I realized my uncle had to have known, but my aunt as well?"

"Mrs. Pelford felt strongly that you would not marry me if I approached you yesterday," Trent said flatly. "She was convinced that the wedding had to be presented as a fait accompli, or you would return to Boston. She refused to allow me to speak to you."

Her mouth tightened. "That sounds just irrational enough to be possible."

"She takes your reputation very seriously."

"In Boston, a person's word is his bond." Merry pulled a fold of her veil into her lap and began pleating it. "My aunt is quite pained by my lack of constancy. My family . . ." Her voice trailed off.

"*My* family—Cedric—also played a part."

"So why did Cedric amuse himself by writing me all those letters at the same time that you were presumably acquiring a wedding license with your name on it?"

"He felt that your quarrel at the Vereker ball destroyed his chance of a respectable marriage."

"That is the reasoning he used to force me to the altar," she said, eyes kindling.

"He argued that there were only two ways to preserve both your and his reputations. Either the two of you would marry—which I would not allow—or you and I would marry in a cause célèbre, and Cedric would become famous for having sacrificed himself on the altar of my true love."

"You wouldn't allow the marriage," she said slowly.

"Of course not."

"Why didn't you simply send me a message saying, 'So sorry, my brother has done a bunk, and you won't be Lady Cedric after all. And by the way, I'll stand in as groom, if you wish'?"

Trent curled his fingers around Merry's wedding ring, surprised by how fierce his impulse was to replace it on her finger.

"Mrs. Pelford said you would return to Boston. I didn't want to chase you across the ocean. I wanted to marry you." His voice came out low, rough. "I wanted to marry you from the moment I met you, but I fought it because you belonged to my brother. And when the chance came to marry you, even in an underhanded way, I seized it."

Her mouth fell open, clearly in astonishment. "From the moment you met me on the balcony?"

Hadn't she noticed that he had nearly kissed her?

"Had you any idea who I was?" she asked.

"None, nor did I know that you were betrothed to my brother. You were a complete stranger. But I made up my mind to marry you."

"That is so odd," she muttered, rubbing her forehead. "I thought this sort of thing only happened in books."

He felt a flash of alarm. "Perhaps I should clarify that I'm not talking about love at first sight," he said, a touch of apology in his voice.

"I think we both agree that there's been enough talk of 'love' in my life," she said wryly. "I did not fall in love with you at first sight, either."

"I decided to marry you for far more rational reasons. You are very beautiful, and even better, intelligent and funny." He hesitated and then added, "I also find it appealing that your experiences have taught you the true nature of romantic love: to wit, that it is a shallow emotion."

A reluctant smile curled the edges of her mouth. "I do not believe that love is shallow. But I do agree that it is unreliable." Merry shook her head. "I would never trust myself to choose another fiancé, for example."

"I am deeply hopeful that there will be no need to put yourself to the test," he said.

"Why are you so afraid of love?" she asked.

"I'm not afraid. But I consider love temporary by definition. Our marriage will proceed on the basis of our affinity for each other, our compatibility. Hopefully we will form a lifelong bond based on mutual respect, not a feckless emotion that evaporates like a puddle in summer."

"That is a persuasive argument," she said slowly.

In the back of his mind, Trent couldn't believe that he was having to argue with a woman about the merits of being a duchess. He'd known from the time he was twelve years old that he was one of the most desirable men in England.

But that was the point, wasn't it? He had decided to marry an American woman because she overlooked his title for his own merits. He just never thought that his merits might not be enough.

Trent leaned forward, but he didn't touch her. If he picked up Merry's hand, he might burst into flames, pull her into his lap, and ravish that plump mouth of hers. "I will give you an annulment if you wish. But I would prefer that you remain my duchess."

He cleared his throat. "You told me in the library that you consider us friends. I believe we could have a very good marriage. I find you far more captivating than any other woman I've met."

"I am honored," she said, a trifle awkwardly.

Despite himself, he took her left hand, turned it over, and kissed her palm. "We both understand that romantic love is bollocks. We will have a solid marriage, a rational, respectful, happy marriage."

He watched as she thought about it. "I have two questions," she said. "First, would you allow me to venture to the East End of London, if I wished?"

"Certainly, not that I would wish you to go anywhere dangerous without me. Why—"

She raised a pink fingertip. "Second. Will you accompany me to the Chelsea Physic Garden to see the pineapple stove?"

What the hell was that? "I should warn you that my cook is a bit elderly. I put a Rumford stove and a hob grate into the kitchens in Hawksmede, my country seat, and she refused to make supper for a solid week."

"This particular stove is not for food," Merry said, her dimple appearing. Damn, but he liked that dimple.

"What is it for?"

"Growing pineapple plants."

He judged it a quixotic endeavor, given England's climate, but he didn't care. "My house has nineteen acres of woods and gardens. You could have a pineapple stove on every one, if you wish."

"Bribery," she muttered. But Trent knew her well enough to recognize the light in her eyes.

He kissed her palm again. "May I return your wedding ring, Merry?"

The question hung in the air.

"Yes," she whispered. "You may."

He slipped the ring over her ring finger. "Will you remain my duchess? For better, for worse, and all the rest of it?"

The question hung in the air of the carriage, silence broken only by the clatter of carriage wheels on cobblestones.

Then she nodded. "I shall keep my vows, Duke. I will be your friend and you will be mine. You will take me to see the pineapple stove, and I. . . ." She gave him an impish smile. "I will not fall in love with you."

The carriage rocked to a halt; they had reached Trent's townhouse and Merry added, "I have to admit that it's amusing to realize that you believe you're so irresistible that you have to warn women not to become besotted with your beauty."

The doorway swung open and a footman appeared. His wife descended in a cloud of lace.

And a giggle.

Chapter Twenty-two

Merry walked into the entry of the duke's townhouse and stopped short. Not the duke's house: *her* house. She was the duchess.

These were her footmen, gawking at her under their lashes. Her townhouse, her front door.

Her husband.

The word sent a thrill through her that was very different from the dread with which she'd pictured being Cedric's wife.

Trent came up behind her, putting a warm hand on her lower back. "Your maid is waiting for you in your bedchamber, if you would like to change your gown."

Merry was tired of dragging around mounds of lace, but she couldn't simply walk into a strange bedchamber and explain to Lucy . . . what? She felt as if her life had splintered into a million pieces and she was desperate to glue parts of it, at least, back together.

She knew what English people always did in moments of indecision. She smiled at Trent's butler—*her* butler. "Thank you, but I should like a cup of tea first."

Two seconds later, she was seated on a couch in a small sitting room, her train wadded up at her feet and her husband seated at her side.

The very sight of him struck her like a blow. Trent wasn't pretty. He had the look of an angel cast out for the sin of arrogance, but at the same time, he was all man, from head to toe.

She cleared her throat. "What am I to call you?"

He looked confused for a moment. Then he said, "My mother addressed my father by his title."

"I address you as Duke?"

"Actually, she addressed him as Trent, as in, the Duke of Trent. I would prefer it, but you are welcome to use one of my personal names, if you like."

"Trent sounds like a river," she observed. "And I am not fond of Mortimer."

The side of the duke's mouth drew up in a crooked smile, and he moved close enough to drop a kiss on her neck.

Merry shivered involuntarily.

He kissed her again, on the chin this time. "My first name is Octavius." His arms came around her and pulled her close. "I am the sixth duke, but the eighth Mortimer."

"I couldn't be married to an emperor," Merry said, trying to keep her voice even although her heartbeat had quickened. "I'm an American, and we do not kowtow to royalty."

A wicked smile lit deep in his eyes. "I wouldn't want you to kowtow. But would you submit, Merry?" His voice deepened. "Would you submit to your very own emperor?"

A shiver broke over Merry's skin. How did he make that word sound so alluring? "No," she breathed, because no matter how delectable her husband was, she would not submit to anyone.

He broke into a crack of laughter. "This marriage is going to be interesting."

Merry discovered her fingers were curling into his hair and she was fighting the impulse to melt against him. She was fairly certain that ladies didn't do that sort of thing—at least not in sitting rooms. "I am having trouble believing that you decided to marry me the first time we met," she said. "I could hardly see you in the twilight."

"You spoke to me as if you were already a duchess."

"You liked the way I spoke?"

"Yes. And your facts, and your laugh. Your gown may have also played a role."

She frowned, trying to remember what she had worn the night they met.

"It was dusky on the balcony, but your skin glowed in the poor light there was." One finger trailed down the line of her neck, then lower over the swell of her breast. "Especially here. You were spilling out of the dress. There wasn't a man in the ballroom who didn't want you."

"They wanted my fortune," she corrected him. "My bosom may have been a welcome second." The duke's hands were callused, presumably from riding, and his caress felt so good that she shivered.

"I don't need your fortune. And I have to admit that it gave me some pleasure to know that you had no ambitions to become a duchess."

"I did not," she said. She wasn't being completely honest. There had been moments when she'd dreamed of marrying him—and becoming his duchess was the unavoidable side effect of that—but a woman has to keep her dignity. Her husband already had far too much self-confidence for his own good.

"Your fortune *and* your bosom are welcome seconds to *you*, to Miss Merry Pelford, an American from Boston."

His answer sent a streak of happiness through her. An aching hunger had sprung into being between them, a kind of madness that made her legs quiver so that she could easily imagine sliding onto her back, his weight and raw hunger following her down . . .

He pulled her tightly into his arms, crushing her breasts against his chest. Then he bent his head and kissed her for the first time since they stood before the altar. Even the touch of their lips together made tingles go down her legs.

Trent was a bossy kisser, moving her head into just the right position. But did it matter, when his lips were so firm and sweet, and he was so good at it? He wasn't pushy and wet, either. It was like a conversation, alternately devouring, then gentle and sweet.

When he finally pulled back, he said huskily, "So Octavius won't do, and neither will Mortimer?"

"What?" Merry asked, sounding like a breathless fool.

"Mortimer."

She shook her head. "Mortimer sounds like an uncle whom you wouldn't invite to dinner."

"I hesitate to tell you that, following tradition, our sons will be Mortimers."

"I might have to think hard about annulment," she said demurely. That brought a reaction. Her breath caught as he leaned forward, a wicked light in his eyes, and kissed her so deeply that pleasure flashed down her limbs.

"What about John?" he said a while later. "It's my third name."

Merry tried it out in her head. She could be married to a John. Though it would be better . . .

"Jack," she said decisively.

Her husband's brows drew together.

"Do you not like it?" she asked.

"Cedric used to call me Jack," Trent said, his voice emotionless. "It sounds childish. I would much prefer John."

Merry had only heard Cedric address his brother as "Duke," and always with an edge of sarcasm. She reached up and slid her fingers into his hair. "Jack makes you sound American."

"Have you any notion how disturbing that is to me?"

"Precisely. Please? If only in private? You may call me Merry."

"I would like to take you to Hawksmede, Merry," Trent said. Surely that was tacit permission to call him whatever she liked.

"Your house in the country," Merry murmured. His hands were wandering over her back, leaving delightful heat in their wake. Was she supposed to pretend his caresses didn't make her feel like collapsing to the floor like a marionette without strings? She leaned into the hard lines of his body, flirting with his tongue, tasting him and feeling him.

"My home," Trent said, a while later. "Have you ever visited a great house?"

"My father lived in a large house in Boston. My uncle's house in the country is even larger. But I have the feeling that Hawksmede is quite different."

"It's older, for one thing."

"There aren't many very old buildings in Boston," she agreed. "Do you live in a crumbling castle, the kind described by Mrs. Radcliffe?"

"No. But my mother called it, not fondly, an 'old heap of stone.' There are few conveniences."

Merry nodded. "No water closets, I suppose?"

"Water closets?" Trent looked taken aback. "My mother put in a bathing chamber, which was seen as progressive in the extreme. Between the watermen and the footmen, we manage to stay clean and warm."

"But there are gardens," Merry said simply. "How far is it from London?"

"Only three hours, if the roads are clear. I thought we might ask your uncle and aunt to pay us a visit in a few days. The chapel is said to be haunted by an angry monk; I'm sure it would be inspiration for a thousand lines at least."

That was very thoughtful of him. She did want to see Bess, if only because her aunt had some explaining to do, as Nanny used to say when Merry was naughty.

"What about George and Snowdrop? Can they come?"

"Of course. Though if you don't mind, I'd prefer that they travel with your maid and my valet. I assume that this will be George's first carriage trip."

"He will learn," she said a trifle defensively. "He's already much better."

Trent dropped a kiss on her mouth. "He is an intelligent puppy. I have no doubt of it. What would you think of leaving for the country today?"

He wanted his bride there, in the old sprawling pile of stone that felt *his*, as opposed to this shiny London townhouse that Cedric had been living in.

"Very well," Merry said easily. "I will need a half hour or so to put on a traveling dress and pack a small bag."

His mouth almost fell open.

"Is that too much time?" she asked.

"My mother always required hours, if not days, to ready herself for a trip."

"I do not," Merry said, keeping her explanation simple so as not to further baffle her husband. "I like to travel."

Trent's arms went around her again. "Merry," he said, in

that husky voice that melted her inside. "We are not going to consummate our marriage in a moving carriage."

Her arms wrapped around his neck. "We're not?" she breathed. Her eyes grew wide as a smile shaped his mouth.

"Though it is—"

"A consummation devoutly to be wished?" she suggested, laughing.

"'Devoutly' does not convey my feelings on the matter," Trent replied, his lips ghosting over hers. "I shall take you home to the place where my ancestors bedded their wives for the first time. This townhouse is too new."

"New?" she managed. "How old is it?"

"My great-grandfather built it in 1720."

"Just so you know," Merry said, pulling back so she could meet his eyes, "you and I have very different ideas of 'new.' My *country* is *new*. It is twenty-seven years old."

"This house is new," he replied with a crooked grin. "It is eighty-three years old."

Chapter Twenty-three

An hour later, Merry climbed into the ducal carriage with a net bag containing two novels she had borrowed from the townhouse's library. She never opened the bag, though, because she and Trent started arguing about the treasure of the Mycenaean kings, which Trent had read about in the paper, and Merry had heard about from a friend of Lord Elgin's wife.

"Lady Elgin had to crawl through a hole on all fours to reach the inner chamber," Merry told him. "And later she saw a city built by the Cyclopes! Would you like another piece of chicken?" They were sharing an excellent hamper containing enough food to feed at least three pairs of newlyweds.

"She may have seen a city," Trent said, accepting the chicken, "but I doubt very much that there was any evidence it was built by Cyclopes. Just how would that fact be demonstrated through its architecture?"

Merry cocked her head and laughed, acknowledging the point. "Half windows?"

She was seated opposite him, but Trent pulled her over to his side. "I suppose the houses might be on one level. I've heard that stairs can be difficult without both eyes."

"Homer is a better writer than Shakespeare," she said, snuggling against him. "Obviously he believed in Cyclopes, since he wrote about them."

"Yes, well, Shakespeare wrote about fairies dancing around in the woods," Trent said, offering her a lemon tart.

"No, thank you. I read somewhere that the Cyclopes built a magnificent civilization on an island off the coast of Greece. Oh! And they are credited with giving Zeus his thunderbolt."

"That proves my point, don't you think? They're products of someone's imagination. It's not as if the prime minister goes around handing out thunderbolts." He pulled her a little tighter. "You look sleepy."

"I will admit that the last two nights were wretched," Merry admitted. She gave him a mock scowl. "No thanks to you, allowing me to believe that I was about to become Lady Cedric."

Even hearing that made Trent's blood run cold. He moved along the seat until his back was to the corner, and pulled her into his lap. With his free arm, he felt under the seat and drew out a blanket, which he shook over her.

"This is so soft," Merry said drowsily. "We don't have cashmere in Boston. Do you know where cashmere comes from?"

She felt, rather than heard, his chuckle. "Tell me later," he whispered.

"I think I'll take a nap, if you don't mind." Her head was leaning on Trent's chest, and her hand had come to rest lightly on his stomach.

He was wearing a waistcoat, and a shirt beneath that, but all the same . . . Merry surreptitiously spread her fingers. His skin was so warm that she could feel it through the layers. She felt safe for the first time since Cedric had threatened her at the Vereker ball.

"Do you wish to loosen your corset?" he said, his voice low. "I could assist."

She opened an eye and peered up at him. "What do you know of corsets?"

"Enough." Trent's eyes had a hungry gleam.

"Humph," Merry said, slumping back against his shoulder. "I am perfectly comfortable, thank you. I never wear a corset while traveling."

He made a strangled noise, but her eyes were already closing. It seemed only a few minutes before she heard, "Merry," and then, louder, "*Merry*."

"Yes?" she asked groggily.

"Time to wake up."

"I'd rather not," she said, from the depths of a dream. "Thank you very much, though."

Trent's laugh woke her.

Merry pushed herself upright. Outside the windows, the sky was black, but flickering torches threw an unsteady light around the carriage. They had arrived.

Trent climbed out. When she appeared in the door after him, he effortlessly plucked her from the carriage.

"You seem to be sweeping me off my feet frequently," she said, her eyes searching his.

"I like holding you." His arms tightened. "My American duchess," he whispered, his breath warming her forehead. He set her down, but he kept her hand in his.

When Merry looked around her, she saw that the carriage had drawn into a large courtyard. Torches were bolted to the walls at regular intervals, but even so, she couldn't make out much more than stone walls, rising into the darkness.

A dignified man advanced out of the murk and was introduced as Oswald, the Hawksmede butler.

"The groom you sent ahead noted that the market fair would likely slow down your journey," Oswald said, after greetings had been exchanged.

"Yes, we've been some five hours on the road," Trent replied. "If you would make the duchess's maid and her dogs comfortable, Oswald, I shall take my wife indoors."

Merry was squinting to see if there were possibly turrets—she hoped so, because she dearly loved the idea of a haunted turret—when Trent turned back to her, flashed a naughty grin, and picked her up in his arms.

Merry gasped and lost her grip on her reticule and net bag, which fell to the flagstones with a soft thud.

Trent paid no attention, striding on toward the lighted door to the house.

"This is very romantic of you," she said, after an awkward moment.

"It is expedient. You slept on the journey, but I spent hours trying to think of anything other than your lack of a corset. And frankly, if the household thinks I'm in love, it affirms the idea that I stole you from my brother due to passion."

Before Merry could reply, he was walking in the door. In the entry, footmen stood ready to receive directions, but she scarcely saw them because Trent went straight for the stairs, carrying her up two at a time without apparent effort.

Top of the stairs, to the left, through a pair of magnificent doors attended by another footman, who closed the doors behind them with a quiet click of the latch.

Her new husband tipped her onto the bed and leaned over her, so close that she could see the curl of his sooty lashes. They were long—as long as hers, probably.

She had judged Cedric handsome, but Trent had a raw masculine beauty that put his brother's prettiness to shame. Together with the gleam in his eyes, he was pure, wanton temptation. His eyes slid over her body as if he were starving and she a banquet, lingered on the curves of her breasts, on the swell of her hips.

"Hello, Jack?" she asked, unable to stop herself from smiling. "I'm up here."

It took a moment for his gaze to return to hers. Without answering, he bent his head and his tongue plunged into her mouth. He kissed her just long enough to make desire riot through her bloodstream, before he lowered his body onto hers.

Chapter Twenty-Four

Trent had always chosen mistresses for their beauty and intelligence; none, though, held a candle to Merry. His wife's face and figure made him feel more savage than nobleman. He would like to throw her over his shoulder, take her off to a cave, and lick her from head to foot. Especially now, when her cheeks were flushed and her lips swollen from his kisses.

The women he'd bedded to this point had been skilled courtesans. In turn, he considered himself a punctilious lover, satisfying them once or twice before he allowed himself to come, always sheathed in a condom to prevent a child born out of wedlock.

This time he didn't have to slip on a wrinkled French letter, let alone tie it so tightly that it left a red mark for hours after.

What's more, he liked his wife. Who would have thought *that* would make such a difference?

"We shall consummate this marriage," he said, "and then we shall stay married for sixty or seventy years." He kissed the tip of her nose. "I do want to make one thing clear. Had you been engaged to anyone other than Cedric, I would have stolen you from your fiancé the first night we met. You have been mine since the moment we met on the balcony."

Merry pressed a kiss on his lips. "Then you are mine by fiat," she told him, and a sweet smile echoed in her eyes. "I claim you."

The thick length of his cock was pressed against her leg and he was harder than he'd ever been. Another look at her rosy lips and smiling eyes, and the ache in his groin deepened.

"What is that noise?" Merry asked, turning toward the sound.

"Footmen are filling the tub in the bathing chamber, through that door." Her maid must have assumed that she would want to wash off the dust of their journey. He wanted to make love to her just as she was, with the perfume that was Merry after sleeping. The most erotic scent in the world.

But she was a lady and a virgin. She was looking back at him now, desire in her eyes, but a wary shyness as well.

Trent washed quickly in a wooden bath brought to his room. It was novel—and delightful—to hear light voices of women filtering through from the bathing chamber next door. When Merry laughed, it sounded like music.

An hour later, the sounds from the other side of the door had finally ceased. He decided that sufficient time had passed that he might pay a visit to his wife's bedchamber. He tied his dressing gown tightly, knocked twice, and strode through the connecting door.

Merry was curled on her side on top of a snowy sheet, her inky hair spread across the pillows. He warned himself for the tenth time that he had to be slow and disciplined. This wild urgency he felt had to be kept in check.

"Good evening," she said, as he walked toward her.

Through the frail stuff of her gown, he could see the dark rose of her nipples, the shadow that embraced the curve of her breast, another tantalizing shadow between her legs.

"God," he said, the sound coming from his throat like a tortured whisper. "You're exquisite."

Her smile deepened.

"I would like to remove my dressing gown, but if you'd prefer, I could do so beneath the sheets."

"What are you wearing under it, Your Grace?"

"Nothing."

He saw her throat ripple as she swallowed. "You said that we are to be married sixty years. I suppose I'll grow accustomed to the look of your knees." She looked adorably shy but willing.

"Not just knees," he said, casting aside his dressing gown. His wife looked him over slowly. It was hard to tell what she was thinking. His body was unlike most gentlemen's, and certainly unlike Cedric's, not that he believed she'd ever seen a man naked.

Still, he didn't resemble the sleek Greek statues one saw in museums. He liked to take vigorous exercise, spending entire days on horseback riding around one or another of his estates. His thighs were muscled . . . hell, there was nothing sleek on his body.

He was all lumps and knobs of muscle, with a few scars

to boot: a white one across his right leg, a darker scar on his abdomen where he had tripped on a scythe as a boy.

Lust was pumping through his veins with a rough rhythm that told him that his control was gone, torn away during the journey in which Merry had slept. He had stroked her cheek, her hair, and the curve of her hip while she dreamed peacefully against his shoulder.

Now he followed her gaze down to where his thick, heavy cock strained toward her. "You're all dash-fire," she breathed.

Trent didn't have the faintest idea what she meant, but he understood the wanton desire in her voice, particularly when the edge of her tongue peeked out between pink lips.

He took a step toward the bed but before he could join her, Merry sat up and began pulling up her nightgown. Her generous breasts moved, swaying gently, and he froze in place.

She wiggled until she could free her gown from under her bottom. Then, in one sudden gesture, she drew it over her head. Her face turned pink, but she remained still.

Something primal rose in his gut as he saw her naked for the first time; suddenly Trent understood the sly language of a lady's skirts.

Merry let out a shaky giggle. "You look as if you've never seen a woman's knees—or the rest of her—before."

"I've never seen my wife's knees—or the rest of her—before," Trent said hoarsely, finally moving onto the bed. His weight settled onto her with a feeling of rightness that spread through his veins like wildfire.

Merry gasped, then curled her arms around his neck and gave him her intrepid American grin, the unreserved expression he'd never seen in an English ballroom.

"Aunt Bess told me that bedtime is when married couples frolic," she whispered against his lips.

First they should discuss the act in a restrained, gentlemanly fashion. Right. He cleared his throat and moved so that he lay on his side next to her. "Do you understand what we're about to do together?" His voice came out like a growl, but Merry didn't flinch.

She turned on her side as well and smiled again, surprising him. Hell, she would probably always surprise him, no matter how long they lived.

"I do. Not that Aunt Bess was a font of information other than her explanation of"—she waved her hand—"the essentials. Did you know that ducks can only copulate in running water?"

When she was nervous, Merry dropped facts like an oak did acorns. "Don't worry," he said, putting his hand on her hip and just letting it rest without moving. "The first time may not be wonderful, from what I've heard. But it will improve."

Her eyes drifted down his body like a caress, even though there was nothing soft about him, nothing refined or gentlemanly. He was all muscles and tendons, corded power. Cedric's distaste for his "burly" chest popped in Trent's head.

Merry seemed unintimidated by his size and power. Her eyes were fascinated, small teeth biting her lower lip and turning it crimson.

There was something vivid and present in her, perhaps owing to her origins or perhaps just to her fearless person.

The thought made him grin and he moved closer so he could kiss her mouth. Even that brush with her silky lips shot molten fire down his limbs.

He ran a hand over her belly. She shivered at his touch, and he bent to taste her, running his lips along the curve of her breast. "You have glorious breasts," he muttered.

"My governess, Miss Fairfax, said that I glittered like a cheap trinket. She thought they were much too large."

"Miss Fairfax is an idiot," Trent said thickly. He'd reached a rosy tip, leaving him no choice but to lick it.

Merry gasped and rolled on her back. She made an achy little sound in the back of her throat, so he licked her again.

"Do you like that?" Trent managed, reasonably coherently.

Merry moaned by way of reply, which made him, impossibly, even harder. He lifted his head to inquire just what information her aunt had managed to pass on, but a hand wound into his hair and held him in place.

After that, Trent gave in to a primitive self, and couldn't seem to shape words. Or maybe words just didn't matter. He suckled her, listening to Merry's breathing catch and quicken.

It wasn't until the fingers caressing his chest began to slide south that he caught her hand and pinned it above her head.

"You can't touch me," he said hoarsely. "The frolicking will be over before it starts."

Merry nodded, her eyes trusting, no understanding of how provocative he found her submission. He was the first to touch her . . . everywhere.

The first to kiss her breast. Her stomach. A bit lower. Her eyes widened, but she didn't move. In fact, when his cock jerked against her leg, a shiver went straight through her body.

Mine, he thought, feeling drunk with heady pleasure, with the impulse to claim his woman—so much so that a warning chimed in his mind again. He wasn't a primitive, after all. It was essential that he made the bedchamber—the frolicking—pleasurable for his bride.

Merry lay beneath him, her skin like milk and honey. Everything about her pleased him, every hollow and curve, tint and texture. It took every ounce of self-control he possessed not to fall on her, spread those creamy legs wider, and bury himself in her softness.

Letting go of her hand, he kissed his way down her stomach and a little lower.

"Jack!" she cried, as he nuzzled a curl at the top of her legs. "Jack, what in tarnation do you think you're doing down there? That sort of thing is not proper. I'm *certain* of it!"

"Improprieties are proper within marriage," he told her, stroking his tongue over a sweet bit of pink flesh. Merry had been tugging at his hair, but she froze.

So he licked that soft spot again. She smelled like flowers and pleasure and sin all at once.

His wife squealed, and the sound of it was so enchanting, so innocent and yet so pleasured, that some part of his heart that had frozen years ago melted a bit.

"Do you like this, Duchess?" he whispered a moment later. Merry's legs were twisting under him, and her hands, still clenched in his hair, were holding him in place rather than pushing him away.

"Don't you dare stop," she whispered. He blew gently against her honey pot and she let out a ragged moan.

"I still think this—" she began breathlessly, but Trent didn't want her to think about proprieties or anything else. His finger breached her most intimate, most private spot and Merry made a desperate sound in the back of her throat. His balls tightened to the point of pain.

Damn it, he couldn't possibly lose control now, could he?

His body answered that question. He would spend like a mere boy at the first sight of a woman if he didn't regain control.

Merry's eyes opened.

"You're soft and rosy, and everything I'm not," Trent said.

He moved up, just enough so that he could suckle her breast again, at the same time he slid his hand down past a silky tuft of hair. A gasp broke from Merry's lips as he thrust a broad finger inside.

Slowly he caressed her in little coaxing circles, watching as her white teeth bit down on her lip, as she made little panting noises in the back of her throat, as her hips began moving irresistibly, her hands tightening on his forearms.

"Jack," she whispered.

His tool had never been harder in his life, but he waited until she broke, crying out, her fingernails digging into his skin with the strength of the waves of pleasure that jerked her body against his. He swallowed her cries like a starving man, half his body lying heavy on hers so he could feel every pulse and shudder.

As her helpless trembling quieted, Trent didn't stir a finger, waiting so she could enjoy the last quiver of pleasure. Her skin was damp and curls clung to her forehead. Her legs were flung apart in abandon, her hair spread across the pillow, her closed eyelashes dark against the high flush in her cheeks.

He had never had anything that was truly his. Cedric had battled him for the house, for the estate, for his parents' love. By the time his mother and father died, he hadn't much more of a relationship with them than he had with the butler—in fact, it could be argued that he and Oswald had a better relationship.

But Merry was *his*. In a queer way, he was even glad that she hadn't known who she was marrying.

She was with him now, in this bed, because she wanted to be, not because she wanted to be a duchess. If she hadn't wanted him, she would have taken passage to Boston in a rage.

That was one thing he knew about Merry: she didn't lie. Her cries of pleasure were as real as the scolding she gave him in the carriage.

It took her long moments to open her eyes, but she was his bride, his virgin bride, and he refused to ruin her experience by leaping onto her. Into her.

When at last her eyelashes fluttered open, she peered at him and said, "Unless Aunt Bess is much mistaken, the evening is not supposed to end there."

A smothered bark of a laugh burst from his throat.

"When I first met you, I thought you looked like a man who hadn't laughed in years."

He slid one of his legs between hers, nuzzling her neck, drinking in the faint perfume of flowers that clung to her skin. "I hadn't."

"You've laughed three times tonight," she said with satisfaction.

He couldn't help himself: his hand went back between her legs and a rough moan caught in his throat, because she was drenched and ready for him.

"It's my turn," Merry whispered, giving him a gentle push. "You told me not to touch you, but that's not fair. I want to, and you'll simply have to put up with it."

Trent had never felt anything like his urge to be deep inside his wife. Somehow the idea that he was the first was making him crazed, possessed. But he forced himself to lie back and allow Merry to drop kisses on his chest.

Her fingers were velvet caressing him, more enticing than if the most celebrated courtesan in the world had him in her grasp. Merry touched his nipple, and a shiver went through him, as if a stone had struck a lake.

He watched as she traced the muscles that laced his chest, leading to a stomach carved by hard physical work, the sort no duke ought to do. The kind he had always done, in an effort to separate himself from his mother's perfumed boudoir and his father's brandy-soaked nights.

"This will sound foolish," Merry said, raising her head. She was heavy-lidded, the unmistakable look of a woman who'd been pleasured. "I love the way you look. It's manly."

"American?" he suggested, mouth quirking up.

"Nationality has nothing to do with it," she murmured. She had kissed her way down to proximity with his cock and was staring at it with fascination.

"Touch me," he said, managing, barely, to keep a pleading note from his voice.

She wrapped her hand around him, causing an explosion of searing heat that made his back arch instinctively and his lips draw back in a hoarse snarl. Any lady he knew would have squealed and dropped him, frightened by his rough response.

Not Merry.

Instead, her hand tightened and slid. Trent's mind went blank and he only dimly heard his own hungry groans.

He kept his eyes open, though, so he could see her watching as her small hand slid tightly up and down. She licked her lips, and that was it.

He lost all control.

He surged up and flipped her over so the hard length of his cock met her softness.

"I want—" He gasped, and tried to collect himself. He was never like this, never.

But Merry's hands wound into his hair. She tugged his face to hers and licked his bottom lip. It was so tantalizing that he leaned down to nip her in reply.

"Jack," she whispered, "I want you."

He growled something, fighting to keep himself in check. Braced above her, he let his head hang, closing his eyes so that he couldn't see her. But it didn't help because his other senses just flared more keenly, and his muscles quivered, dangerously close to thrusting into her.

"This part is going to hurt, Merry," he managed. "Or so they say."

She shocked him again by arching up and whispering against his mouth, "I *want* you, Jack." And then she tilted her hips, rubbing against him.

With one last breath of sanity, he moved backward, pulled open her legs, and looked at her pretty folds. He lapped her like a cat, holding her down as she twisted against his hand, shrieking.

She was loud, his American wife. The thought came dimly because he concentrated on giving pleasure, learning which touches she loved until she burst into flames in his hands and came again.

Enough. He cut the fragile threads of his self-control.

He reared over his wife and slowly pushed the plump head of his cock inside her.

Merry's fingers tightened on his shoulders, her eyes grew wide, and she whispered something he couldn't hear.

She was so tight that he instantly broke out in a sweat. He'd never felt anything like it. He was thrusting into molten honey. He started shaking. How could this not be painful for her? Her eyes were closed and she looked puzzled, not in pain.

He took a deep, rasping breath. "Does it hurt?" he whispered.

Merry opened her eyes and shook her head. "No, but it's very odd."

"You feel so good," he said in a voice that rumbled in his chest. "I wish I could stay like this forever. Never move." He meant it, too. Though at the same moment, he thrust forward again.

Merry took a deep breath and wiggled under him, forcing another groan from his lips. Then she tilted her hips and curled her legs around his waist. The tight grip of her body relaxed and let him in.

Just like that, the blazing ache in his loins went to his head. Pleasure made him mindless, nothing more than a body, sweat beading on his chest in the effort not to plunge into her.

Yet he dimly recognized the sharp bite of her fingernails in his shoulders, her husky moan. He dragged his mouth down the clean line of her jaw, pulled back and waited a second, just enough so that her eyes drifted open again.

There was nothing more delicious in the world than the look in Merry's eyes. Dazed, longing. "Jack," she whispered.

Jack was the new him, the him that finally had someone of his own, someone to cherish and to protect and to make happy. Trent felt a strange sensation all over his body, a trembling intense kind of heat that licked his skin and made him feel raw with . . . something.

"All right?" he whispered.

"Mmmmm."

He began to move, steady and slow. Words came out of his throat without conscious thought, rough, harsh words that grunted as he thrust. Merry couldn't be feeling too much pain, because her eyes were half shut, sloe-eyes, pleasured eyes, and she was clinging to him with her arms and legs.

She was giving permission.

Finally Trent really did let go—or was it Jack who let go? He went a bit mad, his body surrounding Merry, hers surrounding him, warm, fragrant Merry who was his wife to have and to hold, to *know*, as the Bible said.

She started meeting his thrusts, awkwardly at first, forcing him even deeper inside with every stroke. He could feel a storm gathering in his loins. Her hands were curled around his forearms, so tightly he felt the prick of her nails again.

He clenched his teeth, not willing to let go of the delirious pleasure of it, thrusting short and deep, watching a fever spread over her damp, creamy skin. He suckled her breast, tasting salty sweet Merry-sweat, loving the way she twisted under him.

He was covered with sweat, chest heaving, hips pounding into the woman who clung to him, panting, kissing him with pillowy sensual lips.

Freezing when her body finally clenched around his cock, setting him free.

Trent let his head fall forward, and with a rasping groan, he emptied himself into her. Again, and again.

His, and his again.

His only, his first, his last.

Something had broken inside him. Or dissolved. Something hard and cold. He finished . . . but he hadn't softened. Instead of withdrawing, he watched a drop of sweat run down Merry's temple and disappear into her lavish hair.

"Was it painful?" he asked. "Should I withdraw?"

Merry's eyes blinked, then opened, met his. Indigo blue. He catalogued that: gray when she was angry, the violet-blue of sea-water when the sun clouds over when she was satisfied.

No, not just satisfied: happy.

The look in her eyes went straight to the base of his spine and he nudged forward. He was still with her, in her.

"No," she said, gleeful. "That is, it was uncomfortable for a minute, but then it was more than comfortable, if you know what I mean." She wiggled her hips, and he felt it in the soles of his feet. Another groan broke from his throat.

He pushed back toward her in a silent question, watched as she cocked her head to the side and smiled. Then she bent her knees and nudged back up at him, an invitation, a challenge.

"Are you certain you can take me again?" He thrust, a voluptuous slide that sent fire through his body. "We should wait, a day or two. A week."

He didn't mean it. He'd go mad not touching her for a week. But he was a gentleman; if she was sore, he wouldn't go near her.

She matched his thrust, still awkwardly, but she did. "It stings, but it feels good at the same time. Especially when you do *that*."

Heat spread through Trent's limbs as if he'd taken a gulp of peppered brandy. "This?" He thrust, loving the way Merry's mouth fell open as he struck home, eyes dazed, fingers curled into a fist before her hips rose a little and she pushed back.

The sound that came from her lips was so desirous, so sensual that Trent lost his head completely. Again.

He started all over, as if the last hour hadn't happened, his balls as tight as if he hadn't given her everything—in fact, he must not have, because already he could feel coal-heat at the back of his knees and his groin. She made another sound and bit his neck. Bit. His. Neck.

Trent felt his face contort and he lost himself, thrusting into her over and over, so fast and low that she gasped every time he slammed home, her head tossing, her hands looking pale against his skin, slipping over his body.

"You're—" he said finally, growling the word.

She opened her eyes, pleasure-drenched. "Jack."

She was clinging to him and then he realized with a jolt that tears were slipping down her cheeks.

He instantly stopped and whispered, "Tell me you're not crying because you're in pain."

"It doesn't hurt," she whispered back. "It doesn't hurt. I never imagined this."

God, but she had the most beautiful eyes he'd ever seen: eyes he could look at every minute of his life.

"This isn't what I expected," she said with a gasp, because even though she was talking, he couldn't stop himself from thrusting forward, slow and soft.

He dusted her lips with a kiss. "No?"

"No."

A moment's silence. She was getting the rhythm of the thing now, rising to meet him. He braced himself on one arm again, and thrust low, playing with her pink nipple, loving the peach color rising in her cheeks and the way her breath was coming short and choppy.

Then Merry suddenly said, "If you ever do this with a woman other than myself, I'll have to kill you, Jack."

"I will not," he said, keeping it simple. No need to tell her that he felt raw and new inside, as if he'd never bedded a woman before. He couldn't imagine ever having another woman in his bed. Not after this.

Her eyes searched his, and then she nodded. That warning heat at the base of his spine was turning to pure fire, so Trent hunkered down and threaded his shaking hands into Merry's curls, pulling her face to his and ravishing her mouth.

He couldn't have stopped if he tried. He concentrated on kissing her, hungry and wet. Their mouth melted together, each kiss fading into another, and all the time, he kept moving.

"*Jack!*"

Pleasure chased across Merry's face, her eyes shut tight, her heart beating so fast that he could see her pulse beating in her throat. She threw back her head with a cry and he felt her body go rigid.

Down below, her velvety softness suddenly gripped him so tightly that he let out a grunt, and he was lost, falling forward, one last thrust . . . madness. Mind gone. His stones pulled tight, a shout burst from his mouth, and he gave her everything.

Everything he had.

It was as if he'd struck his head, and opened his eyes to find that he was blind. Blind to everything but his body's shuddering ecstasy.

When he finally lifted his face from her hair, he discovered gratefully he was still braced on his elbows—at least he hadn't collapsed onto her like a water buffalo.

Would Merry have noticed that his mind had cracked? That he had bellowed like a madman?

What they had done together bore no relation to the purposeful, genial intercourse he'd shared with mistresses. His mind shied away from the memories. The women were in the past.

He withdrew carefully and slipped to the side, pulling her head onto his arm, willing her to open her eyes and say . . . something. Tell him that she wasn't disgusted by the sweat that had rolled off him onto her. By the way he'd grunted, and lost himself. By the way his breath still sawed in his chest.

She didn't say a word, and when he looked down, he discovered she was cuddled against his shoulder, fast asleep. Not so overcome that she couldn't find words . . .

Peacefully asleep, fingers spread across his chest. Her

hair was damp and as his heartbeat slowed, he heard the echo of her voice calling his name.

She woke as he gently washed her, but went straight back to sleep. And she didn't stir when he decided that her bed was too narrow for both of them, gathered her up, and carried her to his chamber.

That night Trent lay awake for hours, looking at the delicate filigree of Merry's hair, the strength of her jaw, the curve of her earlobe. The plump contour of her breast.

Around him, the world turned, but his internal world turned as well.

Everything shifted places.

He had cared for the dukedom because it was his duty. It was the birthright that he had won from his brother by rushing into the world. It was a prize—everyone told him it was a prize.

It had never felt like a prize. It felt that the thing that made his mother and his brother loathe him. Nothing was worth that.

Tracing swirls on his wife's smooth shoulder, he discovered that Merry now stood at the center of his world, and the dukedom to one side.

When he finally drifted off to sleep, the world was in a new order.

Chapter Twenty-Five

Merry woke the next morning feeling she'd forgotten something. She stretched, her mind hazy, body sore . . . body sore?

And she remembered. Jack. Trent. Husband. That . . . whatever that was called, what they did last night.

She turned her head . . .

Nothing but an expanse of linen sheet beside her. She was no longer in her own bed.

The ducal bedchamber was deeply masculine, with dark curtains tied to the four bedposts, heavy curtains at the windows, a crimson rug on the floor.

Then, with a thump of her heart, she saw, off to the side and one step up, an alcove, large enough to hold a desk and chair.

And Jack.

Merry sat up slowly, pulling the sheet to cover her

breasts. Her husband was seated in profile to her, intent on whatever he was writing, wearing nothing more than a pair of smalls. His shoulders shifted fluidly as he wrote, hardly stopping to dip his quill in ink.

Every once in a while he would pick up one of the sheets of foolscap, consult it, and return to his writing.

"Jack," she said softly.

He didn't turn. She'd never seen such concentration. He thrummed with life and determination.

When he didn't answer, she shifted to the edge of the bed and slid off, bringing the sheet with her. He raised his head only when she stepped up into the alcove, trailing the sheet like an echo of her wedding train.

Stared at her.

"I'm your duchess," Merry prompted, grinning at the confused look in his eyes. "Remember me?"

Trent surged from the chair and before she took another breath, she was off her feet and on her back on the bed.

"My goodness!" she squeaked.

"Have you any soreness?" he demanded.

"No," she breathed. It wasn't entirely true, but that didn't matter, not when her blood was suddenly heated and she felt empty with longing.

He bent his head and kissed her fiercely. "Nothing matters that came before this," he said a while later. "Do you hear me, Merry?"

"Yes," she gasped, arching her throat so that he could kiss her again.

"I'm going to take you now." His voice was dark and low but there was a question there.

"Please," she begged. Her breasts ached for his touch.

As if he knew her thought, one hand cupped her right breast and the other pushed her thighs apart.

"You're wet with my seed," he murmured in her ear.

His fingers slid between her folds, sending jolts of feeling through her body.

"I should bathe," Merry gasped, self-consciousness streaking through her.

"Later," her husband said, a casual command. The broad head of his cock breached her, and she went rigid.

Part of her wanted to pull away, to run to the other room. The other side ordered her to wrap her legs around him.

A cry involuntarily burst from her as he thrust into tender territory.

His lips nuzzled her ear. "I love the way you respond to me," he said.

Merry was responding, all right. Every inch of warmth in her body had fled and she was hanging on to him from pure instinct, her arms and legs tight. She had to tell him the truth. It hurt.

"Bloody hell," he groaned. "You're so hot and tight."

She buried her face in his shoulder. She opened her mouth to tell him, but his hand was on her breast, and somehow that pleasure outweighed the pain. Trent moved to kiss her, and without thinking, her spine arched so that he slipped deeper inside her.

"That's it," he said, reaching down with one hand and pulling her leg higher around his hip.

He pushed forward and there was something about that angle that changed everything.

The harsh sting drained away. Her hands slid down his back, rounding his arse and hanging on. She felt surrounded by him, his scent, his growl, the strength of his arms and legs.

"You're astonishing," Trent murmured in her ear. He began thrusting faster and it hurt and didn't. It burned and yet it was bliss. A shudder started somewhere deep in Merry's body.

A sob broke from her throat, an undignified sound, but his big hand landed on her hip, caressing it, hauling her a little higher so that he created yet another kind of pressure . . .

Heat shot down her spine. But at the same time, it hurt. Her mind veered one way and then the other.

His fingers tightened on her hips, so much that they might leave bruises, and somehow that tiny pain assuaged the soreness, allowing pleasure to flood in.

Her body flushed suddenly, from her cheeks down to her toes, and she cried, "Jack!" startled, shocked by the joy of it.

Her husband's chest heaved as a bellow ripped from his lips.

"Ow," Merry whispered to herself a moment later, too softly to be heard. When he withdrew, tears sprang to her eyes. It stung like the devil.

"What's the matter?" Trent whispered, his thumbs smoothing away the tears that had escaped down her cheeks.

"I'm a bit tender," she confessed.

He frowned at her. "You should have told me."

Merry felt that pink climbing her cheeks. "I didn't want you to stop." She wasn't certain how to meet his eyes. Even thinking of the noises she had made turned her face hot.

Trent seemed not to notice. He wrapped her in his arms, nuzzling her neck. "I'll ring for the bath to be filled, shall I?"

A moment later, she once again wrapped herself in the sheet and made her way stiffly toward her own room. Shortly thereafter Lucy appeared, and after her, footmen with buckets of steaming water.

An hour later, Merry felt much better. Lucy had discreetly poured salts into the bath water and she had soaked for a long time, thinking over the night. She was no longer the same person she had been the day before; everything was different.

Her aunt had maintained that intimate marital acts were pleasurable, and she had been right.

But marriage wasn't merely about bedding. Though the truth was that she'd like to walk back into the bedchamber and catch her husband in his bath, water sluicing off all those muscles . . .

Right there, sitting at her dressing table, she felt herself blush. Luckily Lucy didn't notice. Of course, she wasn't going to look for Trent in his bath, not that he would even be in his bath. Almost certainly, he was already working.

She would go downstairs and meet the household, and then she would begin to explore the gardens. Getting to know the grounds thoroughly would take days; in fact, the very idea of nineteen acres to work with made her smile.

Days? It would take years!

She stood with sudden resolution and informed Lucy that she wished to wear a pair of sturdy walking shoes under her yellow morning gown, not the silk slippers that Lucy had laid out.

Once dressed, she was on the verge of leaving her chamber when she heard the clicking of toenails and George scampered in from the corridor, promptly lost his grip on the floor, and slid into the wall with a thump.

She'd actually forgotten all about George last night. How could she? "Hello, sweetheart!" she cried, leaning down to pick him up. "Where's Snowdrop?"

"In the duke's study," Lucy replied. "His Grace called for a footman to take her away, but she scratched at the door until she was allowed back in."

"Oh no," Merry said, chortling with laughter. "I'm

afraid that the duke doesn't care for dogs, or at least, not for Snowdrop."

Downstairs, Merry bade Oswald a good morning and allowed the butler to escort her into the breakfast room. It took a few minutes, but she managed to pry from him that he'd served the dukes of Trent in one position or another his entire life.

"My husband is extraordinarily fortunate to have you," she said, finally. "And I am very grateful that you are here to ease my way into being a duchess." She smiled at him.

Oswald bowed. "It will be my pleasure, Your Grace." He hesitated. "Will you dine in the breakfast room daily, Your Grace? The former duchess took a light repast in bed in the morning."

"I don't care to eat in bed," Merry said, looking at the eggs, sausages, toast, and blood pudding laid out on the sideboard. "If you'd be so kind, Oswald, I would like some eggs, a tomato, one of those sausages, and a piece of cheese."

Then she seated herself, smiling her thanks when Oswald brought her a plate. "Mrs. Honeydukes is wondering if she might attend you after your meal," the butler said.

"With a good housekeeper," Aunt Bess had told Merry once, "one can survive even an act of God." And then, at Merry's inquiring look, "Oh, you know what I mean. Swarms of locusts. Rivers of blood . . . I can't remember the rest."

Oswald bowed and withdrew, leaving a young footman named Peter, who quickly overcame his reticence and began chattering about the local village, Aylesbury. He was describing the village baker—who wore a canary-yellow waistcoat and had ambitions to be an actor—when a scrape at the door interrupted him.

Peter abandoned his sentence mid-word and snapped against the wall as still as a statue. Mrs. Honeydukes entered the room silently. She was perhaps fifty, with an inherent severity wrought into the very bones of her face.

Merry came to her feet and walked around the table. "Good morning," she said, offering her hand.

The housekeeper looked doubtful, but took Merry's hand and shook it at the same moment that she bobbed a curtsy. "Good morning, Your Grace. I should like to offer the felicitations of the household."

"Thank you," Merry said. "I shall look forward to meeting everyone in the next few days, but in the meantime I would be grateful if you could extend my thanks. But for the moment, Mrs. Honeydukes, I presume you have many things to teach me about the house, and we shall spend a part of every day together. Won't you please have a seat?"

"That would not be my place, Your Grace," the housekeeper said, clearly shocked to her core.

Merry smiled and said, "Mrs. Honeydukes, do you know anything about me, besides the fact that I am the new Duchess of Trent?"

"No, I do not, madam."

"The most pertinent fact is that I am American."

As well as the mistress of the household.

A twenty-year-old duchess was still a duchess, Merry reminded herself.

Mrs. Honeydukes said, "I ascertained as much from your accent, madam."

"As a nation, we are a plain-speaking people. And unaccustomed to the kind of formality that one finds in an aristocratic English household."

Silence.

At length, the housekeeper said, "Ah." She sat.

By a couple of hours later, Merry felt that she had a good

sense of the household. Mrs. Honeydukes used words sparingly, "as if they were silver coins," Aunt Bess would say.

But she seemed to be doing an excellent job as housekeeper and as time went on, she would probably get used to sitting down in Merry's presence while they discussed the day ahead.

The cook, Mrs. Morresey, had also been with the household her entire life. Merry was beginning to see that English aristocrats had responsibilities more or less unknown in Boston: in short, they employed people whose relatives had been serving the family for generations.

"I'm not knowing how to make American food, Your Grace," Mrs. Morresey confessed. "I'm not even very good with French, if the truth be told."

"As long as you can make strong tea and hot crumpets, I'll be happy," Merry said. "I discovered crumpets when I came to England a couple of months ago, and I could eat them morning, noon, and night."

Mrs. Morresey beamed. "My crumpets are as light as the air itself."

After that, they sat down over a cup of tea and talked about important things, like how quickly the spices lost their freshness, and where in London to procure the best tea. Four crumpets and two pots of tea later, she and Mrs. Morresey were fast friends.

Once Peter had been recruited to ensure that George received regular outings and Oswald informed that no puppies were allowed in the drawing room, Merry felt all was well.

Which meant that she was finally free to explore the gardens.

Chapter Twenty-six

Soon after inheriting his title, Trent recognized that he needed a study large enough to manage the operations attached to the dukedom's several estates. His father had got around this problem by leaving his secretary to scamper after him, pleading for signatures.

For his part, Trent took over the library, designating one large table for the administration of Hawksmede, another for the London house and parliamentary matters, and a third for the smaller estates and miscellaneous business like the slate mine.

In the last seven years, he'd spent whole weeks in that room, working from morning to evening. Sometime back in the Stuart days, when the family was relatively new, the windows had been hung with green velvet curtains, embroidered around the hem with interlaced small tin medallions.

The morning after his wedding, Trent found himself examining the room with new eyes. The curtains were faded, and the tin medallions were dull. Many of them were missing. He went to a window and cautiously tugged to see whether the curtain would fall, but it held.

Other than Cedric, his relatives rarely acquired new clothing, let alone drapery and furnishings.

As he and his secretary, Brickle, attacked the stack of mail that had accrued since he'd last been in residence, Trent listened to the heavy silence in the house. He'd imagined it would be different once he had a wife, but he couldn't hear Merry anywhere.

By now she would be finished with her bath. He kept thinking about that, even as he signed contracts and read through a long letter describing a canal that might make a great deal of money for the duchy—or might not, he decided, putting it to the side.

That afternoon, he was going to find his wife and they would go to bed.

During the day.

As it happened, Trent had never cared to remain through the night after an assignation with one of his mistresses, and he had never invited any of them to his house. Thus he had never made love except in the evening, even though, like any man, he tended to think about it all day long.

It was all different now. He had a wife. Moreover, he had a wife who appeared to have a healthy appreciation for bedtime sport.

He repeatedly lost his concentration, thinking about her, until finally he could bear it no longer. It had to be close to the midday hour.

"What is the time, Brickle?" he asked.

"Nearly eleven o'clock, Your Grace."

He pushed back his chair. "Right. Time to stop for luncheon. No, let's stop for the day."

Brickle's mouth fell open, but Trent headed for the door before he could offer a reply.

Merry was nowhere to be found. He stalked through the dining room, looking around with a twinge of discontent. The walls were hung with paintings blurred by layers of varnish and candle smoke. A study of two dead pheasants might as easily depict a bunch of feathery flowers.

His wife came from a new country. He had a shrewd notion that Bess and Thaddeus Pelford lived in a large house whose rooms were whitewashed from floor to rafter, and austerely decorated with furnishings that were newly made, not handed down through generations.

If he hadn't found Merry, at some point he would have entered a ballroom and picked out someone not unlike Lady Caroline, but more tolerable. She would have come from a house just like this, where everything was old and nothing was pristine.

Hawksmede had forty-eight rooms and almost all of them had ceilings so high that they got lost in the gloom on a foggy evening. He turned to enter the drawing room. Looking with newly critical eyes, he noticed that the dark oak chairs lined up along two walls were tired and battered, like a regiment returning from a losing skirmish. Most of them probably dated to the reign of Henry VIII, so they had reason to look worn.

There were a couple of cabinets and three sideboards, lamp stands, and two fireplaces. There was a suit of armor, missing its right arm, leaning next to a genuine Egyptian mummy case, minus its occupant. The case was one of the most colorful things in the room, brightly painted with a depiction of its former occupant, a lady who'd apparently enjoyed lining her eyes with shoe blacking.

One of his uncles had brought it back from Alexandria with the mummy intact, but when they'd encountered a storm at sea the crew had tossed the body overboard with the justification that a female was a female, even if she'd been dead for some time. Millennia, one had to assume.

So the painted case had arrived empty, and had joined the suit of armor; they leaned together as if in cozy conversation.

He was appalled to see a stuffed crocodile poking out from under a table. When he was a child, it had been fixed to the wall, but he vaguely remembered that a rousing country dance held in the ballroom above had shaken it loose at some point.

The table that summed up the room held two brass pieces, cheek to jowl: an eagle with spread wings and a sphinx. The might of Empire had met the might of Egypt, and neither had triumphed.

Hawksmede was stuffed with things that his great-great-great-grandfather had bought, and his great-great-grandfather had used, and his great-grandfather had deplored, but kept using because the things were good quality and had been expensive, once.

Passed down along with a thirst for brandy.

He still had not found Merry, and the house was starting to feel like the moldering nest of an ancient bird that should have had the courtesy to die years ago. At last he located his butler, who reported that the duchess was out of doors.

"In the back gardens, as I understand, Your Grace," Oswald said.

He should have guessed that.

It was far better to be outside the house than inside, as the sun was shining and it smelled like mown grass. He strode into the gardens, skirting the old hedge-maze, though he couldn't help noticing that it was not only derelict but punctuated by gaps where yews had died.

Instead, he marched through the rose garden, discovering that the bushes had become overgrown and black with age and neglect.

Damn it, he should have paid better attention. He paid at least one gardener's wages; he was sure of it. But he couldn't remember walking behind the house once in the seven years he'd been the duke.

At the bottom of the rose garden sat a greenhouse, and it was inside that he finally found his wife. Merry was chatting with an old man—the gardener, he presumed—as she repotted a plant that he would have sworn was irretrievably dead.

She was wearing a long canvas apron and a pair of what looked like satin gloves. They extended past her elbows and were encrusted with dirt.

"Good morning," Trent said, as he entered.

The gardener turned so quickly that he stumbled, and Merry grabbed his arm to steady him.

"Yer Grace," he rasped, pulling his forelock.

"By God, it's Boothby, isn't it?" Trent said, recognizing the man's overly long upper lip. Back when he and Cedric were boys, Boothby had been one of the under-gardeners.

"That's right, Yer Grace."

"It's good to see you're still with us."

"Hello, darling," Merry said. She smiled at him as she pulled off her gloves and laid them on the wooden table.

Everything in Trent's world froze for a moment. No one had ever called him "darling."

"Duchess," he said, bowing. Because that was how he'd been taught.

Boothby cleared his throat and said, "I'll just be on my way, then, Yer Graces."

"Oh, do wait, Boothby," Merry said, untying her apron. "Trent, may I hire some more gardeners?" She looked at him with an expression of great earnestness. "Gardeners pay for themselves in no time, I assure you. Boothby tells me that there was once a kitchen garden so large that it not only supplied the house, but gave cabbages to the whole village."

"I had no idea," Trent said. "How many gardeners were there in my grandfather's day, Boothby?"

"Fifteen in all, Yer Grace," the man said, from the door. "Now there's only meself, and I'm getting on. Yer father let all the rest go."

Not surprising. The late duke had been too busy drinking his way through the cellars to bother with cabbages.

"In that case, we need around fourteen more gardeners," Trent said, crossing the room toward Merry while thinking that he'd like to kiss her. But, of course, that would be unseemly.

It seemed his wife was unaware of that rule—or didn't care. To his enormous pleasure, she came up on her toes and kissed him. Right there, in front of the gardener.

Trent cleared his throat. "Do you know some good men we might take on?" he said, turning to Boothby.

"Aye, that I do." The gardener was grinning.

"I *am* American," Merry told Boothby impishly. Clearly, they had already become the best of friends.

She turned back to Trent. "I plan to extensively redesign the gardens and grounds, unless you have an objection?"

"Of course not. They are your domain, Duchess, to do with as you please."

"We can do it slowly so that the expense is spread over years."

"There's no need for that." Clearly, Trent would have to have a conversation with his wife about finances. "Boothby, I'd be grateful if you could find Oswald and inform him of your needs. Mention any names that you have in mind."

Boothby touched his forelock again, gave the duchess a familiar grin that would have made Trent's mother terminate his employment on the spot, and took his leave.

"Where is George?" Trent asked, looking around.

Merry bent down and peered under one of the potting tables. "Asleep."

Sure enough, the puppy was curled up on a dusty sack.

"He's going to need washing again," she said, straightening up. "Boothby said that he is definitely part ratter because he exhausted himself trying to unearth the occupant from a hole."

In Trent's opinion, George had a motley appearance that might include any number of breeds. He moved to the door and closed it tightly. He was quite certain that no one could see in; the greenhouse was so old that it was glazed with thick, semi-opaque crown glass. It had never been transparent, but the accumulated grime of many years had obscured everything but the strongest sunshine.

He removed his coat and tossed it on the table next to Merry's gloves. Then he picked her up and placed her curvy bottom on it.

"Where is Snowdrop?" she asked him, her dimple showing.

"Resting from her labors. This morning she managed to chew the hem off one of the green curtains in my study."

"For such a small dog, she is extraordinarily aggressive," Merry said. "I rather admire the way she makes up for her size."

Trent didn't want to talk about Snowdrop. His wife looked like a flower sitting there, prim and straight-backed, pretty ankles peeking from the hem of her skirt. He placed his hands on her knees and slowly pulled them apart, watching her face for signs of protest.

Instead, the color in Merry's cheeks deepened, and

small, even teeth bit into her bottom lip, which sent such a flare of heat through him that he almost groaned.

Thank God, her dress wasn't one of those narrow ones that hobbled a woman around the ankles; it was full enough that he could step between her legs, close to the heart of her.

When he bent his head, her mouth opened instantly, and her hands stroked into his hair. They kissed as if they had been kissing for years, his hands moving down to grip her hips.

Merry took a shuddering gasp, air shared with him because he hadn't let her mouth go. But he supposed she had to breathe, so he licked his way from her lips to the line of her jaw, to the slender column of her neck.

She let her head fall back and a little murmur escaped her lips, something between a prayer and a song.

"I want you again," he growled into her ear before kissing her.

A long time later, he pulled away. His wife's eyes were heavy, her mouth deep red, bruised from his kisses. She looked like a courtesan in a naughty French painting, a woman sated, yet still shimmering with desire.

"I would like to carry you back to our bedchamber," he said, his voice deepening as he spoke.

He saw her throat move as she swallowed and whispered something so softly he couldn't make it out. He lowered his head again and ran his lips along the pale skin of her forehead.

"All right," Merry said, clearing her throat with a little cough that made his heart jerk because it was abashed and lustful, all at once. More color spilled into her cheeks.

He shook his head. "We can't. You need time to heal." His mouth drifted over her cheekbones. Was there ever a woman so beautiful?

No wonder Adam followed Eve, and Abélard followed Héloïse, and all those other foolish men followed their women through the ages. The turn of a woman's lip had them on their knees.

"It isn't unbearable," Merry said, looking bashful but desirous. "Isn't it peculiar to think that we are husband and wife?"

Trent had no interest in discussing the philosophical implications of their unexpected marriage. "I have an idea," he said casually, and began pulling up her skirts.

Instantly Merry's hand caught his wrist. "We're surrounded by glass, Trent!"

"Jack," he corrected.

"In private, you said," she flashed back. "This is hardly private!"

"Surely you noticed that no one can see through these old panes?"

"Of course I have. I'm afraid that we'll have to build a new greenhouse at some point, but not until I find the perfect location. This is a bit far from the house."

"As I approached," Trent said, "the only reason I knew someone was inside was that I saw motion."

"And what if someone sees motion?"

"We have no gardeners yet, and Boothby is no fool. He won't come back for hours."

She stopped protesting, because Trent had one hand under her skirts and his fingers were caressing private places. Plump, sensuous flesh.

His wife's hands clenched his forearms and her eyes turned smoky. Her mouth eased open, but no sound emerged.

Trent leaned closer and dusted a kiss on her right cheekbone, and one on each eye, and then on her sweet, pouting mouth.

A pleading sound came from the back of Merry's throat.

"Do you like this?" he asked. There was something about her desirous murmur that reached into his chest and squeezed his heart: his funny, articulate wife, caught in an emotion, an experience, that she couldn't explain.

Lost in desire—for him.

"You are mine," he whispered, as one finger slipped through silky sweet, wet flesh in a way that made her visibly tremble and her hands clench even harder.

"You must stop, Jack. We can't do this here." Her voice was thin, airy.

Merry's body had taken possession of the space where her brain used to be: the world narrowed to Trent's smiling eyes and the way he was stroking her with his callused fingers. "I really can't," she whispered, falling forward and burying her face against his chest. "We mustn't."

This raw emotion, fire under the skin, surprise and desperation—no one had talked of this. Aunt Bess had never said that she might find herself in a greenhouse with her skirts pulled up and her legs disgracefully apart, air cooling her skin, unable to pull away.

Frolicking had nothing to do with a feeling so powerful that she kept shuddering closer to her husband, heart thudding in her chest as if she'd run a furlong at top speed.

With her face buried in his waistcoat, she could smell Trent, coffee and starched linen, a whiff of horse and male sweat, a touch of his skin and soap.

He was bent over her now, one arm curving around her back, his cheek resting on her hair. He provided the walls that she needed as he pushed a second, broad finger into her, past swollen flesh that should have been tender but somehow wasn't.

He held her in the privacy of his arms, shielding her and trapping her at once, making what the two of them did—what they were doing—into a strictly private matter, not for the open air and green lawns that stretched in all directions.

An orgasm slammed into her, making her cry out and shudder from head to foot, coming in a storm of craving and heat.

"I have you, Merry," Trent said, voice dark and reassuring. "I have you."

She hardly heard him, drunk with pure physical pleasure, clinging to him, her mind fixed on the last shaking streaks of pleasure she felt. His fingers slid in liquid heat and he growled her name.

She answered with a sound, not a word, not even a syllable. Just a note, like a bird in its nest.

"Again," he commanded, and his hand moved, his palm rubbing a voluptuous caress to her most sensitive part, fingers sliding easily now, hard and slow and utterly controlling.

"I couldn't," she cried, but the honey mead on his fingers changed everything. She gasped and shook her head, but he was relentless, his fingers owning her body.

"You can." His voice was like steel wrapped in velvet. He wrapped his free hand in her curls and tugged gently so that her head tipped back and he could kiss her again.

Merry lost sight of everything, everything but the aching, empty feeling that had her rocking against his hand, her breath choppy, her tongue desperately mating with his.

She was dimly aware that he was tearing open his breeches with his left hand. They were about to make love in a greenhouse, where anyone might walk in. But she didn't care. She just pulled him closer, moving her legs apart like a wanton.

"Do you want me?" he said, his voice raw.

All she could do was groan because of the clever press of his fingers. Blood rushed through her body, making her head reel as if she'd started to move in circles, faster and faster until she was spinning like a drunken top, legs wide, cries swallowed by his mouth, her body jerking, shaking, taut.

In the middle of that storm his hands came around her hips and he thrust forward. Instinctively Merry curled her legs around his hips and pulled him closer. She was so wet that he came into her in one smooth stroke.

It was like the stroke of a hammer, breaking and reshaping her, body and soul. "Jack!" she cried, hands touching him, caressing him, wherever she could, mouth seeking his. "Jack," she whimpered against his lips because he was rocking into her, thrusting so hard that the table was groaning under her. No pain, just fullness, wild fullness where before there had been emptiness.

Pleasure burned through her in waves, not so much leaving, as settling into her bones like the echoes of a lingering joy. Trent had his hands braced on the table at her sides, his hips grinding into the cradle of her legs. His face had taken on a ferocious severity, a beauty focused on one point.

His eyes were so beautiful, thickly lashed, intelligent, the gaze of a man in his prime. But she thought she saw something else there, too: a recognition of *her*, Merry, with all her weaknesses and strengths, all the confidence she had, and the frailties she hated.

"Merry," he said, his voice deep as a well. "My wife."

She was wrong about the echoes of joy: in fact, those twinges were the harbingers of new pleasure. They caught fire at the look in his eyes and the slow, pounding motion of his hips, and even the sobbing breath in her own throat.

Her fingers curled into him like claws. He groaned and slammed into her once more, pushing her into some other place where there were no gentlemen and ladies, no countries, no polite society, just Merry and Jack and an old wooden table.

She closed her arms and legs around him, and came in pulses that took away his control just as he had taken hers.

As he came, he jerked forward with a low cry that came from clenched teeth, his face buried in the curve of her neck and shoulder as his body shuddered again and again.

And again.

Chapter Twenty-seven

Merry decided that while she was very fond of the greenhouse, she wasn't as appreciative of what followed lovemaking in what may as well have been the outdoors.

Trent was no comfort when she pointed out that one of her sleeves had ripped.

"It probably happened when you were pulling at me like a woman possessed." He'd buttoned up the placket on his breeches, run a hand through his hair, and dropped onto an old wooden chair. He now looked precisely the same as when he'd entered the greenhouse, if decidedly more satisfied.

Whereas there was an unladylike gloss of perspiration on Merry's brow, her hair had come loose from its pins, and of course her dress was torn.

"Come sit with me," Trent said coaxingly. He shifted his

weight. "On second thought, better not. This chair won't survive it."

She shook her head and went back to looking for hairpins. Her hair was so thick that she knew from long experience that two pins—all she could find—would never hold it in place.

"I like your hair down," her rascally husband said.

Merry pounced on a pin. Three would have to do.

"I adore your breasts in that dress." His voice was deep and worshipful.

"Don't even think about it," she told him. "How I will ever face Lucy without fainting from pure humiliation, I don't know."

"You never faint."

"Well, spit!" she cried.

"What?"

"There's—" She stopped. They had been intimate, but this was private.

He got up, came over, and kissed her ear. "What?"

"Something wet," she muttered. Turning her back to him, she used her chemise to dry her leg.

Trent wound his arms around her from behind before she realized what was happening. Then he said, in her ear, "I love the way you smell. But I love the way you smell even more now because I can smell myself on you."

"Oh, ugh!" Merry cried, wiggling. "I shall run all the way back to the house and take a bath."

They left the greenhouse on a bellow of ducal laughter, and walked around the house, following an uneven brick path. George ran ahead of them, occasionally crouching and pouncing at something only he could see.

"I had no idea that the gardens had been allowed to deteriorate into such a wilderness," Trent apologized.

"I shall enjoy restoring them. Do you see that section

over there?" Merry waved toward a stone wall overgrown with vines and lined by gnarled rose trees. A semicircular recess in the wall held the remains of a moss-covered stone bench, which had cracked into two pieces and fallen over, though flower urns on either side remained upright.

"Those rose trees aren't dead," she said, beaming. "Mr. Boothby and I went about with a penknife, and he proved to me there's life there still. The strongest roses have actually thrived on neglect."

Trent asked the obvious question. "They look half dead to me. Why not plant new ones?"

She tugged him off the path and led him to a great tangle of branches hanging over the wall. She pointed to a fresh green patch where Boothby had scraped away the bark.

"Come summer, this will be a fountain of roses," she told him. "My uncle's head gardener, in particular, had very fixed notions and wouldn't listen to me half the time."

"Whereas Boothby is well under your thumb," Trent said, yielding to impulse and pulling her snugly against his side.

Merry couldn't argue with that; she already knew that Boothby and she would be great friends. He didn't care that she was American, and he didn't particularly care that she was a duchess, either. "Your only gardener hasn't been able to do more than keep a small kitchen garden going," she told Trent, "but we have great plans."

"You may hire however many gardeners you like."

"I should like an architect as well, the sort of man who works in landscape gardening. I adored Humphry Repton's work in Kensington Gardens, for example; perhaps we could lure him here. I could use my money—"

"No. Your inheritance will go into a trust for our children."

She stopped. "But—"

"I will support my own wife," Trent said, suddenly looking very ducal indeed. "Your inheritance will ensure that our second son has an estate of his own, which," he added with a touch of ruefulness, "might prevent the sort of resentment that Cedric has always felt. Last year I stopped paying his bills, which just made him angrier."

"You were trying to force him into financial prudence?"

"If Cedric were to decide to live within his means, he would live comfortably, and support a wife. If he were to marry an heiress, he would be extremely well off."

Merry digested that. "Yet he has extravagant tastes."

"He might do better away from England. The constant comparison with my estate was galling. It ate at him."

"Where did you say that he went?" Merry asked.

"He left for the Bahamas," Trent said. "I hope he will thrive there."

Merry wasn't so certain, and given the reserve in Trent's eyes, neither was he, but the last thing she wanted to do was ruin their afternoon by talking about Cedric. "I do not have extravagant tastes," she promised, leading him back onto the path. "The greatest expense in a garden is the head gardener, and I wish to perform that role myself. Mr. Boothby doesn't mind," she added, a bit defiantly.

"You are the Duchess of Trent. You may do precisely as you wish."

Sunshine glinted on her husband's hair, lending the strands surprising depth and revealing hints of amber here and there.

"May I infer, then, that you have so much money that you don't need my inheritance?"

He gave a crack of laughter, his eyes lighting up. "I suppose I shall grow accustomed to your American bluntness."

"I hope so," Merry observed, slipping her hand through his elbow.

"Men of my rank are supposed to live on the income from the estate. But when I inherited, I saw that fields alone could never take us out of debt, and I invested the income rather than putting it back into the estate. Only in the last two years have I been able to put money into the land."

"Of course."

"There's no 'of course' about it. My brother was furious."

Merry briefly considered how Cedric would have greeted her gardening plans: with fury, most likely. She intended to get her hands dirty every single day. Yet Trent didn't seem to mind. He was like some sort of dark melody that she couldn't quite place: unpredictable, unknowable. Fascinating.

"I imagine that you appalled your brother on a regular basis. Cedric told me that no one but shopkeepers wear brass buttons, and here you are with just those buttons."

He responded to her teasing glance instantly, pulling her into his arms and not bothering to answer before he ravished her mouth.

When he finally stopped, her breath was coming in little puffs and she was trembling again. She managed to push him away. "You mustn't . . . in public!"

"'Public' would be the town square," he pointed out. But he drew her off the path again, to another, duplicate alcove in the wall. The stone bench in this one, though equally mossy, had not collapsed. He sat and pulled her onto his lap.

"Trent!" she gasped. "This is so improper."

"The seat is less than pristine," he said, shifting backward so he was leaning against the wall and she was snug in his arm. He tilted her chin and said, "I have two demands for our marriage—no, two *requests*. Will you grant them?"

"Your Grace, I'm sure you know as well as I that one should never agree to a demand without first hearing the nature of it," Merry said, giving him a mock-severe look.

"Make that three requests."

She sighed. "You English are terribly inclined toward rules. I had to make up a list just to survive the season."

"A request is not the same as a rule," Trent said.

"It will be once I have agreed to it."

He thought about that. "What if I told you that if you were ever to address me again as 'Your Grace,' I will resort to violence? Would that be a demand, a request, or a rule?"

"Violence? You?" She wrinkled her nose. Obviously, she knew that he'd sooner cut off his right arm than inflict violence on any woman, let alone his own wife. "You'd have to give me an idea of the kind of violence . . . *Your Grace.*"

He moved as swiftly as any wild animal, bending her back over his arm like a bow, kissing her until she was gasping. Her three hairpins gave up the fight and her hair fell down again.

"That kind," he growled.

"I'll take it into consideration," Merry gasped.

"My second request is that you never fall in love with anyone else."

The words hung on the air and in the interval she heard the twitter of birds and the distant sound of a horse clopping down a dirt road.

He thought she might be unfaithful? He was of the opinion that she was that sort of woman?

But her own lamentable history flashed through her mind. She had never given anyone reason to trust her constancy, so she could scarcely be insulted by the hard truth of it.

"I shall not," she promised, keeping hurt out of her tone. "I may not have known to whom I gave my wedding vows, but I did make them, and I never break my promises."

His smile eased the awkwardness between them. "Oh, I know that. I do not refer to your bedding another man; rather, I don't want you to give your heart away." His lips smiled but his eyes were wary. "Our friendship means a great deal to me."

"I shall not fall in love," she promised. "It seems to me that you feel love when you are expected to, in other words, when a handsome man kneels at your feet and recites parts of a Shakespearean sonnet."

"If I see any man dipping toward the ground in your vicinity, I shall punt him out the door," Trent promised.

"I have no intention of ever falling in love again," she said flatly. "So far, I think your requests reasonable. What is your third?"

"When you have a new greenhouse built, I would like a daybed in one corner."

"For goodness' sake, why?"

He bent his head close and his teeth tugged at her earlobe for a moment, sending a stab of sensation down to her belly. "I have the distinct impression that my wife will be spending considerable time in the greenhouse, will she not?"

"She will," Merry whispered, tipping her head up so his lips skated across her jaw to her mouth.

"I've had a cockstand all morning, Merry. Have you any idea how uncomfortable that is?"

She shook her head.

"I want you to walk into the greenhouse and glance at the daybed, and remember being there with me. I want you to crave me, the way I craved you all morning. Perhaps the memory will drive you into the house in search of me."

"I would never interrupt you for such a motive!" she cried, feeling her face warm.

"Even if I *request* you to?" he murmured in her ear.

"Intimacy belongs in a bedroom," she told him. "Whereas you . . . on a *daybed*?"

He swooped in and kissed her, whispering about how he'd like to make love to her in a field of daisies, and on a riverboat. Merry was quite certain that she was as red as an apple by the time he drew her to her feet again.

But he held out his elbow to escort her back to the house as if they'd been engaged in nothing more indecorous than discussing how to prune a rosebush.

"George!" she called.

There wasn't even a yip in reply.

Trent hardly raised his voice. "George."

The puppy erupted from some overgrown grass, looking even dirtier than he had before. He headed straight over to the duke and began trotting more or less obediently at his heels.

"I find that very annoying," Merry observed. "Snowdrop has completely fallen in love with you, and now George obeys you." She bent down and scratched the puppy's ear. "Don't you understand, George, that Americans *never* obey the English?"

Arms wrapped around her waist and a wicked voice said, "Never, ever?"

By the time they began walking again, George had disappeared.

"Speaking of riverboats, I am considering investing in another canal," Trent said, as if those kisses hadn't happened.

Merry scarcely heard him; she was trying to pull herself

together sufficiently to reenter the house. It was becoming clear that married life meant one had to accustom oneself to storms of desire. "Why would anyone dig a canal?" she asked, willing the flush in her face to go away. "Is it for moving goods, like a river? The Charles River, in Boston, has some ships sailing up from the harbor, but I believe that most goods are sent by mail coach."

"Rivers don't always flow where the merchandise must go, and the mail requires carriages, drivers, horses, exchange of horses, places to stop along the way, food for the horses. A canal, on the other hand, can go directly between two points and carry much heavier goods than can a carriage."

"Uncle Thaddeus is quite interested in the development of steam engines," Merry said. "Did you know that the first steam engine was built back in 1698 by an English engineer? My uncle has invested in an engine being designed by an American, Peter Evans; Thaddeus is certain that goods will be moving all the way from Boston to the Carolinas in carts pushed by steam rather than horses."

"I have read something about them," Trent said slowly. "I believe steam is already powering boats."

They had reached the house and later that day—after Merry had startled the household by taking a second bath—they enjoyed their first supper as a married couple. They ate at a small table in the morning parlor because Trent told Oswald that the dining room was all very well when they had four or more, but it was entirely too gloomy for an intimate meal.

They spent the first course discussing the particularities of steam engines. Because Thaddeus talked of little else than inventions that might or might not become important, Merry turned out to know considerably more than her husband about the new engines.

By the time the third covers were taken away, Trent had pulled out a screw of paper and was jotting down notes.

"Do you know what I like about you?" he asked sometime later, stowing the paper away.

"I have no idea," Merry said sedately, but then she laughed, and added, "but as you will guess, I am longing to know."

"You are as intelligent as you are beautiful," Trent said matter-of-factly. "I intend to take your advice. I will not back that canal; I'll investigate who is working on steam engines in England instead."

"My uncle and aunt arrive tomorrow for a short visit," she reminded him.

Trent looked up swiftly. "In case you're wondering, Duchess, you are not free to return to Boston. This marriage has been consummated several times over."

Merry broke into laughter. "What I meant was that my uncle will know precisely who is working on steam engines in this country. But you should expect him to urge you to invest in Mr. Evans's American engine."

Trent had never before considered investing in an American invention, but now that he had an American wife . . . why not?

Chapter Twenty-eight

$\mathcal{F}$ollowing breakfast the next morning, Merry arranged with Mrs. Honeydukes to review the state of the household linens in the afternoon. Then she set out for a ramble around the estate, with George at her heels. Or rather, scampering ahead of her.

She kept to the gravel path that wound from the bottom of the formal gardens, over a gentle hill past a wheat field, where she nearly bumped into a portly man in homespun. He introduced himself as Mr. Goggin, one of her husband's tenant farmers.

Goggin was clearly horrified to find his mistress—the duchess!—in his field, but he recovered enough to invite her to his cottage.

"I've milk from the cow this morning," he said, ushering her to a chair placed next to the door before he nipped inside.

Merry stretched out her legs and tried to convince George that he wanted to sit when she instructed him to do so.

George rolled over a few times, and then stayed on his back, begging to be scratched. Just then a woman wearing a cap tied under her substantial chin ran out of the cottage, stopped short, and threw her hands into the air. "Why, I never!" she cried.

Merry was rubbing George's plump tummy, but she came to her feet, smiling. "I do apologize for arriving unannounced, Mrs. Goggin. I met your husband in the fields and he insisted that I return with him for a glass of milk."

Mrs. Goggin bobbed so low that her knees creaked. "I never imagined the honor of it. If only it weren't washing day!" she cried, looking with agony at the drying undergarments spread over the shrubbery surrounding the cottage.

Merry took her hostess's hand and squeezed it. "I would have known without this evidence that you are a superb laundress, Mrs. Goggin, merely from the snowy cap you wear."

The farmer's wife stared down at their joined hands, her eyes wide. "I'll fetch some milk!" she cried, running back into the cottage.

"We never met the auld duchess," Mr. Goggin, who had reappeared in his wife's wake, explained. "Please do sit down, Yer Grace."

"Have you lived here long?" Merry asked.

"I'm a tenant of yern—of the duke's," Mr. Goggin confirmed. "As was my father and his before him. We've always worked this land."

Merry was still getting used to the idea that most of the people she met in and around Hawksmede had been linked to the duchy in one way or another for the whole of their lives. Mrs. Goggin returned with a jug, from which she filled a mug with cool, frothy milk. Merry sipped it while they discussed the weather, and the fact that wheat production could fall by a third in the event of too much rain.

Mrs. Goggin was interested to learn that Merry's uncle maintained that a raised bed could protect cabbages from drowning in rain. She knew nothing of wheat, but she'd discovered that lettuces loved rain and cabbages did not.

Back at Hawksmede, Merry clambered down from Mr. Goggin's dogcart with the help of a footman. She banished George to the stables until he could be bathed and entered the house, where she discovered her husband loitering in the doorway of his study, Snowdrop at his feet.

"I gather my wife has been out driving with another man," Trent said, suppressing a smile. Merry's hem was dirty, her bonnet was in her hand, and her hair had fallen down yet again, but she was radiant. Happy.

It gave him a peculiar feeling in his gut. Pride, maybe. Yes, definitely pride. He was damned lucky.

Merry danced over to him. "Mr. Goggin told me stories of you and Cedric as small boys," she said, reaching up to kiss him, disregarding the three footmen milling about in the entry and pretending not to watch.

Trent drew her into the study. "Goggin is a very good man. I must apologize for this room, by the way."

Merry looked around the room. "What's the matter with it?"

"No attention has been given to its appearance in decades."

"If you are nurturing the hope that I shall redecorate the entire house in the best Egyptian style, I fear you'll be disappointed. I have very few opinions about furnishings."

"Yet in the garden, you intend to examine every bulb before it goes into the earth."

"That's about the size of it," she said cheerfully.

"Would you prefer to stay here year-round, rather than live in London during the season?"

"I suppose you have to be in London for the Parliament, isn't that right?"

"I do my best to follow events from here, with the help of a secretary," Trent said, "but yes, I do have to attend on occasion."

"Well, then, I shall be wherever you are," she said, walking over to examine the mantelpiece.

Merry's casual assertion that she would follow him anywhere sharply twisted something in the region of Trent's chest. It took an effort to stay where he was.

She was peering at a bust of King Henry VIII that his father had adorned with an eye patch because he said the old Tudor was as close to a pirate as a monarch could be.

"I have a new marital rule," Trent said, once he remembered how to speak.

"Goodness gracious, England is such a rule-bound country."

Unable to stop himself, Trent strode across the room to her and took her face in his hands. "I am deadly serious, Merry. I want you to promise me that you will *never* get into a vehicle if you know the driver has been drinking."

"Unless Mr. Goggin's milk is intoxicating—" She stopped when she saw the look in his eyes. "I promise that I shall not."

He took her by the arm and guided her toward the door. "In fact, I'd prefer you never enter any carriage not driven by myself or Roberts, my coachman."

"That promise seems impractical. But I don't see why I'd be anywhere without you in the evening, anyway. You aren't planning to go on long trips without me, are you?"

"Would you mind traveling to Wales now and then?"

"Of course not." A minute earlier, they had been standing in front of the fireplace in his study; now they were headed up the stairs. "Jack, where are you taking me? I promised Mrs. Honeydukes that I would inspect the linens."

"I see the necessity," he said, pushing open the door to his bedchamber and giving her a gentle shove.

The door clicked shut as Merry turned, rather surprised. "You do?"

He was stripping off his coat.

"Your Grace," she said with a gurgle of laughter, "you do nothing but take that coat on and off all day."

"Now I know that you are merely trying to provoke me. I gather you wish for a kiss . . . Duchess."

His shirt was already over his head; it billowed and fell to the floor. He prowled toward her, his eyes intent and his hands doing something at his waist.

"We cannot return to bed!" she said, falling back a step.

"I beg to differ. You want to inspect the linens, and I want to make love in such a way that you will have a very close view of them."

"I don't know what you mean by that, Your Grace," Merry cried, falling back another step and holding out her hand for good measure. "I bathed twice yesterday. I cannot ask the poor men to carry cans of water yet again!"

"Watermen are hired to haul water," he said, swooping down on her. "I'll have to have pipes installed." His lips slid up her neck and Merry shivered despite herself.

"Not if it means you'll have to discharge the watermen," she said, trying to keep her voice steady. "They've probably been watering you and your family their entire lives."

"That's how it is," he said with a shrug. "I wouldn't dismiss them. They could become gardeners; there's always a place or two open somewhere. But now I mean to tup my wife, and the only thing that might save you is if you tell me that you are still too tender to allow it."

The Duchess of Trent was a woman who never lied, and her husband knew it. So he discovered in her eyes exactly what he hoped to find.

His arms tightened ruthlessly.

Mrs. Honeydukes sat in the housekeeper's room waiting, but no linens were inspected that day, in any room other than the duke's bedchamber.

Chapter Twenty-nine

At four o'clock the following afternoon, Trent glanced out his study window as a carriage trimmed in shiny brass pulled into the drive. The Pelfords had arrived.

Before his marriage, Trent was not the sort of man who contemplated his state of being on a regular basis or, indeed, ever. But he had been giving his new circumstances an unusual amount of thought, and had decided to make it absolutely clear to Merry's relatives that the marriage had indeed been consummated, and they should not dream of taking her home with them.

A few minutes later, the door to the study flew open and Merry poked her head in. "Jack!" she cried. "I suppose you didn't hear the carriage, but my aunt and uncle have arrived. Do come greet them!"

A duke did not greet his guests in the entryway. But neither did a duke bow, greet his new relatives, and then wrap an arm around his bride as if concerned that she might be stolen from him.

His gesture did not go unnoticed. Mrs. Pelford beamed and said, "Now didn't I say you'd be as merry as bees in clover? Didn't I, Thaddeus?"

"You did," Mr. Pelford confirmed.

"Thaddeus and I are too old and American to adapt to English ways," Mrs. Pelford said. "Neither of us likes being around people without greeting them, and that's a fact." She looked at Trent expectantly, but he was at a loss.

"My aunt believes that entering a room without greeting its occupants is akin to treating people like wallpaper," Merry whispered.

"That is remarkably progressive thinking, Mrs. Pelford. May I introduce my butler, Oswald, along with Albert, Thomas, and Oliver?"

Oswald showed himself to be more flexible than Trent would have predicted, insomuch as he'd been butlering for some thirty-odd years. He shook hands with alacrity and mentioned that he considered America a marvelous country.

"Really," Mrs. Pelford said. "Now why is that, Oswald?"

Apparently Oswald admired an American scientist named Benjamin Franklin, who had received a medal from the Royal Society years ago.

"One of our nation's founders," Thaddeus Pelford said, rocking back on his heels. "If I'd had anything to say about it, I would have kept him away from politics and set him to doing nothing but thinking up inventions. Waste of time, politics!"

"Isn't he the man who flew a kite to catch lightning?" Merry asked, joining in.

Mrs. Pelford paid no attention to the resulting conversation but turned back to Trent, and said, "Now, Duke, you mustn't worry about our comfort; I shall have a bit of a rest, and I imagine Thaddeus will as well."

Trent tried to imagine his father's response to being reassured that he ought not to worry about his guests' comfort, and failed. No one could have imagined that the duke had any such concerns.

"Mrs. Honeydukes has prepared a lovely suite for you," Merry said, turning around. "You'll feel as if you are in a novel, Aunt Bess. I will take you there myself."

Trent thought his wife had adjusted remarkably well to the bridegroom switch, but he guessed that her aunt was in for an uncomfortable hour. "I shall look forward to seeing you this evening, Mrs. Pelford."

"We're family now," she said, tapping his arm. "You'll call me Bess, and Mr. Pelford, Thaddeus. But not to worry, we've no disinclination to addressing you as Your Grace."

Trent could feel the fascinated eyes of three footmen and one butler behind him. "My family addresses me as Trent," he said, bowing. "I would be honored if you would do the same."

Trent was really the practicable choice: Octavius sounded like an emperor, and Mortimer as an unpleasant uncle . . . and Jack was a private name.

"Trent," Bess tried. "It sounds like a river, but it's a good, strong name."

"Your niece said precisely the same thing," Trent observed.

"Aunt Bess really is my mother," Merry put in, "so you'll have to expect it. When I grow older, I might begin spouting verse. Couplets before tea, that sort of thing."

Trent was looking at Bess and he saw her eyes grow

misty, but the lady turned away quickly and bore down on Oswald like a genial siege engine, informing him that her husband's gout required a list of foods that ranged from asparagus to herring.

"Aunt Bess," Merry said, "do allow me to bring you to your chamber now."

As Trent watched them go up the stairs, Thaddeus turned to him with a little shudder. "Wouldn't want to be in Bess's shoes, explaining the whole marriage business," he said frankly. "My wife is fond of creative solutions. Her intuition is generally right, though." His eyes searched Trent's face.

A duke rarely smiles.

Trent couldn't stop himself.

"Right," Thaddeus said, nodding. "Well, that's set, then. Why don't you show me your stables, Duke? It's best to leave the two of them to sort it out on their own."

The minute they entered Bess's chamber, Merry put her hands on her hips. "I am very, very annoyed with you, Aunt," she stated. "You raised me to be honest and straightforward, but I can only characterize your own behavior as *sly*."

"I'm so sorry, dear." Bess looked agonized—but resolute. "You would have got your back up, and marched back to Boston. Then you'd have hidden in the garden, reputation ruined, or worse—fallen in love with another unpleasant fellow."

"That doesn't give you the right to make a game of my wedding!"

"Your uncle had every right to choose your spouse," Bess pointed out. "We allowed you your choice *three times*."

Merry wilted onto a sofa like a deflated balloon. "And I made a dreadful decision each time."

"Yes, you did," Bess said baldly. "If you jilted a third fiancé, the scandal would have marred your entire life. The duke's offer was a godsend."

"As far as you knew, he could have been simply scoring points against his brother," Merry said.

Bess huffed and sat down beside her. "Do you have even the faintest belief that a brother or anyone else could force His Grace to do something against his wishes?"

"No," Merry admitted.

"You may not be in love with your husband, but to my mind, that's an advantage. To be frank, my dear, you've got a fickle streak. You no sooner have a man at your feet than you start to think he smells like a seven-day herring in velvet slippers."

It was true. Merry knew it was true. Her aunt was saying precisely what the duke had said—and what she herself had worried over for weeks.

"I say that as one who loves you as much as I ever could a daughter of my own flesh and blood." Bess leaned over and kissed her cheek. "Probably more."

"I love you, too." Merry's voice caught.

"The duke not only offered to marry you, but he brought along his solicitor, who wrote up the most favorable settlement that I have ever seen. I like Trent, Merry. I like him far better than Lord Cedric, to tell the truth."

"I do as well," she whispered.

Bess cleared her throat. "The duke also led me to believe that there had been some imprudent behavior that suggested you would be a happy couple." She raised her hand. "Do *not* tell me the details, Merry. I shudder to think what your governess would say of your behavior."

"Miss Fairfax would collapse at the idea a duke even spoke to me," Merry pointed out.

"He wouldn't have admitted it, of course, but I'd say that His Grace was close to desperate to marry you," Bess said with obvious satisfaction.

The word "desperate" spread like warm honey through Merry's veins.

"Of course, we argued that he could follow you to America and woo you there. But he wanted you now, not a year in the future. And *that*, my dear child, is the real reason why Thaddeus and I believe the two of you will be happy."

Merry leaned against her aunt's shoulder. "How can I have been in love with Cedric a mere month ago, and now be married to his brother?"

"Why not? The duke would do well in Boston, and Lord Cedric, for all his polish, would not."

By the end of the first week, Trent was growing accustomed to a new feeling that he examined in quiet moments in his bath, or in the middle of the night, and which he determined was happiness.

He and Merry spent their days apart, she out of doors and he in the study or even farther afield, riding the estate with his estate manager. But they often came together at midday, and always at day's end.

He had always exhibited a blithe indifference to scheduled hours for meals, and as such had habituated the kitchen to leaving out bread and cheese. Now he astonished his household with his attention to time.

His valet had been accustomed to his returning home in breeches and a broadcloth coat, after which he ate in the study before bathing and going to bed.

No longer.

On occasion, Trent was unable to take luncheon at home, but he was always back in the house in time to bathe, change for the evening, and join the family for dinner. He, who had rarely taken breakfast before, now joined his duchess and the Pelfords every morning.

"It'd be a scandal if they weren't so right pretty together," the cook, Mrs. Morresey, told the housekeeper.

"Nothing she could do would be scandalous," Mrs. Honeydukes said.

Even the crusty housekeeper had fallen under the spell of the American duchess, with her friendliness and sincerity, her command of odd and interesting facts—which arose from a lively curiosity about any area of knowledge—and her ease in dealing with the household.

Their affections were returned: Trent was reasonably certain that no member of his household would ever again be dismissed, short of having committed a capital crime. Even when one of the second housemaids turned "all over funny" and dropped two dishes dating back to the reign of Good Queen Bess, his wife had an explanation.

"She's that age," Merry told him, when he pointed out that the girl had broken a teacup the week before. "Her head spins because she's growing. Did you know that her father is Squire Montjoy's dairyman? I'll ask Mrs. Honeydukes to place her in the dairy, and we'll see how she gets on there."

"It's not that she's overfamiliar," Trent heard his stable master telling the farrier. "She's American, you see. They don't do things the same way over there."

That she was American seemed to excuse any number of things that would otherwise have made people uncomfortable. Part of him—the indelibly English part—still recoiled when his wife danced into a room and, before he could rise, wrapped her arms around his neck from behind, and whispered things in his ear.

But a thirsty part of him welcomed every kiss and touch

and smile and allowed them to nurture ground that had years ago fallen barren for lack of affection.

Meals became lively affairs. After a week, the Pelfords announced they must take their leave, but Merry wouldn't hear of it, and in the end her aunt and uncle agreed to delay their passage to Boston.

At dinner, Bess and the vicar traded verse, and Thaddeus regularly dissected the workings of yet another invention, such as the steam printing press that was being developed. It was not yet functional, but Thaddeus was certain its shortcomings would soon be remedied.

"It will change everything," he told the table at large. "Only two hundred sheets an hour can be printed these days, but once steam takes over, it will be more than a thousand!"

"Who will read all those sheets?" Bess objected. "I scarcely have time to read a book as it is."

Thaddeus didn't care about that. "People will start to print all nature of things," he said vaguely. "I shouldn't be surprised if they started printing wedding invitations and the like."

"Never," his wife said firmly. "An appalling idea."

Chapter Thirty

About a fortnight into her aunt and uncle's visit, Merry invited their immediate neighbors—Mr. Kestril, Squire and Lady Montjoy, Lord and Lady Peel—to dinner, acknowledging the calls they had paid her after the *Morning Post* announced their wedding.

Merry had believed that Mr. Kestril would abandon his courtship once she married; instead, he continued to give her longing glances whenever they encountered each other. Still, he was their nearest neighbor and it would cause gossip if he were excluded.

The dining room at Hawksmede was dark and somber, but one hardly noticed, thanks to the impressive quantity of gleaming silver that Oswald had placed down the center of the table. A pair of massive epergnes, a dish hoisted in the air by two cupids, and even a sugar caster dating back to King Charles II in the shape of a lighthouse contributed to the air of elegance.

In between the silver were intricately cut pieces of leaded crystal, from paired glass urns to a pedestal jar with an ornate ormolu mount. The crystal threw off sparks of light that made the party look otherworldly—as Aunt Bess characteristically observed—as if every one of them had been "anointed" by fairy dust.

Lady Peel, who was too elderly to engage in flummery, crushed Aunt Bess's flight of fancy by saying that *she* thought that the speckles of reflected candlelight made them all look as if they had had the pox. "Smallpox scars can't be concealed by rice powder," she informed them. "Queen Elizabeth plastered hers over with a mixture of white lead and vinegar, which explains why she always looks like a cadaver in portraits."

This was just the sort of information that Merry loved, so it led to a lively discussion of cosmetics. Mr. Kestril offered the opinion that cosmetic preparations signaled selfish vanity. He followed this with a doting look at Merry's unadorned face.

Lady Peel snorted—speaking across the table—and roundly told him that if she wished to put white paste on the end of her nose, she would, and he could keep his opinions to himself.

While not precisely agreeing with Kestril, Squire Montjoy disclosed that he preferred it when ladies presented a natural appearance.

Lady Peel laughed aloud at the squire, and declared he wouldn't know "natural" if it struck him in the face.

Merry managed to keep her eyes away from the squire's wife, who had made lavish use of rice powder, among other preparations.

"I presume you think I am naturally this beautiful," Lady Peel announced.

Merry met Trent's eyes and saw that she was not alone in suppressing a violent impulse to laugh.

Bess rose to the occasion, and expressed the opinion that if Lady Peel used cosmetics, she did so in a remarkably natural fashion.

"I color my hair," Lady Peel said triumphantly. "I have for years. I use cumin seed, saffron, and celandine. I'd recommend it, Mrs. Pelford. A lady cannot afford to let her hair turn white, as yours seems to be doing."

Merry rose to signal the ladies' retirement to the drawing room, judging that the gentlemen had learned as many intimate details as they cared to about their wives' toilettes.

Bess showed her disgruntlement with the mention of her fading hair by sweeping the squire's wife onto a settee for a chat, leaving Merry with Lady Peel.

"Young Kestril is gaping at you like a trout trying to catch a bug," Lady Peel observed. "My goodness, but that man is as foolish as they come."

"You don't suppose that he thinks I might return his regard, do you?" Merry asked.

"Oh no. He realizes that you're newly married, and anyone can see yours is a love match, even if all the newspapers hadn't told us as much. Did you see how he's drinking himself into a standstill? He'll wake up one of these days, as dry as a raisin, and realize that he's been yearning after a married lady who hasn't the faintest interest in him. I shouldn't be surprised if he went off to India for a spell."

"That seems extreme," Merry said, taken aback.

"Everyone is saying that he's lost the estate to creditors. A gamester, but not in the usual way, since he put his money behind an expedition to bring back an orchid as big as a dinner plate." She snorted. "As if such a thing existed!"

That made sense. Trent invested his money in a flint mine and now a steam engine in Philadelphia, whereas Kestril bid on a dream flower bigger than his head that might exist in a land he'd never been to.

"I like what you're doing with the grounds," Lady Peel said, leaping from exotic to domestic horticulture. "I've told my gardener that I want raised cabbage beds."

"You are the third person tonight to mention cabbages," Merry said with some amusement. "I certainly hope the beds live up to their promise."

"That remains to be seen," Lady Peel said. "God knows what the soil is like in America."

Merry started to defend her country's soil, when Lady Peel gave a bark of laughter and patted her hand. "There, there, Your Grace. I only meant that there's a powerful amount of clay in the Buckinghamshire soil. We'll be watching like hawks to see how your experiments work out."

"Oh," Merry said, stunned by the idea her gardens were being so closely watched.

Lady Peel gave her a sympathetic look. "I imagine it will take some getting used to, being an American and all. The Duke and Duchess of Trent are as close to royalty as we get around here. If you decide to eat a blackbird for breakfast, there won't be a single black feather left within ten miles. Everyone will insist on dining on a songbird that very night."

"Why on earth would I eat a blackbird?" Merry asked, startled.

"Don't," the lady declared. "I ate one once and it was all bones. Better in shrubbery and out of sight—like drunken young men, now I think of it. Hopefully your duke is wresting the brandy away from Kestril. He suffered quite enough of that behavior from his brother and father, I should think."

Did everyone know everything, here in the country?

Lady Peel's next comment confirmed that the country-side did indeed know all about everything. "I approve of all that time you're spending out of doors. You're likely already carrying the heir, after all, and my mother always maintained the fresh air was best for a woman in that condition. None of this shutting ladies up in stuffy bedchambers, as they do in London."

She hoisted herself up from her chair. "You've turned pink," she observed. "I suppose that's owing to young love. I didn't experience it myself, thank goodness. It seems an uncomfortable condition, based on Mrs. Radcliffe's novels, at least. Now if you will excuse me, I must visit the retiring room."

Merry took her ladyship's arm and helped her down the corridor.

"I had doubts about you," the lady said, a few steps later. "An American and all. As a duchess—*our* duchess!"

Merry cleared her throat. "I apologize."

"But you'll do," Lady Peel went on. "The way you're holding my arm, for instance."

"Yes?"

"The former duchess wouldn't have soiled her fingers." She hadn't an ounce of resentment in her tone. "High and mighty as the queen herself, she was. My family goes back to fat Henry—you know, the Eighth—but that wasn't far enough for her. I don't suppose you know the difference, do you?"

Once again, Merry couldn't decide on an appropriate answer, but it didn't matter, as Lady Peel just kept talking.

"The Duchess of Trent wouldn't know *Debrett's* from a book of sermons. The world's a queer old place."

There didn't seem to be anything to be gained from announcing that she had memorized *Debrett's* all the way through H, so Merry held her tongue.

"You ain't a duchess in the old mold," the lady said. "But I'll be jiggered if I don't like the new mold even better!"

Trent had watched Kestril grow more inebriated throughout the meal. With every glass, he threw another longing look at Merry, until Trent had a nearly irresistible urge to toss him out the front door.

After the meal, Trent endured Kestril's lecture about orchids until the clock finally inched to the time when he could bid their guests farewell.

When they had seen the last of them off, and the Pelfords had retired to their chambers, he followed Merry upstairs, adjusting his pace because it was difficult to walk after a four-hour cockstand. Along the corridor. Through the bedchamber door.

Closed the door, trying not to slam it.

As if they were magnetized, they flew at each other, Merry laughing and Trent too overcome to laugh, buttons flying now and then, the wall brought into use.

Afterward, he hung over her, panting, sweating. She was so damned beautiful. He couldn't decide the color of her eyes, because they were always changing, different in candlelight, after making love, when laughing.

Later they lay face-to-face, their legs entangled, and talked.

"What was your father like?" Merry said, following some train of thought in her head.

Trent didn't care for the question. He ran one hand in a

caress down his wife's back, sweeping up the gentle slope of her arse, but he didn't answer.

"Jack, I asked you a question!" Merry said it severely, but he saw a gleam in her eyes, and her bottom wiggled under his hands.

"My father was a drunkard," he said, squeezing the words from a mind that was going foggy with desire. "Drunkards are . . ." He shrugged.

"Are what?"

"They're all the same," he said, getting on with the explanation because he wanted it over. He rolled on top of her, elbows braced at her sides. "Cedric and my father were very different when sober, but not when they were drunk. One fuddled man is just like another: ill-behaved, quarrelsome, and often vulgar."

"Cedric's behavior at the Vereker ball was certainly not admirable," Merry acknowledged.

"His worst self," Trent said. "My father was the same when he was soaked."

Merry's legs moved restlessly under him, desire expressed without words. "What does that feel like?" he asked.

"What?" she replied, her breath catching as he rocked against her.

"This."

"Oh." Her forehead creased. He pressed forward again. Pink was rising in her cheeks and her fingers curled, holding tightly on to his shoulders.

"Empty," she whispered. "I suddenly feel empty, as if I remember that you aren't there and I need you so much."

Trent's grin went all the way to his toes. "Let me help you with that," he said hoarsely.

The following night, words flowed out of Merry like

a stream, something about a plant called the *Campanula portenschlagiana* that she had read about in *Curtis's Botanical Magazine*.

"Some sort of rare plant?" he roused himself to ask. He found it hard to think after making love to Merry, whereas she became more talkative. It turned out that she was talking about the bellflowers that could be found on any roadside.

After years of having no one to listen to, he discovered that he loved listening to her. Some people didn't like American accents, but he thought her voice sounded like water in a river, light and sparkling.

Their discussion wandered into uses for gravel (bellflowers require excellent drainage), and from there to farming methods in Wales compared to those in Massachusetts. Then innovations in plumbing and whether they might work for garden irrigation—and by extension for field irrigation.

That led to canals, not as a means of transport, but as a means of helping to control flooding.

One night, they found themselves talking about his father again until Trent managed to change the subject around to *her* father. Merry was lying across his chest, her hair trailing off the edge of the bed.

"He was an inventor and a diplomat," she said, "but I just thought of him as my father. Do you know what I find one of the hardest parts about his death?"

Trent shook his head.

"We never said good-bye. I saw him at luncheon, and we only talked about silly things. I had a doll named Penny and I was trying to persuade him to build me a small boat so that I could sail her on Boston Common. All the boys had boats and the girls didn't."

"Was he good at building boats?"

"He could make anything," Merry said, her voice husky with sincerity. "I do think he was a genius, Jack." She lifted her head from his chest so she could meet his eyes. She kept talking about her father, but Trent lost the thread . . . because she was so damned beautiful.

"Beautiful" wasn't the right word. It sounded merely physical, whereas everything about Merry glowed from inside. He was thinking about that when he realized that she'd paused and was looking at him expectantly.

"Ah."

She dropped a kiss on his nose. "The last thing that my father said to me was that he'd be home to tuck me into bed. Do you remember what yours said?"

He did remember. His father had been drunk, very drunk. He'd called Oswald a goatish pignut, and then he called the coachman a lout. Cedric had tried to stop their mother from getting in the phaeton and their father had turned on Cedric and called him lily-livered. And worse.

"No," he said. "I can't remember."

He saw in her eyes the moment that she decided not to challenge his fib. "It must have been so difficult to lose both your parents at once. I can't imagine."

Cedric had engaged in public bouts of weeping. Trent had not.

He ran a hand down her slim back. "My father was a drunkard, Merry. No one mourned him."

There was a flash of sympathy in her eyes, but rather than speak, she decided to kiss him and make it better.

Trent had never liked drinking. But if drinking were like Merry's kisses, he'd be a drunk. His head spun when their tongues slid against each other, and she made that achy little sound in the back of her throat . . .

He was drunk on her.

Besotted by kisses.

At the beginning of July, Thaddeus decided that given the French navy was back in operation, delay would mean a risky journey. So he and Bess took off for London and thence to America, promising to return the following spring. Later, Merry cried, and Trent kissed away the tears and seduced her out of her sadness.

She taught Trent about the intricacies of hothouses, and he taught her that a woman's time of the month was no reason to avoid intimacy, after which Merry taught her husband that laughter makes the most awkward of situations more easily borne.

There were moments to treasure: the time when his wife appeared in the study and asked him to spare a few minutes in the greenhouse to consult about new plantings. Or the evening when the bedroom door closed and Merry dropped to her knees and ripped open his placket.

It was mildly humiliating to realize that he wanted more than her body. A man's worth is measured by his sense of self. Or by his title. Never by what his wife thinks of him. Yet he went to the greenhouse in search of Merry when he came up with a new scheme to make the local gravel pit into a going concern.

Of course, they were friends, which explained it. Trent actually found himself wondering if he'd had a true friend before Merry; he even told her about the uncertain years after he inherited the dukedom, when he had been forced to leave Oxford and fight to return the estate to profitability.

For Merry, as far as Trent could tell, lighthearted behavior came naturally. One day they took a blanket and pony cart and went just far enough away from the house to be out of sight—which turned out to be in the middle of field of flax blooms, as blue as the sky.

As blue as the violet in his wife's eyes.

He spread the blanket and devoted himself to worshipping her body. He tried to memorize the sultry curve of her hip, the low rise of her back above her arse, the perfectly shaped bones of her feet.

"Your ankles are as beautiful and fragile as ivory," he told her, lying on that blanket later in a haze of sun and satisfaction. He was tucking periwinkle-blue flax blossoms between her toes.

"That tickles!" she protested. And then, "Did you know that we think of ivory as coming from an elephant, but the same word refers to the tusks of a walrus? Or a wild boar?"

"I did not," Trent said. He was having trouble concentrating, because her slim hand had slipped below his waist.

She leaned closer. "If *you* were an elephant, you would have a magnificent tusk."

That was life with Merry: one moment they were laughing, and then next they were kissing, starved for each other, fumbling, panting with the need to come together.

Chapter Thirty-one

That evening, Merry lay in her bath staring at her toes. For the last few days, she'd been in the grip of a horribly unsettling feeling.

In the first few weeks of marriage, she'd found herself thinking a lot about the moments when Trent would pull her through the bedchamber door, into his arms, and crush her mouth under his. Frolicking, as Aunt Bess called it, was a brand-new activity and had quickly become her favorite.

Sometimes it was more interesting than the raised beds Boothby was constructing in the kitchen gardens, though it felt like betrayal to admit it, even to herself.

But these days she didn't think merely about bedding her husband; she thought about *him*.

All the time.

A few days ago, he had taken her down to the kitchen in

the middle of the night. They had sat at the kitchen table and ate rough brown bread that tasted even better than Mrs. Morresey's crumpets, along with a cheddar cheese that bit the tongue.

She had even drunk some of his ale. It frothed and went up her nose and tasted like liquid bread. But she loved it because he loved it.

That was the problem.

She had the odd feeling that she was falling off a precipice, turning into someone else. A new person.

The next morning she woke up early, though not as early as Trent, and watched him work at the desk in his chamber. She knew perfectly well why he was sitting there, writing in his smalls.

He was waiting for her to wake up. His mouth would soften when he saw she was awake, and he'd push away from the table as if whatever he was working on was irrelevant. He wouldn't even finish the sentence.

Then he would say in a growling, morning voice, "Good morning, Beautiful." By the time he got to the bed, she would be already tingling behind her knees.

Testing her hypothesis, she sat up, pushing a mop of curls behind her shoulder.

Sure enough, Trent's quill dropped, and then he was striding toward her. His body . . .

She could write a thousand lines about the way his stomach rippled when he tore off his smalls, the way he was doing now. About the way he wrapped her up in his heat and passion so that she couldn't do anything but moan.

A half hour later, he rolled over and ran a finger down her sweaty, undoubtedly red face, and asked her how she was.

As if *that* wasn't obvious.

"I am very well." She grinned at him. "You?" She peered

down his body. "Do you realize that I almost never get to see you looking tired? It's so much smaller in this state."

"Smaller?" He looked taken aback. As she watched, that part of him surged with life again.

"Do you call it your lance?" she asked. "Aunt Bess made a joke about that once. Or would you prefer poker? I heard that word in the stables."

Trent snorted, and Merry poked him in the chest. "Young women are never taught about a man's body, you know."

"I can teach you," he said. The look in his eyes was pure wickedness, designed to make a woman weak at the knees. "What would you call these?" He curled his hand around himself. Two parts of himself.

Merry could feel herself turning pink, which was ridiculous, considering what they had just done. But she was discovering that talking could actually be more intimate than intimacy itself, a fact that seemed to surprise Trent as well. "Gooseberries."

"You must be joking." Laughter rumbled from his chest. She shook her head. "There might be other words, but the only one I know of is gooseberries."

"I have a problem with that," Trent observed. "I am neither green nor pea-sized."

"But you *are* hairy," she said with a giggle.

He rolled his eyes.

"What word do you use?" she prompted.

"Testicles, if you want to be precise. Stones. Or bollocks."

"Bollocks!" she cried. "I knew that was a naughty word, but I could hardly ask someone what it referred to."

Trent moved his hand. "Penis. Cock. Shaft." Watching that big male hand circling, pulling at himself, was one of the most erotic things she'd ever seen. "There's nothing feminine about the word because there's nothing feminine about *this*."

Merry rolled her eyes, and he tipped her onto her back, cupping one of her breasts. "So am I holding some sort of fruit?"

"You will laugh."

"Probably."

Making her husband laugh had become one of Merry's happiest activities. "My governess used to call my bosom the Milky Way."

That did it; he let out a bellow of laughter. "That's got to be one of the silliest names for breasts that I've ever heard. How about your nipples?"

Merry wrinkled her nose. "It's an odd word, nip-nip-nipple. Not romantic."

"If I were the poetic sort, I would write odes to your honeyberries." He bent his head and dropped a kiss on her.

"Honeyberries? How is that better than gooseberries?"

"You are as sweet as honey, and not green. If I were that sort of man, I could rival your aunt with three hundred rhymed couplets, and bring you bunches of flowers to boot."

The idea made her feel dizzy, though not because she wanted flowers or a poem or anything like that.

What she was thinking—

She couldn't be thinking that again.

But she was.

Love was like canary wine: it fizzed in her veins and made the world a sweeter place. With a grimace she threw an arm over her eyes.

"Merry?"

She felt Trent drop another kiss on the curve of her

breast, but for the moment she just concentrated on keeping those three words from bursting out of her mouth. He didn't want to hear them. *She* didn't want to hear them.

She'd said them before, too many times. She'd cheapened them with overuse, because she hadn't even understood the emotion.

He kissed her lips this time. "Are you all right, Merry mine?"

Trent called her that sometimes. Because he was possessive. Because she was *his*, mind and body and soul.

Merry actually groaned, realizing what she'd just said to herself. Her eyes popped open. "Cedric thought I was an easy woman because I had been betrothed so many times."

"Why are you thinking about him?" There was an edge to Trent's voice that she found thrilling. Her duke disliked thinking about any of her suitors; every time Mr. Kestril sidled over to her, Trent's jaw would tighten.

"I wasn't thinking about Cedric. I was wondering whether you thought I was a strumpet for the same reason."

"Absolutely not."

His answer was prompt and should have satisfied, but it didn't. "I don't mean in terms of bedding," she said, struggling to find the right words. Finally, she just blurted out the truth. "I have told three different men that I was in love. Do you think that I misled myself? That I never was in love at all?"

She knew the answer. She had had no idea what love was . . . until now.

"You are an emotional person," Trent said, running his finger down her nose. "I don't think you misled yourself any more than other humans who run about making rash promises."

Merry sat up, pulling the sheet up around her because she wasn't as comfortable unclothed as Trent was; he was leaning back against the headboard, naked as the day he was born. "Love is a fickle emotion," he said. "Here today, gone tomorrow. You just had the bad luck to discover that truth while in the public eye."

"I don't entirely agree," Merry said, feeling her way through it. "Mothers love their children. My father loved me. Aunt Bess and Uncle Thaddeus love me. *I'm* the fickle one."

"You're talking about a different emotion than romantic love."

"I don't see why the distinction is relevant."

"When a man tells a woman 'I love you,' he generally wants something from her. Most of those exchanges lead to bed, which means they're really about desire, not love."

Merry bit her lip. "You think desire is the only emotion between a man and woman?"

"No, not at all. Look at us." His grin eased the bleakness in her heart. "You're my friend, Merry. Bloody hell, I never imagined anything like it. You're my friend *and* you make me never want to leave this bed." His voice dropped with the last few words, and then he pulled down her sheet.

She forgot what they were talking about.

But it came up again the next night.

Trent had asked about her father at dinner, and she had come up with story after story about her father's quirky brilliance as an inventor and politician.

Trent said all the right things in response, but Merry had been making a study of her husband. Something changed when she told him about the very prim lady—Merry's mother—who had arrived from England and won her father's heart.

Trent's shoulders had gone stiff, and later that evening, for the first time since they married, he didn't follow her out of the drawing room and up the stairs.

Instead, he gave her a kiss and said that he had work to do. Ten o'clock came and went; the house became still and quiet.

Finally, she climbed out of bed, pulled on a wrapper, and headed down the stairs, her bare toes curling against the silky wood of the great staircase.

She expected to see Trent at one of the three big tables in his study, but instead he was in a sofa at the far end of the room, staring at embers burning down in the fireplace. She padded over to him and sat down.

He wasn't holding papers, a book, or even a drink. Merry slid closer and rubbed her head against his shoulder. "Hello," she said softly.

Trent put an arm around her, and gave her a lopsided grin. "You needn't have come down; I was on my way to bed."

"Every once in a while, a lady can 'fetch' a man," she said, stretching up to kiss his chin.

He pulled her into his lap, but he didn't kiss her, just held her and put his chin on her head.

"What are you thinking about?" she asked.

"Your father."

"I wish you had known him. You are very similar."

"I hardly think so."

She leaned back against his arm so that she could see his face. "You are. All the investments you've made and the way you've made your estate profitable? My father would have done that as well."

"As would any man of sense."

"Any man with the capability, and those are far and few between. I know that you fought in the House of Lords for the Quaker anti-slavery bill, because Cedric told me so, and Father would have done that. What's more, you built the wing on that charity hospital."

"Cedric's project, not mine."

"Without your money—the money you *made*, not inherited—that wing wouldn't exist." She sounded proud, because she was proud.

More and more Merry realized that she could never have been truly happy with someone like Cedric, a man who inherited some money and married into more. She wouldn't have developed the deep respect that she felt for Trent.

"I don't agree, but it's not relevant. I was comparing your father to mine."

"Your father might well have been a different man had he been tested," Merry suggested. "My father *had* to succeed, as did you."

"I was actually thinking about the way your father wooed your mother."

She smiled, leaning back against his chest. "He was a bit of a madman, wasn't he?"

"Love poems—"

"All written by Bess, may I point out. He didn't confess that to my mother for over a year."

"Flowers, jewelry, even a serenade. It makes me wish for your sake that I was a different man."

"Well, excuse me, if I don't agree with you," Merry said, laughing. "I am happy with you just as you are. A different man might not have your lance."

Trent groaned at her jest, but then he lapsed into silence again.

He was in a bloody bad mood and he should probably just take his wife up to bed.

"Or your gooseberries," Merry added, with a mischievous twinkle.

"Listening to your uncle's stories, I felt as if you were cheated."

"Because no one has recited poetry that was actually

written by his sister-in-law? Or from Shakespeare, pretending the sentiments were his? Gave me a ring made from his own hair?"

He winced. "I see your point."

"Three men wooed me. Diamonds have so little meaning that Cedric didn't even bother to buy me one." They had tacitly agreed to leave the late duchess's diamond ring in the safe in Trent's study; it was snarled in too many emotions for Merry to wear it.

His wife didn't sound bitter, but all the same . . . Didn't every woman want those things—not to mention a proper marriage proposal? Merry hadn't even known whom she was marrying. Sometimes he was haunted by that in the middle of the night.

"I suppose that's one reason why we are such good friends," he said. "We understand the emptiness of those gestures."

He had the uneasy feeling that he was trying to reassure himself.

"I know why I dislike gifts of poetry and jewelry," Merry said, "but why do you?"

Trent's hand slid down the curve of her side. "I brought flowers to my mother once," he said, the memory coming from nowhere.

"How old were you?"

"Around six or seven." He hadn't thought about that afternoon in years. He'd been old enough to suspect that his mother didn't care for him, young enough to feel hopeful that he could change her mind.

"What happened?" Merry asked.

"Nothing much. I brought them to her chamber."

"She wasn't pleased by them?"

"I suppose she was. She was fond of roses and I had carefully chosen all the fattest ones I could find."

She frowned. "Something happened."

An acid taste came into his mouth. He'd been so young.

"I asked a maid to tie a ribbon around the posy," he said, turning back to Merry, wanting a distraction. He watched his fingers run over the dip of her waist so that he didn't meet her sympathetic eyes. "After which, I went to my mother's room."

"Oh dear! I can imagine several scenarios that could go wrong after that sentence. We'll have to put a lock on our door once we have children."

"It wasn't as bad as that."

She interlaced her fingers with his and brought his hand to her mouth for a kiss.

"My brother and I weren't supposed to go to her boudoir, of course. As far as I knew, my mother showed absolutely no interest in us, except on rare occasions when we were summoned to the drawing room before tea."

Merry nodded.

"I wanted to give her the flowers before they wilted, so I knocked on her door, and she called 'Enter,' likely thinking I was her maid."

"And?"

"She was sitting on a low chair, with her back to me. She didn't turn around, but Cedric looked over her shoulder. He was sitting on her lap."

"You hadn't known that your brother was there?" There was a steely disapproval in her voice.

"No. I'd had no idea."

"I gather you had not been invited to visit her chamber."

"Never."

"That must have been a deeply painful moment." Merry's hand tightened around his. "Please don't tell me that Cedric looked triumphant."

"No, no, he was sorry. I knew immediately that he'd been to our mother's room many times, but had never mentioned it because he didn't want to hurt me."

"What did you do?"

"I just stood there. He said, 'Mama, Jack brought you some flowers.' I was Jack in those days because my father was still alive."

"What did your mother say?" Merry prompted.

"She gave Cedric a kiss on the top of his head, ruffled his hair, and put him on his feet. She thanked me for the flowers and sent us both back to the nursery."

For a while, neither spoke, and the only sound Trent could hear was Merry's soft breathing.

"I'm sorry to say this because she has passed away, but I rather hate your mother," she said, finally.

"She had every reason to favor Cedric, believe me. I was the sort of boy who was always dirty and often bleeding, with smudges all over my face, no doubt. Thoroughly unattractive."

She twisted about until she was sitting astride his lap, able to give him a kiss. "No wonder you don't want me to call you Jack. I won't do it again, I promise."

He shrugged. "That's not important. I learned something that afternoon, something valuable. I had thought that I could buy the emotion she showed Cedric by being more like him."

"More flowery?"

He nodded, meeting her eyes, wanting her to understand. "A useless gesture. That's why I have no more trust in empty words and gifts of jewels than you do. But the fact that we're friends, Merry? That is something very rare, and it means so much more than empty trifles."

"Friends?" she whispered, so quietly he barely heard.

He began pulling out her hairpins and tossing them to the floor.

"Yes, friends," he repeated, his voice gone gravelly with lust.

She pushed back ever so slightly, her hand on his arm. "I want to be more than your friend, Jack."

He felt his thoughts go still as he watched her gather her courage.

"I love you, Jack. I'm in love with you." She cupped his face in her hands. "I love you more than I could have imagined possible."

Trent's heart stopped for a moment. Merry loved him . . . and she was looking at him expectantly. For one searing moment he felt a stab of pure happiness.

But on the heels of that came something else. Something darker. How many times had she felt exactly what she was feeling at this moment—attached to the laundry list of men she had been betrothed to?

Another man would tell her what she wanted to hear. That he loved her, too. As much as she did, if not more.

But he wasn't that man. He wouldn't lie to her.

He didn't love her. No, he wouldn't *let* himself love her.

Love, romantic love, simply wasn't something he would allow to cloud his judgment.

Instead of speaking, he swept her into his arms and carried her upstairs to bed. Ravishing her would have to be answer enough, sliding into her tight heat with a sigh of pure relief. He thrust wordlessly, over and over, drinking the expression in her eyes. Letting her whimpers and moans drive him and waiting, waiting . . .

Merry's sleek thighs tightened around him and her head jerked back. She cried out, words falling disjointedly from her lips, "Deeper, now, *yes* . . ."

And then, "Love you."

Despite himself, the words had a primal, raw effect on him, driving the air from his lungs. Deep pleasure thrummed in his bones. He wove his fingers into Merry's and lost himself, bliss rolling through him like the tide, leaving him clean and fresh, beached on some foreign shore.

Chapter Thirty-two

For once, Merry woke up earlier than Trent. He was lying on his back, arms flung out, taking up most of the bed. She looked over every inch of him, heart aching.

It was awful, this love.

She had always been happy to see one of her fiancés. But when she looked at her husband, she felt raw and vulnerable.

This kind of love was different. It was complex, and made up of a million strands of emotion. It hurt to feel it alone. She knew exactly why her father had commissioned poems from his sister, and sang tunelessly, and showered her mother in jewels.

She would do anything to persuade Trent to love her. He was her missing piece; he made her complete.

With him, she wasn't American, or a duchess, or even Merry.

She was home.

With that thought, she bent her head and brushed her lips on his. "I love you," she breathed, kissing him again, her tongue sliding inside his mouth.

He didn't kiss her back. In fact, when she opened her eyes and looked at him, he was just waiting for her to finish.

He put her gently to the side and sat up. "We have to talk, Merry."

"You sound like Aunt Bess," she said. "I didn't mean to demand that you respond in kind, Jack. I truly didn't."

He was silent for a moment. Then, "The truth is that I had hoped not to join that particular club: to wit, Bertie, Dermot, and Cedric."

Merry took a deep breath. Of course, Trent didn't understand. She had been infatuated with her former fiancés, an emotion as thin as a grape skin. The love she felt now was woven deep in her bones and her heart. "It's different this time," she tried to explain.

His eyes flashed with a hint of emotion that chilled her as effectively as an ice bath. "Those are the precise words you used at the Portmeadow ball—while talking of my brother. You assured me that your feelings for him were 'different.' "

"It *is* different this time." Merry faltered at the look on her husband's face. Naturally, Trent didn't like the reminder that she'd been in love with his brother—not that she had ever truly loved Cedric. "I never felt anything for him that is close to what I feel for you."

She should have kept her love to herself, allowed it to grow while both of them got used to it. But the words and emotions had spilled out without warning. And she couldn't, or wouldn't, take them back.

The fact was, everything she felt for him had been growing more and more powerful every day. If she found herself in a room with her husband, she leaned toward him as if he were the true North. If she glanced up at the dinner table and merely caught sight of his dark eyes and deep bottom lip, her heart skipped a beat and her knees turned weak.

Even when she was in the gardens, her thoughts constantly strayed back to him. She missed him when he was as close as the next room.

"It feels different to you because we are physically intimate," he said flatly. "You didn't sleep with your fiancés; if you had, you would understand how powerful desire can be."

Merry did understand desire. If truth be told, she lived for the moments when they climbed the stairs together in the evening. Her breath came faster with each step, a heady sensuality slamming over her like a tidal wave. By the time they entered the room, she was frantic to feel his skin against hers, to have his cock in her hand, or her mouth, or herself.

But that madness wasn't love.

Love was something more tender and quiet. It made her pop into Trent's study and drag him away from his work. It made her rack her brain to come up with intelligent and engaging subjects of conversation. It made her want to sleep in the curve of his body, their fingers interlocked.

"Love is not a disease!" she said, finding words to defend herself. "You'd think that I was confessing to having the pox."

Trent swung his legs off the bed and walked to the window, stark naked as he was. Without turning around, he said, "I am uncomfortable with extremes of emotion. In my experience—*and* in yours—people fall in and out of love with startling regularity."

Merry knew with perfect certainty that she would never fall out of love with Trent. He was her missing half, the only man in the world for her. What they shared felt as true as hunger and cold. As joy.

Still, dread soured her stomach: the fear that she wasn't beautiful enough, that she wasn't ladylike. That she was unlovable. Cedric and Dermot obviously hadn't loved her, and Trent had taken her in his brother's stead. He hadn't wooed her.

She couldn't expect that he would love her the way she loved him.

"Don't be angry," she said, hating that she sounded needy. "Please come back to bed."

"Of course I'm not angry." He sighed and turned, coming back, sitting on the edge of the bed. To her relief, his face had softened. "My only concern is that when you fall out of love with me, Merry, you will be disinclined to be my wife, in all meanings of the word."

"No!" she cried fiercely. "How can you say such a thing? I will never fall out of love with you."

"I'm brutally rational. How long did you experience feelings for the infamous Bertie?"

Merry swallowed hard before answering. "Two months." This was so humiliating, being diagnosed as if she were suffering from a case of the measles. She blurted out the sorry tally rather than endure more questions. "Six weeks for Dermot, and a mere week or two for Cedric."

That wasn't the truth. She had met Trent shortly after accepting Cedric's proposal, and in her heart of hearts, she would put the demise of her infatuation at the moment she met a stranger on the balcony.

"Summing that up makes me feel as shallow as a puddle," Merry said, trying to make a joke of it and not succeeding.

No wonder Trent wouldn't even consider the possibility that he might come to love her someday. Who could love someone like that? No one in his right mind would risk it.

Trent leaned over and pressed a kiss on her lips. "I think you're in love with love itself," he said kindly. "You wouldn't be my American duchess if you weren't exuberant and emotional."

"Flighty, you mean." Her heart ached, not knowing how she could ever convince him of her feelings, given her well-deserved reputation. "What I feel for you truly is not the same."

He was silent for a moment. "I do not wish to lie to you, Merry."

"Please don't," she replied. But her stomach clenched. She didn't want to hear the truth.

"I don't feel that emotion for you. For anyone. It is not an emotion I believe has merits."

The words hit her like a blow, and for a moment she struggled to breathe. He was staring down at his hands, choosing his words carefully.

"I value you, and respect you as my duchess. You have become my closest friend in the world. But love, romantic love . . ." He shrugged. "That isn't going to happen."

"How can you be so certain?" Merry asked, knowing she sounded like a whimpering fool. "What if I wanted to turn this into a real marriage, in all senses of the word?" Tears stung her eyes, but she refused to allow them to fall.

"Then you'd be disappointed," he said bluntly.

She pressed her eyes closed, telling herself to accept it.

But she *couldn't*; the stubbornness that was her strength was also her weakness. The ache in her heart drove her, the one that was whispering that Trent could have loved a different woman, someone more ladylike than she. She refused to accept that.

"Why? Why is it not even a possibility?" she persisted.

Trent had a beleaguered look on his face. "I'm a *duke*, Merry. I do not engage in excesses of emotion."

She frowned. "Your title precludes tender feelings?" Anger came to her aid, making her braver. Anger and love together. "I don't agree. Why couldn't you fall in love with me? Am I so objectionable? Too talkative? Excessively emotional? Too *American*?"

"None of that is relevant," he retorted.

"The heck it isn't." Merry jumped off the bed and put her hands on her hips. "I am standing in front of you, Trent. I've just told you that I love you, and you have responded by telling me that you could never feel the same for me. Why not?"

Irritation began to burn up Trent's spine. This wasn't the way they had agreed their marriage would go. They had arrived at a rational agreement that precluded just this sort of hysterics, and now she was ignoring it.

"Bloody hell, Merry," he said, standing up. "I'm the fourth in a line of men you've fallen in love with."

"And the last," she said defiantly.

"One can only hope. At this rate, I'd expect you to be infatuated with another fifteen in my lifetime."

She turned pale, but he kept going because he never wanted to have this conversation again. They had to get all this clear between them, for once and for all.

"You'll have to accept that I won't fall in love with you. I doubt it's in me." He paused and then forced the words out. "I don't love you, Merry, not that way, and I never will."

"Because of who I am," his wife said with a little gasp. Her eyes were shiny with tears.

"No, because of who *I* am." Trent felt a wave of guilt but damn it, she had brought up the subject. "This is just what our conversation in the carriage was supposed to prevent," he growled.

"I must have misunderstood what you meant by marriage."

He shoved his hand through his hair. "Must you be so dramatic? I feel tremendous regard and affection for you, Merry. I lust after you as if I were a boy of fifteen. Isn't that enough, for God's sake?"

Trent prayed that she didn't start crying. He hated crying women. It had ripped him apart when Merry had wept at the Vereker ball, and now, all these weeks later, he was much more fond of her. He treasured her.

Frustration ripped words out of him. "Marriage isn't about a veil or a gown; it's about ordinary days spent together. Our marriage will not survive if you dish up emotional nonsense."

"By 'nonsense,' do you mean my hope that you will love me someday? Or do you mean my loving you? Which is it?" Damn it, a tear was rolling down her cheek. Even so, her voice came out with angry force. "What do you want from our marriage?"

The one thing Trent wanted was to get out of the bloody room. His words came out like the hailstones she was throwing at him. "I refer only to the nonsense about love which you brought up. I don't want it. I don't want anything to do with it."

She flinched. "Yes," she said faintly. "I see."

Trent was willing Merry to understand him. "I have infinite regard and respect for you, as my duchess and as a woman. Our marriage has been about as damned near perfect as I could have imagined. Could we simply put this to the side, Merry?"

"Of course." She straightened her back and nodded. "I will do my best." Her voice wavered but she visibly pulled herself together. "I won't bring up the topic again."

"I think that's better than discussing the precise moment

when you fall *out* of love, don't you? I think we'd better act as if this never happened. I certainly don't want to be informed when your feelings change, as they will."

"Right," she said. "I understand. I really do."

He nodded, inwardly surprised that her promise didn't prompt a sense of triumph. He'd won the argument, hadn't he?

A couple of hours later, Trent found himself in his study, staring at the green brocade lining the windows. Snowdrop had managed to rip the hem off two panels and she was working on a third, filling the study with the sound of little growls.

He couldn't stop thinking about Kestril, the neighbor who was violently in love with Merry. He was well on the way to detesting the man, never more so than when he showed up at dinner with that piece about gardening, from some book Trent had never heard of.

There were likely many such books in the library downstairs. He could start sprouting hoary facts about walnut trees, except everyone would know what he was doing. If he so much as opened his mouth in a discussion of horticulture, everyone would guess he was competing with Kestril for his wife's attention.

He'd be damned if he did that.

The man didn't even know Merry. How could he claim to love her?

Trent himself might be incapable of romantic love, at least as people defined it, but he wasn't incapable of possessiveness.

Merry was his. His for life. He should have dodged the question of love, telling her how much he wanted her, emphasizing the fact that he wanted her so badly it made him weak.

The truth of that made his stomach lurch. If he wasn't

careful, he'd find himself bringing her bouquets of flowers just to make her happy.

They got through dinner that night by being exquisitely polite with each other. Merry didn't say a word about the report in the papers that Napoleon was preparing to invade the English coast, even though they'd had lively discussions of it every evening. Instead Merry excused herself after only two courses and said she was going to bed early.

A few hours later Trent walked through the door that connected their rooms. Embers on Merry's hearth still smoldered, lending her chamber a rosy glow.

His wife was a dark lump on the bed, curled on her side. If she fell asleep after making love, her hair would tangle in curls that felt like corn silk.

Tonight she wore her hair in a thick braid.

Trent drew back the covers as carefully as he could and slipped between the sheets, hoping she wouldn't wake.

Hoping she would.

She didn't stir, even when he carefully undid her braid and set her hair free, tucking her into the curve of his body with one leg over hers, pinning her down.

No, keeping her safe.

It hardly mattered. The tight feeling in his chest eased as soon as he had his arms around her, when Merry sighed in her sleep and snuggled her bottom against him.

Trent stifled a groan and pushed away the idea that he should roll her onto her stomach . . . Slip his hands under her nightdress.

No.

Merry was a will-o'-the-wisp, but she would return to him. Bees slipped from flower to flower, but they flew home at night.

His arms tightened and he buried his face in her fragrant hair until finally, the duke and the duchess both slept.

Chapter Thirty-three

Merry was awakened the following morning by Trent's hand stroking her leg, his fingers asking a question. Without thinking, she let her thighs fall apart, and a silent sigh came from her lips as he accepted her invitation.

She didn't roll over and kiss him, though. She felt bruised inside her chest, as if she'd suffered a physical blow. She was being absurd. A duke lay in her bed, all his restless masculinity focused on her pleasure: what woman would have the right to complain?

Trent kissed his way down her body, slowly and sweetly, the first rays of morning sun making his skin glow like honey. She let her love pour over him as silently as rainwater, voiced only with kisses, touches, moans.

At last she came in a flurry of sparks that hummed through her blood, and returned to herself to the sound of panting—her own panting—in her ears.

Trent turned her over and pulled up her hips, his touch turning her body supple again, awake to every intimacy. He caressed her until she was whimpering, mindless, desire rushing through her body like a tide.

Only when she was trembling with anticipation did he finally thrust inside, their bodies brought into perfect alignment by the hands gripping her hips, his large body rhythmically surging over hers again and again.

They made love like that, in utter silence. Merry hung her head as tears slowly trickled over her cheekbones before disappearing, drop by drop, into her hair.

Yet at the same time, that delicious tension grew within her, winding tighter and tighter until she couldn't feel anything but the imminent burn spreading through her limbs. She pushed back, desperate and hungry for more.

"That's it," Trent growled.

"Please," she said, her voice coming on a sob. "Jack, please. Harder."

He responded with a savage maleness, a wild strength that shocked her into the deepest pleasure. She had scarcely recovered before he put a hand between her legs.

His hips moved again, his body hunched over hers, on and on until she cried out again and convulsed, such violent heat sweeping her that she scarcely noted the deep groan that broke from his chest, or the way his fingers tightened on her hips as he gave a final thrust.

The next moment Merry slipped flat onto her stomach, boneless and enervated. Hair tumbled over her face but she didn't move to brush it away, just lay still, dragging air into her lungs.

She could hear her husband's harsh breathing behind her as he toppled to the side, onto his back.

She felt as tender and vulnerable as a baby bird that had fallen from its nest. Her love for him felt like a mark branded on her skin that he could read, no matter how sophisticated she pretended to be. She lay quietly, and prayed that he would leave without speaking.

"Merry," Trent said, after a time. Of course he wouldn't leave without speaking. It would be ungentlemanly. Her husband was never ungentlemanly.

"Yes?" She tried to sound half asleep, but she sounded alert, even alarmed. "I'm very tired," she added hurriedly.

"I'm sorry about our argument last night."

"As am I," she said.

"Could we simply put this all behind us?"

Put behind her the fact that her husband would never love her? What had made her weep for a full hour the day before was her fixed idea that out of everyone who knew her, Trent alone had known her inner heart.

She had believed he was the one person who didn't find her fickle and shallow.

She was being stupid; she knew she was being stupid. But every one of her insecurities had rampaged through her mind in the night, reminding her of all the things that she was hopeless at, even the way that Lady Caroline looked at her.

Yet when they made love, as they just had . . . He might say that he didn't love her, but the way he'd ravished her said otherwise. He was seductive, yes, but always tender.

The thought gave her backbone. That was the way to show him that he already loved her, because of the tender intimacy they shared. She sat up and looked him in the eye. "How would you characterize what we just did? Was that making love?"

Trent's expression was perfectly blank. Then he said, "Making love is just a more palatable label for intercourse, Merry. Like 'gooseberries,' in fact, which is a word that is misleading in almost all aspects. So is 'making love.'"

"What would you call what we did? How do you think of it?"

His reply was instant and didn't spare her on the grounds of delicate sensibilities. She flinched when he said the word. She'd heard it a few times, but always charged with hostility. It didn't correspond to what they did together.

She couldn't bring herself to repeat it. "Is being with me precisely the same as it was with your mistresses, then?"

"I would prefer not to discuss it," he said, with the kind of polite restraint that called attention to itself.

"Why not? Essentially, you are saying that making love to them is the same as making love to me. Although perhaps I am not as skilled as they."

"There is no comparison between you and my . . . those women." Finally, she saw an emotion in his eyes: distaste.

"But you're saying that you don't make love to me." She got herself out of bed and grabbed her wrapper. "Presumably, you didn't make love to *them*, either. If love plays no part in intimacy, there can be no difference between bedding me or them."

If he refused to call it love, she would try to accept it. But it wasn't friendship, either. One didn't make love to a *friend* as her husband made love to her. It was the only ammunition she had, and by God, she was going to use it.

"That being the case, I'd like to know how I compare in the bed to your last mistress, the most recent one," Merry said. "The one to whom you gave a ruby."

Trent's eyes narrowed. "How did you know that?"

"Cedric told me."

Darkness swept up his face as if a storm had blown in from the sea. "I find it intolerable that you and my brother discussed the subject."

"I am sympathetic," she retorted. "Nor was I happy that you and Cedric chatted about my supposed erotic experience. But I digress. You do not love me, and there is no such thing as 'making love.' Emotion other than lust plays no part in the matter. Therefore, you probably enjoyed it more with her, since she is presumably more experienced?"

"You are my *wife*, Merry. That changes everything." His lips barely moved and every muscle was taut.

Merry felt as if she were outside her own body, observing herself prod a lion in its cage. Why was she pushing him? And yet her heart was beating with an anguished fury, raging at the idea that their couplings had been nothing more than what he had shared with his mistress.

"Why did you give her a ruby?" she demanded. "Cedric thought you wildly overpaid her."

His eyes met hers directly, without emotion. "She announced that she was in love with me. She became distraught when I did not reciprocate."

Just like that, the supposed comparison she had set up—between his mistress and herself—fell to pieces. She loved Trent. Just as his mistress had loved him, and he certainly hadn't fallen in love with the poor woman as a result.

In truth, there was no difference between the acts. Neither she nor his mistress experienced it as Trent did.

"I married you for better or worse," he said now, "and I will never break my vows. Our friendship means a great deal to me, Merry. I believe that we will have—we do already have—an excellent marriage. It's all a matter of control. I shall control my temper, and you shall ignore this infatuation until it disappears."

Merry didn't trust her voice, so she just nodded. She was trapped. He didn't believe in love, and her romantic history merely confirmed his skepticism. She had to accept what he was saying because she had no credibility.

There was no sense to demanding words that he couldn't

or wouldn't give. She took a deep breath. She could prove herself over time. They made love every night; she would just have to show him, without words.

Love him silently.

There was one part of all this that she couldn't get out of her mind: Trent's mistress, the woman dismissed with a ruby, the one who loved him.

Merry wanted Trent to think that bedding her—Merry—was the best experience he'd ever had. Later that night, after her bath, she slid into Trent's bed with a plan in mind. She had decided to put into effect everything she'd learned about his body and drive him mindless with desire.

Damn it, if there was a competition between his mistress and herself—even if it was only in her own head—she was determined to win. She didn't have to ever say again that she loved him, since he disliked hearing it. But she could *show* it. She could make love to him as no other woman ever had.

Yet within moments, she was putty in his hands, whimpering, her heart pounding a crazy, blissful rhythm. Trent had never said much in bed, other than growling appreciation of her body, or cursing as she caressed him, learning to please him. When she licked his shaft, for example . . .

But she had to make him speak to her. "Is there anything you'd like me to do differently?" she asked, pitching her voice to a silky, seductive murmur.

He frowned. "Pardon me?"

"I asked if there is anything you'd like me to do differently," she whispered, peeping at him from under her lashes. At the same moment, she curled her fingers tightly around his "cock," as he called it.

Maybe he would say that he had never had such a wonderful experience in bed. Ever.

She was just beginning to smile, her heart singing, when he nodded.

Nodded?

Well, spit.

Before she had time to think about it, Trent smoothly took on the role of a tutor, adjusting her body as if she were a wooden model. "I enjoy having my stones caressed," he told her.

As if he was noting his preference for ale over lemonade.

All the time, he was caressing *her*, and damn it, the man had learned everything about her body. She was on fire, her hands shaking as she obeyed his instructions until he captured them and held them over her head, using his body and his teeth to make her writhe under him.

A dark voice said in her ear, "Beg me, Merry."

"*Please*," she gasped, without a second's thought. Over the weeks of their marriage, she had turned the word into a hymn that reverberated in the air between them.

Tonight he made her say it over and over, expertly re-arranging her body until her limbs ached with frustrated desire. She started to protest, but at that very moment he pulled her legs apart and thrust inside.

For the first time that evening, she thought he was on the verge of losing control. He looked mad with desire, a groan deep in his throat breaking free. Yet she soon realized that he was changing his rhythm every time the burn began to creep up her legs. By the time he allowed her to have an orgasm, she was sweating and panting.

Pleasure crashed over her with a kind of brutal, melting ferocity such as she had never before felt.

Trent hung over her, panting, and said, "There are other things we can try . . . maybe next time."

That hadn't been what she hoped for.

Not at all.

Chapter Thirty-four

Merry spent the day working in the garden with Mr. Boothby, but even the simple pleasure of transplanting lettuce seedlings that she herself had sown a month before didn't lessen her heartache.

When the last seedling was in place, she wandered around the side of the house to the stone bench where she'd sat with Trent on her first day in the garden. Only the calls of swallows high above broke the song of the honeybees.

Trent had his own odd logic, and he had held firm from the beginning. He had warned her that he loathed excesses of emotion.

She felt both humiliated and foolish. How could she even dream that he would return the wild emotion that she was experiencing? How could she have thought that her meager skills in the bedchamber approached that of the undoubtedly exquisite woman who had been Trent's mistress?

With all her heart, she wished that she'd never disclosed the stupid, stupid fact that she was in love with Trent. It hadn't ruined everything . . . but it had changed things. Before, she had felt beautiful and desired.

She no longer felt that way. She couldn't help thinking that if she were more beautiful, more talented, more amusing, better in bed . . . then he might have fallen in love with her. He wouldn't have been able to stop himself.

No, that didn't make sense, because he didn't fall in love with his mistress.

All the same, she refused to give up. The idea brought to the forefront all the stubbornness that had driven her father to woo a young English lady who'd shuddered at the very thought of a penniless American.

If her father could do it, *she* could do it.

She had made a good start last night, asking how to make their bedding more enjoyable. In fact, she was ashamed to think that she had never asked him before. She had just taken and taken, so overwhelmed by his skills that she lost sight of everything but her own pleasure.

No more.

She would not be a selfish bed partner.

And outside the chamber?

Trent hadn't come to her with a list in hand, but all the same, he desired something that was not so far off from what Cedric had wanted.

In his heart of hearts, Trent wanted her to be more English.

She had behaved like a child, running around kissing her husband in front of others, and calling him that childish name—Jack—which he disliked. She would hate it if he started chanting, "Mary, Mary, Quite Contrary." And yet, Trent had never objected when she called him whatever *she* wanted.

From now on, he would be Trent to her, just as he requested.

She could tell that he disliked being kissed in public. She'd felt his body stiffen. She would stop.

Finally, she could not continue to besiege him with protestations of love, nor could she nourish the hope that learning better skills in the bedroom would win his love. She was only demanding something that he didn't feel.

He had accepted her as she was. He might not like everything about her, but he was a true gentleman. Likewise, she had to accept him as he was—but it didn't mean that she had to accept herself.

Over time, she could prove that her love wasn't shallow. English gentlewomen didn't fall in and out of love like jackrabbits. They didn't kiss in public or call their husbands pet names.

Love meant you wanted the other person's happiness more than your own. If you loved a person, you made yourself better.

Glancing down, she discovered that she'd been idly drawing with a stick in the dirt, outlining a plan for including raspberry bushes in Boothby's expanded kitchen gardens. She scuffed it out with her toe.

That day and all the next, Merry adhered to every precept Miss Fairfax had drilled into her. She was affectionate but not extravagantly so with her husband. A few times, her hand trembled with the instinct to reach out and push back a stray lock of hair, but she refrained.

More than once, she fought an errant wish to weep, but she kept reminding herself that she wanted to make Trent happy. She loved him.

You make people you love happy.

Her aunt had once told her, when she was a little girl and missing her father, "Smile even if your heart is breaking. The grief will still be there, but you are giving it permission to ease. And one day, it *will* ease and you'll feel better."

Merry had done her best then, and she did her best now.

The true challenge came when they were making love. Caught in passion, sweating and trembling, she had to bite her lip ferociously in order to stop herself from uttering love words Trent didn't want to hear.

She was determined not to impose on him again.

Fortunately, most of the time she was busy making certain that she performed the caresses Trent taught her, in both the proper order and manner. If some spontaneity was missing, she was the only one who seemed to notice.

Married couples do settle into a pleasurable routine, of course.

Chapter Thirty-Five

Trent made it through the days that followed Merry's declaration of love in a haze. He still didn't know exactly what had happened between them. Thank God, it had blown over quickly, or so he told himself.

On the face of it, nothing had changed. Though why that made him feel like grinding his teeth and cursing, he didn't know.

His wife seemed to have got over their disagreement promptly and without holding a grudge.

But she had changed. She wasn't herself. At luncheon the next day, he caught her pronouncing "schedule" with a "shed" sound and not "sked," as she had before.

She laughed when he pointed it out, and said that their children would be English.

Trent scowled at her.

"All right, I won't try to adopt an English accent," she

said, putting a hand on his arm. "But I would never want our children to feel that they owed allegiance to two countries. It would be confusing."

She was right . . . was she right? He didn't know. But he didn't want Merry to put a hand on his sleeve as if she were Lady Caroline.

The evening meal was surprisingly tedious, because she didn't take him to task for the inadequacies of the English government, as she usually did. The newspaper reported the despicable treatment of the begums of Oudh by the East India Company, but Merry only remarked on the prospects for a good harvest. She seemed to have made friends with every one of his tenant farmers.

On the second evening, it struck him that she hadn't told him any facts all that day or the one before. It felt like a clutch at his heart, the idea that his wife would no longer inform him, out of the blue, that King Henry III had a polar bear that used to swim in the Thames.

She'd spent the whole morning going about in that damned pony cart. Holding babies, she said. Talking to tenants.

"What did you talk about?" he asked.

She rolled her eyes. "We argued. Mr. Middlebryer is in favor of Lord Ellenborough's bill extending the death penalty to violent crimes. It's well known that penalties do not discourage criminal activity."

She was sharing all those facts she had stored in her head with others, but not with him.

Merry must have seen a shadow on his face because she added, "Not to worry, Trent. I didn't offend him; we both enjoyed ourselves."

"Why the hell are you calling me that name?" he demanded.

He saw the confusion on her face. "Because it's your name?"

He felt churlish but couldn't seem to stop himself. "You said that Trent sounded like a river and you'd prefer Jack when we were alone. We're alone."

Merry gave him that charming smile, the one she gave to footmen, and said, "I called you Jack for all the wrong reasons, simply because it was an American name." It wasn't *his* smile. The smile she gave Jack.

Trent nodded at the dog she was cuddling and said, "What about George? He's named after your president."

"George is a name that can also honor the king," she said, scratching the puppy's head. "George the Third. I'm sure my George is a king among dogs, after all."

"You may call me Jack," he said lamely.

"You told me that it was your childhood name, and I didn't understand how much you disliked it. I apologize," she said earnestly, obviously meaning it.

Trent finally managed to identify the storm of feelings that was making him feel sick.

He felt as guilty as if he'd killed a robin in its nest.

It turned out he had a conscience. Yet what had he done, precisely? He'd never asked Merry to turn mealymouthed or English.

He had liked her just as she was. He liked being called Jack.

Now she was every inch a duchess: affable to all, irreproachable in her kindness, courteous to her husband. The household eddied around her like leaves caught in a river, and she seemed to effortlessly keep it all going.

The thought sent him, brooding, into his study. He suspected he knew what was going on: in her courageous, cheerful way, Merry had determined to make the best of things. He had as much as told her that she was immature and shallow, but he was an idiot.

She was at the mercy of her emotions, after all. It wasn't as if she'd said, *I think I'll fall in love with Cedric today.* Or Bertie, or that other idiot over in Boston.

Or him.

As far as he could see, emotion stormed over her like a hurricane and left as quickly. The harsh pain in his chest was hard to ignore; he wanted to turn back the clock. Why in hell hadn't he luxuriated in her love while he had it? He was damned sure that Bertie had been wildly happy for the two glorious months that Merry loved him.

The reminder that she'd fallen out of love with Bertie made Trent feel like a feral dog chained to a tree. Something uncontrollable rose up in his gut, demanding attention. Some . . . feeling. Worse than his attack of conscience, worse than lust, worse than anger.

It took the discipline of a lifetime to shove that emotion back into the locked box where it belonged.

Chapter Thirty-six

After a few days, Merry was pretty sure that Trent didn't appreciate her efforts to become more English. His mouth tightened when she tried to modify her voice. He growled at her when she praised British policy.

Perhaps he wanted her, the real her.

Unfortunately, she was growing confused about who the real her was.

Being a duchess was a lot of work. It seemed selfish to spend time picking flowers when so many people living on her husband's land were in need: sometimes of no more than a friendly word, but often, once she sat down to talk, she learned that Mum had rheumatism, or the roof was leaking, or their only cow had died and they hadn't milk for the children.

Who would listen, if not the duchess?

Today she had to visit a new widow, and she'd promised to stop by the vicarage. The late duchess's orphanage urgently needed beds; the littlest ones were sleeping in threes and fours. At home, Mrs. Honeydukes wanted to show her samples of serge for the footmen's new livery.

Merry sighed and turned away from the window. It was time to bathe and dress. All she wanted to do was garden, but it was out of the question. Maybe tonight she could find some time for the design of a new hedge maze to replace the decrepit one.

No, tonight the squire and his wife were giving a dinner party to celebrate the fact that their only son had graduated from Cambridge with highest honors. Her heart sank even further: Kestril would be in attendance.

Kestril spilled his adulation for her as easily as a bag of grain pours out its seed, and her marriage only seemed to have exacerbated things. It had become intolerable. Tonight she would have to make a stand and tell him plainly that if he didn't change his behavior, she would have no choice but to exclude him from her social circle.

That evening she put a gown whose leaf-green skirt showed through translucent silk gauze trimmed with ribbons the color of cherries, along with high-heeled Italian shoes that matched the ribbons. She might not act like a perfect duchess, but she was reasonably certain that she looked like one.

She was fidgeting around the drawing room, sipping a glass of sherry, when Oswald informed her that His Grace was unavoidably detained, and had requested that she precede him; he would join the party as soon as he was able.

Merry put down her glass. Could it be that Trent was avoiding a carriage ride with her? "Of course," she said to Oswald, managing a smile. "My wrap, if you please. The carriage can return for His Grace."

She had made such a foolish mistake when she'd told

Trent that she loved him. By pushing him, she had ruined everything they had between them.

No, that couldn't be true.

He would love her someday. She simply had to give him time.

Look at the story he'd told her about his mother. What's more, his only sibling was Cedric. She shuddered at the thought. Trent had never been loved; how could she expect him to recognize the emotion when he felt it?

If only she hadn't told him. *That* was what had created this painful awkwardness between them. It was always there in the room now. He felt she was fickle and shallow, and then she'd demanded an emotion he didn't feel for her.

His words beat through her head, creating a repeating memory as powerful and painful as it had been the first time she'd heard it. *I don't love you, Merry, not that way, and I never will.*

She wrenched her mind away. Enough. She would prove her constancy by loving him, and after a year, or five years, or however many it took, she would mention it again.

Meanwhile she had to love him silently while becoming who he wanted.

He would fall in love with her. It would just take time.

She was learning to be a duchess as fast as she could. She was already better in bed, making certain that she caressed him in all the right ways every single time. She hadn't called him Jack once, although he didn't seem to notice either way.

What's more, she hadn't let herself cry in front of Trent, no matter how anguished she felt, because she knew how much he hated it. It turned out that if a woman clenched her fists hard, driving her fingernails into her palms, she could stop tears from falling. Then she could pull on gloves and cover up the white marks left on her skin.

Part of her wanted to run into the library, pull him away from the desk, and make him go to the dinner party with her. Didn't he care in the least that Kestril would take it as blatant encouragement if she appeared alone?

But a duchess didn't do that sort of thing. A duchess didn't shout the way an American woman might. A duchess just climbed into the coach and silently ground her teeth.

The squire's drawing room was unusually full; in addition to the usual neighbors, Lady Montjoy's son had brought home with him four young men from Cambridge. With one glance, Merry could tell that all five young men were well into their cups.

Kestril popped up at her elbow the moment she turned from her hosts. Merry's spirits sank when he greeted her with a tipsy grin.

"The evening is very fine, Your Grace, and our hostess has opened the doors leading to the garden. There is a magnificent prospect to the east and I am convinced you would find that it rivals even the finest such in America."

Merry hesitated, but she might as well get it over with. She had to inform Kestril that they would no longer converse until he put a stop to his ardent compliments, not to mention his feverish glances.

"Montjoy built a splendid stone staircase, as straight as Jacob's ladder, behind the house," Kestril said. "You simply *must* see it, Your Grace. May I have the pleasure of escorting you there?"

This was her opportunity.

His breath was so brandy-filled that it was likely flammable. He leaned closer and slurred, "I will *always* take the greatest care with the woman who holds my heart in her keeping."

Kestril understood love about as well as she had before

her marriage. She should explain to him that love—*true* love—was something that came quietly in the night, like a thief who stole your heart.

It wasn't a cheap emotion, to be given away to a pretty neighbor. Or to the three men with whom she'd been girlishly infatuated.

"All right," she said with a sigh. "I would be glad of your escort to see the stairs."

The staircase lay on the other side of a short rise, out of sight of the drawing room. Kestril had not exaggerated; it truly was splendid. It stretched all the way down the hill, with no obvious purpose other than to please.

"There are one hundred steps in all," he told her.

"Why is the marble wet?" she asked. "It hasn't rained today."

"Hydraulics," he explained, drawing her down several steps and pointing to a small opening at the top. "When the squire pulls a lever, water pours down the steps, cleansing away leaves and dirt."

"That's quite brilliant," Merry said, immediately thinking of three or four places at Hawksmede where a staircase would be not only beautiful but useful. Likely her uncle would have ideas about the hydraulics. "Do you know—?"

She stopped because Kestril had dropped to his knees, awkwardly balanced on the step above her, still clutching her hand.

She gave a little tug, but he just brought her gloved hand to his mouth and started to kiss it.

"Mr. Kestril," she scolded, pulling harder. "You are being entirely improper."

"You remind me of an orchid, a neglected orchid blooming in the deepest forest," he said, slavering kisses on her gloves. "You are my American orchid."

"Stop kissing my hand this very moment!" Merry cried.

"I will never love any woman the way I love you," he said soulfully. In contrast with Cedric, it was obvious that he had over-imbibed. His words were slurring together.

Merry tugged again, with more force. "Let go of my hand, sirrah!" Perhaps she ought to give him a kick. Her shoes were quite pointy. She moved up a step so that she was on the same level. "If you don't let go, I shall kick you straight down this flight of steps, Mr. Kestril!"

He simply looked up at her, eyes wide and glassy. "I know you desire me as much as I desire you, Merry. I've seen it in your eyes."

"How dare you use my first name?" She finally wrenched her hand free and wiped it on her gown.

Kestril scrambled to his feet. "I'm planning to travel into the jungle where I will discover a new orchid, which I will name after you. Perhaps a *Comparettia merriana*. Or *Phalaenopsis americana*, depending on what I discover."

"You are a blackguard," Merry snapped, "and exceedingly fortunate that my husband didn't accompany—"

"What care I for husbands? Your hand is a white, white orchid. I love you; I adore you; my heart is in your hands!"

Before she could stop him, he again grabbed her hand and fell to his knees. But one of those knees slipped on the slick stone, and he pitched forward into Merry. She rocked on her high heels, moored by Kestril's grip on her hand.

For a long second she swayed at the top of Squire Montjoy's stone staircase, but then her weight pulled her hand from Kestril's and she pitched down the steps.

There wasn't time to scream.

Chapter Thirty-seven

Trent knew he was in a wild temper. He shouldn't go to the squire's dinner because if Kestril even looked at Merry, he would clip him on the jaw.

She hadn't mentioned love in bed last night, or the night before, or the one before that. Perhaps she'd already fallen out of love. After all, that was the pattern. She fell in love; she fell out of love.

Maybe she'd succumb to Kestril next. The bolt of pure jealousy he felt shocked him into action. He leapt into the carriage as if he were heading to a fire.

His vehicle was forced to wait to enter the squire's courtyard as another was obstructing it; he was startled to see grooms shouting and footmen darting about looking inefficient.

A hand grabbed his shoulder as Trent descended from the carriage. He turned to find his coachman behind him.

"Yer Grace," John shouted, "they're saying the duchess . . . the duchess—" His voice was drowned out in the clamor.

In that moment, Trent registered that the carriage that had blocked the courtyard was that of the village doctor, who was unlikely to be an invited guest. His heart began pounding in his ears.

He didn't wait to clarify what John was trying to tell him; he took off for the front door at full speed, following the sound of voices through open doors into the back garden.

Erupting from the house, he saw guests clustered at the top of the squire's famed cascade of steps, peering down. Even as he ran past them and down the hill, his brain was piecing together the scene in front of him: people were kneeling beside someone . . . the doctor, too, was on his knees . . . there was a woman lying on the grass.

Trent's lungs constricted in a silent howl. It was Merry. Her face was white; her eyes were closed and her forehead was bloody.

Dread wasn't an emotion; it was bigger than that. It buckled a man's knees and poisoned the air in his lungs.

When he reached the group, Trent shoved the squire to the side, dropped to his knees, and put a hand on his wife's cheek. "Merry, what happened, darling? Are you all right? Can you open your eyes?"

Her eyes opened. Thank God, her eyes opened. Her forehead was scraped, but he didn't see signs of a more serious injury.

"Trent," she said in a wavering voice.

He felt a wave of relief so acute that he was almost unable to speak, along with a searing need to gather her into his arms and hold her. But first he had to know what was wrong, and whether she'd broken anything. "Are you hurt? What happened? Did you slip on the steps?"

"I'm not sure," she said weakly.

"The duchess is suffering from *commotio cerebri*."

Trent looked up and found a young stranger with a weedy beard crouching across from him. He went on importantly, "To put it in terms you can understand, she has a commotion of the brain caused by a concussive blow. But she has not broken any limbs."

Trent shifted his eyes to the village doctor, who said, "Her Grace doesn't recall the precise events which led to her injury, but Mr. Kestril has informed us that she slipped and tumbled down the steps while he was explaining the water feature of these steps."

"Where is he?" Trent asked, keeping his voice even. Bloody Kestril.

"Hysterical fit," the young man said. "Lady Montjoy took him off for a dose of bitters."

"Her Grace tumbled around halfway down the steps," the doctor said. "After ascertaining that her neck and spine appear to be uninjured, we moved her here while the grooms put together a provisional litter."

Carefully, unable to stop himself, Trent pulled his wife into his arms. She turned her cheek against his chest without saying a word. His arms tightened until he was probably causing her pain. Without speaking, he buried his face in her hair, swallowing hard, aware that everyone could see he was clutching her but beyond caring.

"Your Grace, I am Simon Swansdown, Esquire, at your service," the weedy stranger announced, though no one had asked. "I attended Cambridge University, then studied medicine for a year at the University of Edinburgh. I am now bound for London, where I'll take my degree. I can assure you that memory loss is common in cases of injury to the brain."

"'Injury to the brain,'" Trent repeated. Merry was pale,

but she appeared unharmed, other than the graze on her forehead. He ran one hand over her head, his other arm still holding her. He couldn't find a bump.

"I can't remember anything about the fall," she said faintly. "I'm trying . . . but I just *can't*."

"You may never remember anything, Your Grace," the doctor put in. "The more important point is that you have survived with a quite mild injury."

"*Commotio cerebri* may cause memory loss of a few hours, days, or even weeks," Swansdown said. "Patients frequently lose the memory of a length of time before the accident. Your Grace, do you know where you are?"

"On the grass," Merry said wearily, closing her eyes. "Trent, can we please go home?"

"Can you tell us what day it is?" Swansdown asked.

"Will her memory come back in time?" Trent asked, ignoring Swansdown and looking to the doctor again.

"In my experience, it may or may not. It is impossible to say; there is much that we do not understand about this type of injury. He turned to Merry. "Your Grace, I would echo my . . . colleague's question. Do you know what day it is?"

"The newest treatment to induce memory recovery is an injection of oil of turpentine," Swansdown said importantly.

Merry's brows drew together. "I'm not sure what day it is," she whispered.

"It's Saturday," Trent said. "But it doesn't matter. It's not important."

"You will suffer headaches on and off for a few days," the doctor told her. "Oil of turpentine may be the latest treatment, but I am of the firm conviction that it is best to do as little as possible. I advise strict bed rest in a darkened room for the next several days."

"What is the last thing you remember?" Trent asked, rocking Merry a little. She was a perfect bundle of soft woman and silky hair and everything he ever wanted in life.

"I can't remember the accident at all."

"You came to a dinner party at the squire's house," Trent said.

"I came by myself?" She looked confused. "Where were you?"

Regret made his chest convulse. "I didn't accompany you. I am told you went for a walk with Mr. Kestril." Kestril, who would answer for allowing Merry to topple down the stairs, though Trent didn't voice it aloud.

"We don't well understand the effect of blows to the brain," the doctor said. "But clearly your wife knows who she is, Your Grace, and who you are. That's all that matters."

Trent nodded and rose to his feet, Merry in his arms. "I'll take her home."

"Don't push Her Grace to remember, or allow her to become frustrated by what she has forgotten," the doctor said, straightening. "In these cases, it's important for the patient to remain tranquil. Racking her brain will do no good, and it might do harm."

"I strongly recommend an injection of turpentine," Swansdown piped up.

"As much rest as possible," the doctor said firmly.

The Montjoys were waiting at the top of the steps. Trent nodded and thanked them for summoning the doctor. He was on the point of asking about Kestril's whereabouts, when he glanced down at his wife's blanched face and decided that Kestril could wait.

Trent managed to climb into their carriage without letting go of Merry. Inside, he propped himself in the corner, keeping the dearest person in his world safe in the circle of his arms. "What's the last thing you remember?" he asked her again.

A few moments of silence, then: "Luncheon."

That wasn't bad. He dropped a kiss on her hair. "I was out of the house, so I don't know how you spent the afternoon. You've forgotten an uneventful few hours. It's possible your maid could jog your memory but perhaps you shouldn't bother."

She raised her head, frowning at him. "You weren't out of the house, Jack. We had a picnic in the flax field."

Trent's heart skipped a beat. That was almost a week ago. They had spread a blanket and made love five . . . six days ago.

"Don't you remember anything after that?" he asked carefully. "Our disagreement?" His throat felt rusty and dry.

"Disagreement?" Unease crossed her face. "This afternoon? Have I forgotten more than a single afternoon?"

"It was nothing important," he answered quickly, brushing a kiss across her lips.

"What did we quarrel about?"

"Nothing," he said. "A trifling matter."

She snuggled back against his chest. "I've never had a headache quite like this one."

"What does it feel like?"

"A clamp on my head. And I'm so tired."

"Go to sleep, darling," he said quietly. As her eyes lowered, he slowly caressed her back, like a lullaby his mother had never sung to him.

Chapter Thirty-eight

Merry spent the next few days in bed, as the doctor had ordered. The first day was the worst, because not only did her head throb intolerably, but she woke in the grip of the sort of nausea that almost made her wish the fall had finished her off.

"This is so humiliating," she moaned, after losing yet another battle with the urge to retch.

"The doctor assures me an unsettled stomach is commonplace," Trent said matter-of-factly. He handed the basin to her maid and seated himself on the edge of the bed, wiping her face with a wet cloth.

Merry kept falling asleep. Every time she awoke Trent was there, sitting beside her reading or working at the desk in his alcove.

He wasn't the only one in the room. Snowdrop scratched the door until she was admitted. George, who usually ran in terror from the little white dog, ignored her altogether and fretted until he was allowed to curl up next to Merry on the bed.

The second and third days passed in the same way as the queasiness gradually went away. Trent brought her broth, and made her drink cup after cup because the doctor thought liquids were a good idea. He read the newspaper aloud to her, because words swam about on the page and made it impossible for her to even skim the headlines.

On the fourth day, Merry woke with the dawn to discover her husband's strong arm curled around her middle, holding her firmly against his body.

Her head didn't hurt, and the room wasn't spinning. She felt neither queasy nor lethargic.

In fact, she felt splendid, entirely returned to normal. Except she wasn't normal, was she? She'd lost a few days—she wasn't sure how many—and would never get them back. It was the queerest thing, to have a slice of one's existence simply vanish.

But did it matter? What mattered was that her husband was here and she loved him—

Just like that, it all came back. Everything. Well, everything up to the moment Kestril knelt at her feet and called her "his American orchid."

An involuntary shudder went through her. It was probably just as well that she couldn't remember the rest.

The quarrel—the one that Trent had asked her about in the carriage—*that* memory was back, too. She swallowed hard, remembering that her husband had said their disagreement was unimportant. A trifling matter, he'd called it.

He didn't want her to remember, because she had embarrassed him by expressing feelings he didn't share.

In short, she had the miracle she had devoutly hoped for.

When Kestril had said, "I love you," he had made a claim on her feelings. For the first time, she understood exactly what it felt like to be trapped by someone else's emotion, their unreasonable demand for a response one couldn't give.

Trent wasn't disgusted by her, as she was by Kestril. But it was no wonder that his eyes darkened with distaste when she insisted on expressing herself. Considering her regrettable history, he had shown considerable forbearance during their disagreement.

She *did* love him, but that didn't matter.

The accident, frightening as it was, had given her a gift: she was able to turn back the clock. No more babbling of love, making her husband uncomfortable. Over time, she would prove that she wasn't shallow or inconstant.

For now, she would bury the whole idea deep in her heart. Perhaps she'd mention it in five years. Or ten.

She didn't care if Trent ever said, "I love you."

Well, not very much.

She stretched, happy to realize that her body was singing with health . . . and desire. Her marriage was reborn, fresh and new, and this time she wouldn't make a mess of it.

When Trent awoke, it took a few minutes to persuade him that she didn't need broth, and that her head no longer ached, and that she was fit as ever.

But once he calmed down, handed the dogs over to a footman, and came back to bed, Merry leaned her head against his shoulder and said, "I have to thank you for everything you've done since my accident to nurse me back to health."

"In sickness and in health," he said, putting his arm around her.

"It was more than most husbands would do," Merry

pointed out. "That was the action of a true friend, and I'm so grateful."

For some reason, he didn't seem happy with her thanks. His eyes narrowed and his jaw clenched.

But Merry was confident she could coax him out of a bad mood. After all, she possessed all those new skills he'd taught her.

In the days following their quarrel, Trent had imagined Merry telling him bluntly that she had ceased to love him. In his bleakest moments, he had even imagined her declaring that she meant to return to America on the next boat.

But he had never imagined she would forget that she loved him.

Yet that's what happened. Her love for him vanished along with her memory of the accident.

No matter how many times he ravished her, the word "love" never passed her lips. She screamed with pleasure, sobbing, panting, hoarse, undone. He turned her into the picture of debauched womanhood, glistening with sweat, her chest still heaving, her lips swollen and glossy from his kisses.

Desire, not love.

A drop of bitter irony found its way into his mind: he hadn't wanted a wife who loved him, and now he had just that wife: Merry, without the awkward emotions and unspoken expectations.

She had even thanked him for taking care of her, as if he were any acquaintance. As if that was all they were. *Friends.*

He hated that word.

Yet if the accident robbed him of Merry's love, she was

nevertheless still his. She was in *his* arms, in *his* bed, in *his* house.

The irony was that he knew to the core of his being that possession and friendship weren't enough anymore. Having been loved by her, he wanted more.

Back in his study but unable to concentrate, he finally decided that the solution was up to him. He had to make her fall in love with him again.

He would woo her, as her father had wooed her mother. As her other fiancés had done, Bertie and Cedric and that other fool.

Kestril as well, now he thought of it.

According to the squire, the young fool had bankrupted himself over an orchid, and fled the country the night after Merry's fall.

Trent was reasonably certain that most of the county had assured Kestril that it would be better to leave England than to face his wrath.

Instinct told him that the man precipitated the accident somehow. Maybe he tried to kiss Merry. Trent came back to himself to find that his hands were in fists and he was vibrating with rage.

A few days later, when he was absolutely certain that his wife had fully recovered—after she had started swatting him every time he inquired about her head—he woke her early in the morning and made love to her so passionately that she barely stirred when he kissed her nose and left for London.

He had two items of business in London. The first was a brief visit to Rundell & Bridge. He selected a superb diamond ring that was significantly larger than the one Cedric had stolen.

As long as he was there, he picked up an emerald

diadem as well, with a matching emerald manteau clasp, a pair of earrings, and an armlet. He hesitated over a pearl necklace that reminded him of Merry's skin but decided in the end to return with her and let her choose what she'd like herself.

His second errand took a bit longer. But the power of his title—and the ducal purse—eventually triumphed.

He returned to the toll road and managed to arrive at Hawksmede at six o'clock that evening. His butler was shocked. "It's a full three hours to London, Your Grace," he kept saying. "The horses must have been running full out."

"We made good time," Trent said, handing over his hat and gloves. "I've given the gardeners a task that must be seen to immediately, Oswald. I'd be grateful if you'd send a couple of footmen outside to see if they can provide additional help. Where is the duchess?"

"One of the grooms drove her in the pony cart to the village, Your Grace."

Trent took his hat back.

"I believe she is paying a call to the vicar," Oswald called, as Trent barreled out the door.

Sure enough, he found Merry chatting with the vicar's wife amid the crumbs of a tea cake.

Trent's wholly unexpected appearance in the doorway made the duchess blink. For a thrilling moment, he thought Merry was about to jump up and throw herself into his arms.

But she didn't. She was charming and friendly, but she had stopped kissing him in public.

When she fell back in love with him, he would demand it. She had to kiss him whenever they met or parted. No exceptions.

Later that evening, after they returned home, dressed for dinner, and met again in the drawing room, he scarcely bade her good evening before he presented her with the emeralds.

"They're beautiful!" Merry cried. Her eyes lit with pleasure; she examined each piece with delight; she danced over to a glass and put them all on, even the diadem, which she wore throughout dinner.

She thanked him extravagantly, but said nothing about love. Nor did she make any witticisms about an American wearing a crown, which frankly was half the reason he had chosen that set. He thought it would make her laugh.

He couldn't give her his second gift until it was ready. And he had made up his mind to save the diamond ring until she fell back in love.

Later that evening, they scarcely made it up the stairs before tearing off each other's clothing. He seduced her with a feverishness that approached madness . . . but she still said nothing about love.

Afterward, he couldn't sleep. He lay on his back, Merry tucked against him, and alternated between cold sweats at remembering how she'd looked, seemingly lifeless on Montjoy's lawn, and hot fear at the idea that he'd lost his chance.

The injury to her brain had not diminished her desire for him, but it had erased her love, leaving affection in its place. Not love.

Who could have dreamed those words meant so much? Not he.

The galling thing was that he knew exactly what it was that he was feeling. After all, he had never stopped loving his mother, even after he was aware of her clear preference for Cedric.

In the morning, Trent waited until after breakfast before he took Merry's arm and asked if she might accompany him to the gardens.

She looked up at him in surprise. "The gardens? I don't really have time, Trent. I promised Mrs. Honeydukes that—"

"I want to show you something," he said stubbornly. Merry still looked as if she might object, so Trent was forced to kiss her until she gave in.

If she wasn't going to kiss him in public, he would have to kiss her instead.

Outside, Merry forgot about Mrs. Honeydukes and began pointing out all the ways in which the gardens were improving.

It was a damp morning, and she clung to his arm as she picked her way down the decrepit stone walks. Trent made a mental note to get the walks repaved by the following week, no matter how many stonecutters had to be brought out from London. He refused to contemplate her falling ever again.

They walked into the greenhouse.

"What is that?" Merry gasped, staring down into a gaping hole that had replaced two old tables.

Boothby stepped forward. "Morning, Your Graces! That's a pit," he said, stating the obvious.

"Yes, but what are your men doing to it?"

"Lining it with tanner's bark," he answered.

"For the cultivation of pineapple seedlings," Trent put in.

Merry turned to him with a gasp. "You didn't!"

Trent grinned and turned her to face the opposite corner where a shiny black stove with a brass pineapple on its door squatted. "We'll have to build another forcing house for plants that don't like as much heat the way pineapples do, but Boothby seems to have it all in hand. I brought along a man from Chelsea Physic Garden who'll get the seedlings set up as soon as the men finish with the pit."

"Oh, Trent!" Merry cried, laughing and crying at the same time. "This is so wonderful!" She came up on her toes and kissed him. "You make me so very happy. I think I am the luckiest duchess in all of England."

"And America?"

"That goes without saying," she said, twinkling at him. "I am the *only* American duchess."

Nothing about love.

He watched as Merry ran outside to talk to Boothby about pineapple seedlings. Her silence was a gash in his heart.

It wasn't possible that a crack on the head could excise someone's love, was it? As decisively as a surgeon removed a bad tooth?

It took a few minutes before he understood what he had to do. He couldn't simply hand over the pineapple stove—or the emeralds, for that matter—and expect them to do the work for him.

He had to say the words himself.

Right.

He could do that.

He had felt the cursed sentence welling up in his chest in the last two days, as if it were fighting to be said. He walked outside and got rid of Boothby and his crew with a jerk of his head.

Then he led Merry back into the greenhouse, lifted her onto his favorite table, braced his arms on either side of her so she couldn't escape, and said, bluntly, "I love you, Merry."

Her mouth fell open. "You what?"

"I adore you." He could hear Merry's voice in his memory, saying the same words. He cupped her face in his hands. "I love you more than I could have imagined possible."

"Trent, are you saying this because I hurt my head?" she asked, narrowing her eyes at him.

"No. I'm saying it because it is true." He snatched her up, burying his face in her hair. "I love you." His voice was a husky growl. "I couldn't stop myself, no matter how much I pretended not to feel the emotion. I pretended not to be making love to you, but I was."

She pulled away, her eyes searching his. "Before, you preferred another word to describe that."

"Fu—" He stopped.

The exchange she was talking about took place during their quarrel—the quarrel she had supposedly forgotten. And now he thought about it, she hadn't gone back to calling him Jack in private, the way she had before they fought.

He stepped back and stared at her.

Shame swept through Merry like a cold wave as she met her husband's eyes. The words he had just said went straight out of her head. Guilt and shame warred for a place in her heart.

"Merry, is there something you forgot to tell me?" Trent said in a quiet voice. "And I use the word 'forgot' quite deliberately."

She swallowed hard. "I'm sorry. I did remember our disagreement."

"Did you *always* remember it?"

"No, no! All the day of the accident I had been wishing that somehow you would forget what I had said, and we could go back to the way we were. At first, I honestly remembered nothing after our picnic in the flax field. But on the fourth day, I suddenly remembered everything."

"Why didn't you tell me?"

"Because you didn't want to hear about love from me." She bit her lip but kept her eyes on his. "I never felt anything like this for my other fiancés. I know you don't believe that, but so it is. So I fibbed—no, I *lied* to you, but it was with the best of intentions. I only want you to be happy, and you didn't want to hear about that—about love."

"I'm not happy."

"I'm sorry," Merry whispered, her eyes falling. She started pleating a fold of her dress.

He took a step closer. "You should be."

Surely she hadn't ruined everything again?

"I know," Merry said earnestly. "Trent, if I promise *never, ever* to—"

"*Jack*," he said. "I hate it when you call me Trent." His mouth met hers; his tongue teased hers, flirting, promising, seducing . . . loving.

By the time he raised his head, she could hardly breathe, let alone speak.

"I love you," her husband said. *Jack* said those words. "Please, Merry, will you tell me that you haven't forgotten to love me?"

She knew that tears shone in her eyes. "Is that what you thought?"

Trent's smile was rueful, but there was real pain behind it. "Emeralds, the pineapple stove . . . I could think of nothing else to give you. You have all the flowers you could possibly wish for."

Her duke was looking at her with an expression that seemed to fulfill every promise she had ever longed for.

"Even when I forgot our quarrel, I didn't forget what I felt for you," she told him.

Her hands were trapped between their bodies and she didn't pull away from his kiss until she could feel his heart beating madly against her palms. He buried his face in her hair. "I was afraid the accident might have knocked sense into you."

"I'll never stop loving you," she whispered.

"But then I realized that even if you didn't feel it any longer, even if you had fallen out of love with me, I would never stop loving you, to the end of my days."

A tear ran down Merry's cheek. "Oh, Jack."

"You just have to understand that I'm very new at this."

"*This?*"

"Loving."

He meant it, Merry could see. He was serious. She felt a deep pang in her heart at the certainty in his eyes.

"You are wrong," she told him. "If you will forgive me for my bluntness, your mother was a monster. But you loved her anyway."

His eyes were so dark that she could hardly read them, but with one fierce movement his mouth swooped onto hers again.

"Jack," Merry whispered sometime later, "you don't mind that I'm American, do you?"

"Hell no."

"If I embarrass you by kissing you in public?"

"I am never embarrassed by you. Never. I just don't want you to fall out of love with me, the way you did Bertie." He pulled her so close that she could feel the hard contour of his shaft between them.

"I shall always love you," Merry promised. "You are my one and only."

A smile crept into his eyes.

"I never loved Bertie, nor Cedric, either. I didn't even know what that sort of love was until I discovered it with you. I love Bess and Thaddeus, but they are my family. My love for you . . . it's bigger than a river." She colored. "That sounds stupid."

"No, it doesn't." Trent kissed her again, almost compulsively, as if he couldn't stop. "Mine is deeper than a tanner's pit."

She choked with laughter.

"Higher than—than a flax plant," he finished, realizing that his poetic ability was as laughable as he'd always thought it would be.

One more thing was left to be done.

Trent pulled back and sank down on one knee before her, right there in the greenhouse. "Merry Pelford, would you do me the very great honor of becoming my wife?"

His wife appeared to have forgotten how to speak—a simple yes would do. She had a hand clapped over her mouth, and tears were slipping down her cheeks.

So he prompted her. "'Deeper than a tanner's pit' is poetry. I'm on one knee and I have a diamond to give you. Those two things, Miss Pelford, mean that you will fall madly in love with me, and promise to marry me. Luckily for me, I can tie you to my bed if you try to resist me."

Her hand fell from her mouth. "Are you teasing me?" Merry demanded.

"Yes," he said instantly.

"In the middle of your marriage proposal?" Her voice rose a little.

"Yes," he said. And then added, "You make me laugh, Merry. But do you suppose that you could answer me? A brick is cutting into my knee."

His wife leaned forward, which put her breasts at a delicious distance from his mouth. But he kept his eyes above her chin.

"Yes," she whispered. "Oh yes, Jack, yes, I will. I will love you, to the top of an aspen, and to the bottom of that pit, and all the way to London and back. I'm already your wife and I shall never change my mind."

He stood up and took her left hand in his. Then he slid a diamond on her finger that glittered in the sunlight filtering through the thick panes.

"You are my *American* duchess," Trent said gruffly, his finger tracing the shape of her cheek. "You pour milk into tea at the wrong time, but you do everything else the right way. I love the way you speak. And I love what you say. I've never met another woman who is as fascinating."

Merry shut her eyes to listen to what her husband was saying.

To *memorize* what he was saying.

His hand slid down over her breast with an affectionate pause over her nipple and then continued down the curve of her stomach.

"When you are carrying our first child," Trent said, his voice dropping to a deeper register, "I will hope she's a girl, because she will keep her younger brothers in line."

Merry's mouth curled into the biggest smile of her life. She opened her eyes.

"I'm not practiced at this, love, but I will give you everything I have. I only hope our children have your laughter and your curiosity and your gift for love."

Another tear ran down her cheek.

He smelled like wintergreen soap and clean sweat and everything she loved most in the world. He tasted like happiness.

Sometime later, she opened her eyes again and said huskily, "I wouldn't be your duchess, but for a rented pineapple. Do you suppose that we should send a crate of them to Mrs. Bennett, once we have harvested our first crop?"

A slow grin spread across Trent's face. "I believe it's time for bed," he said conversationally.

"It's not even time for luncheon," she protested.

Her husband's smile hadn't a trace of that quiet darkness that he usually carried with him.

"That was a ducal order," he clarified, eyes gleaming.

It was foolhardy to let him know how much she adored

that commanding tone, so she just slipped from the table. He grabbed her arms. "All those things I taught you how to do in bed?"

Merry grinned. "I'm getting better, aren't I?"

Trent shook his head. "That was bollocks."

Her smile evaporated.

"Making love to you has nothing in common with anything I've experienced with any other woman. Nothing. There's no need for those things; you look at me and I'm hard. Wiggle your hips and I want to come, sometimes in my breeches, like a mere lad."

"Oh," Merry breathed.

He gave her a hard kiss. "Right now, we will make love and it's all going to be for your pleasure."

What woman would say no to *that*?

Inside the house, Trent escorted Merry to her bedchamber and gave her another kiss in full sight of a chambermaid, who promptly fled. Merry tugged at his hand, but he shook his head. "I'll be back in five minutes." His eyes promised wicked things.

Merry managed to wriggle out of her dress—because she'd rather die of shame than summon her maid—and lay down on the bed naked, pretending to be as bold as her husband always was.

The door between their rooms opened and Trent strolled in, carrying a bowl covered with a white cloth.

"What on earth is that?" she asked, sitting up.

He stopped short and his eyes flared with desire so heady that she started tingling all over. Particularly in her breasts, which happened to be where he was looking.

With a visible effort, he looked back at her face. "May I just say how unbelievably lucky I am to have you?" His voice was a husky rumble.

Merry gave him a smile that was only a bit shy. It felt

odd to be naked in the daylight but right then and there she realized that she would stroll through the whole house without a stitch of clothing if she knew that Trent would look at her in that fevered way.

He walked across the room—no, he *prowled* across the room—and sat on the edge of the bed. "We will sleep in my bed tonight."

Merry was having trouble keeping her breath steady. It would never do to let her husband know how melting she felt when he issued commands. At least, this sort of intimate command. "We will?"

"Yes. Because we're going to play in this one now. Afterward, the sheets will be rather sticky." He pulled off the cloth.

The bowl was filled with chunks of sweet, ripe pineapple.

"I brought more than a stove from London," he said with a devilish smile. "Now lie back, Duchess."

"Jack! What are you planning to do?"

He took a cube of the fruit and shook a drop of juice into the bowl. "Eat some," he said meditatively. He held the scrap of sweetness to her lips. "Actually, I'm going to feed it to you."

"I'm quite hungry," Merry said huskily. She opened her mouth and he slipped the fruit inside, bending to lick a stray drop of juice from her lips.

"As am I."

He took a second piece, but didn't feed it to her. Instead, he leaned back, gazing at her body as if it were a work of art.

Her eyes widened.

Then she squealed. The pineapple chunk that slid over her nipple was chilly. But the tongue that followed was blissfully warm.

Chapter Thirty-nine

*T*he letter arrived around six months later, when the duke and duchess were sitting down to breakfast. That very morning, Merry had deduced that she must be carrying a child because—among other clues—the smell of wintergreen soap made her stomach lurch.

Something was obviously not right.

She was drinking a cup of tea and nibbling a piece of toast while Trent read aloud bits from the newspaper so they could argue about them later.

In the middle of an article predicting an invasion by Napoleon—which Merry feared, but Trent scoffed at—she started wondering whether she ought to tell her husband about her suspicions now, or hold off as long as possible.

She had the idea that he might be intolerably protective upon learning she was *enceinte*. She'd never known anyone like Trent, someone who would do literally anything for someone he loved.

That was a surprise: this man who swore he would never love, loved more fiercely and passionately than Merry could ever have imagined.

When Oswald entered with the post, Merry perked up. "Is that letter on top from my aunt?"

"I'm afraid not, Your Grace."

Trent took the letter, his brow furrowing. "From Cedric," he said. "Posted a month ago."

Merry gasped and straightened. They hadn't heard from her brother-in-law since he left England. They hadn't discussed it, but she knew that her husband worried about his twin, for all he growled at the mention of him.

"This is a first," Trent commented, tearing open the letter.

"Have you written to him since he left?" Merry asked.

"Once or twice."

Of course he had. Trent would never give up on his foolish brother.

She took her last bite of toast, thinking about family. Then she heard a deep chuckle and looked up.

"Did I ever tell you that arrogance runs in the bloodline?"

"I ascertained that by myself," Merry said demurely.

"Read this." He tossed over the letter.

To His Grace, the Duke of Trent

Dear Jack,

    I shall keep this brief, because I find apologies ill-bred. I realize that implies that genteel behavior precludes vulgarities, which is clearly not true in my case.

I received your letter, and although the draft on your bank was much appreciated, it is not needed. I suppose that surprises you, but the fact is that I have landed on my feet. No need for money, so you will find it enclosed here, along with some part of what I owe you.

You are likely shocked to your core, but you will have to wait until I return to England to hear the story. I am not sure when that will be, since I embark for India on the tide tonight. I might not be in touch for quite a while.

I did want to say one thing, though. I know you think that I do not love you, but you are mistaken. In fact, you are the only person I love in the world, although I rarely showed it.

I did show it once, though. I had only one possession in my life worth anything, and I gave it to you.

I mean Merry, of course.

It took me some time to understand that you and she belonged together. And it took a few nights of drunken plotting to get around the fact that you would bungle it, and she would leave for America and meet some fellow on the boat who would stick a fourth ring on her finger, and by the time you found her again, the captain would have married her off.

So I arranged things for you. One of my few triumphs!

Spare your sons that ghastly name "Mortimer," will you?

Your brother, Cedric

Epilogue

Merry endured her labor in her own inimitable American fashion, from Trent's point of view. He had the vague idea that British ladies were given laudanum and slept through the whole experience.

The Duchess of Trent, however, had read an article that suggested that laudanum might have ill effects on the child, and refused it.

Instead, she howled and clung to her husband's hand, and swore at the midwife when the woman suggested it was time for His Grace to leave the room.

Thus, Trent was the first man in his acquaintance to be present for the gory, astonishing experience of childbirth.

To be truthful, he would rather not have been there. But it did mean that he got to hold his son within a minute of his birth.

Trent had accepted the alarming passion he felt for his

wife, but still worried that he wouldn't be able to muster it for a baby. But he no sooner looked at the annoyed, red face of the seventh duke—who had his nose, poor scrap—and he knew that he would do anything for Thomas, who was named after his wife's father. Thomas Cedric John Allardyce, the future seventh Duke of Trent. His heartstrings were tied to a little scrap of humanity as tightly as they were to Merry.

He looked up, his heart full, and found her smiling at him.

"He looks just like you, doesn't he?" she asked softly.

So much joy filled his heart that it felt as if it might crack. He sat down beside her, arranging Thomas so that he could see his mother. Or could see his mother if he cared to open his eyes.

"I love you," Trent whispered. "God, Merry, I love you so much."

She reached up, and he leaned down, and their lips met in the middle. It was the sort of kiss that carried a husband and wife through bad times and good times. Or perhaps it was the love they shared that did it.

That love got them through another baby, Fanny, and then a third, Peter. After Fanny learned to walk, she loved nothing more than to pull a small red wagon containing her brother Peter.

No one except Trent understood why his wife laughed so joyously at the sight of her beautiful children trundling about in that shiny red wagon.

It got them through the sad day when Snowdrop died, and all three children were inconsolable. George did his best to comfort them, with help from three butterball-shaped puppies named John, Thomasina, and James, after the next three American presidents. Merry was raising her children to honor both English *and* American traditions.

And finally, Merry and Trent's deep love was there on the joyful, miraculous day when Lord Cedric Allardyce strolled through the door of the townhouse in Cavendish Square, healthy and hearty, his clear blue eyes set off by skin tanned to the color of dark honey.

He was hand-in-hand with a smiling black-haired young woman whose skin was darker yet, a color that no English lady—no matter how many times she forgot her bonnet—could attain.

But that's a tale for another day.

Author's Note

A Note about Americans in London

This novel began as a simple story, a novella about an American marrying a British lord. I thought up the plot because I was living in London for a year with my family, running Fordham University's London program. But Merry and Trent demanded far more space than a piddling hundred pages, especially after the rented pineapple made its appearance.

I discovered that fascinating phenomenon during a tour of the marvelously preserved Georgian townhouse, No. One Royal Crescent, in Bath, England. The museum had set the dining room for an elegant party—and somehow my family and I ended up talking with the docent about why a pineapple sat in the place of honor. After that, I turned myself into a pineapple expert, even attending a lecture on the history of the Chelsea Physic Garden, the better to learn about pineapple stoves.

If pineapples were rare in 1803, so were American heiresses; the phenomenon of these young ladies marrying into high society actually began around twenty years later. The most famous American duchess is Consuelo Yzagna, who became Duchess of Manchester in 1876. But she was not the first; in 1828, the American heiress Louisa Caton married the heir to the Duke of Leeds. Louisa's grandfather had signed the Declaration of Independence.

While this novel owes a great deal to the historical sites I visited in England, it is just as indebted to the dear friends I made during the year. Rachel, Cecile, and Jessie tirelessly listened to stories of Merry, lending their stories of culture clashes to my experiences as an American abroad. Thank you, my dears!

Seven Minutes in Heaven

Edward Reeve may be the son of a marquis, but he's more interested in the hurly-burly world of business than the rules of high society. However, when Ward inherits two young half-siblings whom he never knew existed, he realizes they need a governess.

He hires someone from the very best registry, Snowe's—but quickly discovers that what he really wants is Mrs. Eugenia Snowe herself, a witty, beautiful widow.

Sparks fly as Ward pursues Eugenia with charm and determination, but Eugenia refuses him at every turn. She was married to a man she adored, and in her opinion, nothing could surpass those years of bliss.

But Ward will take any risk to prove Eugenia wrong. He'll stop at nothing—not even kidnapping—to convince her that they're meant to be together. He promises her heaven, if she'll just give him a chance . . .

She'll give him seven minutes.

My Dear Readers,

While each of my twenty-five novels has fans, one series has proved a particularly enduring favorite: the Essex Sisters quartet. A few years ago, a reader named Jody Gayle proposed an e-book companion volume that would include my introduction to the series, the "extra chapters" I wrote in response to reader requests, and a series of essays exploring Regency fashion, horse racing, and publications.

Over the last two years, I wrote a hundred-page introduction that traces the writing process from my first idea to publication. Then we faced a vexed decision. *Kiss Me, Annabel* exists in two versions; the last two hundred pages of my original draft are sharply different from the published novel. In essence, I had written two novels. We decided to include the original pages in the companion, so you can come to your own conclusion about which *Kiss Me* is your favorite.

Once I was deep in the Essex Sisters world, I wanted to spend time there! The companion also includes a brand-new short story with an appearance by Josie and the Earl of Mayne. And what's more, *A Gentleman Never Tells*, a full-length novella, will be published in tandem with the companion. Josie and Mayne appear again, this time with their daughter!

If you loved the Essex Sisters novels, I hope you will enjoy diving into the companion. If they're new to you, all four novels are being reissued by HarperCollins with gorgeous new covers, just in time to accompany the companion.

Following this letter is an excerpt from *A Gentleman Never Tells*, as well as an excerpt from *Much Ado About You*, the first novel in the Essex Sisters quartet. I hope you enjoy them!

With all best wishes to you and yours,

A Gentleman Never Tells

August 13, 1826
Telford Manor
Fontwell, Sussex

"*I* would prefer to take supper on a tray." Lizzie didn't look up from her book, because meeting her sister's eyes would only encourage her.

She should have known Catrina wouldn't back down. "Lizzie Troutt, your husband died over a year ago."

"Really?" Lizzie murmured, turning a page. "How time flies." In fact, Adrian had died eighteen months, two weeks, and four days ago.

In his mistress's bed.

"*Lizzie*," Cat said ominously, sounding more like an older sister—which she was—with every word, "if you don't get out of that bed, I shall drag you out. By your hair!"

Lizzie felt a spark of real annoyance. "You already dragged me to your house for this visit. The least you could do is to allow me to read my book in peace."

"Ever since you arrived yesterday, all you've done is read!" Cat retorted.

"I like reading. And forgive me if I point out that Tolbert is not precisely a hotbed of social activity." Cat and her husband, Lord Windingham, lived deep in Suffolk, in a dilapidated manor house surrounded by fields of sheep.

"That is precisely why we gather friends for dinner. Lord Dunford-Dale is coming tonight, and I need you to even the numbers. That means getting up, Lizzie. Bathing. Doing your hair. Putting on a gown that hasn't been dyed black would help, too. You look like a dispirited crow, if you want the truth."

Lizzie didn't want the truth. In fact, she felt such a stab of anger that she had to fold her lips tightly together or she would scream at Cat.

It wasn't her sister's fault. It wasn't anyone's fault except her late husband's, and he was definitely late—i.e., dead.

"I know you feel ashamed to be in company," her sister continued, energetically digging her own grave, as far as Lizzie was concerned. "Unfortunately, most people are aware of the circumstances of your marriage, not to mention the fact that Adrian was so imprudent as to die away from home."

That was one way of putting it.

Imprudent.

"You make it sound as if he dropped a teacup," Lizzie observed, unable to stop herself. "I would call the fact that Adrian died in the act of tupping Sadie Sprinkle inconsiderate in the extreme."

"I refuse to allow you to wither away in bed simply because your husband was infatuated with Shady Sadie," Cat said, using the term by which the gossip rags had referred to Adrian's mistress. "You must put all that behind you. Sadie has another protector, and you are out of mourning. It's time to stop hiding."

"I am not hiding," Lizzie said, stung. "I take fresh air and moderate exercise every day. I simply like reading in bed. Or in a chair."

Or anywhere else, to tell the truth. Reading in a peaceful garden was an excellent way to take fresh air.

"Moderate exercise," her sister said with palpable loathing. "You used to ride every day, for pleasure. We would practice archery on a fine day like this, or roam about the countryside, not sit inside reading."

"Adrian's stables were part of the entail, and went to his cousin," Lizzie said, turning the page. She hadn't read a word, but she was hoping that a show of indifference would drive her sister from the room.

"Not the mare that Papa gave you when you turned fourteen!" her sister gasped.

Showing masterly control, Lizzie didn't roll her eyes. "A wife has no true possessions," she said flatly. "Under the law, they belong to her husband, and Perdita was, therefore, transferred to the heir."

"Oh, Lizzie," Cat said, her voice woeful.

"It wasn't so terrible," Lizzie said, meaning it. "I went to the auction, and Perdita went to a family with a young girl. I'm certain that she is well cared for and happy."

"Do you realize that by staying home and wearing black, you give the illusion that you are grieving for your husband?"

Lizzie's hands tightened around her book. "Do you know what being a widow entails, Cat?"

"Wearing ugly black dresses for the rest of your natural life?"

"It means that I never again need put myself under the control of a man—*any* man. So, no, I have no interest in joining you at dinner. I know perfectly well that Lord Dimble-Dumble has been summoned to audition as my next husband. I don't want him. I'd be more likely to come to dinner if you had invited the butcher."

"I couldn't do that," Cat said, in a sudden digression. "Mr. Lyddle has developed a most unfortunate addiction to strong ale, and he's regularly found lying about in the gutter singing, rather than butchering meat."

"Who does the butchering now?" Lizzie asked, deciding to take a walk to the village and see this interesting musical event herself.

"His wife. My housekeeper says that she can get better cuts at a lower price these days. You're trying to distract me with talk of singing drunkards," Cat said, unfairly. "Let's discuss your future."

"Let's not."

"We might begin with the fact that you were never in love with Adrian." Cat began walking around the bedchamber, waving her hands as she waxed eloquent about her late brother-in-law's flaws.

She was preaching to the choir, so Lizzie stopped listening and just watched Cat pacing back and forth. How could it be that her older sister was positively frothing with life and energy and passion, while Lizzie felt like a tired, pale shadow?

Her hand crept toward her book. It wasn't the most interesting novel in the world, but it had the inexpressible charm of being new.

Over the last eighteen months, Lizzie had read every

novel she owned three times over. She would be quickly bankrupted if she bought more than two books a week, so one of the best things about visiting Telford Manor was access to her sister's library.

Cat appeared to be hopeless at arranging a refurbishment of the manor—which desperately needed it—but she was very good at ordering novels. And clothing. If Lizzie looked like a black crow, Cat was a chic French peacock.

Lizzie raised her knees, surreptitiously propped her book against them, and slipped back in the story of Eveline, a sixteen-year-old girl being forced to marry an old man. She herself had been twenty when she walked down the aisle.

On the shelf.

Beggars can't be choosers, her father had told her.

Her book suddenly vanished. "No reading!"

Cat was holding the novel above her head, for all the world as if they were children again. Lizzie used to hope that someday she'd grow up to be as commanding as her sister, but she had given up that idea long ago.

It wasn't just a question of height. Her sister was the type of person who gathered everyone in a room around her, and Lizzie was the type of person whom they walked over on their way to be with Cat.

That sounded resentful, but Lizzie didn't actually feel bitter. She would hate to be the center of attention. She wound her arms around her knees and propped her chin on them. "Cat, may I have my book back, please? It was a hard journey, and I'm tired."

"What do you mean, a hard journey? It can't have been more than a day and a half!"

"My coach is over twenty years old and the springs are worn out. It bounced so hard on the post road that I couldn't keep my eyes on the page, and my tailbone still hurts."

"If your jointure won't extend to a new vehicle, Joshua or Papa would be happy to buy you a coach."

Lizzie turned her head, putting her right cheek on her knees, and closed her eyes. "No."

She heard her sister drop into the chair by the side of the bed. Then she heard a sigh. "Papa is getting old, Lizzie. He made a terrible mistake, and he knows it. He misses you. If you would just pay him a visit . . ."

"No."

Why would she visit the father who had turned her away when she ran to him in desperation? The father who had known precisely what a disaster her marriage would be, but didn't bother to warn her?

An hour or so after their wedding ceremony, Adrian had brought Lizzie, still wrapped in her bridal veil, to his mother's faded, musty house, and informed her that he had no intention of living with her.

Not only that, but he was late to meet his lover for tea.

It had happened almost six years ago, but she could still remember her stupefaction. She'd been such a silly goose.

"But where do you live?" she had stammered.

"I bought Sadie a house, and we live there," Adrian had said casually. When she frowned in confusion, he had added impatiently, "*Sadie*. Didn't your father tell you her name?"

"Sadie?"

For the first time—and in her experience, the last time—her husband had been a little defensive, even a trifle ashamed. "I never lied. He knows perfectly well that we will lead separate lives."

"Perhaps you should explain to me," Lizzie had said,

"because my father unaccountably forgot to mention it. As did you, I might add."

Adrian had unemotionally laid out the terms of her marriage. It seemed her father had paid a great deal of money to buy his daughter the title of Lady Troutt. For his part, Adrian had wed her for her dowry, and because he needed someone to care for his mother.

"The estate is entailed," he had told her, glancing around the musty sitting room. "It goes to some distant cousin, along with the title, of course. I told your father that I wouldn't be averse to trying for a child, once we've had time to get used to each other."

Lizzie had just gaped at him.

"But we can't bother with that now," Adrian had told her briskly. "Sadie is upset about this mess, naturally enough. I promised her I'd be home by four. My mother takes her luncheon on a tray. There are a couple of maids, but it would be good if you could bring it in yourself. She complains of being lonely."

After that, he left.

A few minutes later, Lizzie left as well. She went home.

Only to be sent back to her husband's house.

There was no point in revisiting her father's line of reasoning. Suffice it to say that no woman—even one who had abundant sensuality and beauty, which Lizzie did not—was capable of seducing a man who didn't return to the house for a fortnight.

A man who doesn't bother to consummate his marriage until he's suffered a heart seizure and has, as the vulgar might put it, been given notice to quit.

A man who despises his lower-class wife, and never bothers to hide it.

Read on for an excerpt from

Much Ado About You

the first novel in the
Essex Sisters Quartet!

Available wherever books are sold!

September 1816
Holbrook Court, seat of the Duke of Holbrook
On the outskirts of Silchester

In the afternoon

"*I* am happy to announce that the rocking horses have been delivered, Your Grace. I have placed them in the nursery for your inspection. As yet, there is no sign of the children."

Raphael Jourdain, Duke of Holbrook, turned. He had been poking a fire smoldering in the cavernous fireplace of his study. There was a reserved tone in his butler's voice that signaled displeasure. Or perhaps it would be more accurate to say that Brinkley's tone signaled the disgruntlement of the entire household of elderly servants, not one of whom was enchanted by the idea of accommodating themselves to the presence of four small, female children. Well, the hell with that, Rafe thought. It wasn't as if he'd *asked* to have a passel of youngsters on the premises.

"Rocking horses?" came a drawling voice from a deep chair to the right of the fireplace. "Charming, Rafe. Charming. One can't start too early making the little darlings interested in horseflesh." Garret Langham, the Earl of Mayne, raised his glass toward his host. His black curls were in exquisite disarray, his comments arrogant to a fault, and his manners barely hid a seething fury. Not that he was furious at Rafe; Mayne had been in a slow burn for the past few months. "To Papa and his brood of infant *equestriennes*," he added, tossing back his drink.

"Stubble it!" Rafe said, but without much real animosity. Mayne was a damned uncomfortable companion at the moment, what with his poisonous comments and black humor. Still, one had to assume that the foul temper caused by the shock of being rejected by a woman would wear off in a matter of time.

"Why the plural, as in rocking *horses*?" Mayne asked. "As I recall, most nurseries contain only one rocking horse."

Rafe took a gulp of his brandy. "I don't know much about children," he said, "but I distinctly remember my brother and me fighting over our toys. So I bought four of them."

There was a second's silence during which the earl considered whether to acknowledge the fact that Rafe obviously still missed his brother (dead these five years, now). Mayne dismissed the impulse. Manlike, he observed no benefit to maudlin conversation.

"You're doing those orphans proud," he said instead.

"Most guardians would stow the children out of sight. It's not as if they're your blood."

"There's no amount of dolls in the world that will make up for their situation," Rafe said, shrugging. "Their father should have thought of his responsibilities before he climbed on a stallion."

The conversation was getting dangerously close to the sort of emotion to be avoided at all costs, so Mayne sprang from his chair. "Let's have a look at the rocking horses, then. I haven't seen one in years."

"Right," Rafe said, putting his glass onto the table with a sharp clink. "Brinkley, if the children arrive, bring them upstairs, and I'll receive them in the nursery."

A few minutes later the two men stood in the middle of a large room on the third floor, dizzily painted with murals. Little Bo Peep chased after Red Riding Hood, who was surely in danger of being crushed by the giant striding across the wall, his raised foot lowering over a feather bed sporting a huge green pea under the coverlet. The room resembled nothing so much as a Bond Street toy shop. Four dolls with spun gold hair sat primly on a bench. Four doll beds were propped atop each other, next to four doll tables, on which sat four jack-in-the-boxes. In the midst of it all was a group of rocking horses graced with real horsehair and coming almost to a man's waist.

"Jesus," Mayne said.

Rafe strode into the room and stamped on the rocker of one of the horses, making it clatter back and forth on the wooden floor. A door on the side of the room swung open, and a plump woman in a white apron poked her head out.

"There you are, Your Grace," she said, beaming. "We're just waiting for the children. Would you like to meet the new maids now?"

"Send them on in, Mrs. Beeswick."

Four young nursemaids crowded into the room after her. "Daisy, Gussie, Elsie, and Mary," said the nanny. "They're from the village, Your Grace, and pleased to have a position at Holbrook Court. We're all eager for the little cherubs to arrive." The nursemaids lined up to either side of Mrs. Beeswick, smiling and curtsying.

"Jesus," Mayne repeated. "They won't even share a maid, Rafe?"

"Why should they? My brother and I had three nurses between us."

"Three?"

"Two for my brother, ever since he turned duke at age seven, and one for me."

Mayne snorted. "That's absurd. When's the last time you met your wards' father, Lord Brydone?"

"Not for years," Rafe said, picking up a jack-in-the-box and pressing the lever so that it hopped from its box with a loud squeak. "The arrangement was just a matter of a note from him and my reply."

"You have never met your own wards?"

"Never. I haven't been over the border in years, and Brydone only came down for the Ascot, the Silchester, and, sometimes, Newmarket. To be honest, I don't think he really gave a damn for anything other than his stables. He didn't even bother to list his children in *Debrett's*. Of course, since he had four girls, there was no question of inheritance. The estate went to some distant cousin."

"Why on earth—" Mayne glanced at the five women standing to the side of the room and checked himself.

"He asked me," Rafe said, shrugging. "I didn't think twice of it. Apparently Monkton had been in line, but he cocked up his toes last year. And Brydone asked me to step in. Who would have thought that ill could come to Brydone? It was a freak accident, that horse throwing him. Although he was fool enough to ride a half-broken stallion."

"Damned if I thought I'd ever see you a father," Mayne said.

"I had no excuse to say no. I have the substance to raise any number of children. Besides, Brydone gave me Starling in return for acting as a guardian. I told him I'd do the job, as soon as he wrote me, and no bribe was necessary. But he sent Starling down from Scotland, and no one would say nay to adding that horse to their stables."

"Starling is out of Standout, isn't he?"

Rafe nodded. "Patchem's brother. The core of Brydone's stable is out of Patchem, and those are now the only horses in England in Patchem's direct line. I'm hopeful that Starling will win the Derby next year, even if he is descended from Standout rather than Patchem himself."

"What will happen to Patchem's offspring?" Mayne asked, with the particular intensity he reserved for talk of horses. "Something Wanton, for example?"

"I don't know yet. Obviously, the stables aren't entailed. My secretary has been up there working on the estate. Should Brydone's stable come to the children, I'll put the horses up for auction and the money in trust. The girls will need dowries someday, and I'd be surprised if Brydone bothered to set them up himself."

"If Wanton is for sale, I'm the one to buy him. I'd pay thousands for him. There could be no better addition to my stables."

"He would do wonders for mine as well," Rafe agreed.

Mayne had found a little heap of cast-iron horses and was sorting them out so that each carriage was pulled by a matched pair. "You know, these are quite good." He had all the cast-iron horses and their carriages lined up on the mantelpiece now. "Wait till your wards see these horses. They won't think twice about the move from Scotland. Pity there's no boy among them."

Rafe just looked at him. The earl was one of his dearest friends, and always would be. But Mayne's sleek, protected life had not put him in the way of grief. Rafe knew only too well what it felt like to find oneself lonely in the midst of a cozy nursery, and cast-iron horses wouldn't help, for all he found himself buying more and more of them. As if toys would make up for a dead father. "I hardly think you—"

The door behind him swung open. He stopped and turned.

Brinkley moved to the side more nimbly than was his practice. It wasn't every day that one got to knock the master speechless with surprise. "I'm happy to announce Miss Essex. Miss Imogen. Miss Annabel. Miss Josephine."

Then he added, unable to resist, if the truth be known, "The children have arrived, Your Grace."